Stubby Amberchuk
& the Holy Grail

Stubby Amberchuk
& the Holy Grail

Anne Cameron

Harbour Publishing

Published by
  Harbour Publishing Co. Ltd.
  P.O. Box 219
  Madeira Park, BC
  Canada   V0N 2H0

Cover design and art by Gaye Hammond

The author gratefully acknowledges the assistance of the Canada Council
in the completion of this book.

  Cameron, Anne, 1938 –
    Stubby Amberchuk and the Holy Grail

    ISBN 0-920080-22-7

    I. Title.
    PS8555.A44S88 1987   C813'.54   C87-091392-1
    PR9199.3.C34S88 1987

Printed and bound in Canada

For Nancy and Stanley
Thora and Jerry

Alex
Erin
Pierre
Marianne
Tara

and especially
Eleanor

Part One

Stubby

1

Stubby Amberchuk was born five months after her parents got married, a matter of timing that had varying degrees of significance upon her life at different times.

Stubby's mother Vinnie was one of the several apples of her parents' eyes. The other apples were Vinnie's two sisters and the biggest apple of all was her brother Gordon, on whom rested most of the aspirations and expectations of the family, none of which were ever realized. Stubby's grandparents were convinced the sun rose and set in the cracks of the children's backsides and so, of course, there was no way any prospective mate was ever going to be really good enough for any of them. Gordon believed this so implicitly he never did get married, so the supposed immortality which presumably reposed in Gordon's scrawny loins never amounted to any more than Gordon himself did. Both of Vinnie's sisters, however, while they believed they were, indeed, marrying beneath themselves, did marry, and the men managed to justify their existences by providing the seed for several children.

Stubby's mother, the youngest and therefore the one preferred only slightly less than Gordon, knew for a fact she was marrying beneath her but, as the timing of Stubby's birth showed, Vinnie had very little in the way of choice. Vinnie truly believed she had been betrayed by her body, shoved down the garden path, so to speak, by her own hormones, lured into a lifelong trap by moonlight, the sound of the surf and the effects of a goodly portion of a bottle of sloe gin, which Vinnie had believed to be little more than soda pop.

Her parents gazed at her with shock, then gazed at her intended with horror. ''A lout,'' Vinnie's mother decided. ''Goddamn asshole,'' Vinnie's father spluttered, and resisted the impulse to tapdance on the face of his son-in-law apparent. Perhaps the fact the despised creature was six foot two-and-a-half inches tall, weighed almost two hundred pounds and was layered in muscle and sinew helped Vinnie's father behave like a civilized person.

Vinnie and Dave Amberchuk were married quietly in the courthouse with only their immediate families in attendance. On one side of the small room Vinnie's mother and father, her brother Gordon and her sisters stood huddled together, their faces suggesting they each and all detected a faint odour of rotten starfish coming from the half-open window. They were huddled together not only for comfort but because the immediate family of Dave Amberchuk filled what might be called "their side" of the small room and overflowed into the side Vinnie's family felt ought to have been theirs and theirs alone. Neither of Vinnie's brothers-in-law attended; they couldn't afford to miss work, they said. All of Dave's brothers and brothers-in-law took the day off and crammed their enormous forms into dress suits. Feet more used to caulk boots thumped in highly polished oxfords, hands normally grimed and grease-smeared were scrubbed with brushes and lathered with dish detergent, then hung, red, knob-knuckled and calloused, from the starched cuffs of snow-white shirts. Necks suntanned to a shade approximating the reddish bark on the arbutus trees pushed up and out of collars left unbuttoned—the designers of shirts pay no attention to the needs of men who work with their muscles. The working men hid the gap between collar button and buttonhole with the knots on their ties while in the small room in which the ceremony was held, but as soon as the brief ceremony was finished, the ties were loosened and the fun began.

Dave's sisters and sisters-in-law were brightly and beautifully attired in an assortment of skirts and blouses and dresses from the Eaton's catalogue, and if there was more than one version of the same style, well, there was no duplication of colour, proof of the depth of co-operation exhibited by the family. Of course Cora would have preferred her dress in mauve but Louise had already made her choice, and two mauves at the same show would never do so Cora chose the green, knowing Rose would want the blue.

From the court house the families moved to the banquet room of the White Lotus hotel for what Vinnie's mother called a cold buffet and the Amberchuks called a smyorgybyorgy. Vinnie's mother had flatly refused to have any of the lout's relatives in her house. Pete Singh, who had bought the White Lotus from Justin Wong the year before, on hearing the buffet was intended for the Amberchuks, changed his usual menu. Ordinarily Pete charged a set price for setting up the tables, chairs, plates and cutlery, then charged so much per head-by-tens as he called it. So much for ten people, and a sliding scale going on up from there, the more people who attended, the less-per-ten Pete charged.

"What if only eighteen people show up?" Vinnie's dad tried to bargain.

"Same as for twenty," Pete said firmly.

"But that means I pay for two people who didn't eat!" the stingy little man squealed.

"Invite two extra," Pete shrugged. "And don't forget," he reminded, with no trace of a smile, "I'm not charging you twice as much for twenty as I am for ten. I don't make anything at all if twenty show up. The only profit I make is if someone doesn't show up."

Usually Pete did okay on wedding buffets and graduation buffets, there's always someone who can't make it because a kid stepped on a rusty nail or fell out of a tree and broke a collarbone, and the people throwing the party usually overestimate anyway, not wanting to be caught short and made to look cheap. Pete's buffet was usually an assortment of thinly sliced cold cuts, several kinds of green salad, large bowls of potato salad, a couple of dozen stuffed devilled eggs and a roast turkey or a big ham studded with cloves. But when Pete heard who the groom was he quickly amended the usual menu. His deal was that for a stated price he would provide all the food a party could eat. But there was no limit to the number of stuffed devilled eggs that could disappear down the gullet of any Amberchuk.

No limit to the platters of thinly sliced cold beef or the number of turkey carcasses apt to be stripped. Why, even the Amberchuk children were legendary for their ability to just pack it away, whatever it was, by the bushel and peck, by the gallon and quart, metric or imperial, it was all the same to them.

Pete Singh wisely took his beef and, instead of trying to slice it thinner, cut it into beef curry—and far more curry than beef. Rice, he reasoned, is a hell of a lot cheaper and more filling than fancy little sandwiches. Instead of leaving entire turkey drumsticks lying around to be swallowed happily, leaving only the bare bone and sometimes, somehow, not even that, the turkey dittoed the beef, cut into small pieces and drowned in curry sauce.

"What's this called?" a young Amberchuk asked, grinning with pleasure and shovelling in another forkload.

"Chinese food," the older Amberchuk instructed, scooping up a mouthful of curried ham and rice with a large piece of the spicy flat little pancake things Pete had supplied.

"Chinee, huh?" the younger one said, around a bulging load of something that made his eyes well with tears and sweat pop out on his forehead. "Sure is good, whatever it is."

Even Pete was aghast at the mountains of rice that vanished into the maws of the family of gyppo loggers. Vinnie's parents nibbled and picked and yearned for cucumber sandwiches or salad with three colours of macaroni, but Dave's family burped, belched, laughed and went back for more, and in the kitchen Pete Singh ladled out the rice and buckwheat chapatis, relaxed and even began to smile. He'd make a profit on this one, after all.

Usually when one of the Amberchuk females got married the whole family worked for weeks preparing for the party, and whatever else got roasted, fried or barbecued, nothing got curried. Curry was something you did with a comb to a horse, not something you put into your belly. But this idea of exotic cooking was catching on fast. "Poppa," Phyllis asked, eyes hopeful, "when I get married, can I have this kind of food?"

"Let's go talk to Pete," her father replied, unable to deny any of his kids the kind of sendoff they wanted. That was when Pete Singh went from smiling to laughing and began to talk business on a scale he hadn't previously dreamed of. "Oh hell," Dad Amberchuk guessed, "maybe three hundred, maybe four hundred people, she's marrying up with one of the Colville boys and god knows we're up to our knees in Colvilles."

"Not to worry," Pete soothed, "you just give me a week or two's notice and we'll fix up a real wingding for the kids."

The Amberchuks had class of their own sort, and if it wasn't the same kind of class as Vinnie's parents thought they had, that was the fault of Vinnie's parents, who had arranged, grudgingly, for just enough cheap domestic plonk to be available for the toasts to the queen, the bride and the attendants, and for the rest had ordered pots of tea and coffee. The Amberchuks noticed this, of course, within five seconds of walking into the room. It never occurred to them that Dave had married into a family of cheap shits; they naturally assumed that in the glee and excitement of the happy occasion someone had overlooked something, and no shame in that, hadn't Uncle Max shown up for his own daughter's wedding without his socks, and hadn't he walked down the aisle with his bare ankles poking out between his new patent leather shoes and his rented tuxedo pants? Well then, say nothing about it, just fish into your pocket and chip in, show the people we know how to act, and before the first huge bowls of curried ham and rice were empty the stacks of beer cases were growing by the door. Pete Singh didn't usually drink alcohol at all, but he went home quite undeniably sozzled, causing his wife to tell him a good many things, most of which he pretended not to hear and some of which he passed out before he had a chance to hear.

Vinnie and Dave left the reception after the customary tossing of the garter and throwing of the bouquet, then drove to Victoria, checked into a hotel and had a reasonably enjoyable honeymoon. Dave enjoyed the sex and Vinnie enjoyed the chance to visit the museum, see all the Indian artifacts and go to a different movie every night for a week.

It was God's own mercy Dave Amberchuk didn't give a flying fit what anybody else thought of him because first Vinnie's parents, and later on Vinnie herself, lost no opportunity to let him know their opinions of him, his line of work, his social status and or lack thereof and what a damn shame it was Vin had ruined her life. He shrugged, he grinned, he ignored it all with the best possible grace and took increasing satisfaction in just doing his job the best way possible. He put Vinnie's increasing snarliness down to her delicate condition and deliberately forced himself to stay around home in the evening rather than do what he wanted, which was put as much distance as he could between himself and the virago who was his bride. Precisely because he forced himself to do it, it was exactly the wrong thing to do; Vinnie would have preferred to have seen virtually nothing at all of Dave, even though only a few months ago she had practically grown into the small table on which the family phone stood as she waited for Dave to call and invite her to a slow-pitch game or a ride down to the river. Vinnie would have preferred to have lived as her mother lived, seeing her husband's face over the breakfast and supper tables and only briefly on weekends. Vinnie would have loved to have packed the black-painted metal lunch bucket while the breakfast bacon sizzled in the pan, call Dave as she put the eggs in the bacon fat, then disappear into the bathroom while he ate his breakfast alone. She would have preferred to have seen only his back as he walked down the path to the road to catch the crummy to work and then to have the next ten or eleven hours all to herself, with nothing to tolerate in the evening except the supper ritual. After that, she fervently wished Dave would disappear to do whatever it was men did when they left the house after supper and came home in time to fall into bed in their longjohn underwear.

Instead, Dave was there from supper till bedtime, chopping wood, mowing the lawn, fixing the hen coop, re-shaking the roof in preparation for the winter rains. He was there measuring, sawing and hammering in place a new board on the back steps. He was there ripping apart the gooseneck under the sink, cleaning it, replacing it and smiling proudly as the sink drained quickly and easily. He was there as surely and as impossible to ignore as her growing belly. And she heartily wished she could see *that* walk off down the path on its way to China or Peru.

Had Stubby looked like Vinnie, or even like either of her maternal grandparents, her life might well have been quite tolerable. Instead, she came into the world with the Amberchuk look stamped on her and none of them, not her mother, grandmother, grandfather, uncle or aunts ever quite forgave her for that. Dave, of course, was delighted and would have liked nothing better than to wait the briefest possible of intervals and start another one right away.

"Forget it," Vinnie said coldly, and went to the doctor to get herself fitted for a diaphragm. She also bought a cream to lubricate the diaphragm and fight sperm and, just to be sure she wasn't taking any chances, she also used a sperm-killing gel; it's a wonder Dave could keep it up when he found himself in the vicinity of it all.

"What did you get married for?" he asked, puzzled, hurt and very horny.

"I was pregnant," she said with undeniable truth. "And I don't ever intend to get like that again."

"Oh," he said, at a loss for words.

Vinnie wanted Dave to go into camp, to disappear into the green wall for months on end and come home only for fire season, snow season or the occasional inevitable strike. All Vinnie had been raised to expect from a husband was someone who brought money into the house and took the garbage out of the house. Instead she got a husband who didn't care if he never earned enough money to buy a cabin cruiser. "What good would it do me," Dave asked, "if I was only home once in a while and never got to use it? I'd rather have a clinkerbuilt and an outboard and use it whenever I want."

"That's what you get when you marry that kind of person," Vinnie's mother said with what she thought was wisdom. "No aspirations, no upward mobility, no ambition at all."

But Dave had ambition. Dave had aspirations. And most of them centred around Stubby. She hadn't been christened Stubby. She had been dressed in a long, lacy dress, stuffed into a lace-trimmed bonnet and plunked in the arms of the Anglican minister, who duly sprinkled her with water and dedicated her and her life to God, then informed the world, or at least that portion of it attending the ceremony, that the child's name was Sheilagh May Amberchuk. Dave had no part in naming his daughter and had even tried to protest the spelling of Sheilagh, but by this time nobody seemed to be paying any attention to him. He had done his part, worse luck, and done it unthinkingly, and certainly wasn't needed any more.

Sheilagh May Amberchuk had brown hair and brown eyes and a strong, square body. "Stocky," her mother defended. "Stubby," her maternal grandfather insisted.

Dave was angry but damned if he'd show it, so he picked up his daughter, held her, laughing, over his head and jiggled her the way she loved to be jiggled. "Is that you?" he asked. "Are you Stubby?" and Sheilagh May chortled. "C'mon, Stubby, let's us go get us an ice cream."

"She's too young for ice cream," Vinnie argued, "you'll freeze the lining of her stomach and she won't ever be able to digest food properly."

"Who says?" Dave laughed.

"Everybody," Vinnie declared grandly.

"Gimme one name," he challenged and, tucking Stubby under his arm, walked out of Vinnie's parents' house and up the gravel road to the general store, where he bought a double-decker and sat with it on the porch, licking the ice cream, holding the cone for Stubby to suck the half-melted parts and jawing with his friends.

"When you having the next one?" someone asked.

"Me?" Dave laughed. "I didn't even have this one, Vinnie did."

"You know what I mean, you clown."

"No rush," Dave announced, saving face in spite of his broken heart, "Some people have to try, try, try again until they get one worth keeping, but we got us perfection first crack off the reel."

"Oh, yeah, then how come there's so many Amberchuks?"

"Oh, you'd have to ask my mother about that," Dave laughed. "Maybe she ain't satisfied with none of us." He turned the cone so Stubby could get at the softening strawberry scoop. "My mother," Dave expanded, "isn't someone to settle for less than she thinks she can get."

The strawberry dripped onto Stubby's dress and mixed with the chocolate and made one hell of a mess, but Stubby didn't care and neither did Dave. "You obviously have no idea how hard it is to wash, starch and iron those little dresses," Vinnie raged.

"Put 'er in jeans 'n' a T-shirt, then," Dave suggested.

"My daughter is a *girl*, not a *boy*," Vinnie stormed.

"Who'n hell cares *what* it is until it's into pooberty?" Dave argued, beginning to feel more than a little bit shirty. "As long as it's strong and healthy and has the right number of eyes, nose, mouth, arms, legs and such, who gives a shit? Kids don't got no sex at all until they're into that pooberty thing," and to all intents and purposes he promptly wiped from his mind the fact that Stubby was a girl. Which is not to say he treated her exactly like a boy. He just didn't care if she was clean or dirty and never once helped force her feet into little button-strap patent leather slippers. Vinnie kept Stubby dressed the way everyone knows girls are supposed to be dressed, right up until a half hour before Dave came in from work, then she changed her into overalls, a cotton T-shirt and little sneakers and consoled herself with the thought that it was just for an hour or two.

With Dave's help, Stubby learned to shinny up a rope, she learned to climb fences, she learned to put her own worms on her trout hook, she learned to set the oarlocks in the little holes and she learned to row. When she fell into the water she learned to swim. For her fifth birthday, Dave got her a softball glove and that kicked off the argument that was the straw that broke the camel's back. Vinnie packed her suitcases, commanded Stubby to follow her and stomped out of the house on her way to her parents' place where, as she had so often been told, the door had been closed to keep out the breeze, the dust and the flies but would always open to let her back into the family.

"Stubby," she snapped, "come on!"

"Do I gotta?" Stubby asked.

"I said," Vinnie yelled, "to come *on*!"

Stubby turned and looked at Dave, who looked back at her and thought his heart would break. "Do I gotta?" she repeated dolefully.

"Not if you don't want to," Dave answered. "You do whatever you want to do, whatever you know is right, and I'll back you all the way, Stubbzers."

So, instead of following Vinnie, Stubby got her little can of dried bugs from its place on the shelf under the sink and went to feed her turtle, Myrtle, who lived in a little clear plastic dish with a clear plastic island under a brown-trunked, green-leafed plastic palm tree. She sprinkled dried bugs on the water and watched as Myrtle poked her head out of her shell, blinked her tiny round black eyes, then stretched her neck longer, longer, longer and even longer. Myrtle blinked again, opened her mouth and one of the dried bugs was gone. Stubby could see Myrtle's throat wiggling. She knew the bug was on its way down into Myrtle's stomach. Bubbles appeared at the corner of Myrtle's mouth, then the strange thing started all over again, jaws opening, neck stretching, bug disappearing.

Vinnie waited all of two minutes for Stubby to follow her. When she didn't appear, Vinnie stalked off by herself, a suitcase in each hand.

Stubby put herself to bed when she got tired and didn't bother with her usual bath. She just wiped at her hands and face with a damp cloth and crawled on top of her bed, exhausted by her own puzzlement and unease. Before Dave went to bed he pulled the quilt up over Stubby's sleeping form and reminded himself to suggest to her that she really ought to strip off her clothes and sneakers, put on her pajamas and wipe the bits of leaf and grass from the bed before she crawled onto it at night, the grime was apt to raise hell with her bedclothes.

He didn't go to work the next day. He took Stubby to his mother's house and she played with a back yard full of assorted cousins while Dave and his mom talked seriously over a pot of tea.

"Vinnie's walked out on me," he said.

"Oh my," said his mother, who had actually been expecting something very much like this to happen.

"I think she pro'bly won't be back," he admitted.

"Oh, my dear," she consoled.

"Stubby didn't want to go with her."

"Then it's best that she didn't," his mother agreed.

"If they try to take her I'll kill them," he vowed.

"No," his mother corrected, "you'd go to jail as sure as if you'd killed human people. You'll just go and get her back. If need be, we'll all go and get her back. Unless, of course, she changes her mind and wants to be with her momma. In which case, David, you will have to allow her to live with Vinnie."

"If Stubby wants to do that," he said softly, "then I'll go along with it. Breaks my heart to think about it," he admitted, his eyes suddenly damp and shiny. "But what breaks me up worse is the thought they'll make her go somewhere she don't want to go, or do something she don't want to do. Seems as if we all wind up having to live like that soon enough, no need for it to come down on her when she's small."

As much as Stubby loved her mother she did not, not ever, want to live in the same house as her maternal grandparents. She didn't mind visiting them briefly, but she didn't like hearing her father called an asshole or a fool or a jerk or a dope or a loon, and she didn't like the way nothing she said or did was ever good enough. Visiting was enough for Stubby, especially if it was a brief visit.

But it wasn't enough for Vinnie's brother Gordon or for his father. They arrived at Grandma Amberchuk's at ten in the morning several days after Vinnie had hied herself off with her suitcases. Dave was at work, Stubby was staying with Gran and Gran was busy in the basement putting clothes through the washing machine. Gordon and his father scooped Stubby from the back yard, Gordon's hand placed firmly over her mouth to stop her yells. She was stuffed into the car, made to sit on Gordon's lap and driven to Dave's house. She was handed to her grandfather, who put *his* hand over her mouth while Gordon went inside and scooped her clothes. Within minutes she was at their neat and tidy house with the close-cropped lawn, regimented flower beds and no sign at all of swallows' nests in the eaves. (Everyone knows birds are messy creatures and leave embarrassing white stains on the side of the house if you allow them to nest.)

Grandma Amberchuk knew immediately what had happened. She knew Stubby would never have left the yard without saying where she was going. She knew as surely as if she had seen what had happened. She didn't call the RCMP or pitch a fit or take hysterics or do anything but go about her day-to-day routine. She waited until the crummy dropped Dave off at the corner and then she dropped the bomb on him.

Dave arrived at his in-laws' neat and tidy house halfway through their supper. He didn't say a word. He simply kicked a hole in the screen door with his heavy boots, stepped in through the hole and stood, still in his bushy-smelling work clothes, grinning an unspoken invitation to his father-in-law and brother-in-law, neither of whom were suicidal enough to accept what the grin offered.

"Never needed to lock my door in my life," Dave said, "but I'm getting me a new deadbolt first thing Saturday morning. Got a bunch of thieving assholes in the neighbourhood, I guess. Most'a Stub's clothes has been swiped."

"She's *my* daughter!" Vinnie screeched.

"That's true," Dave agreed, "and you can see her any time you want for however long you want as long as it's fine by her." He turned to Stubby. "So, Stubbs, what say? You stayin' or comin' home with me?" Instantly, Stubby slid off her chair and ran to him, leaving her supper unfinished on her plate.

"She hasn't finished eating," Vinnie protested, stricken.

"I'm not hungry," Stubby said as she stepped through the hole in the screen door and raced for the pickup where it was parked at the side of the street.

"You'll hear more about this," Vinnie's father promised.

"By me," Dave gritted, "ya got a helluva nerve. Things get forgiven when people's family. When they ain't family, things done stay done. Best ya fix yer door," he laughed, "or the 'skeeters'll get ya." He stepped through the hole and stomped across the porch and down the steps to the pickup, then drove to the White Lotus, where he and Stubby packed away the Special for Two.

Grandma Amberchuk went over and talked to Vinnie and her folks and came home with an agreement that almost satisfied the majority. Stubby would spend Monday and Tuesday with Vinnie and her family and would arrive at Grandma Amberchuk's in time for lunch on Wednesday.

"It's only two days," Grandma Amberchuk pleaded.

"Two 'n' a half," Stubby argued, but only for the sake of arguing, not because she wanted to kick off round two of the overall uproar. If Monday, Tuesday and part of Wednesday would keep the screen door intact and the faces from going brick red, Stubby was all in favour of it.

Of course it all changed when she started school anyway. Instead of her dad dropping her off at Grandma Amberchuk's on the way to work and picking her up on his way back home, everything got very silly for a while. They tried having him drop her off at Grandma's and then

Grandma taking her to school, but Stubby had to get up early, then miss her afternoon nap, and she caught it in the ear from the teacher for daydreaming or dozing at her desk. Then Grandma tried coming over as soon as Grandpa and the uncles finished breakfast, but Vinnie objected because it still meant Stubby was alone in the house for as much as fifteen minutes between the time Dave left to catch the crummy and the time Grandma arrived. "What if the house caught fire," she screamed. And there was no arguing with that. They even tried having Dave drive Stubby to Vinnie's place in time to go to bed so she could wake up to a healthy, nourishing breakfast, get dressed and go to school, but everyone argued about what was a decent bedtime for a growing girl. Then they argued about whether or not Stubby should go to Grandma Amberchuk's after school and wait for Dave there, or whether she should go to Vinnie's parents' house and wait for Dave under the loving eye of her mother.

It snowed like a bugger that year and by mid-November Dave was off work because the snow pack was a foot too deep for anyone to fall trees or set chokers safely. Since Dave was home full time the problem died down for a while. That was great as far as Stubby was concerned: she woke up in her own house, had breakfast at her own table, went to school, came home to her own house and had supper with her father who, she was convinced, cooked far better meals than anyone else except Grandma Amberchuk. Stubby just did what she was told and went where she was told. Finally the fate that had sent a deep pack of early snow sent a rare, very dry spring. By June the bush was shut tight for fire season and there was, again, no need for a set-to over how and with whom Stubby would spend her time. Summer holidays were not going to be a problem after all. Dave was home and nobody was going to argue with him!

Except Dave wasn't a saint, and he wasn't an angel. He was, in fact, a very healthy young man, and he had, as they say, appetites.

It was just the chance Vinnie had been waiting for. When Dave started getting a babysitter to come in after Stubby was asleep in bed, Vinnie, her mother and father and, of course, follow-along-Gordon, got a detective and in no time flat there were photographs to prove it all. Vinnie sued Dave for divorce on the grounds of adultery. And demanded full custody of Stubby.

Dave counter-sued for custody, claiming and proving that Vinnie had abandoned Stubby when she walked off with her suitcases. The lawyers grinned at each other. They met for coffee, they met for drinks, they met for lunches, they met for dinners and they talked about hockey, football, soccer, fly fishing and imported versus domestic beer. Both billed their clients heftily for these many and varied business meetings.

Vinnie got her divorce and even got custody of Stubby, but Dave had evening visitation rights, weekend visitation rights and half of the school holidays. Nobody was satisfied, least of all Stubby, who wound up wearing more dresses than she wanted to wear and didn't have Myrtle with her any more. Everyone knew, said Gordon, that turtles harbour salmonella germs, which would cause the whole family to get sick and die of food poisoning, gastrointestinal inflammation or diseases of the genital tract.

''You mean the outhouse shuffle,' replied Stubby.

''Don't talk like trash,'' Vinnie's mother scolded.

Stubby couldn't understand what it was that was so trashy about saying outhouse shuffle. It was a lot better than green apple two-step or the running shits. She had, however, enough good sense to keep her questions to herself at this point.

Vinnie didn't want any more children and she didn't want any more to do with a husband than she'd already had to endure, but she did not enjoy being dependent on her mother and father. If she went to work, a number of problems would immediately present themselves. For example, she had absolutely no training of any kind and even if she did, there weren't any jobs for women, at least not any jobs that paid well enough to make it worthwhile getting out of bed in the morning. Vinnie had been raised to a certain role, a position in life, and through her own youthful folly had almost, but thank god not quite, excluded herself from any chance of being who she was raised to be. Besides, if she got a job Dave would immediately reopen the custody battle; it had been only Vinnie's twenty-four-hour-a-day availability as a mother that had swayed the court in her favour in the first place.

Dave paid child support, he grudgingly paid the absolute minimum his lawyer could arrange as spousal allowance and he prayed to the Good Lord Above that Vinnie would step out of line, just once, step out of line and give him grounds to go back into court for yet another round of appeal and dispute.

Vinnie could have afforded a very small apartment on the money she had coming in from Dave, but there was no way she was having her child sleeping on a fold-out couch. She was far better off staying at home. Except that it was, beyond any doubt, a pain in the face having to continue to do as her mother told her.

Every weekend Stubby raced to Dave's pickup, jumped in and they drove off together to spend their time playing ball, camping, fishing or visiting the cousins, aunts and uncles.

Vinnie began to think that, without the burden and responsibility of Stubby, she should be having a good time too. The first thing she saw when she ventured out of her matronly shell was Earl Blades, who was, as Vinnie's mother proclaimed from the very first, more the kind of person

Vinnie had been raised to marry. Earl was a teacher, and if he didn't make as much money in a year as Dave did, he at least went to work clean and didn't shove Copenhagen snuff behind his bottom lip or wear filthy jeans with wide suspenders or push his peas onto his fork with his thumb. He didn't laugh as if he was trying to break the windows with the sound of his voice either, and probably wasn't going to want to roll sweatily and lustily for hours on end and turn the bedsheets into wrinkled, stained embarrassments.

Vinnie married Earl. Stubby was her mother's flower girl, which everyone thought was real sweet. Except Stubby, who had to hang around all through an otherwise perfectly decent Saturday smiling at people she didn't know, even when they said how happy she must be to have a new daddy. As far as Stubby was concerned she didn't have a new daddy, she didn't need a new daddy, she had her Dad and that was more than enough.

Vinnie and Earl left on their honeymoon and Stubby went to spend two weeks with her Grandma Amberchuk and her dad. "It's not a fair bargain," Vinnie had argued. "You're getting two extra weeks."

"Listen, Vin, you won't even *be* there, so it's no skin off your ass," Dave had countered. "And if you don't like it, fine. I'll just pick Stubbs up after school on Friday night like the court says I can do, and you can have the whole shiteroony without her."

Stubby knew there was something going on. She knew it from way before the wedding but she didn't know what it was until more than halfway through summer holidays and by then it was too late.

Vinnie and Earl took off on their trip, Stubby had a wonderful two extra weeks, then Vinnie and Earl came back and life went on as it had been going on, except Stubby now lived with her mother and stepfather in a rented house in what they called the good end of town.

Finally it was summer holidays and Stubby could go back to Dave's place and have a taste of life the way she liked it. They headed off in the pickup truck together, leaving Myrtle's plastic pond safe at Grandma Amberchuk's house. They pitched tent wherever they wanted and fished for trout to cook over a campfire. They sent postcards home and had their pictures taken in one of those jokey places where you can shove your head through a hole in a cardboard cutout and there you were, a convict in a striped suit, a sheriff or a Mountie. Stubby had her picture taken as a clown, as a fat lady in front of a circus tent and as a rodeo rider on a bucking horse. Dave shoved his face through the hole with a big cigar stuck in his mouth and had his picture taken in a dancing girl's costume. They had a wonderful time. They got suntanned, bug-bitten and ate what they wanted when the spirit moved them. But eventually Dave had to take her back to the rented house, where Vinnie and Earl were waiting.

Everyone was very quite and secretive and there was a lot of smirking and smiling and not letting Stubby in on what was obviously a great big secret. A week after she was back from her holiday with her dad Stubby was—she thought—off on another holiday, this one with Earl and Vinnie. They got in Earl's car and drove away from the rented house on their way down-island to Victoria, where they spent two days riding double-decker buses, eating fish'n'chips and admiring the hanging baskets of flowers. Then they drove onto the ferry. When they drove off the ferry on the mainland, Earl and Vinnie were laughing at some joke they didn't share with Stubby.

She fell asleep in the car and when she finally woke up it was pitch black, they were still driving and her bladder was fit to burst. They stopped at a roadside cafe so she could use the facilities, but nobody suggested having supper and when Stubby said she was hungry they told her, "We'll be there soon," and "It won't be long," and "Not far to go now." For lack of anything better to do, Stubby fell asleep again, and when she woke up, Earl was lifting her.

"I can walk," she snapped, pushing off his arm. "Don't touch me."

"Here, here, little miss," he said, his voice cold and angry, "you watch your tone of voice! Nobody talks to me like that."

Stubby ignored him and got out of the car on her own steam, followed Vinnie up the stairs of a house, yawning, and wondering aloud where they were.

"This is your new room," Vinnie said happily. Stubby gaped. It was exactly what they showed in the magazines, exactly what Stubby had never particularly wanted.

"What do you mean *my* room?"

"This is our new house."

"What do you mean?" Stubby stammered. "We don't live here!"

"We do now," Earl said happily.

"Not me." Stubby could feel something starting to shake inside her. "Not me though, eh? I live in our old place, right?"

"You live with me," Vinnie said, satisfaction virtually dripping from every syllable. "I have custody."

"We do," Earl corrected, and Vinnie nodded.

"But my *dad*!" Stubby wailed.

"You'll see him for holidays," Vinnie smiled.

"But weekends, too! It's supposed to be weekends, too."

"Well, that's obviously not possible, is it," Earl lectured. "I mean, after all, I have a new job here, and it's too far to go back and forth every weekend, you'd no more than get there and it would be time to come right back again. I'm sure if he wants to see you he can arrange something, but until he does, you'll have to wait to see him at Christmas.''

''You cheated!'' Stubby screamed. ''You cheated, the both of you, and you just wait until I tell my dad about it!''

Earl lifted her by one arm, took her to her new bed, dumped her on it and told her she'd better start learning how to control her temper, then told her until she did learn how to control her temper she could just stay in her room and work it off by herself. He closed the door behind him when he left. And locked it.

Stubby sat on her new bed with the white bedspread, staring at the little lamp that looked like a lady in a pink hoopskirt with a lightbulb growing out of her head and a lampshade instead of a hat, and she raged. Silently and internally. Stubby was learning the politics of silence.

It took her almost a week to find out where in hell's name she was. The day the men came to install the new phone in the new house, Stubby picked up the new phone book and opened it. At the top of every page, the name of the town. Vetchburg. That's all she needed to know. She put the phone book back, went to her room and sat on the new carpet, her back against the pink wall, and read *Trixie Beldon and the Red Trailer Mystery*.

Both her mother and Earl had been watching her very closely as if expecting her to pull some kind of stunt. They were right. Stubby waited her chance to pull one, and to pull it good. She ate her supper quietly, did not glare when Earl corrected her table manners, helped stack the dishes in the sink, bathed, cleaned the tub out when she was finished, then went to bed. She fell asleep immediately, as she always did, and woke up in the middle of the night to go to the bathroom, as she always did. But instead of going straight back to bed, she picked up the new phone, dialed for long distance, then dialed Dave's phone number. He answered on the sixth ring and Stubby told him where she was. ''Earl's got a job here,'' she said quickly, ''and they've got a new house and everything. And they say I have to live here too.''

''What's the name of the place again?'' Dave asked.

''Vetchburg,'' Stubby answered. ''I don't know where it is, though.'' And that was all she got a chance to say. Earl was there, in his pale blue pajamas with the darker blue stripe. He took the receiver from her hand, replaced it on top of the desk phone, then slapped her backside three times, hard, and told her she wasn't allowed to use the phone without permission and wasn't to make long distance calls until she had the money to pay for them herself.

Stubby didn't care. She went back to bed and fell asleep in spite of the place on her round little bum that burned long after the sound of Earl's slaps had faded.

Dave didn't arrive the next day but he arrived the day after that and there was one hell of a go-round. Stubby missed most of it because the first thing Earl did when he heard Dave's voice was grab Stubby, shove her in her bedroom and lock the door. But after the police arrived Stubby was let out of her room and then everyone had to go down to the courthouse to see a magistrate and some child welfare workers.

Earl had the divorce and custody papers right there where he could lay his hands on them as soon as they were needed and he took them with him. The upshot of the whole thing was that Stubby had to stay with Earl and Vinnie until a proper hearing could be arranged. Dave had to return to Bright's Crossing and get his lawyer back to work on it all, but Stubby had a chance to spend some time with him, time enough for them to make a few plans of their own.

She started school in September and it wasn't too bad. Nobody was interested in giving her much of a hard time, even if she was the new kid in town, because, after all, Earl was vice-principal. She didn't bother telling anyone Earl wasn't her dad, and she didn't bother raising a fuss when she found out she'd been registered as Sheilagh May Blades. She just waited, she bided her time and waited for the lawyers to do whatever it was lawyers were supposed to do in order for her to go live where she wanted to live.

She waited all fall and all winter. Whatever was going on didn't seem to be much of her business. Earl had a lawyer and Dave had a lawyer and a couple of times Earl and Vinnie went down to have meetings with people, but nobody would tell Stubby what it was all about no matter how often she asked. What's more, nobody listened when she said she liked Bright's Crossing a lot better than Vetchburg. So Stubby waited for the letter Dave had told her he would send, but it didn't arrive. Every night she came home from school and asked, "Any mail for me?" and every night Vinnie said, "No, but we got a new catalogue," or "No, but there's a free sample of toothpaste in that big envelope if you want to try it."

Sometimes in the evening the phone rang, and a few times it was for her and she was allowed to talk, with Earl and Vinnie hovering over her trying to hear what Dave was saying.

"Did you get my letter?" he asked.

"No," she said, "did you get mine?"

"Did you mail it yourself?" Dave asked.

"No, I wrote it and Earl said he'd mail it when he went to the post office. Didn't you get it?"

"I guess it'll come tomorrow or the next day. Don't worry about it,

Stubbzers, the post office is as slow as a snail. Who gets the mail at your house?''

"It comes through a slot in the door when I'm at school, nobody has to go to the general delivery in the store or anything.''

"Tell you what,'' Dave tried to sound casual, "I'll talk to a guy here about the slow mail delivery, okay? Some guy'll come out to the house to see you. All you have to do is tell him you aren't getting your letters, okay?''

"How's Grandma? She said she'd write me but I never got nothing.''

"Grandma's fine. You tell the guy who comes to see you that you didn't get Grandma's letters either. Grandpa's fine, too; he's been doing a lot of trout fishing. Just wait until you see the place he's found, Stubbs. Fish as big as your arm!''

The guy came out to the house and asked some questions and Stubby said no, she hadn't got any letter or cards at all, not even one. Then the man spoke to Earl and said something about registered mail, and about the law insisting letters belonged to the person to whom they were addressed, and Earl got real mad and went to his bedroom and came back with a half dozen letters and some jokey cards. All of them addressed to Stubby Amberchuk, and all of them opened.

"He says,'' Stubby challenged, looking up from the letter on her lap, "that there's ten bucks in here for me, but it's not here.''

"It's in the bank,'' Earl gritted, "in an account for your education.''

"He didn't say it was for education,'' she snapped. "He says it's to go to the show.'' She felt very brave with the government man sitting on the new sofa, watching Earl carefully and making notes in his little notebook.

"If you want to go to the show,'' Earl answered carefully, "I'll give you the money.'' His tone was reasonable but his face was nearly purple.

"I don't want to go to the show,'' Stubby argued stubbornly. "I just want my money that my dad sent to me.'' Earl nearly choked but the man nodded, so, emboldened, Stubby forged ahead. "And if I've got money in the bank, I want to see my little book.''

At Christmas Stubby went to Bright's Crossing and had six days with Dave. Six days of Grandma Amberchuk's cuddles, six days of cousins, six days of not having to remember a thousand rules, six days of jokes and teasing and being swooped up and tossed around from one set of heavily calloused paws to another. But on the seventh day it was into the pickup truck and back to Vetchburg.

"Snow,'' Stubby said gloomily, "that's all it seems to do here in the wintertime.''

"Sure is cold,'' Dave agreed.

"Look at the trees,'' she dared.

"What trees?" Dave agreed. "Them's just shrubs and bushes. Someone pruned them too heavily. Not good for a thing." He laughed. "Hell," he elaborated, "a woodpecker'd have to carry a lunchpail between 'em!'"

"Yeah," she agreed sourly, "and I have to live here!'"

"Give the lawyer a chance," Dave soothed.

"It's taking too long," she was sobbing, trying to knuckle the tears from her eyes. "It's just taking forever and ever!'"

"Easy on, Stubbzers." He put his big strong arm around her and pulled her against the comforting bulk of his huge body. "It might take some time, but that only means they're bein' real careful, dotting all the i's and crossing all the t's and making it all ticketyboo.'"

So she gave the lawyers a chance. But nothing seemed to happen. There wasn't time during Easter holidays for her to go to Bright's Crossing to see Dave, nor for Dave to come up to see her, what with work and all, but there were cards and letters from Grandma and Grandpa, from all the aunts, who signed for the uncles and cousins as well, and she had a big chocolate egg full of jellybeans delivered by the postman. In spite of its trip through the mail it hadn't broken, even if some of the hard candy flowers had chipped off the outside. She got a chocolate hen and a chocolate bunny from Earl and Vinnie, and she phoned Dave collect and had a good long yack, so it wasn't too unpleasant.

But in spite of it all, it was still a bit disappointing. Quite, in fact.

Still nothing seemed to be happening with the lawyers or the court. When school was out Vinnie told her she was going to summer camp.

"I'm s'posed to spend the summer with Dad!" Stubby screamed.

"Not this year," Vinnie said coldly.

"Why?"

Nobody would tell her. She kicked up a stink, she argued and pitched a fit, and still there were no explanations. The phone got taken from its jack and disappeared into Vinnie's bedroom and the door was locked most of the time. Earl tanned her backside twice because of the stink she was fomenting and she spent several hours locked in her room, then Vinnie let her out for supper and Earl pitched his fit about how Stubby was supposed to stay in her room, without supper and with no distractions. So back into the room she went while Earl and Vinnie had a big row, and after that was over Stubby came out of the room and was told that the reason she wasn't going to spend the summer with her father was that he'd broken his leg in the bush and was in the hospital in traction and wouldn't be able to look after her.

"Then I'll stay with Grandma Amberchuk!'"

"No you won't. For one thing, she's an old woman and doesn't need to have some kid hanging off her all the time. And for another, the visitation order says nothing at all about you staying with her, it says you have to stay with your dad. Well you can't stay in hospital with him, so I don't have to send you and I'm not sending you anywhere but camp.''

''You're supposed to!'' Stubby dug in her heels. ''The judge said!''

''Just so you won't be too disappointed about missing your trip to Bright's Crossing, we're going to go to Calgary to see the Stampede. Now, isn't that generous of Earl?''

She was supposed to be satisfied with that. But Stubby wasn't, not the least bit satisfied at all. In fact, Stubby was furious. And it showed. ''You fix your face, young lady,'' Earl ordered. Stubby knew she was supposed to replace the frown on her face with a look of bland acceptance, but she didn't even try.

She glowered. Earl got up to give her a damned good whack on the butt and Vinnie stopped him. ''Of course she's disappointed,'' Vinnie said. ''After all, a summer in Bright's Crossing is a lot nicer than summer here.''

''What's wrong with here?'' Earl demanded, stung to the quick.

''Well, what *isn't* wrong with here?'' Vinnie scoffed. ''There isn't a lake worthy of the name within a ten-mile radius of the town, the river isn't fit to swim in, it's so dusty you practically wear the enamel off your teeth eating a sandwich and the blackflies have a person anaemic within five minutes of going outside the house.''

Then they had a big argument, with Earl saying Vinnie had spoiled Stubby rotten and that Stubby was ungrateful and sullen and a brat to boot, and Vinnie saying Earl might be a teacher but he didn't know bugger-nothing about kids and Stubby wasn't spoiled, she just had a good strong mind of her own and wasn't about to be dictated to by someone who didn't seem to be able to let another person have any opinion but one that he, Earl Wonderful Blades, had handed to them on his own silver platter. Earl said he often wondered if Vinnie knew how little sense such statements made. Right about then was when Stubby went to her room. She sat on the floor so she wouldn't mess her coverlet and she glared at the dresser which both Earl and Vinnie had told her repeatedly was the very best one money could buy from the Eaton's catalogue. When she heard the sounds of the argument dying down to what promised to be an icy four-day silence, Stubby crawled into bed, pulled the covers up around her ears so nobody would notice she was still fully dressed, and pretended to go to sleep.

Vinnie looked in on her and saw her snuggled in bed. She turned off the overhead light and closed the door. Two hours later Stubby was out of bed, quietly busy. She got her pack from the back of the closet, shoved in her bathing suit, a spare pair of jeans, a few shirts, a warm sweater and lots of underwear and socks. She tied her good sneakers to the strap of the pack, put on her laceup winter boots that doubled as hiking boots and pulled on her last year's blue denim jacket.

Then Stubby got her bankbook from her top drawer, checked to be sure she had her student card for identification plus her wallet-sized birth certificate, put them in the left breast pocket of her jacket and stepped on the snap to make sure it was properly fastened. Under the doily which sat under the fancy silver-backed brush and comb set Vinnie and Earl had given her for Christmas, hidden there just in case of emergencies, was the money her dad had put inside the big Easter egg, the money neither Vinnie nor Earl knew she had. And what's more, Stubby knew where there was even more money. Stubby knew where Vinnie kept her secret, her mad money, hidden under the paper-wrapped cigar-looking things in the pale blue box in the cabinet under the bathroom basin.

Moving as quietly as she could, Stubby went to the bathroom, pulled out the blue box, removed the cylinders, and hauled out Vinnie's stash. Without counting it, she put it in her pocket, tiptoed back to her room, shrugged on her pack and left by the side door from the kitchen. She got her bike from the garage and pedalled furiously away from the nice new house.

She didn't get far. The police drove past and saw her and, as they explained to Earl a short time later, they couldn't think of one good reason why the vice-principal's seven-year-old daughter was out on a bike with no light at one-thirty in the morning.

"Thank you," said Earl, "I'll take care of it." He lifted Stubby clear off the floor, plopped her down on a straight-backed kitchen chair and told her to sit tight while he showed the police to the front door. When the police had left, Earl came back and stood there in his grey pajamas with the wide maroon stripe, demanding answers. When Stubby didn't give him any answers at all and just met each question with absolute silence, Earl blew his cool and backhanded her across the cheek, knocking her from the chair to the floor. Vinnie started yelling, Earl started hollering, Vinnie screeched, Earl slapped Vinnie's face and Stubby, shocked and horrified, cracked like an egg and spilled everything.

Stubby got chased back to her bedroom by an icily enraged Earl. She was barely asleep when there was Vinnie, with a look of absolute determination on her face. "Ssssh," she said conspiratorially, "he's sleeping." Stubby followed her mother, and mere minutes later they were driving away in Earl's car. By next afternoon Stubby was sitting in front of a plate of supper listening to Vinnie explain things to her mother and father.

"I couldn't take the thought of an entire summer in that dust bowl," Vinnie lied, with a wide and happy smile. "Besides," she added deceptively, "with Dave in the hospital and all, it seemed like the thing to do. I mean, I'm sure a visit from Sheilagh would cheer him up no end."

What it really was, of course, was all that money in Stubby's pocket. Earl had wanted to know where it had all come from, and Stubby, spilling her guts like any amateur, had told him. Right about then was when the heat of attention got shifted from Stubby and her little escapade to Vinnie. "Summer in Vetchburg," Vinnie said brightly, "really explains that old saying, I've enjoyed about as much of this as I can stand. Why, the mosquitoes come in over the horizon in V formation, with outriders searching for a good place to take the carcasses. They've got forks and knives, but the official butchers cut it out of you with little chainsaws!"

Lying in bed that night, Stubby remembered the way Vinnie had walked out on Earl and how much it was like the way Vinnie had walked out on Dave. What would life have been like if she'd followed Vinnie that first time? The thought was almost as horrible as the vision of what life would have been like if Vinnie hadn't walked out the second time.

Stubby went to the hospital to see her dad and knew right away it was all far worse than anything anybody had told her. A broken leg isn't a big thing to a gyppo logger; they usually wear their cast for only as long as it takes them to get gassed up and break it off so they can hobble off to the next bar. But Dave wasn't going to be on Unemployment Enjoyment, he wasn't going to be going bar-hopping, he was in bed with his leg hanging from a plumber's nightmare of pipes, pulleys, ropes and canvas slings, and the cast on his leg was bloodstained where the big metal things stuck out the sides.

"Does that go right into your leg?" Stubby gulped.

"Right through to the other side," Dave replied, his face the colour of cottage cheese left in the sun to go sour.

"How bad is it?"

"Well, the doctor says I'll be able to dance once the cast is off," Dave tried to joke, "which is great because I couldn't dance worth a damn before they put it on me."

"They weren't going to let me come," she blurted.

Dave looked at her and nodded, his eyes dark-rimmed with fatigue.

"You knew?" Stubby felt as if a big black hole was opening in the world and she was in dire danger of falling into it.

"Stubs," Dave pleaded, his voice thin and weak, "the paper said you were to spend summertime with me, not with Grandma. I phoned the lawyer. He said summer'd be over before we even got into court about it all. Do I look," he demanded bitterly, "as if I could fight anybody, even a blind man?'' He didn't look as if he could stand his ground against a half-grown barn cat. ''If it would'a done any good, Stubbs, I'd'a tried, but what's the use when you'd'a been back in school before we even got our say?''

''They're cheating,'' she said firmly.

''Yeah,'' he sighed, ''well, everyone to their own taste as the vicar said, licking the cow's ass.''

Stubby went to see him every day. She was there at eleven in the morning when visiting hours started and stayed until they brought his lunch to him. Then she headed off on a bike borrowed from her cousin Jim and joined the other kids at the wading pond in the playground. Just before suppertime, when she knew Dave's afternoon nap was done, she got back on her bike and returned to the hospital for another half-hour or so. Then it was home to Vinnie's parents' house to have supper, a bath and go to bed.

Every night Stubby sat up in bed staring out the window at the washblue sky, watching the pastels of Island twilight change from pink to flame, then back to pink again, and she listened to the sounds of kids playing softball in the park. It was hard to figure out what to do next. Not knowing what anyone else had in mind made her problems seem all the bigger.

Then Earl arrived. Vinnie's mother and father and even arsletart Gordon took a firm grip on their best company manners and smiled pleasantly, even though they knew from the look on Earl's face that Vinnie's reasons for showing up had been severely edited and were not exactly accurate. Which is not to say they thought Vinnie was a liar, but all of them knew from personal experience how one person's edit is another person's censorship.

Earl had supper with the family, then he and Vinnie went off in his car. They weren't back when Stubby went to bed, they weren't back when she finally went to sleep, but they were back when she got to the table for breakfast in the morning. From the look on Vinnie's face she hadn't had much sleep and hadn't enjoyed being awake. Stubby headed off right after breakfast and went to see Grandma Amberchuk, then went to the hospital to see her dad, and when she came home for supper Vinnie looked even more tired than she had in the morning. After supper Vinnie and Earl headed off in the car again. They both had hoarse voices and Earl looked as if he had Old Dutch cleansing powder in his shorts. His every move was controlled and his smile sat on his face with the grim determination of a constipated person on a warm toilet seat.

The following morning Vinnie looked exhausted. She had obviously been crying, her voice sounded as if she'd been eating gravel for a week and there didn't seem to be enough coffee in the pot to satisfy her. "Pack your clothes," she said in a tired voice, "we're leaving this afternoon."

Instead of packing, Stubby went to her bedroom, closed the door, opened the window, went out it and got on her cousin Jim's bike. By the time Vinnie and Earl realized she was gone, she was at Grandma Amberchuk's place blurting out her story. Before Earl could drive his rented car to Grandma's place, Stubby was in Grandma and Grandpa's car and the lawyer had been phoned.

When Vinnie and Earl walked into the hospital room, Stubby was sitting on Dave's bed holding his hand and Grandma Amberchuk was standing like a grenadier guard at the foot of the bed. Grandpa stood off to one side smiling quietly, and that smile took all the starch out of Earl's stuffed shirt. Still, Earl had to try. He just had to let these workies know he was not going to just fold like a wet noodle.

"This is all ridiculous," he started, and Grandpa Amberchuk smiled even more widely. "There is no way at all Dave can look after Sheilagh and there's nothing in the court order says we have to hand her over to someone else."

"Who in hell are you," Dave asked tiredly, "to decide what will or will not be done with Stubby? You got less to do with it than my mom or dad. At least they're related to her."

"I'm her stepfather," Earl said proudly.

"Seems to me," Grandpa Amberchuk said in his soft rumbling voice, "that before anyone starts calling themselves anything special in regard to a kid, that kid ought to have some say. And what Stubby has had to say so far don't sound to me like you've got much claim."

"The lawyer's on his way up," Dave said. He wanted to roar and shout, to holler and bluster and kick ass, but he was barely able to hold his head off the pillow.

"Oh for christ's sweet sake," Vinnie sighed.

"Gonna fight this one, Vin," Grandpa Amberchuk warned. "Gonna fight 'er every inch of the way. Gonna show you something you never even imagined before in your life, because that kid don't want to live in any place with no trees and no grass."

"Vinnie," Earl commanded, "you're that child's mother. Just pick her up and let's get out of here."

"Shut up, Earl," Vinnie said softly. She was exhausted from the fight she'd just been through with Earl, and she knew with a kind of hopeless sick certainty that the feathers were about to really hit the fan between Stubby and her stepfather. And would continue to hit the fan for the next who knew however many years. And Vinnie had used up all her yelling and shouting, had used up all her defiance and spit, she'd worn out all her standing up for her rights and come to the end of her ability to put up with one emotionally charged row after another. It was one thing to go into court in a town where nobody knew Dave or any other Amberchuk, but it was something else altogether to go into court in Bright's Crossing and try to explain why she had never mentioned to anyone she was planning to leave town with Stubby.

Any judge in his right mind would give custody to the mother of a child born in Bright's Crossing and living in Bright's Crossing, but nobody, not even a judge, was going to sentence any child to leave the Island and go live up country, where if it wasn't dust blowing in the window it was snow blowing in the door. And Earl wasn't apt to want to move back to Bright's Crossing, where he'd be a teacher again instead of vice-principal. He probably wouldn't want to move back to Bright's Crossing if they gave him the entire school system, because Earl did not like the Amberchuks, not a single solitary one of them, and that included Stubby, glaring at him with open defiance now that she was safely surrounded by her relatives.

Vinnie stared at her daughter and thought over the past number of years, starting with the day she had realized she had missed one menstrual period and was overdue for the second. She looked at Earl and knew that there was nothing at all Stubby could ever do that would make her acceptable to Earl. Besides, Stubby couldn't stand Earl's guts and Earl felt the same way about Stubby.

"One day," Vinnie said sadly, "One day you'll be sorry, Sheilagh." Then she turned and headed for the doorway.

"Vinnie," Earl snapped, "come back and get your child."

"Earl," Vinnie gritted, "shut your face until you're asked your opinion, okay?" Suddenly Vinnie was out the door and down the hallway without so much as a goodbye. Earl hesitated, not knowing exactly what was expected of him.

"I'll ship her things down at the beginning of next week," he finally managed. Nobody answered him, so he left in pursuit of Vinnie.

Vinnie packed her belongings, Earl put the suitcases in his car, arsletart Gordon promised to return the rented vehicle to the company and Vinnie and Earl drove off in silence. Vinnie's mother, father, brother and sisters stared at each other in puzzled silence, not at all sure why Sheilagh was going to stay with her Grandma and Grandpa Amberchuk, but too polite to ask each other any questions. Vinnie fell asleep in the car while they waited in the lineup for the ferry and she slept almost the entire crossing to the mainland. When she woke up she had a good rip-roaring five-minute argument with Earl, mostly about her telling him to mind his own business, after which she refused to talk to him for the rest of the trip to Vetchburg. They had something to eat at a roadside pancake house. Earl told her she'd feel better after a good night's sleep, and when she didn't answer, he decided that meant she agreed with him. After all, everyone knows silence means consent.

Stubby played softball until it was too dark to see the ball, then she went to Grandma Amberchuk's place, had a good scrub in the tub and went to bed naked. She fell asleep listening to the peeping call of the mosquito hawks and the scratchy noises made by the claws of Myrtle the turtle against the sides of the little plastic pool.

2

Stubby was back at school before Dave got out of the hospital. Nobody asked her, but if anybody had, Stubby would have said her life hadn't been this good since the softball glove kicked off the final straw. She and Myrtle had a room all to themselves, Grandma Amberchuk had been around enough kids in her lifetime not to get bent out of shape over ordinary everyday things and grade three had a lot more going for it than grades one and two had ever had. Besides, Stubby now had a bike of her own and didn't have to borrow a clunker from her cousin. It might not have been a great bike, it might not have even looked like very much of a bike, it wasn't a ten-speed or a five-speed or even a three-speed, it was just a standard street bike, and whatever colour it might originally have been, it was now painted with dark blue enamel. On the fenders Stubby put strips of bright orange reflective tape. There were no handgrips on the handlebars and the carrier rack had seen better days long before Stubby salvaged it from the garbage dump. But it got her to and from school or anywhere else she was going and Stubby thought it was quite wonderful.

Dave came out of the hospital with a limp and two canes. It was obvious to anyone with half an eye he couldn't look after himself, let alone look after himself and Stubby. So he moved in with Grandma Amberchuk too, back into the room he had shared with his brother all those years ago before he met Vinnie and invested in a bottle of sloe gin.

"If it hadda been my arm," he tried to grin, his face pasty, the new lines cut between his eyebrows and around his mouth standing sharp in Stubby's eyes. "If it hadda been my arm I could'a gone to the second *hand* store and got me a new one," and Stubby laughed at his joke, even though she didn't much feel like laughing.

Dave insisted he could cut the kindling by himself, thank you, he might be a cripple but he wasn't a helpless one. What's more, he could carry the kindling into the house and pile it behind the wood stove. Every morning he got up, sucking his breath in sharply when the muscles in his smashed leg cramped and ached. He dressed himself and made it down the stairs without help, the metal brace clumping, the two canes tapping. No matter how dark the circles under his eyes, he smiled as he moved toward the table, feeling his way with his two shiny aluminum sticks and if, when he sat down, his mouth tightened until his leg was bent at the knee and lifted to its proper place, everybody else was too polite to comment on it. Grandma Amberchuk had his vitamin pills and aspirins waiting for him and while he washed them down with orange juice she poured him a cup of strong coffee. About halfway through the coffee the aspirins started to work and Dave could speak without that hot-wire sound in his voice, the sound, Stubby knew, that meant he was gritting his throat muscles to hold back a groan or a whimper.

There were things she mustn't do, like bump his chair or sit on his knee the way she used to do. She could sit on the arm of his easy chair and from there she could lay her head on his shoulder or feel his big arm warm around her waist, and that was almost as good. They explained to her that her weight not only hurt him, it slowed the circulation of blood in his bad leg and slowed the healing. She tried hard not to think of what it used to be like sitting on his knee and snuggling. You didn't do anybody any good at all thinking things like that.

They also told her she mustn't snitch one of his aspirins, that they were special ones, special for bum legs and not good for anything else. Sometimes the aspirins were white, sometimes pink, sometimes they were pills, sometimes capsules or tablets. When she asked she got told that they came from different factories and everyone does things a bit different. But sometimes he'd take an aspirin and be fine, other times he'd take an aspirin and be asleep within fifteen minutes, the sweat standing in beads on his forehead.

While Stubby was at school, Dave chopped kindling and invented six dozen different ways to carry firewood into the house. Determined not to just sit around like some kind of gibble, he took to helping out with chores he normally never would have considered. He could put T-shirts, underwear, socks and jeans through the wringer as well as anybody could and, balancing carefully on the porch, his belly pushed against the porch rail to help him keep from teetering, he could hang clothes on the line at least as well as Stubby, although neither of them came within a prayer of being as fast or as neat as Grandma. Every three hours he took a couple more aspirins and if the pain was particularly bad he spiked his tea with something from the Liquor Control Board. After a while there was always a faint smell of LCB on his breath, which everyone said was no wonder if you saw the mess his leg was.

By Christmas the leg was strong enough to support him without suddenly collapsing and sending him sideways. He only needed one cane, and didn't need that one all the time. He was, he decided, about as good as he was going to get for a while. So he and Stubby moved back home.

The house smelled funny, almost like the school—old stale air and clothes left hanging in the closet, the water in the toilet bowl and tank gone rusty, the stain dark and large on the old white porcelain sink where the tap dripped. Stubby and Grandma scrubbed every floor in the house but applied wax on none of them for fear Dave would take a tumble because of it. They stripped and aired the beds and mattresses and while Stubby scrubbed out the toilet, basin and tub Grandma did the sink and counters. Still the house smelled like an old school. "It'll be okay," Stubby promised her doubtful-eyed Grandma. "You'll see, just wait. I'll get some incense sticks or something."

She and Dave put up a small Christmas tree and piled presents under it but did not consider, not even for one brief second, cooking Christmas dinner by themselves. They had the big meal at Grandma's place and took lots of leftovers home with them that evening.

After they got home Dave sat in the living room with his sore leg up on the new footstool, drinking LCB brandy and watching television. Stubby tried hard to think of something she could say to him that would make her seem like interesting company instead of just a kid, but she couldn't think of anything so after a while she just went to bed. Then the phone rang. She had to get up to answer it because Dave was having trouble getting out of his chair.

It was Vinnie and Earl phoning to thank Stubby for the presents she had sent them, and Stubby thanked them for the stuff they had sent her. Earl wanted to know if the dresses had fit. Stubby confessed the pink one was too big around the waist, but Grandma said it would be no problem at all to adjust it to fit. What Stubby diplomatically left unsaid was that the pink dress would be adjusted to fit her cousin Patsy, who thought it gorgeous and had been allowed to take it home with her after Stubby loudly declared she'd go naked before she'd wear anything with ruffles all down the front. "It makes me look like a pink beachball," she glowered, and it was true, it did. Looking like a beachball of one colour or the other was something that happened quite often to Stubby who, while not fat, had not, as Grandma put it, started to get her true growth yet. Patsy was eighteen months younger than Stubby and already a full head taller.

"Don't worry, Stubbzers," Dave grinned blearily, "good things come in small packages, it's only shit has to be heaped in high piles.''

''Poison comes in small packages, too,'' she countered.

''One man's poison is another man's something-or-other,'' Dave grabbed her and pulled her close. ''If you want we can tie your feet to the porch and your head to the pickup and put a bit of a stretch on you.''

''No thanks,'' she decided.

Nick Zambovski could ride his two-wheeler along the railroad track. He was the only kid Stubby had ever heard of who could lift the bike onto the glistening rail, start running alongside, then jump, land on the seat, swing his leg over the bar, pedal and not have the bike dump him flat on his back in the gravel alongside the track. Even people who had seen him do it, even people seeing him do it, said it was impossible. But impossible or not, Nick could do it. Not all the time—he himself would have been the first to admit there were times he knew ''in my bones'' that it wouldn't work, times when he was tired or too excited or sleepy or not feeling quite up to it, and those times Nick just shrugged and said he didn't think he could do it today, maybe tomorrow or the day after that.

Stubby yearned to be able to ride her bike along the rail. Every day she tried and every day she wound up in the gravel, flat on her back, flat on her belly, flat on her side, but still she tried. She could walk the rail, balancing carefully, arms outstretched, but she couldn't ride her bike on the rail. ''Hell,'' Dave scolded, putting iodine on the skinned palm of her hand, ''you can't even *push* your bike along the rail!'' But that didn't stop Stubby from trying. Just before Easter, she picked herself up from the gravel rail bed one more time, glared at the rail, glared at her bike and gave it up for a bad job that day. She picked up the bike and started pushing it alongside the track.

One day, she hoped, she'd get to see the other end of those glistening rails. One day Stubby intended to get herself a scooter or a speeder and pump herself from Bright's Crossing clear across the prairies to Montreal, then, before pumping on to Newfoundland, she would see a National Hockey League game. She had it all planned. She'd sit in the Montreal section and cheer at the top of her voice for whoever the other team was. She was sure it would kick off a wonderful fight, maybe even as good as the one they had when Rocket Richard was kicked out of the game and the whole city went nuts. Stubby didn't remember that game, it happened before she was paying attention to much of anything at all, but she'd heard her dad and her uncles talk about it often enough, even though all they knew about it was what they'd heard on the radio. They made it sound as if they'd been right in the thick of it all, punching and kicking, hitting and gouging and having a right good old time.

Stubby stopped to tie the lace on her once-white now-grey sneaker and, while bent over double, frowning with concentration, she saw, some fifteen feet behind her, the dog. It had obviously been following her and now was sitting in between the two glistening rails, one ear cocked, head tilted, waiting. Waiting to see what Stubby was going to do next. Waiting to see where Stubby was going to go next.

"Where did you come from?" Stubby asked. The dog tilted her head to the other side, keeping the same ear cocked. "Think you're cute, eh?" Stubby growled, still ticked off at her constant failure to ride the rail the way Nick could. Shoelace retied, Stubby once again lifted her bike and pushed it along the small path beside the tracks. Everybody knew you weren't supposed to walk the right-of-way. Everybody knew if you got caught the E&N would take you to court and you'd get fined. Everybody walked the track anyway. It had been so many years since the E&N paid any attention to all its trains nobody ever expected to ever hear tell again of anyone getting seen by a railwayman, let alone stopped by one. Looking back over her shoulder, Stubby saw the dog following, and now Stubby could see that she was tired, limping, and that somewhere in her undoubtedly spotty parentage there had been terrier. Wire-haired terrier, in fact.

"C'mere, dog," Stubby invited, snapping her fingers. The dog limped up, mouth open, tongue lolling, and Stubby scooped her up and put her in the wire basket clattering from the handlebars. The dog promptly lay down as if she had been whelped and raised in that basket. Stubby stroked the brown ears, scratched the white head and examined the travel-worn paws. "You've been covering the miles," she muttered and the dog panted agreement. "Looks like you've been travelling for weeks. Days, anyhow."

She rode the bike down the embankment from the railway tracks and pedalled home. Naturally the first thing Dave saw was the dog. He stared at it, then at Stubby. "Where'd you get that poor excuse?"

"On the tracks."

"Looks like someone threw it away," he laughed. "If I had a dog like that, that's what I'd do with it. It's just the right size to chuck from a moving train."

"She's got sore feet," Stubby said stubbornly.

"Yeah? Just hope she didn't get sore feet by walking for ten, that's all I got to say."

As it turned out, the dog hadn't been walking for ten, she was only walking for six, but they didn't arrive for almost a month and by then the dog was in much better shape. Her feet had healed and she was six shades cleaner because of the baths Stubby gave her. Stubby called her Daisy for no reason except she liked the name, and Dave called the dog Dozey because he said she was too stupid to learn more than to lick her chops.

People looked at Daisy and grinned. Whether she was riding in the box Stubby put in the wire carrier or whether she was racing after the bike, her whiskers blowing in the wind, people looked at her and smiled. Shaggy coat, bewhiskered face, cutoff tail, Daisy was a grin inducer. She was white when she was clean, except for two brown ears and a brown patch on her back just above her tail. And most of the time Daisy had her mouth open in what Stubby insisted was a big grin of her own.

"How old's your dog?" they'd ask.

"My dad thinks she's three, my grandma thinks she's five, and I've only had her a little while," Stubby answered.

"Is she going to have pups?" they asked, looking at the round belly.

"I hope so," Stubby laughed, "but my dad says there's a good chance they'll be jokes, just like she is."

Ten days after the pups were born they were all spoken for, in spite of the fact that Stubby, in a vain attempt to have them around for a while, had said they would cost ten bucks each. "I didn't think anyone would pay ten bucks for a dog without papers," she mourned.

"Next time ask for fifteen," her dad laughed.

"Wonder who their father was . . ." Stubby puzzled, looking in the box at the squirming pups.

"Looks to me like their father was the six fastest dogs in sight," Dave laughed. "You've got every colour in there except maroon. Who knows, next time you might get maroon."

When it came time to give the pups to their new owners, Stubby determined there would be no next time. Daisy howled and Stubby bawled, and even Dave obviously didn't enjoy any of the six farewells. Stubby meant to make an appointment with the vet but she forgot and by the time nature reminded her it was too late; Daisy was out making her own choices and decisions. The male dogs barked and snarled, growled and fought, they raced and chased and slobbered hopefully; Labby mutts and spaniel crosses, Dobie-looking studs of all sizes and even a hopeful Maltese. There were cockapoos, peekapoos, pugapoos, and multipoos. There was even one small poodle named, predictably enough, Pierre, and it was he whom Daisy chose to bring home with her. Pierre didn't stay long but he stayed happily and when he left, against his will, in the back of his owner's station wagon, Daisy gulped water until she ought to have split down the middle, then waited until the first time anyone went out the door and that was it, Daisy was off again.

"There she goes!" Dave yelled, and Stubby raced for her bike. Daisy cut through the front yard, slithered under the fence and was gone before Stubby had her bike out of the shed. By the time Stubby made it to the road, Daisy was a dot disappearing in the distance. Stubby went after her, legs pumping frantically.

She didn't find Daisy for more than an hour, and then it was only the yiping, yelping and yodelling that gave her the clue and led her to the scrambling mass of assorted dogs and wotzit-poos. Daisy was grinning wider than ever but was too tired to evade Stubby. "You oughtta be ashamed of yourself," Stubby scolded, snapping the leash to Daisy's much-slobbered collar and fastening it to the handlebar of the bike. "Just sit in that box and behave."

She was almost at the bridge over Haslam Creek where the road turned onto the four-lane highway, the last place in the world she expected to see an old woman, but there, for sure, was an old woman, an old woman with blue-tinted hair, an obviously expensive grey suit, grey stockings and grey shoes, holding in her grey-gloved hands a white cane. Walking down the side of the road toward the highway.

"Hey, lady," Stubby called, pedalling to catch up to the woman, "Hey, lady, there's a lot of traffic on that highway."

"Highway?" the woman turned her face toward Stubby, and she could see herself reflected in the tinted glasses. "I didn't expect to get anywhere near the highway."

"Well, that's where you're heading," Stubby insisted. "Can't you hear the traffic?"

"Is that traffic?" the old woman shook her head. "I thought it was the sound of the creek. I seem to have got myself turned around somehow."

"Which way did you think you were heading?"

"I meant to walk home," the old woman said peevishly. "I had an appointment at the clinic and I thought I'd be much longer than I actually was. I told the driver to come for me but then, when I was finished so quickly, I decided to walk back. I suppose the driver arrived, found me gone and just drove back home again. If that's the highway,"—she peered toward the noise—"then I've turned left where I ought to have turned right. Or perhaps I turned right where I ought to have turned left."

"Perhaps you didn't turn at all when you ought to have," Stubby suggested. "Where are you going?"

"Do you know the large grey house at the top of the hill?" the old woman asked.

"You mean Richardson's Farm?"

"I do indeed," the old woman nodded. "That's where I was going."

"Well, you sure did get yourself turned around. It's in exactly the other direction. I could ride up there and tell that driver guy to come get you."

"You could also," the woman suggested sharply, "give me a ride there yourself."

"On the bike?" Stubby gasped.

"Do you have a seat on your bike?"

"Yes, ma'am, and I'm used to doubling, but. . . aren't you just bit. . . old. . . to ride double on a bike?"

"And aren't you just a bit. . . young. . . to be asking questions of your elders?" The old woman managed to get up on the seat of Stubby's bike and cling tightly to the waistband of Stubby's jeans while the girl pedalled toward Richardson's Farm. Daisy curled up in the cardboard box and went to sleep in spite of the indignity of having a white cane poked in the box with her, and Stubby was less burdened with the weight of the old woman than she was when one of her softball team caught a ride home with her.

"I'm going to stop," she warned. "There's a gate across the driveway." Stubby braked, then jumped to the ground, holding the bike as upright as she could. The old woman let go of the waistband of Stubby's jeans just before Stubby parted company with the bike, and, reflexively, reached out and managed to grab the handlebars. "I'm sorry," Stubby gasped, "I didn't mean to almost tip you off into the dirt."

People were running from the house, a man in a grey suit with his pantlegs tucked into high black boots, like a lion tamer or something, and a woman in a cotton housedress with a big apron over it. They stared as Stubby got back on the bike and pedalled toward them with the old woman still perched on the seat.

When the driver and the housekeeper realized Stubby was heading for the front steps, they turned and raced back toward the house, arriving just in time to help the woman down off the bike. The driver glared at Stubby as if something was her fault, but the housekeeper smiled at her and patted her shoulder.

"Please come in," the old woman said, her voice weak. "I think we both need a cup of tea."

"I've got my dog with me," Stubby blurted.

"I doubt the dog will drink tea," the old woman said as she headed toward the stairs, "but I'm sure we can find something for her. Wright, please make sure that the young lady's bicycle is safe." Stubby picked up Daisy and followed the old woman into the house.

She had always wanted to see the inside of the Richardson farmhouse. The story was, old man Richardson's only child, a girl, had up and left in the middle of the night, walking from the farm to the train station, buying a ticket to Victoria and leaving on the three a.m. Red-Eye Flyer. The old man shrugged it off, claiming all the Richardsons had always been gamblers, witness the fact there were so many farmers in the family. She'll do okay, was all he said, and never divulged to anyone the contents of the letters that arrived every two weeks, regular as clockwork, from more cities than a person could remember. Vancouver, Calgary, Saskatoon, Montreal, Halifax, London, Paris, Detroit, Chicago, San Francisco. When the old man died, the neighbours looked after the stock until Ada Richardson's lawyer could make arrangements for a tenant to move onto the place. Every year the farm taxes were paid by the lawyer in Vancouver, but slowly over the years the farm began to get run down in spite of the regular coats of paint the lawyer ordered applied every five years.

When the last tenant retired the neighbours waited to see who would replace him. Then, without warning or explanation, Bright's Crossing was invaded by journeymen, journeywomen and artisans. The old roof was ripped off and new shakes hammered in place, the outer walls were scrubbed with a wire brush until all the old paint was flaked off, then new paint was applied. Front steps, side steps and back steps were replaced, the porches were checked for sturdiness and repaired. Inside, walls were plastered, painted, or papered, all the plumbing was checked, repaired, replaced if necessary. The kitchen was virtually torn apart and put back together again, and when the flurry of activity finally stopped, those few locals who had been inside and who had known what the house was like originally, vowed everything looked as it had when the place was brand new. "Not a speck of formica in the kitchen," they marvelled, "it's all blond wood, hand oiled," and they shook their heads, wondering at the kid of mentality would spend so much money without availing herself of the modern conveniences.

The farm land was plowed, spread thick with manure and plowed again. Then it was levelled, the split rail fences replaced with new cedar rails and the duck pond, which had gradually filled with silt until it was good for little more than a goldfish pool, was redug and stocked with some kind of fancy duck nobody had ever before seen. A new hen coop housed a flock of chickens, again of a breed nobody had ever heard tell of, some kind of middle-sized hen that laid eggs with coloured shells. Two enormous old Clydesdales arrived and were retired to the once again lush fields and then, finally, Ada Richardson returned home, arriving in a long grey car with a uniformed driver.

Stubby followed the old woman into the huge room where one entire wall was taken over by a brick fireplace. She gaped at the hundreds of books, she gaped at the incredible sofa, she gaped at the chairs that even she knew had cost a fortune, and she gaped at the rugs on the floor.

"It's gorgeous! It's absolutely gorgeous!"

"I'm glad you like it." The old woman sank into one of the chairs, leaned back, and sighed with fatigue and relief.

"I've never seen anything like this," Stubby confessed. "There's stuff like this in the antique store in Nanaimo, but not as much. And," she said candidly, "I don't think it's as nice, either."

"Would you like tea?"

"Oh yes, please."

Stubby tiptoed to the sofa, trying hard not to touch the carpets with her decidedly grubby sneakers. Once at the sofa, she tried to find a way to sit on it without letting her hands touch the fabric.

"Perhaps," Ada Richardson suggested, when the housekeeper brought the tea tray, "you could take the young lady's dog to the kitchen and give it some sliced ham."

"Be careful," Stubby warned. "If she gets away from you she'll take off and the whole silly thing will start up again."

"Is she wild?" asked the housekeeper warily.

"No, ma'am," Stubby answered, smiling. "She's in heat." The housekeeper looked both shocked and shy. Ada Richardson laughed softly to herself and Stubby wondered if maybe she was a little bit tetched, like old people sometimes get, talking to people who aren't there and laughing at things nobody else can hear. But she tucked her sneakers politely out of sight and drank her tea with all the proper manners she'd picked up from observing Grandma Amberchuk.

"Is there a good restaurant around here?" Ada Richardson asked, looking and sounding much better after her second cup of tea.

"Well, there's Pete Singh's White Lotus," Stubby offered, "and closer in to Nanaimo there's a couple of ribs'n'chicken places."

"I see." The old woman thought for a few minutes, then smiled as if she had come to some kind of important decision. "Would you come to supper with me at the White Lotus on Saturday night?"

"Me?" Stubby gasped.

"Please," Ada Richardson smiled. "It's the least I can do after the way you helped me get home in one piece. I'd have looked a bit ridiculous smeared all over the front of a Mack truck."

Stubby rode home with her head in the clouds, but not so far in the clouds she neglected to make sure Daisy was leashed to the handlebars of the bike.

"Well, then," said Dave, eyes wide, "we'd better get ourselves into town and get you some new clothes suitable for the occasion. Or,"—he looked away politely—"you might want to wear one of the dresses your mother sent you."

"I've got almost new jeans," Stubby insisted, "and my nice shirt from Christmas is still in real good shape, got all its buttons and everything." Stubby knew Worker's Compensation wasn't much more than welfare under a different name and didn't really leave much room for things like new clothes, new shoes or fancy jackets.

"Okay," Dave said, resigning himself one more time to Stubby's apparent refusal to even begin to approach the outer limits of puberty. "How about a new pair of shoes, anyway. And *not* sneaks."

"What have you got in mind?" Stubby bargained. What Dave had in mind was a nice pair of one-strap patent leather maryjanes, but he knew just about how far he'd get with that idea. "Oh, maybe a nice pair of loafers." He waited to see and hear if Stubby was going to spit on the idea. Stubby might have if all they'd been talking about was school clothes, but they were discussing Saturday night supper at the White Lotus with Ada Richardson, and even she knew a person had to get herself spiffied up for an occasion like that, Worker's Compensation or not.

When Ada Richardson and her driver arrived on Saturday night Stubby was decked out in the best stuff she'd been able to put together. Her jeans were freshly washed and she'd ironed them herself, getting a crease down the front almost sharp enough to slice cheese. Her Christmas shirt, pale blue with dark blue plastic buttons, was similarly well ironed and her new oxblood loafers gleamed. The driver shook hands with Dave, then walked Stubby to the car and held the door open for her. Stubby climbed into the back and sat next to Ada, then found her hands sweaty and her mouth dry.

"Hi," she managed.

"Relax," Ada smiled. "It's just me. I'm the same old bat rode double on your bike, aren't I?"

"I didn't know when you got up on my bike," Stubby confessed, "that you were a millionaire."

"So what if I am?" Ada laughed. "Aren't I still the person who took the wrong turn and nearly walked herself into the middle of traffic? And aren't you the one got me safely home?"

"Yes, ma'am," Stubby admitted.

"Then relax," Ada commanded. Stubby tried, but it wasn't easy. Obviously wherever Ada Richardson went things became a big deal. Pete Singh himself met them at the front door of the White Lotus and showed them to a table next to the window, overlooking the sea. The driver disappeared as if he'd vanished into thin air and so did the car. One minute it was out front, the next it was gone. Stubby hoped the driver would be back when it was time to leave, because she knew for a fact Ada would never make the walk home.

Pete Singh himself waited on them and everything went as smooth as clockwork. Stubby could see the people on the other side of the White Lotus, over in the booths where she usually sat, all pretending not to be sneaking glances at the two seated at the white-linen-covered table in the rarely used dining room.

Stubby read the menu because, as Ada herself said, she couldn't see her hand in front of her face. And when supper arrived, Stubby got a lesson in manners. Ada put her left hand on her soup bowl, holding it lightly, orienting herself so her soup spoon, in her right hand, never once clanked against the bowl she could not see. And when the meal arrived, Ada daintily touched her plate, first the rim, then the portions of food sitting on it. "Do you suppose," she asked quietly, "you could cut anything that's big into little pieces?"

"Sure," Stubby agreed, and hopped out of her chair, walked around to Ada's side of the table, and quickly, unselfconsciously, cut the food into bite-sized pieces.

"Thank you," Ada smiled, not exactly at Stubby, but in the direction she thought Stubby was.

"Must be a bit of a nuisance," Stubby dared.

For a while," Ada admitted, "I refused to go anywhere. I was used to being as independent as society allows anyone to be, and having to be babysat stuck in my throat. Sideways. My ego was in shreds, and my ego was what it was made it possible for me to be independent. A friend of mine,"—she smiled fondly, remembering—"took more of my sulkiness than you'd expect a body to endure, and finally she yelled at me that I was the one hurting my own pride, I was the one making myself be a helpless and dependent pain in the butt. She got me so angry that when she dared me to prove I wasn't a coward by going to a concert, I screamed back at her that of course I could go, and I went. You don't have to see the tuba player to enjoy the music."

"I was real scared of coming here with you," Stubby confessed. "I was afraid I'd slurp my soup or something and embarrass you. My grandma said just pretend you're having supper with the Queen of England and you'll make out okay. That only made me more nervous. I could see my knife slipping and skittering my potato across the floor or something disgusting like that."

"I understand." Ada's eyes, hidden by the dark-tinted glasses, were turned to Stubby and for a moment Stubby almost thought Ada could see her. "I hear that you live with your father."

"Yeah," Stubby nodded, forgetting Ada could not see. "Vinnie, my mom that is, lives in Vetchburg, with Earl."

"Where in heaven's name is Vetchburg? It sounds almost like a disease—or a town named after a disease," Ada laughed. "I'm sorry, said the doctor, there's nothing modern science can do, she's got vetches."

Stubby entered the game happily. "We could invent an ointment, and run ads in the *National Enquirer*. 'Beat the agony of the vetches,' or maybe 'Do you suffer the embarrassment of the vetches?' . . . I think it's a kind of a fungus," she decided, "the kind that gives you dry scaly skin that itches and flakes off in your bed so when you lie down, there's this little snowstorm of flakes."

"I take it," Ada smiled as the index finger of her left hand unobtrusively located her meat, "you do not exactly admire Vetchburg."

"Hate it," Stubby acknowledged, her voice lacking the undertone of laughter that was usually present. "Scrawny trees, dried-out grass, and so cold in winter that when you walk the snow squeaks under your boots. In the summer all you hear is whup-whup-whup as the little dealybobs on the water sprinklers spin. Whup-whup-whup, twenty-four hours a day, whup-whup-whup, and you can tell exactly where the water stops falling, there's a line between the green grass and the yellow stuff that never got any water. Some places there isn't even any yellow grass, just this sort of grey dust, not dirt, more like the stuff you sweep up from under the bed. And every living thing bites," she added fiercely. "Spiders bite, and your whole arm, say, swells up. Or your leg if that's where they got you. Mosquitoes, boy, they come in V-formations, like when the geese fly north, and the ones in the front of the V, they have sawblades on their noses. Even the snakes and lizards snap at you."

"Do you miss your mother?"

"Not really. I think the time when I would have missed her I was so mad at her that I didn't bother with any of the being sad part of it. Earl," she pronounced, "might not be the world's biggest jerk, but I bet he comes a close second. He told everyone he was my dad, and when I said he wasn't my dad, just my stepdad, he got real mad and told me I was making a big deal out of nothing much at all. So I said if it was nothing much at all there was no reason for him to get owly about it, and he whapped me. He doesn't like me one little bit and he never did, which is fine with me because the feeling, as my grandma says, is totally mutual."

Ada Richardson enjoyed Stubby's chatter more than she enjoyed the meal, although she could tell from her companion's little murmurs of appreciation that in Stubby's opinion the food was incredible. And when dessert arrived Ada knew from Stubby's gasp that the look on the girl's face was one of awe and disbelief.

"I didn't know they could do that, make whipped cream stand up by itself!"

The driver reappeared as if by magic and the ride back was over too soon as far as Ada was concerned. Once over her initial awe at being in the presence of a real millionaire, Stubby had relaxed and talked to Ada much the same as she talked to Dave or to her Grandma Amberchuk. Ada was used to polite and respectful yes-ma'ams and no-ma'ams; the giggles and teasing made her feel years younger, reminded her of days and nights when laughter was the rule, not the exception.

"Thank you very much," Stubby smiled, and even if Ada couldn't see the smile, she could hear it in Stubby's voice. "It was absolutely wonderful. I never had candles on the table all through the meal before in all my life."

"Can you play cards?" Ada asked, surprising herself.

"I can play snap," Stubby replied, "and Dave's teaching me cribbage."

"Could I interest you," Ada teased, "in learning to play poker?"

"I guess. If I can learn. I'm not very good at cards," Stubby admitted. "I usually get kinda bored. Dave says it's a sign of low-grade intelligence if you've got an attention span of less than seventeen seconds."

"Let's see if Dave is right," Ada invited. "You come to my place next week and I'll teach you to play poker."

"How can you play if you can't see the cards?" Stubby blurted.

"Why," Ada laughed, "I have a few decks in Braille."

Stubby brought home a little bag of scraps for Daisy, and entertained Dave with her description of the candles, the tablecloth and the incredible dessert. Dave grinned blearily throughout the entire recital, his sore leg propped up on the footstool, his hand curled around his glass. After Stubby had gone to bed Dave checked his TV schedule, then tuned in the late show and watched while he finished his bottle and fought the pain in his shattered leg.

Ada Richardson played poker with a degree of skill and concentration that lifted it out of the realm of game and placed it close to the areas of eating, breathing and drinking. In spite of the Braille markings on the cards, Ada did not cheat. She wore soft grey gloves when it was her turn to shuffle and deal and removed them to read with her fingertips the hand she had been dealt.

"It's not just luck," Stubby realized. "You have to use your loaf too, right?"

"Right," the old woman said firmly. "You don't have any control over the hand you get dealt, but what you *do* with it is what determines if you're a winner or a loser. I call it," she smiled, "the game of life."

Once a week, sometimes more often than that, Stubby went up the hill and played poker with Ada Richardson. Of course Stubby did not win very often in spite of the fact Dave, when he learned Stubby knew how to play, offered her hours of practice as often as she wanted. With Ada, Stubby played for plastic chips, for the fun of playing. With Dave, Stubby played first for jellybeans, then later for quarters, dimes and nickels.

Ada Richardson looked into the circumstances surrounding Stubby's life and learned things even Stubby didn't know. She learned there was very little chance Dave Amberchuk would ever again work as a chokerman, or as anything else for that matter. His leg was too badly damaged to ever again allow him to do anything very physical. Medical records are, of course, private and not to be divulged, but when you have as much money as Ada Richardson, and know as many people in high places as she, little things like confidentiality evaporate. The doctors who, at Ada's request, examined the x-rays and medical records, said it was a wonder Dave Amberchuk could walk at all and tendered the opinion it was more a case of his own stubborn determination than it was a case of expert surgical intervention.

While Ada was more than impressed with Dave's guts, she was less impressed with his brains. Dave was not considered to be any kind of candidate at all for job retraining. There are nicer words for it, but Vinnie's mother's description of Dave as a lout had not been far off the mark. Dave could read, but not well, and could sign his name and write excuse notes for Stubby's teacher, but any idea he would go back to school and turn himself into some kind of success aborted and died before being born into a thought. Dave would never be a bookkeeper or insurance salesman. What he was rapidly turning himself into was an alcoholic, and no wonder, said the doctors, the pain must be almost intolerable.

Ada's investigation into Stubby's potential was more encouraging. Stubby was not very interested in what they were teaching her in school but she learned it quickly, passed her exams and amused herself by reading books, playing softball and disappearing on her bike with Daisy in the carrier basket. She had average ability in drawing and painting, adequate talent in music class and a distinct gift for playing games with the spoken language. Ada nodded, kept her own counsel and appeared to very quickly butt out of most areas of Stubby's life.

"Just a minute," she said quietly, "you've forgotten something."

"Oh yeah," Stubby laughed, "you're right."

"That's the last time," Ada promised, "from now on, you make your mistakes and I'll take advantage of them."

"Hard-hearted woman," Stubby accused happily.

"The purpose of the game," Ada chortled, "is to win. Not to babysit!"

"Go ahead." Stubby dared, "Do your best. I'm gettin' good at this. You won't win all the time." She returned her full attention to her cards.

Stubby enjoyed poker. It reminded her of softball. No matter how good a softball player you think you are, if you don't have a good streak of luck you might never get on the winning team; and no matter how lucky you are, if you haven't honed your skills life can become one boring losing game after another. Poker, like softball, allowed Stubby to concentrate on something she had a half a chance of winning and, for a time at least, forget her slowly growing uneasiness.

Stubby knew she didn't live like people were supposed to live. Stubby knew there were few, if any, other girls her age, whether in Bright's Crossing, Ladysmith, Duncan or even Nanaimo itself, who lived the way she did. The house was offbeat enough. It had been, years and years and years ago, way back when coal was king, one of the company houses for married miners and their families. When the coal became too expensive to cut the company shut the mines, leaving the jobless miners stranded in rowhouses they did not own. As long as people continued to pay their electric bills the company kept the lights burning. As long as the company didn't want their houses back, everybody in officialdom ignored their existence. As one person or family moved out, others were waiting for the chance to move in. And so it was, fortuitously, just as Dave and Vinnie learned they were to be parents and ought to get married, Dave's sister and her husband decided four kids and another on the way were too many for their shabby little company house. They moved out and Dave and Vinnie moved in.

But even in the row of small houses, Stubby's life was different. Other rowhouse kids had both parents living together. Maybe they fought, even yelled and screeched in public, but they at least lived together. Or if they had split up, the kids lived with their mom and whoever else had moved in with her. There were no kids living just with their dad. And somehow, the aspirations and incomes of the people who lived in the Row weren't very high. For reasons Stubby didn't understand, but which seemed none the less to be engraved in stone, low income seemed to either go along with or cause early pregnancy and marriage, untidy yards, peeling paint and broken windows, noisy or missing mufflers on old pickups and cars and the frequent arrival of police.

Dave kept the house painted and his fences repaired and even when his leg was throbbing and the smell of cheap liquor wafted from him with every breath, he found time and energy to tend his roses and cut his lawn. In the back yard he grew a garden and next to it built a hen coop and hen yard. Perhaps not all, but certainly many of his neighbours thought he'd scrambled his wits when the log rolled on him. It didn't make sense to put that kind of energy, not to mention expense, into a place that wasn't your own. Gardens and hens and roses were for those who lived on the other side of Haslam Creek, those who owned their houses and the land they sat on. Nobody who lived on the Row had ever bothered with that. The Row wasn't permanent. The people who lived there laughed and said, ''Hell, I'm here for a good time, not a long time,'' and when times didn't seem good there was always the Liquor Control Board or homebrew, white lightning or homemade wine.

Stubby was certain she stuck out like a sore thumb. That she didn't made no difference—she thought she did. There she was, eleven years old, seeing boys as friends, not as trophies, more involved in learning to play softball, poker and chess than kissing games, more apt to ride off on her bike with her dog than hang around under the streetlight at the corner where the mosquitoes zizzed in the light and the moths flung themselves against the globe with mindless fanaticism. When Stubby went to the river in the hot summer afternoon she went to swim, not to pose carefully in the sunlight, hoping the boys would notice and appreciate. Stubby tanned because she spent most of her time out of doors, not because tanning was supposed to make you look sexy.

When it came to sex, Stubby decided she was a washout. Girls no older than she was were learning to smooch, giggling about it, exchanging secrets as they stood in front of one mirror or another smearing blue stuff on their eyelids or dabbing thick black gunk on their lashes. Some of them used a tube of lipstick, others painted on a sort of liquid with a tiny brush; a few did both, then applied a layer of clear, shiny vaseline-like stuff to make their lips look as if any minute they were going to drip off their faces and land on the front of their blouses—the usually still-flat front. And Stubby knew as surely as she knew her name that if she were to try to use any of that stuff she would wind up looking like a total jerk.

Looking like a jerk is not a thrilling or inviting prospect. Especially when already you are so different in so many ways, what with your dad growing roses while ruining his liver and your mom living in Black Fly Gulch with a guy who was, for chrissakes, a vice-principal. My god. No need to crown all of that by spreading goo on your face and teetering around in shoes guaranteed to pitch you head first into the nearest blackberry bush.

From time to time Dave had vague thoughts about cutting down on the amount he drank. But they were vague, they didn't come very often and he didn't spend much time on them. He and Stubby pitched in on the chores, their only rule that well-known ''The one who cooks doesn't clean up,'' and Dave knew the meals were mostly humdrum. Work with what works he thought, and anyway, Stubby got to experience fancy cooking occasionally with Ada Richardson. For himself, what difference did it make. Every bite of food tasted to a greater or lesser degree of the aspirins he chewed in increasing numbers because of the growing pain in his leg. Sometimes, when he was half floating on aspirin and rye, he felt Stubby was being sort of cheated, but he wasn't sure how. He wanted to tell her, show her, demonstrate how much he appreciated her loyalty, how much he loved her, but there weren't that many chances to be a hero, not when your leg was held together with silver bolts and pins and supported by a stainless steel brace.

But he got his chance. They were enlarging the airport and the contractor who'd won the tender was from out of town and brought his own workers with him. It's well known that out-of-towners don't have any responsibility to anybody; it isn't their home, it isn't their nest they're shitting in and any veneer of civilization strips off with a speed directly proportional to the amount of time a guy's been away from home.

Daisy was a bum. No doubt about it, Daisy was the world's prime example of a tramp. When Stubby was around Daisy stuck to her like glue, but when Stubby was in school Daisy had no more loyalty to home, hearth or Dave than the out-of-towners had to Bright's Crossing. No matter what Dave or Stubby did to plug the hole under the fence, Daisy got on the other side and zipped off faster than stink, visiting the neighbours, investigating the garbage behind the corner store, mooching sandwiches from the kids at lunchtime, prowling the ditches hunting down mice and rats. A real bum.

Just down the road a bit from where the out-of-towners were working on the airport, a drainage culvert ran under the highway. Daisy was terrified of traffic, but when it wasn't raining, and when the culvert was dry, Daisy would cross under the highway and tend to the squirrels, grouse, mink, weasel and rats in the long grass and broom brush around the airport. And, of course, she mooched from the workers, sitting on her haunches, front feet tucked under her chin, watching each bite of sandwich, or dancing on her back legs, yipping imploringly, begging for a taste, just a small taste of cookie.

"Shoo," they said, waving their hands, and, "Fuck off, mutt," tossing sticks or rocks. The younger ones, the nicer ones, laughed and tossed her a crust or a half a cupcake. It was enough to keep Daisy going back hopefully, ignoring the shouts and the thrown rocks and even tools. The more Daisy ignored the insults, the angrier the assholes got and finally some prime specimen picked up a hatchet and heaved it. Usually the stuff thrown at Daisy missed. The hatchet didn't. It landed, sharp edge first, on her left flank and Daisy screamed, screeched, then took off for home, the hatchet sticking out of her small bleeding butt. "Ya goddam fool!'' one of the younger men yelled. ''Fuck you,'' the prime specimen replied, and the fight was on in earnest.

Daisy made it home, but it took her hours. The concerned workers who had chased after her lost her when she disappeared in the ditch, not knowing about the culvert. Daisy lay a long time in the trickle of stale water in the cool shade of the cement pipe, then she responded to her inner clock and started home, where she knew Stubby was waiting.

Dave hadn't driven much since his accident. He'd traded his standard pickup in on an automatic, but even so he still had to bend his leg to fit it under the dash and that hurt. It hurt so damn bad he was afraid that after five minutes he'd get dizzy and steer into a semi or a bus full of school kids. But when Stubby screamed and raced for the grimly staggering Daisy, Dave headed for the yard and fired up the truck.

Daisy needed help right away but the vet was clear across town. Dave didn't even hesitate. He drove straight to the Bright's Crossing Medical Clinic and limped in carrying Daisy, the hatchet still stuck in her hip bone. Stubby followed, face white, eyes huge, trembling with fear and grief.

''Don't be ridiculous,'' the young doctor blustered, ''I don't treat dogs!''

''Mister,'' Dave gritted, ''you're on retainer from that construction company, everybody knows that. And right there on the handle of that effin' hatchet is the name of that company. So you never mind about me or my kid, or even my kid's dog, you just see to it you get your boss's tool out of that animal's hip. And you just do 'er gentle, and do 'er right, because if the dog dies, they'll find that hatchet shoved so far up your ass it'll take six doctors to get it out again.''

''Is that a threat?'' the young doctor challenged.

''No, sir,'' Dave said, his face white with pain and rage, ''it's by way of bein' a heartfelt promise. You fix this dog or you'll never fix another goddam thing. Especially not your own smile.''

The young doctor knew it would take the police three-quarters of an hour to get to him and by then there wouldn't be much reason for them to arrive. He looked at Dave, then he looked at Daisy, her eyes glazed with shock. And finally, he looked at Stubby. ''Sit down,'' he said, lifting the dog and laying her on the metal-topped table. Stubby sat. ''Keep talking to her,'' the young doctor ordered. ''I have to give her an injection and I don't want her to bite me.''

When the hatchet was out and Daisy was stitched together and sleeping on a clean blanket in her own box in a quiet corner in Stubby's bedroom, Dave heaved himself back in the pickup and drove to the construction site. There was nobody there. All the rage and fury, all the feeling of powerlessness bubbled and seethed until Dave began to fear he would go nuts and use the hatchet to pound to shit every Euclid truck, every earth mover, even the Johnny-on-the Spot. Instead, he returned home with the hatchet and sat up all night watching TV, drinking coffee laced with rye and checking on Daisy. When the dog began to whine, Dave crushed an aspirin tablet and dropped the powder in her mouth, then gave her a few ounces of fresh cool water to drink.

"Sure," he told Stubby agreeably the next morning, "you can stay home from school and nurse her. Be sure you get some water into her every hour, even if it's just a tablespoonful or so."

"Where you goin'?"

"To see some men about a dog," he replied, hefting the hatchet.

Stubby almost phoned the police. But they'd never get there in time to stop it and if Dave murdered the entire crew it wasn't going to be his own daughter who blew the whistle on him. She sat, telling Daisy all her fears, expecting at any minute to hear the sirens.

Dave limped onto the construction site with the hatchet swinging from his huge fist. Work stopped. The men moved aside, letting Dave pass, and he knew from the inadvertent flickering of the eyes of each of them which one it was he wanted. He walked right up to the prime specimen and offered him the hatchet. Without thinking, the moron took it, then looked at it, guilt written all over his face.

"You were fast enough to heave it at a ten-pound dog," Dave invited, his grin chilling the blood of all who saw it. "Maybe you'd like to try to heave it at me." But the moron wasn't that stupid. He shook his head.

"Want to settle it in the dirt?" Dave invited.

"You're crippled," the prime specimen protested.

Dave laughed. "Only where it shows, asshole," he taunted. Then, just in case he hadn't understood the subtlety of it all, Dave grabbed him by the shirtfront. "I've got a crippled leg, but you, you festering ball of shit, you're crippled inside, where it don't show but there's no cure." He used every insulting phrase he had ever heard, calling on his years in the bush where descriptive cursing is a way of life and a point of pride, and still the man just stood, the hatchet in his hand, head dangling toward the ground.

Finally Dave released the shirtfront and limped back to his truck. Not one out-of-towner made a move toward him. They stood watching as the truck backed up, turned and headed back toward the highway, dust rising from its tires.

"Aw, shit!" the culprit cursed, dropping the hatchet and heading for the portable, where he handed in his time and caught a ride into town with the accountant. He had his bags packed and was on his way back to the mainland on the next ferry

Dave figured it was just about his finest moment. He wanted to tell Stubby about it but logger's modesty only allowed you to brag about the exploits of someone else. None of the out-of-towners spoke about it to any of the locals, so Stubby never heard the story. When she asked Dave where the hatchet was, all he said was, ''I took it back,'' and Stubby thought that was all he'd done. She didn't spend much time thinking about it. She was more worried about Daisy than she was about what happened to the hatchet. Dave sat on the front step, the sunlight glittering on the metal brace that supported his leg. He poured a double slug of rye into a water glass, added an ice cube and a hint of well water, then sipped, watching the oily liquor swirl against the ice. If anyone had asked him, he wouldn't have been able to say why he was crying. After all, for once, the pain in his leg wasn't uppermost in his mind. So what if the kid didn't know what he'd done? So effin' what?

3

They were slicing and hacking at Dave's leg again. Stubby wasn't sure what they were doing or why they wanted to do it; something about the pins not being secure, wiggling and causing deterioration of the bone. Whatever it was, Stubby, Myrtle and Daisy wound up at Vinnie's mother's place. Not that Stubby wanted it that way. Stubby figured she was more than capable of looking after herself. After all, for weeks, in fact months, she'd been actually looking after herself and Dave, so it ought to be a snap to not have to look after him, help him up and down stairs, in and out of the bathroom, most of the time so sodden with drink and so crazed with pain he didn't even know she was there. But things have a way of coming down without control, and without control of your life, you wind up in some strange places, doing strange things, like calling Vinnie's mom Grandmother and going to school from the wrong end of town.

Vinnie's mom had showed up a couple of days before Dave went into the hospital for surgery. Dave was sitting in the living room, his leg propped on the footstool, his mouth turned to cotton batten by the 222s, his eyes turned to dull glass by the rye whiskey, when his former mother-in-law knocked at the front door. Stubby answered and invited her grandmother to enter the house. Everything was neat and tidy, the floor freshly swept; the furniture, tatty though it was, seemed clean. Dave, naturally, couldn't string six words into a sentence, but what do you expect, poor man, what with the bone in his leg rotting inch by inch. After some preliminary conversation, Vinnie's mom got right to the nub of the matter. "Sheilagh, I'd like it if you would stay with us while your father is in the hospital."

47

"I usually stay with Grandma," Stubby blundered, forgetting, as she was wont to do, that the woman speaking to her was also her grandma.

"Yes," Vinnie's mom nodded, and even Stubby could see she was very nervous and uncertain, "but your Grandma Amberchuk isn't a young woman any more, Sheilagh, and she's got enough on her plate worrying about your father. And your aunt is only days away from confinement, and that means your cousins will wind up at Grandma Amberchuk's too. It seems just a bit much. I can't do anything about your cousins, or your father's surgery, but I certainly can help where you are concerned. And we haven't seen much of each other in the past little while."

Actually Stubby and Vinnie's mom hadn't seen much of each other in the past big while either. Stubby didn't volunteer to go over and be chided for wearing jeans instead of decent clothes, or for having her hair long and loose instead of cut and curled, or for any of a host of things her maternal grandmother found reason to scold her for, nag her and generally make Stubby feel overwhelmed by criticism. The most Stubby saw of her mother's family was when Vinnie showed up on one of her irregular and seldom scheduled visits, which lasted varying lengths of time depending on how long it took Earl to get enough time off to come down and jawbone Vinnie back where Earl figured she belonged.

Stubby spent a lot of time after Vinnie's mom left staring at the blowsy roses pattern on the wallpaper of her room, feeling very stupid and insensitive. Stubby hadn't noticed, but of course Grandma Amberchuk was getting old; much older than Vinnie's mom, who had only had four kids, and Grandma Amberchuk had nine, and everyone knows every baby adds ten years to the mother's age. Every pregnancy costs the mother one of her teeth. All those jeans to wash and shirts to iron, all those beds to make and lunches to pack, all those loaves to bake and socks to mend, all those fines to pay and bail hearings to attend and, of course, all those grandchildren needing a place to go when something tossed their lives into the air. Stubby convinced herself she had been a millstone around Grandma Amberchuk's neck, a burden the old woman had uncomplainingly borne because of her sense of duty, her maternal conditioning, her uncomplaining devotion to her family.

But when Stubby tried to explain it all to Grandma Amberchuk, she couldn't find the words to tell about realizing what a pain in the face her presence and life must have been. Grandma Amberchuk listened with her own interpretation and concluded Vinnie's mom must be pining terribly to be so devoid of self respect as to go to Stubby and practically beg her to spend time at her place. Why else, she reasoned, would the woman come out with this nonsense about age, when anyone could see Grandma

Amberchuk was as strong and as spunky as she had ever been. Oh, a bit stiff in the hips, perhaps, but that happens with menopause, and no need to dwell on it or feel resentful, just take your calcium pills, wash them down with goat's milk and face life as best you can.

Vinnie's mom, realized Granda Amberchuk, didn't have much going for her to encourage her to face life with any kind of smile. Gordon couldn't be waved around as any banner of success; as the years marched on in their inexorable fashion, the puny pennant he represented had definitely frayed at the edges. And those two daughters, well, not that one would want to be caught out in public being judgmental, but had there been a way to actually have the one-point-five children the statisticians said was average, those two would have done it. Instead the oldest had one, the youngest—determined to come out ahead in at least this area of competition—had two, and of those three grandchildren, Vinnie's mom hadn't managed even one of the fun kind; a boy in short pants and two girls in frilly dresses and all three of them needing training wheels on their two-wheelers up as far as grade three. Of course the poor woman wanted a breath of laughter, a ray of joy, of course the poor woman wanted to have Stubby around, and any excuse was better than none.

When Grandma Amberchuk smilingly agreed to the plan, Stubby was more convinced than ever that she had been a burden, an inconvenience, a huge and enormous imposition. Stubby headed off to Vinnie's mom's place feeling lower than whaleshit.

She couldn't make herself call them Grandma and Grandpa. But with a bit of practice and some iron determination, Stubby managed to say Grandmother Fleming and Grandfather Fleming. What was really uneasiness and lack of practice was interpreted as being politeness, which Vinnie's mom and dad figured must have been the result of Vinnie's efforts on those sporadic occasions when she was in Stubby's life. Certainly none of the Amberchuks had ever been known for politeness, social skill or even respectability, except, possibly, for that poor old woman who had mothered and endured the entire pack.

Stubby's patience was tested sorely. And so was Daisy's. Not allowed in the living room, Daisy tried to content herself by curling under the kitchen chair Stubby most often used. Ousted from the kitchen, Daisy tried settling herself beside Stubby's bed. Chased from the bedroom, Daisy found a corner in the upstairs hall where she might pass unnoticed and curled in a sad ball, out of sight, out of mind and most of all, out of the way of the big clumping feet.

"Sheilagh, whatever are you doing sitting up here?" Grandma Fleming wondered if the child was brooding. It was a dangerous thing, brooding, apt to lead to almost any kind of aberrant behaviour.

"Visiting with Daisy," Stubby answered, forcing her stiff facial muscles to smile. "She's feeling kind of lonely. I think she misses her own place."

Vinnie's mom decided this meant that Stubby herself was homesick, and resolved to nip that nonsense in the bud. "She'll adjust," she said briskly. "Now why don't you come down and watch TV with us?"

"I'm not too interested in TV." Stubby replied. "I'd rather just sit here with Daisy."

"Rubbish," Vinnie's mom declared. "Lawrence Welk is coming on, you don't want to miss that!"

"Yes I do. I don't like his bubble machine," Stubby said, her jaw set. But nobody knew what she was talking about, so finally, she lied and said she was really very tired and thought she ought to go to her room and catch a nap.

"Do you need any Midol?"

"No," Stubby answered, "I never use the stuff." She went to her room confused, wondering why her grandmother seemed to think every day of the month was leading up to those few days of slight inconvenience.

Daisy followed Stubby and curled up on the rug beside the bed. "Don't let her lie on that rug!" Vinnie's mom snapped. "You know how dogs shed. In my opinion, she ought to be sleeping outside in the woodshed."

"She's old," Stubby defied, and Vinnie's mom, rather than face any sort of actual insubordination, retreated.

"Poor old Daisy," Stubby mourned, feeling as sorry for herself as for the dog. "I'd have you up on the bed if I could, but those two would pitch a fit for sure."

Vinnie arrived. Stubby supposed someone had phoned her to tell her about Dave's operation and Stubby's stay, and she steeled herself for what she was sure was going to be a couple of weeks of absolute horribleness.

"How bad is your dad's leg?" Vinnie asked, before she even said hello.

"It's bad," Stubby answered.

"Why didn't you tell me!" Vinnie snapped.

"Why would I do that?" Stubby puzzled.

"'Well, after all!" Vinnie shook her head, amazed at Stubby's obtuse mind. "I *do* have a vested interest."

"No, you don't," Stubby answered, already bored with the entire conversation. "You've got Earl, remember?"

"Have you been up to see him today?"

"Yes."

"Want to go again?"

"He'll have had his shot," Stubby explained, "and he'll be real drowsy, and he doesn't like anyone to see him when he's like that.''

"Come on," Vinnie headed for the door, and Stubby followed, praying for the magical day when people would listen to what she had to say.

Dave was propped up on pillows with an *Argosy* magazine spread on his knee. He looked up, saw Stubby, smiled, saw Vinnie and the smile faded.

"That's not much of a greeting," Vinnie beamed.

"What'n'hell you doin' here?" Dave growled. Stubby wanted to explain, but could hardly do that with Vinnie plonking herself down on the chair Stubby always used when she visited. Stubby moved to the radiator under the window that looked out on the not-too-inspiring sight of the logs boomed in what had once been a small bay rich with shellfish and assorted bird life.

"What am I doing here?" Vinnie smiled determinedly. "I came because I heard about your operation."

"Hope you didn't think that was going to cheer me up." His voice was thick and his words were slurred, as they always were when he'd just had his pain shot.

"I think we should discuss what's to be done with Sheilagh."

"Me?" Stubby echoed, but nobody heard.

"Nothin' to discuss," Dave said coldly, blinking rapidly, trying to fight the effects of the drug.

"But if you're going to be in and out of hospital all the time, we have to come to some kind of decision. After all, it isn't good for a child to have her life constantly disrupted."

"Stubby's fine," Dave snarled.

"Sheilagh deserves more than she's been getting so far!" Vinnie flared.

"I'm fine," Stubby piped.

"Vin," Dave grinned, and it was almost enough to make a person's skin crawl. He raised himself on one elbow, still smiling his wolf smile. "The first big disruption in Stub's life was when you had your little temper tantrum and walked out; and every other disruption since has been thanks to that perambulating asshole you hooked up with, old wotzisname the arsletart school teacher."

"Yeah," Stubby nodded agreement.

"Dave, we have to stop doing this." Vinnie kept her voice as calm as she could under the circumstances. "We're so busy trying to one-up each other that we're losing sight of what really counts."

"Vinnie," Dave yawned, "why don't you go down to the beach with a tablespoon and use it to pick up the sand. Then use a sharp-pointed rock to pound that sand right up your ass."

"Oh, really!" Vinnie rose, jerking her head in that motion that meant Stubby was supposed to follow her. "You're impossible!" Vinnie left.

Stubby got down off the radiator, walked over and sat on the chair next to her father's bed. "You okay?" she asked.

"Nope, I'm so damn mad I could spit. Except my mouth's too dry. You wouldn't happen to have a beer in your pocket, would you?" he asked hopefully.

"No," she laughed, "but I'll phone Uncle Steve and see if he can sneak you in some of them oranges again."

"Love you, Stubs," he sighed, sinking back into his pillow, blinking slowly and trying hard not to let his weakness show. "But get lost now, okay?"

"Sure." She kissed him and patted his hand, noticing how his fingers trembled, noticing how skinny his arms were. "Sure. You be good, y'hear." She left, almost colliding in the doorway with Vinnie, who was on her way back with her shirt in a knot to find out why Stubby hadn't followed her on command.

"What she needs is some kind of stability." Vinnie's voice carried clearly up the hot air register into Stubby's room. "This back and forth between one place and another depending on the state of His Royal Self's health isn't doing her much good."

"Go see the lawyer," her father suggested.

"I already did. To absolutely no avail at all," Vinnie snapped.

"Well," her father consoled her, "after all, if you hadn't left so precipitously you could have planned things a bit and none of us would've been in this bind."

"Oh, of course, it's all *my* fault. You men!" she said bitterly. "You all stick together like gum in a child's hair."

"Now, now," said her mother, trying to keep peace in the family.

Vinnie wearily opened the kitchen door and dropped into one of the wooden chairs on the back porch. She ignored the first nighthawks, ignored the sound of the frogs croaking in the ditches and creeks, ignored the twilight streaking the sky. She lit a cigarette, dragged the smoke deeply into her lungs, stared bitterly at nothing at all, and pulled the small imitation-gold pill box from the pocket of her tailored pants. Vinnie had a choice. She could take an amphetamine and forget about her anger, riding the high, or she could take a sedative and her anger would be smothered under the calm. Vinnie chose the sedative. After all, it was evening, it would soon be time for bed and, she hoped, sleep. She swallowed her pill without water and smoked determinedly, waiting for the calm.

Vinnie wasn't always pleasant, she was often on the verge of hysterics, she wouldn't win any prizes for intellect and she wasn't always as skilled in her manipulative schemes as she wanted to be, but Vinnie wasn't stupid. She knew that in the male-dominated world in which she had been born and still lived, her only worth lay between her legs. And if the form surrounding that worth wasn't up to the standards the male controllers had decided to want at that particular time, Vinnie's value wouldn't be very high. So she had started taking amphetamines to keep herself as slender as possible. The side effect she had not anticipated, but welcomed gladly, was the high that made even ironing white shirts seem interesting, made even vacuuming seem worthwhile. Vinnie got from speed the energy and courage she needed to make it from breakfast dishes to supper dishes, from the laundry room to the bedroom, from the medicine cabinet to what passed with Earl for romance and sex. Far from disapproving, Earl found Vinnie's drug-taking a sexual turn-on; it proved she was willing to go to any lengths to be what he wanted.

But the high sometimes brought with it sudden tantrums. The same doctor who had prescribed the amphetamines was more than willing to write a prescription for the exact opposite kind of pill, the exact opposite kind of effect. This good man, visited by Earl because of Vinnie's erratic temper, looked wise and talked of the upswings and downswings of female biology, soothed Earl's fears and made a note on Vinnie's chart to remind himself that too much of a good thing sometimes had adverse effects, that amphetamines can make women reckless, even assertive, that the high can actually bring about socially unbecoming characteristics, like talking back or arguing.

He gave Vinnie the same story about the upswings and downswings and added a touch or two about lunar cycles, then wrote the prescription. Neither Vinnie nor Earl noticed the new drugs made Vinnie's mind dull and dependent. They in no way interfered with any of her normal domestic tasks. She could still clean house, she was still available for sex when Earl decided he wanted sex. Earl did not in any way miss Vinnie's energy, he did not miss her passion, he did not miss her jokes or her imagination; he had never put any kind of value on any of that crap anyway. He liked her best when she was so zonked she didn't know if she'd been pinned, folded, stapled or spiritually mutilated.

Vinnie slimmed down on her amphetamines until she looked as if she had just walked out the gates of Dachau, and when her hands began to tremble or she felt herself in danger of losing her temper, she took one of the other kind of pills and within a few minutes all the symptoms vanished. She never stopped to tell herself it was no wonder she felt depressed, she never stopped to notice that every women she knew was as depressed as she was, as dependent on drugs of one kind or another as she was, she never stopped to think that maybe depression is a normal reaction when your entire life is dull and boring. Dusting furniture is boring, washing white shirts is boring, shining someone else's shoes is boring. Weeding someone else's garden is boring. Being penetrated twice a week is as boring as shit when it isn't your idea and no consideration is ever given to what you feel. But to not take the pills, to not alternately fly a false high or sit in a false calm, to actually wake up and take stock of your life and do something to change it, is terrifying.

Vinnie knew there were dozens of women out there who would be more than willing to take her place, more than willing to watch the ceiling while Earl worked off whatever it was he was working off, and she knew there was no way she could get a job and support herself in the style to which she was damned well determined to stay accustomed. So Vinnie took the pills. She took them not because she was stupid, but because she wasn't. She knew that without them her entire life was garbage.

"Vinnie," Stubby said firmly, "I think you should stop all this go-round right now. Dad's not feeling well, and they might wind up carving his leg off an inch at a time for all we know, and he doesn't need this kind of stuff. And anyway, I am *not* living with you and Earl."

"Sheilagh," Vinnie sighed, "gimme a break, will you'?

"Give yourself a break," Stubby answered, and Vinnie glared. "You're the one came all this way to try to stir something up, nobody from here went up where you live looking for a row. I'm doing just fine, and if the day ever comes," she invented desperately, "when Dave and I can't do 'er on our own and I have to wind up living with someone else, I will go and live full time with my very good friend Ada Richardson."

Without the pills, Vinnie undoubtedly would have continued the clash of wills. But the pills were doing what they were supposed to do, they were making Vinnie docile, obedient and unable to carry even the simplest of thoughts to anything approaching a logical conclusion. She nodded. She stubbed out her cigarette and lit another. She smiled at her daughter. "I only want to be sure," she said gently, "that your life is going to be better than mine has been."

Stubby stared. Vinnie wasn't having a fit. Vinnie wasn't getting bent out of shape. Vinnie wasn't doing any of the things she usually did. Stubby was almost disappointed.

"You know, darlin'," Vinnie patted the arm of the wooden chair, and Stubby sat down, stiff and not yet trusting, "there was this thing happening in the magazines and movies, and even on TV, and I thought it was happening here. Well, it wasn't. It wasn't even happening out there. Just in the magazines and movies and on TV. They called it the Sexual

Revolution. And it said. . . it taught. . . that if we could all get past our conditioning, if we could all free ourselves of our restraints and hangups, we'd all enjoy sex, enjoy life, and everyone would be free and everyone would be equal. Now I knew my mother wasn't free, and I knew she sure as hell wasn't equal, so I went looking for the stuff she didn't have, the stuff I thought would make me free and equal. Well, what I found was something else. I found that it didn't matter a damn that I was an individual, with my own hopes and dreams. All that mattered was that men are the bosses, in bed and out. You remember that." She smiled and puffed on her cigarette. "Could you get me a cup of tea?" she asked, so sweetly that Stubby jumped from the chair arm and rushed into the kitchen.

When the cup of tea was perched on the arm of the chair, Stubby pulled up the other chair and sat down, almost overjoyed to be actually involved in a real mother-daughter conversation, the passing on of wisdom from one generation to another. Vinnie lit yet another cigarette, sipping her tea, dug out her little box of pills, took another tranquilizer and smiled at her daughter. "You know, of all the men I met, of all the boys who thought they were men, your father was the only one who didn't jaw on at great length about things like how rape was just not possible in a proper society because once women got over being repressed they would want sex, so they wouldn't have to be forced into it. Dave didn't talk much," she said, sadly, "and I was so young I thought that was a drawback, I didn't know it was a blessing in disguise."

"Was he a jerk?" Stubby asked.

"Yes," Vinnie replied, "but they all are. All of them. The only reason any girl had for saying no to sex that made any sense to them at all was pregnancy. They didn't want to wind up listening to the patter of little feet any more than anyone else did. So a lot of them talked a lot about how abortion ought to be legalized. They figured that would make women absolutely available, you see. But it didn't work that way. We got abortion but we also decided we could say no if we wanted. That after all, this is our meat, not theirs. That's what some of us thought." She gulped at her tea and shook her head. "I don't want you to listen to that kind of garbage," she lectured. "I don't want you paying any attention at all to any of that women's liberation nonsense. I tried it, and look what it got me."

"What?" Stubby asked.

"Exactly," Vinnie agreed. "I want you to remember, Sheilagh, that sex is a duty when you're married. How you feel about it, what you think about it, doesn't matter one little bit. If you aren't married, every man in the world thinks you're available and some of them get kind of mean; if you're married, you've only one of them to contend with, and you might get one you can handle. And if anybody ever starts to bend your ear about choice, or control over your body, or equality, you just stuff your fingers in your ears and pay no attention, because as long as men are the boss, that other stuff is just crap. Crap, that's all.

"But—" Stubby blurted.

"No," Vinnie held up her hand. "I know a lot of this is right over your head, but we don't get much chance to talk, so you remember what I just told you. All that stuff is garbage."

There was a lot Stubby wanted to say, but she didn't bother saying it. She knew she wasn't going to remember much of whatever it was Vinnie was going on about, and she didn't suppose it mattered one little bit. Stubby didn't have any intention of getting married. Not for years and years anyway, and surely to god anything that was wrong with the system now would be fixed by the time she was old enough to have to worry about it. Anyway, Stubby wasn't Vinnie and wouldn't make Vinnie's mistakes; for sure she'd never leave anyone like Dave to go live with a nerd like Earl.

"It's getting chilly," Vinnie's mom called through the screen door. Vinnie obediently rose from her chair and went into the house. Stubby picked up the empty teacup, the ashtray and Vinnie's cigarette package and followed her mother, wondering why Vinnie's mom was smiling softly, meaningfully. Vinnie's mother, of course, thought Vinnie and Stubby had been having a nice little getting-to-know-you conversation.

Stubby had no idea what Vinnie had been trying to tell her or why she had taken it into her head to say it. It all came right off the wall and Stubby had no place to put any of it, so she let go of it. Vinnie, on the other hand, thought some kind of wisdom had been imparted, some kind of rapport established, some kind of link forged, and felt closer to her daughter than she had for years. Maybe, she decided, Sheilagh and I don't exactly love each other, but we have a healthy respect for each other, we like each other, and that might even be better than blind loyal love.

Stubby was concerned about Dave. He wasn't snapping back from this operation. Whatever they had done to his leg hadn't improved matters at all. He lived from injection to injection, and only the gentle fog of demerol kept him from trembling with pain, his upper lip beaded with sweat. He wasn't walking yet, he wasn't even going to physiotherapy, the best he could manage was to sometimes get himself into a wheelchair, his leg propped and cushioned, in time for visiting hours. Stubby preferred it when he didn't make the effort to get out of bed. He might look grey and sick in it, but he was worse out of it.

Stubby didn't want to talk to Vinnie about it, especially when so little of what Vinnie said made much sense, and she could hardly go to Grandma Amberchuk with worries about the old woman's son. Grandma Amberchuk had worked hard, raised healthy children, doted on healthy grandchildren and had never expected any of her children to be ill or infirm for years. Sometimes, Stubby was certain, Grandma Amberchuk deliberately blocked out the part of her mind that registered the passage of time, blocked it out so she wouldn't have to face the sum total of days, weeks, months and years her son Dave had limped, suffered, swallowed aspirin and alcohol and tried to grin. Stubby couldn't even talk to Vinnie's parents about anything more critical than the day's TV schedule; there was no way she was going to mention Dave's infirmity. So Stubby went, with Daisy in the wire basket carrier, to see Ada Richardson.

"It has always seemed to me," Ada said bluntly, "that bone fractures either heal quickly and with almost no help or . . . they don't heal at all. I hear they put silver inserts in the leg. I've never had silver inserts in any of my bones, and I haven't known anyone who did, but I don't think it's something that promises well for the future."

"You mean he's going to get worse?"

"He might not. But I think his leg is. If it would set your mind at ease, I can have my own doctor check into it for us."

"Please." Stubby heaved a sigh of relief. Ada would take care of it. There was nothing Ada couldn't take care of one way or the other. But silver inserts sounded terrible. Nobody had said anything to her about that. Nobody was saying much of anything this time around.

Why'd they put silver in him?" she blurted. "Is it like the bolt things they put in that other time?"

"Like that," Ada agreed, "but different. The bolts went from side to side, to hold the broken pieces in place. But the breaks didn't heal. So these thin rods go down the hole in the middle of the bone, like a fulltime splint." She wished she could see the look on Stubby's face, wished she had some idea of what her words were doing. And wished heartily the doctor had taken the time to explain to the child what was being done and why.

Stubby wished she hadn't asked. Even the brief and incomplete explanation made her feel sick to her stomach. It made it sound as if the inside of Dave's leg was just mush and jelly. God knows the outside looked bad enough, all purple-ridged scars and zipper-tracks from stitches. Silver inserts, for god's sake! She didn't want Ada talking about it any more. Maybe if they stopped talking about it she could stop thinking about it and if you ignore things, sometimes they just go away and leave you alone. "Stuke?" she asked hopefully.

Ada leaned her head back, her dark glasses turned to the ceiling she couldn't see. "Not tonight," she said quietly, "I just don't seem to feel like playing cards. I think I'd just like to sit here and visit."

"Do you miss things like books and magazines?" Stubby was amazed at her own brashness.

"Terribly," Ada answered. "And sunsets and sunrises, and going to art galleries and watching crocusses bloom in the spring. But it could have been worse. God, what if I'd been struck deaf!"

"'Blind is worse," Stubby guessed.

"No," Ada smiled. "No, I don't think so. I think I got off lucky. I mean, we're all blind at night, so I had some practice; and even at night, when you can't see anything, there are so many sounds to listen to, so much to hear and share. You can step outside at night and even if you can't see your hand in front of your face you know there's a world out there; frogs and bats and insects and little furred things. Rocks, trees, it's all there, even if you can't see it."

"What happened?" Stubby dared.

"Thou shalt not look upon the face of the Lord thy God Jehovah," Ada laughed.

"Are you saying you tried to look at God?" Stubby gaped. She didn't really believe in God. Not really.

"Not only tried, but did. I saw the face of God." Ada didn't sound crazed or loony.

"What did he look like?" Stubby wasn't quite as atheistic as she had been only seconds ago.

"Beautiful." Ada rested her hand on the chair back and from the look on her face Stubby knew she was remembering. "The radio had been full of it for weeks. Eclipse of the sun. Don't stare at it with unprotected eyes, they said. So we bought these special things, smoked glass, eclipse viewers they called them. My friend also got a thing that would cast the reflection of the eclipse on a wall or screen. Said she didn't trust technology very much. We watched most of it on her screen, but, just like the Lady of Shalott, Ada Richardson the blockhead had to *see*, not just watch the reflection. But the smoked glass viewers weren't effective. There were many of us suffered damage of one kind or another, to some extent or other; not all of us went totally blind."

"But. . . the face of God?" Stubby probed.

Ada laughed, briefly, then even the hint of the laugh was gone. "First my eyes itched. Then they ached. Then they began to burn. My friend phoned the doctor. By the time he arrived at the house, the edges of things were vanishing; I suppose it's like what you see when your TV screen starts to go. He put drops in my eyes, and fussed. . . and the last thing I saw was my friend's face bent over the bed, smiling encouragement and telling me it would all work out just fine.''

"Oh." Stubby felt terribly disappointed. "I thought you meant really God."

"I did," Ada said, her face and voice serious.

Ada lay awake in bed long after Stubby had been taken back to Grandmother and Grandfather Fleming's house. Ada didn't mind being blind at night. There was nothing to miss, nothing to wish you could see, however briefly, however fuzzily. At night she could lie in bed and concentrate on the flashes of colour a doctor had told her were retinal image memories, colours Ada was certain she had never seen before she went blind, zips and darts of blue lightning, whirling swirls of oranges and reds, second-long glimpses of silver and gold light she didn't dare study during the day, didn't dare study because she knew if she didn't control whatever this was, if she didn't ration it out as a treat to herself in those times when sleep eluded her, she would get sucked into it and wind up somewhere else, somewhere the sighted could never go, and Ada was tired of being alone, tired after a lifetime of emotional and spiritual loneliness.

Here in the dark Ada could watch the movies that ran in her mind. She could become an observer of her own past and do it safely, knowing that in the dark of night, nobody else could watch her, possibly read her expression. Ada had so carefully guarded her expressions for so many years it was habit to her, but any habit is a burden to be gladly put down once in a while.

She had always understood why her mother refused to live on the farm. There had never been any uneasiness or puzzlement about it. She even understood why her parents had thought they could make a life together, in spite of being two of the most unsuited people imaginable. Her father, born to love his farm, born to understand animals and crops more easily than people, born to enjoy the smell of damp earth and animal sweat, had taken one look at her mother and jumped eagerly into what he knew would not be easy.

Ada even understood why her mother had willingly and happily married a farmer. She had thought you could marry the farmer without having to marry the farm.

When her mother left, Ada was seven years old. She came home from school and her father was sitting at the kitchen table, his eyes swollen and red, his huge hands folded together, fingers gripping fingers as if he were literally hanging onto himself. He explained to Ada that her mother's departure did not mean she did not love him, and certainly did not mean she did not love Ada. "She just can't stand living this way," he said, and Ada had understood. She herself did not always enjoy the farm. Especially in the winter when the ground was soggy, when no matter what you did the smell of manure never quite left the air, when everything squished and you lived in rubber boots. "If you want to live with her," her father said, "that's how it'll be. I'll send you money every chance I get." He waited to hear the rest of his world collapse. But Ada chose to stay. She wasn't sure why, it just didn't feel like time to make any moves of her own. She stayed and grew up like any farm kid. She went to school and learned about the parliamentary system, the rules of grammar, the basics of arithmetic and mathematics, the approved version of the history of the world, and if she did not swallow the entire pill, she swallowed enough of it to pass every grade with good marks. And when it felt like time, Ada left the farm.

Her mother was living in Vancouver and Ada went to live with her for all of six months. Ada could not understand why her mother had found the farm boring; her life in the city was enough to send a person screaming with horror. Magazines, books, radio programs, an enormous record collection and a small store. Get up in the morning, turn on the radio, put on the coffee and get ready to go to the store. Drink coffee, eat a piece of toast, walk to the corner, catch the bus, ride it to the stop closest to the store, get off the bus, go to the store, unlock the door and go inside. Spend the whole day selling fabric, wool, buttons, zippers, interfacing and patterns to women who have hours to spend looking, feeling, comparing—and often leave without buying. And all the time the soft sound of the radio in the store, voices and music half heard, soothing, numbing. When work at the store is finished, walk to the corner, catch the bus home, and the sound of the radio meets you when you open the door. "It keeps the canary company," Ada's mother explained. Make supper, eat it, do the dishes, tidy the house if it needs it, which it seldom did, then sit in the living room reading and listening to the radio until it is time for a bath and bed. Finally, blessedly, the radio is turned off and you fall asleep gratefully, until the alarm clock goes off, the radio is turned on and another day is ticking itself through the routine. Friday night a movie. Saturday night a concert or a visit to a theatre to see a play. Sunday, if it's a nice day and if, if, if, a trip to the park to walk part way along the sea wall, then return home again.

Ada thought she was going to shriek. Instead she looked around for ways to amuse herself. She joined a women's bridge club and enjoyed it so much she looked for more. And more.

It wasn't difficult to find what she was looking for. Vancouver is a port town; anything anybody would want is available. It might take a while if what you were looking for were illegal, but what Ada was looking for wasn't illegal, it wasn't even immoral. And when Ada moved on to Montreal, she already knew where to go to find the best game in the city. She sat in, playing conservatively, her nervousness hidden, and if she was afraid she would find herself aced out by the big city players, if she was afraid her provincialism would betray her, she quickly found out her fears were groundless. Ada took them as easily as she had taken the small-towners on the coast.

Every society has its own pecking order. Ada Richardson soon was playing for high stakes with some of the most influential people in the biggest city in the country. It was wonderful. Any hint of boredom was gone. Gone with the soft much-used decks of long winter nights at the oilcloth-covered kitchen table, playing with her father, games to pass the time until bedtime. Now the cards were crisp and new, used briefly and discarded, and they became more than cards in a poker game, they became tickets to anywhere she wanted to go. It puzzled her that so few people saw them the same way she did. She hadn't felt at home on the farm, she hadn't felt at home in the store, she felt at home at the card table, although she didn't feel at home with the others seated around it. After all, each one of them was intent on winning, intent on trying to make sure she lost.

Then, after years of feeling alone, after years of using her cards and her skill with them as train tickets, bus tickets, boat tickets, plane tickets and the means by which she paid her hotel bills, Ada found herself in the most high stakes game of her life. Forty years old, with more money than she would ever know what to do with, Ada met the first real friend she had ever had.

When you've won week-long games in Las Vegas, when you've taken the big pot from men who play poker with the same mental outlook the pope has when he celebrates mass, you don't expect to find yourself playing the game of your life while you're on what you consider to be a holiday. But there she was, Ada Richardson, on a small coastal ferry going from Vancouver to Prince Rupert, from Prince Rupert to Alaska, sitting in a lounge playing for no money at all, playing for points and nothing else, against a long-legged jeans-and-silk-shirt clad vacationing librarian who barely studied her cards before looking out the huge plate glass window at the fog, clouds, and mist-shrouded unnamed islets. You don't expect to have the best opponent you've ever faced break all the unspoken rules by saying, "Oh my god, look at that! Those rocks are covered with sea lions!" Above all, you do not expect to willingly put your cards aside and go out on deck to lean on the rail and watch huge brown animals flopping gracefully on shit-encrusted stones.

There wasn't enough to see in Prince Rupert to justify getting off the ferry and taking a cab to see the sights. Ugly houses perched on what had been beautiful mountainsides, small town greasy spoons and pool halls and a couple of extremely ugly canneries. But Ada and Joan spent several hours seeing Prince Rupert, walking up and down the dreary streets looking in windows at things they had already seen somewhere else. Stiffly posed mannequins wearing clothes already out of style in other places, a music store with half a dozen mediocre guitars in the window. Black-haired, black-eyed native kids who ought to have been in school and instead were playing soccer on a side street. They caught a second cab back to the ferry, comparing the stacks of postcards they'd bought, laughing at the number of different angles of pictures of the same few totem poles.

Then they picked up their game where they'd left off, playing for points and talking easily about the most ordinary things. "Do you have a stateroom?" Joan asked.

"Yes," Ada smiled, "and thank god I was warned to reserve the entire thing all to myself! I had to pay double, of course, but at least there's room to bend over and take off my shoes. You?"

"No," Joan laughed, "I've already made this trip once. I learned the first time. I brought my sleeping bag, and I'll be more comfortable on the floor in the lounge than I would be lying in the bowels of the ship listening to the engines pounding and smelling those awful diesel fumes."

Ada thought about that at night, and about how she had hated the stateroom, hated it so much she had finally convinced herself what she had was a bad case of claustrophobia. She stuck it out until they got to Alaska, stuck it out because she didn't have a sleeping bag. She got one in Alaska. On the trip back she slept in her sleeping bag on the carpet in the lounge, with the loggers and cannery workers, with the Indians and rednecks.

And played poker every night, not for money, but for points. It was actually the same game coming back as it had been going there. When the ferry finally arrived in Vancouver, Ada found the courage to invite Joan out for supper.

Lying in bed at night, safe in the blackness, Ada could watch the memories and not have to protect herself. Joan laughing easily, Joan smiling at the waiter, Joan not only quietly sliding a tip under the edge of her plate but personally thanking the waiter and the bus boy. Joan going back to Ada's hotel room, and both of them knowing why.

Morning, and Joan waking up, stretching like a cat, rolling on her side to look at Ada and finding Ada already awake and watching her. "Well," Joan smiled, "hi there."

"Hi there yourself," and then they were both laughing softly, and it wasn't until hours later they got around to thinking about eating.

Ada had known from the beginning that whatever else she felt when she was near Joan, it was not loneliness.

"How would you like to see Paris?" Ada asked.

"Love it."

"Cairo?"

"Who do I have to kill for the chance?"

"Do you have a passport?"

"Yes."

"Will you come with me?"

"Yes."

And it was that easy. Right up until the night in a large soft bed in a small warm room in a hotel in Metz, when Joan had quietly said she was going to have to return to Canada. "I've managed to spend almost every cent I had saved, and . . ." she shrugged, "all the world hates a freeloader."

The silence stretched out for long minutes and Ada thought about what life would be like without Joan. She didn't like what she was thinking. There were, of course, obvious alternatives. Ada could stop travelling and go to wherever it was Joan found work and live there, but why, when they both so loved travel, should they sit nailed to one place most of the time? Or Ada could go back travelling by herself. "I don't know much about relationships," she said finally, "but it seems to me money or lack of it is often used as an excuse for a fight that actually has its roots in some other reason."

"I don't *want* to go," Joan said, understanding immediately what Ada was trying to find words to say. "Believe me, Ada, I *want* . . ." The words stopped, Joan's face flamed and her eyes filled with tears.

"I've got money," Ada said. "I've got lots of money. If we live like this for the next twenty years and I don't make a bean between then and now, we still will not be impoverished."

"But if I do that," Joan sighed, "and five years down the line we have a big fight and I storm off, or you kick me out, or any of the million horrors that seem to happen all the time . . . there I am, looking for a job, five years out of date in my profession . . ."

"If, on the other hand, we don't duplicate other people's errors, if you had money of your own . . ." Ada tried to find the most delicate words to explain what she was trying to formulate.

"Like a child's allowance?" Joan said gently. "Or a mistress's . . . - fee?"

"More like a guarantee of non-dependency," Ada amended. Then she told Joan about feeling alone. She explained how she made her money. Joan listened, and snuggled close, attentive and comforting. They talked most of the night and never needed to discuss it again.

Joan was a very different person than Ada was; she began to study the investments Ada had made so casually. "It gives me something interesting to do when you're out fleecing the fleecers," she laughed.

"Interesting?" Ada laughed. "What could be interesting about banking practices?" Joan explained what she knew, what she was researching and studying. Explained it in poker terms. Explained it so well Ada became interested, too. And from that time forward, Joan and Ada played together, not poker, something even more high-stakes than poker.

Even after Ada had lost her eyesight they played and won. Even after Ada could no longer see the sights, they travelled and Joan explained, described, and shared everything.

Ada made very careful arrangements for her money. She firmly expected she would be the first to go. After all, she was ten years older than Joan and besides, Ada was blind, she could easily miss a stair riser and break her neck in the fall, could step off the sidewalk into the path of a moving bus, or pitch through a window or slip on ice. Joan was the happy, healthy one, the one who cross-country skied and scuba dived, who jogged and swam, who climbed to alpine meadows or rode a rubber raft through white-water rapids. But suddenly it was Joan who was dead, and there was nothing for Ada to do but go home to Bright's Crossing, to deal with the loss of the only thing she had ever really wanted to win.

Ada's physician pulled the same strings he had pulled some years before, and Stubby got the news Dave was determined she not get. "It's got a name as long as your leg," Ada said calmly, holding Stubby's mitt-like paw in both her well-manicured hands. "But what it means is, the bone is not healing. It's deteriorating."

"You mean . . . rotting, right?" Stubby could feel herself starting to shake, could feel a scream of protest welling in her gut. Daisy sensed her upset and began to whine in sympathy. "Like cancer?" she guessed.

"Yes," Ada nodded.

"Are they going to cut off his leg?" Stubby gulped.

"Probably. And so I've taken a very great liberty, Stubby. I've asked my physician to find the very best man for this kind of thing. Before anyone starts chopping, we'll know for a fact that it's the only thing that can possibly be done."

"If he makes that awful joke about the second hand store," Stubby vowed, "I'm gonna yell at him."

"For some people jokes are the only way they can handle horror."

"Do you suppose Dave's . . . scared?"

"Are you?"

"Yes."

"Then in all likelihood, so is he. You can pretty well always tell how a person feels about something by taking a good look at how you'd feel if it was you."

Knowing that if she hadn't said something to someone it was because she didn't want to talk about it, Stubby reasoned Dave's silence came from the same place as hers. Much as she wanted to talk to him about it, sit on his bed, put her face against his shoulder and cry, or let him cry on her shoulder, she bit her tongue, kept her questions and fears to herself, and tried to concentrate on the games of cribbage they played. Cribbage bored her, but it was the only game other than fish and snap that Dave could play; he was too full of sedatives to be able to concentrate on anything more complicated.

"I have to have another operation," he said, with obvious effort.

"I know," Stubby answered.

Dave focused his too-shiny eyes on her face and stared for a long time. "How long've you known?"

"Couple of weeks."

He nodded. His hand, once so powerful, now so skinny, picked at the white coverlet. "How'd you find out?"

Stubby told him of her visit to Ada, and Dave nodded. "You never said nothin'," he accused.

"You never did either," Stubby countered.

He nodded again. His eyes welled with tears, but he made no move to grasp Stubby's hand, so she made no move to invade his privacy. "Couldn't tell you," he gulped. "Helluva thing to have to tell anybody." He looked at her, looked away, and Stubby realized he was terrified. She got off her chair and moved to sit on the bed beside him, flouting hospital rules. He reached for her hand, squeezed it, blinked rapidly.

"Hey," she tried to grin, "too bad it wasn't your arm that was fouled up . . ."

"Just keep that mad bitch of a mother of yours away from me for a few days." He let the tears slide down his face. "I couldn't manage the butcher and Vinnie both at the same time."

"Trade you," Stubby laughed. "I'll take the butcher and you get Vinnie and her folks."

"Bring on the knife," Dave groaned, "the axe, the chainsaw, whatever it takes, but please, dear God, not Vinnie's father." He coughed, and Stubby could tell the coughing hurt him. ''That man makes my ass ache.''

4

The bed looked weird with only one leg outlined under the starched coverlet and Stubby couldn't help staring at the flat place where Dave's other leg had been. Even asleep, propped on pillows, he looked off balance. The tube was gone from his nostril and the awful sucking machine was gone, but the plastic bag of clear fluid was still suspended from the T-frame and the needle still stuck into the back of his hand, forcing the skin up in a tight, painful-looking ridge, seeming, in some weird way, to be more of an insult than the amputation. Somehow, something taken off wasn't as degrading as something foreign shoved in and left.

She'd been sitting on the chair for hours, waiting for Dave to wake up, but it didn't seem as if he was in any hurry to do that. His eyelids were sunken and dark, his lips dry, beginning to crack, and where his scalp showed through his thinning hair, Stubby could see dry flecks of skin. His chest rose shallowly in quick movements that reminded her of the flutter of moth wings. It didn't seem to have much to do with breathing, not really, breathing made your chest go up and down with some kind of determination; whatever Dave was doing seemed hesitant and very temporary.

His upper arm was pinpricked where they slid the needles into him and filled him with things to keep him asleep, keep the pain at bay. Stubby had nightmares about the pain, envisioning it as some kind of stealthy worm with long, thin, serrated fangs, a creepy-crawly from the worst possible television shows, only it wasn't on television any more, it was coiled in the bandaged lump that had once been her father's leg. They hadn't cut far enough, they hadn't cut out the pain and it was snapping and chewing and planning forays into other parts of his body. The injections didn't do anything to the pain, they just put Dave to sleep, where, they said, he didn't feel it. But he did. His hands twitched, his mouth twisted sometimes, and even though he felt so hot, so dry, there was often sweat on his brow or his upper lip.

He hadn't been fully awake in a week, not since they'd wheeled him down the hall in the green gown, green socks and silly green tea-cosy hat. Stubby had walked beside the stretcher as far as the elevator, holding his hand until the last possible minute, and when the elevator doors were closing he had managed to lift his head and grin, even wink at her. Then the doors slid shut, and that was the end of the Dave she had known, the one who could at least walk on his own two feet, the one who had once laced up high caulk boots and gone off to work, stomping up and down slopes, dragging cables, fastening them around felled trees, getting himself out of the way quickly and easily. The one who had come home with his boots tied together at the laces, slung over his shoulder, banging slightly with each step, tapping his chest and back, swinging slightly, the one who had dropped the boots behind the stove to dry, removed his comfortable black romeos and padded around in wool socks, grey with red stripes. The one who had shown her how to climb and walk a split rail fence. Who could fire a kick so fast you didn't even see it coming as the soccer ball whizzed toward the goal, leaving you standing there feeling foolish.

The Dave waiting in the bed when she came after school that first day wasn't the same old Dave at all. Not either of those old Daves. "You don't have to go to school today, Sheilagh," her grandmother said gently, but Stubby had wanted the routine, the sameness, the comfort of having something to do, something expected of her. As soon as the last bell rang, she ran outside, grabbed her bike and pedalled furiously to the hospital. She would have liked to have had Daisy with her, but the rules didn't allow that.

Actually, the rules didn't even really allow Stubby to be there. The rules insisted children could only visit on Sundays, and then only if accompanied by parents, but nobody chased her off, nobody would have been able to chase her off if they wanted to.

She sat by his bed, dry-eyed and terrified, until Vinnie came and got her, took her home, made her eat something and then nagged her into going to bed. The next day Stubby went to school but couldn't pay attention to anything. The teachers ignored it and after school she whipped up to see Dave. But he was still asleep. The third day she didn't bother going to school. Partly it was because she slept in and nobody woke her up, partly it was because she knew she wasn't going to be able to sit there listening to stuff that didn't make any sense to her, worrying herself about her father. She slept until ten-thirty, then woke up, leaped out of bed, pulled on her clothes, had a breakfast her grandmother and Vinnie claimed was totally inadequate, and while they were still trying to get her to have a poached egg, Stubby was heading out of the house.

She sat there all day, ignoring everything and everyone, staring at Dave, willing him to come out of his refuge, trying to force him awake, trying to force him to be well. Trying to force him to live.

Since any excuse to get the hell out of Vetchburg was a good excuse, Vinnie arrived to do her impersonation of Florence Nightingale. Stubby dug in her heels. "You'd better not," she growled.

"It might cheer him up," Vinnie protested.

"Stay away," Stubby flared. "He said he didn't want to see you! Take the hint, Vinnie. The man doesn't want to see you!" It wouldn't have made any difference. Vinnie could have come and gone away feeling good, and Dave wouldn't have known.

"Stub?" he managed. She shot out of her chair, moved to stand by the bed, grasping the hand that didn't have the needle stuck in it.

"Hey," she said, her voice thick with tears. "Not doin' too good, huh?" He tried to look at her but his eyes wouldn't stay open. "Go to sleep, it's okay," she soothed.

He might have said more but the nurse came in and Stubby had to step aside while she checked him over, took his pulse, fussed with something. "I'll get you a shot," the nurse promised.

"Gimme a shot in the head," Dave groaned, "with a three-oh-three." Stubby realized he wasn't joking.

"You stop that!" she snapped.

He managed to open his eyes then, and fixed his gaze upon her. He shook his head sadly, "I figured I'd live to be ninety-six, and I hoped I'd get 'er by bein' shot in the back by a jealous husband while I dove out the bedroom window. This . . . ." He raised his hand, let it drop weakly again. "This is ratshit, Stubby."

"You'll feel better tomorrow," she insisted. "Ada Richardson got you the best doctor in the whole wide world."

"Maybe she never done me no favour, Stubs. I might'a been better off with a hamfisted sucker who'd'a killed me on the table, where it didn't hurt." He went back to sleep even before the nurse arrived back with the injection.

Stubby left the hospital, got on her bike and pedalled to Ada's place, seeking comfort. The housekeeper brought her tea and a sandwich and Ada said all the right things, but still Stubby felt like shit on a stick. "He isn't going to get better, is he?'' she challenged. Ada shook her head, unable to find words.

''What happened?'' Stubby raged.

''Have you ever seen a puffball?'' Ada asked finally. Stubby nodded, then realized Ada couldn't see the nod, so she muttered yes, she had, so what. ''Ever see one just suddenly pop open and all the white powder go floating off on the wind? Well, that's what happened. The bone deteriorated around the silver, the cancer started, and before they got the leg cut off, it had split and sent its seeds out in the blood.''

''They should'a done it sooner then!'' Stubby gritted. ''They just sat with their heads up their bums!''

''It's his own fault,'' Ada said coldly. ''He knew there was something wrong and he didn't go to the doctor until it was too late.''

''But. . .'' Stubby didn't know if she wanted to cry or curse.

''Are you worried about him or about yourself?'' Ada asked.

''My life,'' Stubby said very stiffly, ''might not seem very long to you but it is, after all, my whole and entire life. And even when they wouldn't let me live with him I knew he was there. Soon he won't be.''

''I'm very sorry,'' Ada said softly.

''And then it will all start up again,'' Stubby exploded, ''Vinnie and that jerk husband of hers will step in and there I'll be in Barfsville again, only this time everyone will say how *nice* they are, and how *kind* they are, and isn't it so *wunnerful* how open-minded he is . . . and they'll just gloat, that's all, just gloat, because they'll have won!''

''Vinnie is, after all, your mother.''

''I can hardly be held responsible for that!'' Stubby laughed in spite of herself. ''I mean, Vinnie's okay by herself, but my sweet whistlin' jesus, the company she keeps . . . know what I mean?''

''What is the one thing in the entire world you think Earl would understand?'' Ada asked.

''A poke in the yip,'' Stubby replied immediately. ''Or someone tapdancing on his top lip. A sharp stick in the hole of his ear. Something that would let him know in no uncertain terms that he is not the be-all and end-all of creation.''

''Power,'' Ada laughed, ''comes from money. Not from the barrel of a gun, and not from sharp sticks in ears or eyes, either, for that matter. If you have money you can hire someone to keep the guns and sticks away from you. Most of the people who want power of some kind or other eventually find out that if they have enough money, they have the power they wanted.''

Stubby shook her head. ''Earl don't seem to care for money. Maybe because he's never been without it.''

''If he's never been without it, he doesn't know how to live like most of us have had to live. So he'll be afraid of that. People always fear what they don't know or haven't tried.''

Stubby had no idea what was going on. She didn't even know for quite a few weeks that anything was going on, much less that it concerned her. She went to see Dave in the hospital, and as he slowly gathered some strength and could sit for brief spells in a wheelchair, she pushed his chair down the hallway to the solarium, where he sat at the expanse of glass, staring out at the sea to his right, the mountains to his left. And Stubby sat visiting with him, playing cribbage or watching the TV, rolling cigarettes for him or helping him peel what he called the magic oranges. And she pretended she didn't know her father was dying. Dave, in turn, pretended he didn't know that Stubby knew what he hadn't been able to put into words even to himself.

But Ada Richardson wasn't avoiding any issues. Ada phoned her lawyer, who flew from the mainland on a charter flight, was met by Ada's driver and taken to the huge house. They spent several hours together, then the driver took the lawyer back to the small airport and a charter flight back to the city. The next morning the lawyer made some phone calls and set up some lunch appointments and dinner appointments and the wheels began to turn.

Someone sent an official-enough-looking letter to Vinnie, who was still visiting her parents and having extended long distance arguments with Earl.

''What do you know about this?'' Vinnie asked Stubby, who looked at the letter and shrugged.

''Nothing,'' she replied honestly.

''Is your goddamn father up to something?'' Vinnie raged.

''He's too sick to be up to anything at all,'' Stubby defended. ''What is it?''

''It's a letter saying they want my permission for you . . . and me . . . to be interviewed by someone from the welfare. And they make it clear that without my permission it might take longer, but they'll do it anyway. What's the welfare got to do with me? Or,'' she glared, ''with you either, for that matter?''

''Prob'ly something to do with school,'' Stubby guessed. ''What with Dave not bein' out of the hospital yet and whatnot.''

Vinnie talked to Earl about it on the phone and Earl called the welfare. He tried to push a few buttons and lean on the fact he was a respected leader of the community and a school principal and all. But in the end, as the letter to Vinnie had suggested, the interviews happened. Stubby was interviewed once with Vinnie in the room and twice on her own.

"I don't want to live with Earl," Stubby said flatly.

"Sheilagh!" Vinnie gasped. "What a disloyal thing to say. Why Earl loves you!"

"Earl doesn't know the first thing about me," Stubby argued. "He doesn't want *me*, he wants you, and the only way he can have you is to put up with me. And even if he does want me," she finished, "I don't want him. I don't like him. I don't like anything about him. I don't like the way he bosses me, I don't like the way he bosses you, I don't like the way he thinks it's always his way that's the best and only way, and I *hate* that effin' town he lives in."

"Sheilagh!" Vinnie tried to smile. "Whatever will people think if they hear you talking like that?"

"I don't give a fat rat's ass what people think!" Stubby shouted. "I was asked and I told the truth, and if they don't want the truth then they better not ask!"

"If it were to become . . . impossible . . . for you to live with your father," the welfare worker asked delicately, "what would you prefer?"

"I don't know," Stubby said, her voice shaking. "I don't know where I'd go. They don't let kids like me live on their own. Maybe I'd catch a freight car and become a bum. But I would *not* live with Earl and Vinnie in Dustbowl Heaven."

"Well," Vinnie hedged, "maybe Earl would consider moving back here."

"I wouldn't live with him here, either," Stubby snarled. "The man makes my skin itch. I think I'm allergic to him."

"Oh, don't be ridiculous!" Vinnie snapped.

"You don't be ridiculous," Stubby argued. "It's absolutely ridiculous to think for one minute that Earl and I are going to live in the same house without a fight. He won't be nice to Daisy, he wrinkles his nose up at the sight of Myrtle, he thinks girls who play sports are ruining their reproductive organs or something and he is as stubborn as an old hound dog. Nobody ever told him he wasn't Jesus Christ's little brother. And he isn't bossing me around any more!"

"Sheilagh, I insist you stop behaving in this abominable manner." Vinnie leaned forward and grabbed Stubby by the wrist. "Now you stop it! What will people think!" She turned to the welfare man and tried to smile. "Honest to god," she was nearly crying, "I don't know where she got this bug in her ear about Earl. He's the salt of the earth."

The interview lasted another hour and a half but Stubby said very little. She slouched in her chair, glaring at the welfare man, glaring at Vinnie, glaring at the rug, glaring at the drapes and the windows and the ashtrays.

"How come," she exploded suddenly, "everyone thinks it is just fine if I lose my dad and my Grandma and Grandpa Amberchuk and Ada Richardson and my ball team and my friends and the creek and everything and go live in some place where you never get the sand out of your shoes and the thweet-thweet-thweet of the sprinklers drives you nuts? How come that's just hunky dory with the whole world?''

''What do you mean . . . if you lose your father?'' the worker asked in a soft tone.

''He's dying, isn't he?'' Stubby blurted. Vinnie gasped, her eyes filled with tears, and she looked suddenly very scared. ''Well,'' Stubby demanded, ''isn't he? Isn't that what this is all about? That goddamned Earl stirring dust again?''

''No,'' said the worker, ''this wasn't Earl's idea.''

''Oh,'' Stubby stared. ''Well, I'm sorry. I thought it was. It's something he'd do if he'd'a thought of it in time. He's just *got* to win, you see.'' Then Stubby nearly joined Vinnie in tears. ''I mean, he's *not* my dad. He never was. He never will be. But that's what he always says he is! And everything I have is *here*. I am not the one who married Earl, so why do I have to lose my whole life?''

''And what about me?'' Vinnie wailed, ''Aren't I your mother?'' She began talking about what it meant to be a childless mother, which in her opinion was worse than being a motherless child. Stubby slumped back in her chair and zipped her lip again, returning to her glaring and sarcastic sniffing.

The next interview, without Vinnie, went much better in Stubby's opinion.

''Tell me what you like about Bright's Crossing,'' the worker asked.

''Why'n't you come with me and I'll show you,'' Stubby suggested. They got in his car and Stubby gave directions. They drove to Haslam Creek, they sat on a rock and watched the water, then rolled up their pant legs and, carrying their shoes and socks, walked down the creek to where the trestle went overhead.

''See,'' Stubby pointed, grinning, ''on the crossties and the places where the ties join the supports? See the white stain? Well, that's pigeon poop, and that's where they have their nests. Just hunnderds of them. And if you get them at the right time, just before they fly, they're what the fancy restaurants call squab, and boy, are they ever good! But you never take 'em all,'' she instructed, ''or you'd be out of pigeons in about two years.''

''What do they do when the train comes?''

''Prob'ly put their fingers in their ears, huh?'' she cackled crazily.

Stubby thought she saw the worker's car parked on the far side of the ballpark in the third inning of the game against Wellington, but she wasn't sure, there were a lot of beige cars in the world. She was almost sure she saw his car driving away from the hospital, but Dave didn't make any mention of having had a visitor, so Stubby decided she had worker-itis and made a point of ignoring every beige car she saw.

She had a second interview without Vinnie. This time she took the worker up the old mine road and showed him the ruins of the colliery equipment, the heaps of slag, fireweed growing from it, and explained to him how dangerous it was to try to climb up the heaps. She showed him the river, the rapids, the fossils in the caves. He nodded often, smiled openly and even teased her about the way she talked. "It's Island," she shrugged. "Y'know? Eh? Wodjasay? Huh?" and they both laughed.

"Vinnie won't talk like that," she confided, "because Earl says it shows a decided lack of class." She shrugged. "Earl would know about a lack of class, believe me. My dad says class is somethin' if you get all fussed up about it, you don't have any." The worker grinned and nodded his head.

On the way back, he reached out, turned off the car radio, and asked, "How do you feel about your dad's . . . sickness, Sheilagh?"

"My names's Stubby," she growled. The worker nodded and waited. The pause lengthened.

"He's not sick," Stubby managed, "he's got cancer. It was in his leg, and then it seeded, and now it's everywhere. It's what gives him headaches, it's what makes his ribs hurt. He's not sick at all. He's dying."

"Have you talked to him about it?" the worker asked. Stubby shook her head fiercely.

"Why not?"

"He never talked to *me* about it," she argued angrily.

"There are things people ought to say to each other before it's too late," the worker said firmly. "And if those things don't get said, you wind up for the rest of your life feeling as if stuff never got finished. Some people never finish anything in their lives because they got started that way."

"What if he doesn't want to talk?"

"Ever slow you down before?" he grinned. "I mean, your mother didn't want you to say what you said to me when she was there . . . but you said it!"

Stubby went up to the hospital that evening and handed Dave a bag containing a dozen oranges. "Did 'em myself," she bragged. "Picked out the juiciest I could find, then got a needle from Ada and filled it with vodka, then injected the orange . . . got about two doubles in every orange. Plus," she teased, "all that healthy Vitamin C."

"Oh a'course." Dave managed a smile and began peeling an orange eagerly.

"I was wondering if we should try tequila." Dave raised an eyebrow, grinning widely. "I was also wondering," Stubby dropped her bomb, "if maybe you'n'me shouldn't have a talk about things like what's going on and what it means and what's next for both of us."

"Oh shit." Dave bit into the orange desperately. "Oh shit, Stubs."

"Listen," Stubby quavered, "it's okay. I mean it isn't what I want, and it's not what I'd'a chosen, but...like the guy said, I'll live, y'know?"

Dave swallowed his orange, began hurriedly to peel another. "There was stuff I wanted to do and see," he mourned. "I wanted to see you graduate from high school. I wanted to give you away when you got married. I wanted to hold your babies on my knee..."

"Tell you what." Stubby reached out, took a section of orange from him, popped it in her mouth. "I'll arrange it so you haven't missed a thing. I'll drop outta school, I'll never get married, and I won't have any kids, how's that?"

"Prob'ly just as well," he agreed, chewing furiously, swallowing as though the orange was as big as a basketball. "I mean the thought of your kids turned loose on an unprepared world. Eh?"

"Yeah," she agreed, licking her fingers. He handed her another segment, she nodded her thanks. "Did I tell you today that I love you?" she asked conversationally.

"Hell, you never even told me that yesterday, let alone today."

"Well, I do. And I did. Yesterday, I mean. And last week, and back before that even."

"Glad you told me." He bit into another orange, the juice squirting. "I'm real glad that you told me. When your mom and I got married, it was because she was up the stump, you know that, huh?"

"Yeah."

"But I think you ought to know that I'm not sorry. Some people, well, their kids are kind of a disappointment, or a pain in the ass. But I like you, Stubby Amberchuk. Love you, guess most parents love their kids, whatever love is. But most of all, I like you."

"Gimme some more orange," she hinted delicately. He grinned, tossed her one, told her to peel it herself.

When the afternoon supervisor came in the room to check, she found Dave Amberchuk sprawling on his belly and Stubby giving him a backrub, both of them laughing like loons. "I'll be a ghost," he was giggling, "and I'll come rattle your window at night. Scare the devil out of you."

''I'm not scared of ghosts,'' she babbled. ''But if a seagull craps on my head, I'm sure not going to blame the bird!''

Stubby's courage and laughter lasted all the way to the back entrance of the hospital, where she had her bike parked. Then she couldn't do it any longer. She leaned her head against the wall of the building and cried. When Ada's driver picked her up and carried her to the big black car she hadn't even noticed, she clung to him. He said all the right things—it's okay, let 'er rip, kid, it's a right bitch, howl like a wolf if you want. Then he put her in the back seat, where Ada cuddled her and said nothing at all while the driver went back to get the battered bike and put it in the trunk of the car. Stubby lifted her tear-swollen face, wiped her eyes with fingers still sticky with the juice of two oranges, and fought for control. ''It isn't fair!'' she managed, ''and the whole thing just pisses me off!''

In the morning she was too sick to go to school. Ada's housekeeper brought her breakfast in bed, with a side order of aspirin, and after she had eaten Stubby rolled over and went back to sleep. It didn't occur to her to phone Vinnie. But it had occurred to Ada the night before, so there was no sideshow about it.

5

Stubby had expected Dave to be in the hospital one or two weeks; she had not expected him to be in hospital two or three months. Stubby had expected to have to endure Grandmother and Grandfather Fleming for a very short period of time; she hadn't expected she would have to live with them through the wet and the rain of Island winter. Stubby certainly had not expected Vinnie to stay for more than a few days. But Vinnie stayed. Through autumn, into the winter, Vinnie stayed. Stubby began to fear Vinnie was going to stay through spring and summer too.

Then Earl phoned long distance to say he would be arriving for Christmas, and Stubby pinned her hopes on Earl's powers of persuasion. It wasn't that Stubby disliked Vinnie, because she didn't. More and more, Stubby found it possible to talk with her mother without feeling she might as well be talking to her own armpit. More and more Stubby realized that, in her own way, Vinnie was holding conversations, and not just coming out of nowhere with garble and gab. It was just that Vinnie and her parents did not exactly fit into Stubby's way of life, and Stubby, for sure and certain, did not fit easily nor comfortably into their idea of life and how it ought to be lived. She realized, with something close to sadness, that if only the whole bunch of them weren't related and interrelated, they would undoubtedly allow each other to live their own lives free of interference. They might even manage to be friends. But family ties were choking them.

There was the matter of opinions. Stubby was supposed to not have any. Children, she was told repeatedly, should be seen and not heard. ''If God had'a intended kids not to be heard,'' she replied tartly, ''we'd be born mute and only be given a voice on our nineteenth birthday.'' Had Stubby had reason to say that to Dave or to Grandma Amberchuk or to Ada, her pronouncement would have been met with a grin, a giggle or a guffaw. Instead it earned her a slap that left Grandfather Fleming's palm print on her cheek.

''It's for your own good,'' Vinnie tried to explain. ''Nobody likes a smart-mouthed kid. He loves you and all he wants is for you to learn to . . . fit in.''

''If that's how people treat you when they love you,'' Stubby challenged, ''I can only pray to God nobody else in my whole life ever decides to love me. My enemies treat me better than that.''

''Now, don't be flip,'' Vinnie warned.

''Oh, no *ma'am*,'' Stubby breathed. ''Not I.'' She sat with the blandest possible face until Vinnie gave up and left the room. Then she got up, closed her door carefully and quietly and stood safe in the room, unobserved and unsuspected, pulling every face she could manage, contorting her muscles, grimacing and sticking her tongue as far out as it could go. She stuck her tongue so far out, in fact, the little jigger underneath that kept it connected to her mouth rubbed against her bottom teeth, bled slightly and was sore for two days.

As Christmas approached and Earl's visit was impending, Stubby was consoled only by the fact Dave seemed to be feeling more comfortable. His trips to the solarium were less exhausting, he was able to sit for longer periods of time and he began to taste and enjoy the treats Stubby brought him. At first it was bland things like a bowl of custard, a fruit jar half filled with caramel pudding, a butter tart Ada's housekeeper had made. The day Dave asked her if there was any way she could manage to come by a nice piece of smoked salmon, Stubby nearly wept with joy.

''No problem,'' she promised, and it wasn't. All she had to do was walk down the road, over the trestle and along the bank of the river until she got to the reserve, and then it was easy. She explained to Betty Paul, who explained to Tommy Dick, who nodded and went to see Alma Pete, and before Stubby had finished her cup of tea or had a chance to play with the latest baby, Alma was handing over half a smoked salmon.

''You tell your dad,'' she said softly, ''that we're hopin' he has an easy goin' of it. He's a good man.'' She looked down at the floor, smiling at the toes of her sneakers, and just nodded when Stubby thanked her. Stubby knew enough not to offer money for the fish. She also knew enough to wait a couple of weeks before going back down with a reciprocal thank-you gift.

Dave enjoyed his salmon and the nurses willingly put it in the small fridge on the second floor, bringing him a few slices whenever he asked for them. The next time Grandma Amberchuk baked his favourite soda bread there were extra loaves for Alma Pete, and when Grandpa Amberchuk and Uncle Ed got a deer there were roasts and ribs for Alma and her kids.

Stubby hadn't been able to do much about collecting bottles to return for the deposit or stacking wood for pay or any of the other jobs and chores she had once done to supplement her allowance and, as Christmas drew closer, she was more and more aware of what a pain it was to be broke. She didn't have time to babysit or to clean out garages, carports or sheds, and the prospect of finding presents was starting to look impossible.

"Say, when did I last hand over your allowance?" Dave asked out of the blue. Stubby just shrugged. "Jesus," Dave lectured, "you've got to do better than that, kid. If a person owes you—collect." He pretended to swat at her.

"You had other things on your mind."

"So what's *your* excuse?" he glared. "Go get my bank book and my chequebook and I'll catch up. Retroactive." He grinned again.

When Stubby looked at the cheque, she gaped. "You sure?"

"Sure I'm sure," he growled. "Goddamn compensation still has to pay me. And you're runnin' yourself ragged helpin' me while I'm laid up . . . you deserve every cent." As Stubby began to cry, Dave managed to haul her from the bedside chair to the bed, and he held her tightly. "Hey," he soothed, "it's okay, you know. Whatever it is, it's okay."

"I'm gonna miss you so much," she managed. "How did you know I was really broke? How did you know?"

"Cause I'm your dad," he said.

Earl arrived with a back seat full of packages Stubby knew he hadn't wrapped himself, and immediately the entire house shifted into loon gear. Everybody was busy bending over backward for Earl; or at least busy appearing to the others to be attempting to be bending over backward to please Earl. Grandmother Fleming made scrambled eggs for breakfast, the way she did nearly every morning of the year, but put the plates on the table with a big, cheerful grin and a coy, "I know how much you liked scrambled eggs, Earl." Grandfather Fleming picked up the platter of eggs and handed it to Earl instead of loading his own plate first. "Eat up, son," he said heartily, "it's not every day you get a chance to eat Mother's scrambled eggs." Vinnie made sure Earl got first grabs at the plate of toast, and seemed intent on assuring that at no time would the coffee level in Earl's cup get below the half-full line. Stubby waited her turn for a chance to put food on her plate and dreamed of the day she could push the toast, one slice at a time, up Earl's nose. And Earl sat through it all, smiling as if everyone was only doing what the Good Lord had intended.

Stubby bought Dave a case of Japanese oranges and sat on the floor in Ada's living room, carefully injecting double shots of tequila into every tangerine in the box. "At least we can be assured," Ada smiled, "he isn't going to suffer from scurvy."

"I wonder if it would work with pineapple too."

"Wait until summertime and try it with watermelon. I bet watermelon and vodka would be wonderful." She laughed. "Maybe I'll put in my own order now. When I get old and senile and useless, would you be so kind as to fix me up a beautiful, red, ripe watermelon?"

"It's a promise," Stubby vowed. "But I don't think Dave'll be here come summertime." Ada sighed, content to hear Stubby's voice calm and finally free of the hard edges of panic and rage.

Christmas morning was pleasant. Everybody oohed and aahed and smiled over their presents, even Earl.

Earl unwrapped the package from Stubby slowly, smiling stiffly even before he saw what was inside, and then his smile broadened, became natural and happy, as he held up his gift, a fly-tying kit. "How did you know?" he asked, his voice warm and friendly.

"Me?" Stubby shrugged, unconsciously imitating Dave. "Oh, I'm a smart kid." Although she had intended it as a dig, Earl took it as a joke and laughed, and Stubby began to wish she had spent more time over his present instead of just getting him something because she felt obligated.

She left the house as quickly as she decently could and pedalled her old bike through the rain to the hospital. Grandma and Grandpa were already there and Stubby knew the uncles, aunts and cousins would have carefully scheduled their visits so that throughout the entire day Dave would have company without ever having too much. The small tree was set up on Dave's bedside table, waiting only for Stubby to put the little silver angel in place, and the foot of Dave's bed was covered with presents. When Stubby handed over the gift-wrapped box of tangerines, safe from the rain in its plastic bag cover, Dave grinned and winked at her. "Betcha I know what it is," he laughed. "Betcha it's vitamins."

"I don't bet." Stubby pretended to disapprove.

Dave handed her a plain piece of grocery string. "What's that?" She tugged at it gently. It seemed to go across the floor and out into the hall.

"Follow it," he urged, not even interested in opening his present. Stubby followed the string across the room, out the door and down the hallway to the solarium. The string was tied to Stubby's Christmas present—a brand new firengine red five-speed with a shiny new basket carrier. In the carrier was a blue cushion which someone had embroidered with the outline of a daisy. Stubby stroked her bike and blinked rapidly, wanting to howl and rant with renewed sorrow, but when she heard the sound of Dave's chair wheels rolling down the hallway she swallowed her pain and the smile that greeted him was as wide as the tears in her eyes were bright. Dave and Grandpa Amberchuk were eating tequila tangerines, but Grandma had hers held in her hands. ''I'm driving,'' she smiled, putting it in her pocket.

''Guess what?'' Dave challenged.

''What?'' Stubby bent, cradling him in a tight hug in spite of the awkwardness of his chair.

''I've got a pass,'' he gloated, ''and I'm havin' Christmas dinner with all of you!''

Ada's driver was waiting outside with the limo, and the wheelchair folded up to fit in the trunk with room to spare for the box of tangerines. Stubby elected to ride her new bike, and the old one went into Grandma and Grandpa Amberchuk's trunk. Stubby raced off, stopping by Grandmother and Grandfather Fleming's house to get Daisy.

Everyone at the house seemed to think Stubby had stopped by to share her happiness with them, and Grandmother Fleming bustled around wrapping up Christmas cake, shortbread, and a plum pudding. ''Our contribution,'' she smiled, ''to what I hope will be a wonderful day for your father.'' Stubby couldn't help wondering if it took a case of terminal cancer to move you from the list of louts to the list of acceptable people. It seemed rather a high price to pay, and she wondered if she should tell Dave he had graduated.

She put the Christmas goodies in her backpack and introduced Daisy to the new bike and basket carrier. Daisy wagged her tail and let her tongue loll from a half-opened mouth in a wide doggy grin as Stubby raced across town steering one-handed, her other hand busy squeezing the bulb of the ooga-horn fastened to her handlebars.

They all cried at least once that afternoon, even Grandma Amberchuk, who had vowed to herself and God that she'd make it through the day without tears. But it was a good day and a wonderful party. Ada's housekeeper, who had been openly amazed by the invitation, had cooked herself to a fare-thee-well. Ada's driver had wisely opted to limit his contribution to liquids in bottles of different sizes and colours. Ada herself brought a collection of expensive cheeses, most of which had never been seen, let alone tasted, by any of the Amberchuks, all of whom pronounced each and every one of the new taste sensations delicious. ''Even the one that seems to have. . . gone a bit off,'' one of the cousins said politely, forcing himself to swallow.

Nobody said Daisy smelled, or had fleas, or was maybe getting mange in her old age. Nobody said the living room's no place for a dog, or can't that creature go outside where it belongs. They stepped over Daisy, they scratched her ears and if Daisy wound up on a chair someone else wanted, they asked her to get out of it instead of giving her a shove and dumping her on the floor. When Dave had to lie down on what was ordinarily Stubby's bed when she stayed there, Daisy hopped up beside him and curled up against his leg. ''Got me a watchdog,'' Dave yawned. ''Watch her watch me catch a few Z's.''

He wakened just in time for dinner and, as Grandma Amberchuk said, ''You'd never know there was anything wrong with him to see him put away his food.'' That's when she started to cry, even though she had determined not to, and for a few moments everyone looked around wildly, not quite knowing where to rest their eyes.

''Momma,'' Dave said gently. ''Momma, you knew when I was born that I wasn't going to live forever. Now, didn't you? Come on, didn't you know, deep in your heart, that sooner or later I would die?''

''But. . . not so soon!'' she wiped her eyes, struggling for control.

''I'm just gonna go a few years early is all.''

He cut his turkey carefully, then smiled at her. ''And if you really believe God's in his heaven and that's where we go when we die. . . well. . . I'll be waitin' for you when you finally get your slowpokey self up there.''

''You don't expect your children to go first,'' Grandma Amberchuk explained quietly. ''If you did, you'd probably never have children.'' Her voice quavered again. ''It's very hard, David.''

''Yeah,'' Dave agreed, ''it's a son of a bitch, for sure.'' Then he put his piece of turkey in his mouth and chewed slowly.

Everyone waited for someone to say something wise or clever or consoling or philosophical, but just before the silence became deafening, Stubby broke it. ''Could someone please pass me the stuffing?'' she asked clearly. Dave shot her a look of approval, their glances locked for brief seconds, and then conversation resumed around the enormous table that was really the table plus several boards set across three wooden saw horses and covered with clean sheets because all the tablecloths were too small.

They got Dave back to the hospital without any trouble and he was sound asleep in his bed before the limo was clear of the parking lot. Stubby, her new bike safe in the trunk, sat in the back seat with Ada and Daisy and a large box full of leftovers and samples for her to take back to Grandmother Fleming's house.

''Thank you very much for the new wallet,'' Stubby smiled. ''I always wanted a real leather wallet that would fit in my back pocket.''

''Thank you very much for the tape.'' Ada took Stubby's hand in hers, pressed gently. "I have never in my life had a present like this. Where did you find the tape recorder?"

"Oh, they've got one in the music room at school, so's the kids in band can hear what a caterwaul they make."

"And the jokes?"

"I just asked everybody the same thing. What's the one joke you would never tell your mother or dad. Some of 'em," she warned, "are pretty rank."

"But I bet you had fun taping them all the same," Ada grinned, already anticipating the sound of Stubby's giggles, taped forever.

"I'll tell the world," Stubby laughed. "Some of the best ones are towards the end. By then I was almost hysterical. It's not easy. That's a ninety-minute tape. Takes a lot of jokes to fill ninety minutes. I had to do it just a few at a time or all I did was sputter and giggle."

"Which one is your own joke?" Ada probed.

"I didn't use mine. I was gonna, but at the last minute I decided not to. This way, no matter how rank or awful they are, I can say it wasn't me," she cackled foolishly.

Ada made her next foray while Peace on Earth was still fresh in the minds of all and before Earl's Goodwill to Men had begun to fade in the approaching imminence of his departure.

"Just because she has decided to have Sheilagh as her . . . heir . . . is no reason . . . ." Vinnie spluttered.

"Ms. Richardson has quite an investment portfolio," the lawyer said coldly, "and it isn't something one just automatically knows how to manage. The diversification of the investments requires a certain kind of knowledge and training which, I do not hesitate to suggest, neither of you would be capable of providing."

"Vinnie," Earl said softly, possibly craftily, "it's a wonderful chance for Sheilagh."

"Ms. Amberchuk's father has agreed," the lawyer said smoothly, "and all necessary papers and agreements have been signed with him."

"But why should I have to . . . ."

"Advantages," Earl mused, "of a kind we'd never be able to afford."

"Well, I don't seen why I should have to give up my own flesh and blood just to provide Ada Richardson with an heir. If she'd wanted an heir she could have had one. She wasn't born without ovaries, you know," Vinnie yelled.

"Ada Richardson is not exactly running around this country looking for a place to leave her money." The lawyer fixed Vinnie with his cold blue eyes and didn't bother pretending to smile. "Believe me, madam, people volunteer for the chance. We are not talking just one or two measly million. What we are talking here is big bucks.''

''Oh,'' said Vinnie, her voice suddenly very small and thin.

Earl at some time must have had all the makings of an open-minded person, a person able to see both, or even all sides of a question. When they left the lawyer's office, Earl was talking of advantages for Stubby. By the time Vinnie drowsily turned off the light to go to sleep that night, Earl was talking about how grossly unfair it would be to deprive a soon-to-be half-orphan child of so much when she hadn't even had a chance yet to get over her grief. Every reason Stubby had ever yelled at him in arguments over where she ought to live resurfaced, but as Earl's ideas, not as Stubby's. And that, to Earl, made all the difference in the world.

When Earl packed his suitcase in the trunk of his car and headed off for the bare branches and snow-covered ground of what Stubby now called GumRubberBootsville, Vinnie went with him. Vinnie had never exactly given in; she had never signed anything relinquishing her real or imagined rights to her daughter. But she had signed a form signifying her agreement that in case of the death of one David Amberchuk, Ada Richardson be appointed temporary legal guardian. The word *temporary* soothed Vinnie and satisfied Ada and her battery of high-powered lawyers.

Dave was allowed to leave the hospital and enter a nursing home, where he got the care he needed and which Stubby couldn't provide. He managed, for a while, to pretend to the entire world that he actually liked the place. And as spring sogged its way across the land and the green tips of crocus and daffodil started to show through the mud, Stubby's life settled down markedly.

She moved from Grandmother and Grandfather Fleming's house to Ada Richardson's house. Neither of the Flemings understood any of the reasoning behind it, but they didn't argue any more than Grandma Amberchuk had. They had done their familial duty. They loved Stubby as much as they loved any of their grandchildren, but Stubby was right in her estimation that something about her made them ill at ease and constantly put them off balance. And though they missed her, they did not miss her clattering up the stairs, her energetic movements, her individualistic ideas and attitudes or her dog.

All the Amberchuks knew was that it was what Dave wanted, and whatever Dave wanted was just fine with them. After all, the poor bugger was dying, what else mattered except that.

Every day after school, before she went to the nursing home to see her dad, Stubby pedalled her new Christmas bike to Ada's house and got Daisy. Nobody argued with her about it being inappropriate to take a dog to a nursing home, nobody said it was mean to leave the dog sitting in the carrier of the bike for an hour or more. Nobody thought it weird that the dog would enjoy sitting in the carrier waiting for her person and nobody looked with derision or disbelief when told the patients in the nursing home waved at the dog through the window, tapped on the glass and even, if they were able, limped, hobbled, or wheeled themselves to the sunporch, from where they could coax Daisy into jumping out of the basket and frisking stiffly on the grass.

Once a week Stubby stopped off at Grandmother and Grandfather Fleming's house on her way home from the nursing home, to fulfill what Ada called her familial obligations. She reported on Dave's progress, answered questions about school, dutifully drank a glass of milk and was diplomatic enough, when asked, to say she would very much enjoy staying for supper. Then she phoned Ada to make sure it wasn't going to complicate matters for the housekeeper and after supper Stubby helped with the dishes. She dropped in on Grandma and Grandpa Amberchuk at irregular and unscheduled intervals and sometimes not only stayed for supper but spent the night.

"I want you to play ball this year," Dave told her.

"I'd rather come and see you," she lied bravely.

"I want you to play ball this year," Dave repeated. "I can hear kids' voices from the park. They're yellin' and havin' hell's own good time, and I want to be able to lie here and try to pick out your voice. I want to be able to think to myself, see, you useless fart, you aren't quite ruining your kid's entire life. Besides," he winked, "it'll give me time with my girlfriend."

"Pure D-poop," Stubby scoffed.

"Oh yeah?" Dave tried to argue and joke, but he was getting tired again, his eyes were sunken, his skin looked as thin as parchment and the colour of lemon pudding. "I ain't dead yet." He managed a smile and Stubby knew it was time to leave. She tucked him in, kissed his scratchy whiskered cheek and went to get Daisy.

"I feel like there's something I ought to be able to do," she told Ada, "and I can't think of what it might be. He seems so *sad*. He makes jokes about it, but . . . "

Ada sent Wright, the driver, to the nursing home. He helped Dave into his clothes, then wheeled him to the limo and they drove up Nanaimo Lakes Road to look for curly lilies and drink whiskey. "Ridiculous thing," Dave confided, "I'm half a step from hell and I ought to be preparing my soul for judgement day and all I can think of is I wish I had managed to get myself laid just one more time than I did. Now, ain't that a hell of a thing?"

''Probably a basic survival urge to attempt to assure the continuation of one's genetic pool,'' Wright mused, lighting a cigarette and handing it to Dave. When Dave reached for it, Wright noticed the man's wrists weren't much bigger than Stubby's were, and he remembered Stubby telling him that when she was little Dave had been one of the best wrist-rasslers in the area.

''Well, I don't know.'' Dave didn't really understand what Wright said when he talked, and he sometimes wondered why the man wasn't teaching university instead of driving a limo. ''Maybe I only had the one fish in my genetic pool, but she don't seem to me to be a sucker.''

''I have heard,'' Wright nodded, ''of soldiers dying in battle with erections.''

''Yeah,'' Dave agreed, ''I even heard tell some of 'em had a hard-on.''

Wright grinned and passed the bottle to Dave, who drank from it, but sparingly. He shook his head with regret. ''Goddamn,'' he sighed. ''Was a time I could'a drained 'er, but. . . every goddamn thing I put in my mouth tastes like an old penny is stuck under my tongue. I resent that, you know.'' He nodded, half drunk. ''I mean, you'd think you'd get just one little tiny fuckin' break.''

Wright talked to Ada, who talked to her doctor, who reached out and pulled a few strings Ada's money kept well greased at the nursing home, and Wright did the rest. He rented a room at the hotel, equipped it with absolutely everything the occasion required, then took Dave in the limo from the nursing home to the hotel and carried him from the parking lot to the elevator. There wasn't a soul in sight, thanks to Ada's money.

''Sweet suffering jesus,'' Dave breathed, staring with disbelieving eyes at an elegant creature called Estelle. ''I already died, right? And went to heaven, right? And you're an angel, right?''

''Don't know much about heaven or angels, do you Amberchuk?'' Estelle teased, grinning cheekily. 'Only archangels have red hair. And you aren't in heaven yet. . . but gimme about five minutes, willya?''

''Lady,'' Dave vowed, ''archangel or not, ya can have the entire rest of my life, such as it is.'' Then Estelle's capable hands were untying the belt of his nursing home bathrobe, her blue-green eyes twinkling.

Wright came back to the hotel room three hours later, picked Dave up and carried him back to the limo. Neither of them said a word. When Dave was back in his bed at the nursing home, tucked under the blankets and almost asleep, he focused his eyes on Wright and nodded several times. ''You're okay, fella,'' he said.

''Same to you,'' Wright answered, and left the room knowing Dave would be sound asleep before the limo's engine began to purr.

''You got good friends,'' was all Dave said to Stubby about any of it.

She had no idea at all what he was talking about, she only knew Wright's visits had been good for Dave. Whatever kind of man talk they had, it took the sadness out of Dave's voice.

Once in a while, in the few days remaining to him, Dave smiled at something nobody else could see, and twice, just as Stubby was walking toward his room, a lady with a headful of curly red hair who looked as if she'd just stepped out of *Vogue* magazine came out of the room and passed Stubby in the hall.

"Who's that lady?" she asked, never having heard Estelle's unladylike vocabulary.

"Told you I had a girlfriend," Dave whispered, reaching for Stubby's hand.

He looked like a child. Except for the whiskers, and the nurses were real good about keeping them shaved. The suntan was gone and somehow, with it, the weather lines vanished. He was skin and bone and there was absolutely no way anybody could deny the fact he had a definite odour, something close to but not quite like burnt sugar. But his face looked like that of a youngster, big eyed, big eared and vulnerable.

"Don't let 'em take me back to the hospital, Stubs," he begged. "The effin' place makes me sick." She nodded and wiped angrily at her traitor eyes.

So Dave Amberchuk died in the nursing home, not ten minutes after Stubby and Daisy had ridden off on the bright red bike.

The home had already contacted Ada by phone when Stubby came in after three innings of softball.

"You in the living room?" she called.

"Yes," Ada answered. Stubby walked in, went over to kiss Ada on the cheek and opened her mouth to give Ada all the details of who struck out whom, who hit what, who caught the line drive.

"I have heavy news for you Stubby," Ada said quickly.

"How bad?" Stubby froze.

"Sit down."

"That bad, huh." She sat, gulped, and clenched her hands into fists. "Is it dad?" she managed. Ada nodded.

"He's dead, Stubby."

"God almighty damn," Stubby said, her voice hollow. She slumped back in the big chair and just waited. Waited, but nothing happened. She felt cold, she felt as if the world's biggest boulder was in her stomach, but that was all she felt. "I'd better go over and tell Grandma and Grandpa," she said.

"Wright has the car ready. Please assure your grandma of my deepest condolences, and tell her we would be honoured to have the reception here after the services.''

''Thank you.'' Stubby got up, kissed Ada's cheek again, then went out to where the limo was waiting. Daisy hopped in the back seat and settled herself on the baby blanket put on the seat especially for her, and Stubby rode to her grandma's place in silence.

As soon as Grandma Amberchuk saw Stubby arriving in the limo, she knew. She turned blindly and Grandpa grabbed her and held her in his arms, swaying gently, rocking her, as Stubby joined them, wordless.

6

They were drinking tea and sharing memories, drinking coffee and comparing emotional souvenirs, drinking whiskey or vodka or rum or beer and shaking their heads; not so much in sorrow as in dumb acceptance. Sharon, the housekeeper, had made mountains of sandwiches and gallons of potato salad, Wright had helped slice roasts and chickens and turkeys and hams and Sharon's kitchen had been crammed with aunts, cousins, neighbours, friends and people Stubby didn't know and wasn't expected to know, all of whom had brought food for the mourners.

They were out on the front porch or sitting on the stairs or scattered on the lawn, as if shy of having their voices trapped in the house Ada Richardson had so beautifully repaired and renovated. Outside, their voices drifted softly, weaving and interweaving, not echoing or bouncing from the staircase or tumbling into the carpet to wait for the vacuum cleaner. They were eating and drinking and talking and even smiling, renewing their claim to life, demonstrating their eternal optimism, placing their own mortality on the line and keeping Dave Amberchuk alive in their hearts and minds and in their laughter long after the dirt had filled his hole in the ground.

They had buried him at one in the afternoon, not from the church but from the undertaking parlour. Even Grandma Amberchuk had known what a joke it would have been to take Dave Amberchuk dead into the church he had so seldom entered once he was old enough to direct his feet on his own path, once he had reached the age of about six. The reverend hadn't even asked any questions. He showed up at the undertaking parlour at twelve forty-five and had murmured soothingly and comfortingly to Grandma Amberchuk until it was time for him to move to the front of the room and start his talk. He'd kept it short, to the relief of everyone there, and then had gone with the rest to the cemetery.

Past fields of grazing cows, past old farmhouses and barns, the huge black hearse with the coffin inside led a parade of cars, pickups and vans, all with their headlights shining. Past the road leading up to the Row, past the creek and the railroad trestle, past the schoolhouse and the community hall, moving slowly, crossing the highway one immediately behind the other and to hell with the highway traffic backed up to Ladysmith and Nanaimo, held by respect and tradition as Dave Amberchuk, for the last time, moved through the land of his birth and life.

The hole was raw and ugly and the words of comfort the reverend intoned didn't help Stubby one little bit. She didn't really hear them anyway, no more than she'd seen the flowers on the coffin or the cars following Ada's big limo. Stubby sat in the room staring at the big fancy box, then she sat in Ada's car and stared at the tips of her brand new highly polished oxblood loafers. Then she stood next to the raw hole and looked at her hands clasped in front of her, fingers gripping each other tightly, and she waited to feel something.

Almost everyone was there. Alma Pete and Tommy Dick and Betty Paul and Billy James, Evelyn White and Colleen Sewid and all the Robins family. Every logger Dave had ever known, every friend he had ever made, and all the kids from Stubby's softball league, even the bat boy and water girl. Everyone except the pretty lady Stubby had seen at the hospital. They all stood silent, uncomfortable, not sure what to do next, and then, when the young minister had said the last of his words, they left.

Stubby was glad she didn't have to hear the dirt hitting the coffin, glad she didn't have to watch them filling the hole, trapping Dave in the bottom of it. She didn't know if she believed anything, but there was no way, she was certain of that, there was no way even God was going to cram Dave into a white toga or teach him to play the harp. She was equally sure it would take more than Lucifer to get away with stabbing Dave in the ass with a pitchfork. She could just about picture it, old Lucifer, the star of the morning, whom some said was Jesus' big brother but had been disinherited or something because of his nastiness, just about see old Lucifer thinking he was so great, stabbing and prodding at Dave with his little three-pronger, and Dave turning around, not small and sick and puny, but returned by magic to what he had been, what he really had been and would be again. And Dave laughing and taking the stabber and bending it over his knee and grabbing Lucifer by the front of his shirt and saying Listen here you little bugger, keep your meathooks to yourself or I'm gonna pound sand so far up your ass you'll have to hire a dentist to vacuum it outta your throat. And still grinning he'd up and turf the devil ass over teapot onto the hobs of hell and then Dave would go off to meet his friends. Dave hadn't much stock in religion and had once said his idea of heaven and hell was very basic; in heaven there would be no politicians, in hell there'd be nothing but.

Grandma Amberchuk had cried, and so had Grandpa Amberchuk and the uncles and aunts, but there was no howling or raving or slobbering except when Vinnie had begun to tremble, then shake, then gasp Oh my god, Oh my god, and then Earl had the good sense to get hold of her by the arm and lead her away a few feet and talk to her until she calmed down.

Everyone said what a hell of a good guy Dave was, they ate and they drank to his memory and those of them who took stock in such things offered up prayers for the repose of his soul, which probably did more for Grandma Amberchuk than for Dave. But nobody knew what to say to Vinnie and Earl, nor to Grandmother and Grandfather Fleming. Nobody was very interested in saying anything at all to Gordon Fleming—the dry stick might take it into his mind to respond and there you'd be, stuck for the next half hour listening to Gordon's dipshit ideas, which were hard enough to listen to at the best of times, and burying Dave Amberchuk wasn't one of the best of times.

Stubby wasn't sure Vinnie and Earl's attending the funeral was the right thing for them to do but, after all, Vinnie had been married to Dave at one time, and you don't just wipe that out with a swipe of your hand, and even if it had ended in a foofoorah, it ought to count for as much as, say, setting chokers with him for seven or eight months one year. And you couldn't expect her to arrive alone; Earl wasn't letting her out of his sight. She was too prone to stay at Bright's Crossing for weeks and months at a time, and the long distance bill was enough to make the telephone company smile and Earl himself weep.

Vinnie moved slowly, spoke slowly and her eyes looked as if she had been hit on the head, the pupils small, almost gone. Earl, on the other hand, talked like a machine gun and his eyes were never still. Stubby was supposed to pay particular attention to their needs, see to it they had tea, coffee, fruit juice, liquor, whatever they wanted, but every time Vinnie set eyes on her daughter she dissolved into tears. Then Earl started patting Vinnie's shoulder, and saying There there now and then he would say We mustn't be selfish or You'll see, it will all work out for the best. Finally, Stubby just made herself scarce. Ada knew where she was, Wright knew where she was and Sharon knew where she was. For the rest of the afternoon, when asked where Stubby was, each of the three said vaguely ''She doesn't seem to be here,'' as if that answered the question rather than just repeated it. But it satisfied the questioner and Stubby was left alone, as she wanted to be.

She sat behind the house in the old orchard that was being reclaimed and revitalized by expert pruning, grafting, and fertilizing. Every sort of fly and bug in creation was buzzing and zizzing in the grass but Stubby ignored them unless they landed on her skin or got themselves lost in the canal of her ear. She sat in her new clothes, the oxblood loafers glinting in the sunlight, turning the pages of the photo albums.

There were Dave and Vinnie, looking like nobody Stubby had ever known, standing stiffly, holding hands, grinning at the camera with mouths stretched taut with embarrassment. Vinnie pregnant, sitting on the bank of Haslam Creek, hands crossed as if trying to hide the bulge that would be Stubby. Dave on the henhouse roof, nails in his mouth, hammer in hand, replacing shakes. Dave planting the first rosebush, shirt sleeves rolled to just below his elbows, forearms massive, hands like waterbuckets, then Dave with the rose planted, grinning happily, hands stained with earth and composted cow manure. Vinnie standing by their first pickup, trying to look pleased when in fact she had never liked having a pickup and always wanted a car. Vinnie by the pickup again, this time carrying Stubby—or rather what probably was Stubby but looked like nothing more nor less than a bundle of blanket. Dave on the back steps, frowning with concentration, holding Stubby and staring at her as if trying to figure out what it was he had in his huge arms. Grandmother Fleming with Stubby on her knee, Grandfather Fleming in his big chair with Stubby held in the crook of one arm. Dave building a swing, the ropes hanging from hooks in the doorway and a small wooden box of some sort on the floor. Stubby sitting in the wooden box, propped with pillows, her fat bare baby feet stuck straight out in front of her, looking uncertain even though Vinnie was kneeling next to her, smiling at the camera. A blur in the doorway, Stubby being introduced to her swing. Stubby howling with fear in Dave's arms, and Dave laughing freely, head thrown back, unaware of or unconcerned with the camera.

In every picture he was big and strong and laughing and tanned and nothing at all like the poor little wasted guy in the hospital bed or the scarecrow person in the nursing home.

Someone else had taken this one. Dave and Vinnie with Stubby, sitting on the back porch. Vinnie looking at the camera, Dave winking down at Stubby.

Where were they going all dressed up like that? Why was Dave wearing a white shirt? What had happened to change Vinnie from the laughing girl with the beautiful eyes to the strange woman on the front lawn whose eyes glinted pinprick-pupilled from beneath swollen eyelids?

So many photo albums, so many pictures, things and people that didn't even exist any more. Stubby up on Plevin's old tractor, a kitten in her arms, and Plevin's farm was gone now, expropriated for a highway bypass, the tractor probably put through the crusher and sent off to Japan, lost in the making of a dozen Toyotas or Datsuns. The kitten, white with black patches, mother of a million, turned to dust in the corner of some garden somewhere.

Daisy and her first litter of pups. Daisy and her second litter of pups. Daisy and her fifth litter of pups. Daisy on her back legs, Stubby holding up the front ones, showing off Daisy's shaved belly, the almost invisible line of her spaying operation, the few stitches looking like flyspecks on the photo paper. Billy Gordon with one of Daisy's pups, Elva Stannard with a black pup with whiskers. Daisy begging for a piece of meat in Dave's fingers, and all you could see of Dave was his hand and a bit of forearm but surely, oh God please, he surely was still on the other end of that hand, couldn't you just turn the picture over maybe and see him there?

One whole album was pictures of Dave in hospital this last time. Stubby didn't want to look at any of those pictures. Not today. She stopped looking when she got to the ones of Dave with his leg brace glinting, his face lined and his eyes betraying his knowledge, even then, of what was waiting for him down the pike. All you gotta do, kid, to get through life, is just put one foot in front of the other, a bit at a time, day by day, down the pike, doin' your best, that's all.

But it wasn't always that easy. And still she didn't feel what she was waiting to feel. She could feel the sun warm on her face and arms, feel a bug walking on her leg. Feel the breeze in her hair. Feel the photo albums heavy on her lap. Feel Daisy curled against her, asleep. But none of the other things she had expected to feel.

When the people had all gone home and the place was quiet again, Stubby gathered up the photo albums and took them to the house. Up the stairs. To her room. Then placed them on the bedside table to look at again any time she wanted.

Vinnie had wanted to take a picture of Dave in his coffin, his hair neatly brushed, looking like a dead stranger, not like Dave at all, and Stubby had taken the camera away from her and said, ''Don't you dare. It's gross.'' But she was willing to bet someone had done it when she wasn't there. Rotten thing to do. No privacy left anywhere. Pictures of deaders in their coffins.

She had a bath, carefully brushed her teeth, kissed Ada, Wright and Sharon goodnight, called Daisy in from her nightly pee prowl and went up to her room. She climbed into bed with Daisy and, one hand stroking the aging dog, Stubby waited for whatever it was that would allow her to feel something. She was still waiting when she fell asleep.

7

The Bright's Crossing Women's Senior A Softball Team practised every Monday, Wednesday and Friday evening on the top-field diamond in the schoolyard just down the road from the nursing home where Dave Amberchuk had spent his last days. Very often the Friday night practice was cancelled in favour of an actual game, and any activity on the field Saturday or Sunday was sure to be a league-sanctioned for-real dead serious game. The Bright's Crossing Women's Senior A team wore real leather athletic shoes with cleated soles, real regulation-style ball socks with instep straps instead of feet, white with blue stripes at the knee, white flannel uniform pants that ended just below the knee, overlapped by the wonderful team socks, and a real honest-to-god big-league-style baseball team shirt in royal blue with gold trim. On their heads the women wore blue peaked caps with gold trim and a big gold BC emblazoned on the front. Every shirt had a different sponsor's name on the back: King's Store, Calverly's Gas Station, Scotch Bakery, Price-Rite Meats, Vito's Backhoe, Howie's Bulldozing, Jonson's Hardware, Williams' Well Digging and Blackie's Dowsing. Actually, Blackie's Dowsing and Williams' Well Digging were sponsored by the same person, but rather than have two shirts the same, Blackie Williams had agreed to the name change. Stubby thought the uniforms, and the women who wore them, the most beautiful on the entire Island. She yearned for the day she would be old enough to show up at spring tryouts, even dared dream she would one day be good enough to be allowed to join the team and play for Bright's Crossing.

She was fourteen years old, still square, still stocky, still convinced she was so different from the rest of the world as to be almost a total freak, but her life was back on the rails again, and all she had to do was what her dad had told her to do, just put one foot in front of the other, keep your head on your shoulders and move one step at a time down the pike. School was okay, life with Ada, Wright and Sharon was more settled and comfortable than anything she could remember, the damp sog of early spring had passed and the warm soft days of sunshine and blossom were on them. Daisy was old and almost crippled in the hip that had been damaged by the thrown hatchet; she had trouble getting up and down steps, it wasn't easy for her to find a comfortable position to lie down in and she would never again jump up quickly from her nap when she heard the sound of Stubby's feet on the stairs. But there was aspirin for her discomfort and something stronger for those damp winter nights when she whimpered softly with pain and her appetite was as good as ever, so good, in fact, Stubby had been forced to put Daisy on a diet. A diet Daisy hated and ignored, and which she got around in ten dozen different ways.

"Didn't you give Elva Stannard one of Daisy's pups one time?" Ada asked at supper.

"A female," Stubby nodded, "sort of airedale-coloured, but a lot smaller. Why?" Stubby finished cutting Ada's meat into bite-sized pieces, and moved back to sit at her own place at the table.

"Wright tells me Elva's dog has puppies, and that the father is the Bevan-Colson's registered cocker spaniel."

"Really?" Stubby laughed happily. "That'd be something to see, I bet."

"You might consider having a look at them," Ada said, wiping her mouth with the linen napkin, and smiling across the table in the direction of Stubby's voice. "Poor old Daisy isn't getting any younger, and it might cheer all of us up to have a puppy around the house."

"Are you suggesting Daisy's about to die?" Stubby said, her voice carefully neutral.

"Sooner or later she's sure to die," Ada replied, "although I doubt if it's going to happen very immediately. What I was actually trying to suggest in the most diplomatic way I could think of was that she's too old to get much pleasure out of tramping around with you any more, and you might have more fun with a younger dog. Then Daisy and I could sit here in a manner more befitting our advanced age and dowager outlook and...." She stopped talking and joined Stubby in disrespectful laughter.

"Sure," Stubby agreed happily. "Maybe I will check 'em out."

She intended to do that after she'd watched the Bright's Crossing Women's Senior A Softball team practice after supper, but somehow, without exactly meaning to, she wound up at Elva Stannard's place before she went to the park. So, when she arrived halfway through the first inning of a practice game between the Women's Senior A team and the Men's Teen Town team, tucked down the front of her shirt, warm and comfortable against her belly, was a very small six-week-old replica of Daisy.

Stubby parked her bike against the fence and moved to sit in her usual place well back of the line, on a small knoll halfway between home plate and first. She was peering down the front of her shirt grinning and talking to the pup, only half aware of the game in progress.

"Watch it!" a woman's voice screeched. Reflexively, Stubby did everything at once, launched herself anywhere except where she was while turning to try to see the danger. Her left hand came up to clutch the pup safe against her belly and, when she saw the white blur coming at her, her right hand moved without her thinking about it and she had the softball caught securely in suddenly throbbing fingers. She landed on her left hip and somehow managed to hang onto both the puppy and the softball.

"Close call," the umpire said, sighing with relief.

"My fault," Stubby admitted.

"It happens," the first basewoman grinned. "Glad you didn't get your head split open."

"Me too," Stubby grinned, then dared put her dream into words. "If that had happened I might've died before I had a chance to show you just how bad your team needs a good third basewoman like me."

"Oh yeah?" the first basewoman laughed. "That good, huh?"

"Better," Stubby promised.

"Hey coach," the first basewoman yelled, "we got a kid here bragging about how good she is on third."

"Put up or shut up," the man at bat yelled.

"Who'll hold my pup?" Stubby blurted. "And I got no mitt with me."

The scorekeeper for the night, who was actually the second string shortstop for the men's Teen Town team sitting out a sprained thumb, took the pup and loaned Stubby his glove. "Don't ruin the pocket," he warned dourly. Stubby didn't answer; it was the kind of thing not really worth answering.

"I'll take the bench," the regular third basewoman offered, grinning, as she pulled a package of cigarettes and a lighter from her shirt pocket. "Eat your hearts out," she teased, lighting her cigarette.

Stubby moved to third and touched the bag, kicked it a couple of times to see if it moved loose on its ground peg, and if so how much and in what direction. She scuffed a couple of stray pebbles off her baseline, fidgeted and fritzed for a few acceptable moments, getting the feel of everything, then she turned, nodded, and crouched ready to move in any direction.

She didn't get a chance to show what she could do until the last minutes of the fourth inning. There was the crack of the bat against the ball, the flash of the batter heading for first, the thwack as the ball bounced once and was caught by the shortstop, the yell, the white blur coming at her and Stubby, reaching out with her left foot, slammed it unerringly on third base, caught the ball, tagged the runner, then fired the ball to second and caught the mitt of the second basewoman seconds before the runner forced off first arrived.

"Way to *go*!" the chucker yelled happily.

"Way to *be*!" the catcher screamed.

"Double play!" the regular third basewoman jumped up from the bench, yelling and laughing. "Not tacky at all!" she shouted happily. Stubby felt her face going brick red with pleasure and knew the last of the butterflies had gone from her stomach. It wasn't a fantastic play, it wasn't an incredible play, it wasn't something they were going to talk about at post-game parties for years to come, it was just good, knowledgeable, journeywoman ball playing, but she'd done it, she'd done it steadily, she'd done it without thought or fumble or brag or hesitation, and she'd done it in a way that told them more clearly than any words ever could that she was a ballplayer. Not just someone who played ball, and certainly not just someone who said she played ball, but a real ballplayer.

The third out was easy, the chucker just didn't let the batter get any wood on anything and whizzed three past her in five throws. They changed, and Stubby waited until the others were settled before she lowered herself to the player's bench.

"How good are you at bat?" the coach asked quietly.

"Not as good as I want to be," Stubby admitted. "I don't do well on low outsiders."

"How old are you?"

"Be fifteen the middle of August," she said.

"Awful young," the coach hesitated. "You ever think of playing for Women's Teen Town?"

"Yessir," she said, trying to swallow the lump in her throat, blinking so her eyes wouldn't well with disappointment.

"And?" the coach prodded.

"I already play with them," Stubby said. "I'm third base on the junior team."

"Why the junior team?" the coach demanded. "Why not first string team?"

"Too many kids playing ball," Stubby explained. "Nearly twenty on the senior team already. Gotta wait your turn to move up, I guess.'' She half sniffed, remembered she was trying hard not to appear to be a mere kid, and stopped sniffing even though she was afraid the next thing she was going to do was start to cry.

''You're good,'' the coach said, ''but you're too young for my team.'' Stubby nodded, blinking even more rapidly than before. ''Not that I think you'd goof or not play well enough,'' the coach explained, ''but I'm damned if I'm going to be the one encourages you to play above your level and frap the ends of your bones.''

''Yeah,'' Stubby nodded. She knew about the ends of your bones, she knew the long bones in your forearms weren't totally formed until you were almost eighteen, and too much hard pitching and throwing could permanently damage your cartilage, give you arthritis and bursitis later on, maybe ruin your chucking arm years too soon. She knew about bone damage to hips and knees because of overtraining and stress. ''Yeah,'' she repeated.

The coach said she could play out the rest of the game and her disappointment wore off, but now more than ever she coveted the uniform, the peaked cap, the blue and gold colours and the gold-braided sponsor's name on the back of the shirt. One day, she promised herself, one day. She held her puppy on her knee and cheered for her team members when they were up to bat and handed the puppy back to the scorekeeper when it was three out and time to go back to guarding third. When it was her own turn up to bat, Stubby handed the pup to the first basewoman and moved toward the plate.

''Last bats,'' the coach yelled. ''Time's up.''

''C'mon, Scrooge,'' the pitcher roared, ''give the kid a break, willya, she's got her bats comin' to her.''

Other than the pup who looked like Daisy, nothing had gone altogether right since suppertime. She got a chance to show what she could do but was too young for the team and she'd been fanned on her only other trip to the plate and now she was only going to get a bats because they felt sorry for the poor little diddums who couldn't make the team. She saw the softball leave the chucker's hand and she aimed all her frustration and disappointment at it. And knew before she felt the bat connect with the ball, knew before it happened that what she was letting loose was a saunter-around walk-'er-in homer.

She heard the crack, and while the ball was still sailing and everyone was watching it, amazed, Stubby turned to the coach, smiled happily and walked to put the bat in the bat bag. ''Thank you very much for the chance to play,'' she said. ''I really enjoyed it.'' She waved and winked at all the beautiful women in the beautiful uniforms, then moved to get her pup, tuck it down the front of her shirt and walk to her bike. Nobody said anything, they just grinned and let her make her exit, and she was pedalling away from the field before the ball arrived back where the catcher could trap it. The coach grinned and looked at the women sitting on the bench watching her knowingly. "Younger every year," she laughed. "Makes a person feel kinda old."

Stubby rode home grinning from ear to ear. She could remember every split second, from the moment before the pitch actually left the chucker's hand to the time the palms of her hands picked up the first of the vibrations coming through the hickory bat. She remembered how she had tensed her shoulders, loosened her arms, tightened her grip on the black-taped handgrip of the bat, flexed her feet, relaxed her knees and stared at the thin space where the chucker's hand would deliver the ball. She had seen the white blur as it left the pitcher's hand, but she had never actually seen the ball itself. But playing it over and over again in her mind she knew there had really only been one place the ball could have gone. She remembered the position of the chucker's feet and legs, the angle from shoulder to elbow, the cock of the wrist, and though she knew she would never in a million years be able to explain it without first learning mathematics, geometry especially, she knew it had to do with levers and pulleys and balance and thrust and angle and a whole pile of other things she didn't have names for, and she knew none of it mattered, not the terms, the explanations, the analysis, nothing. What mattered was that she, Sheilagh May Stubby Amberchuk had *known*, and in the knowing had gripped her bat, flexed, shifted and swung in exactly the precisely correct way, at exactly the precisely correct arc so the ultimate power of her swing hit that ball at exactly the right second in the right place and the major force of the pitch hit the major force of the swing and the ball flew like a pheasant shot in the ass with salt. And she knew she could do it again if she could just manage to get to exactly that pitch of concentration.

"What are you going to call her?" Ada asked, stroking the ball of wiry fur curled on her lap.

"Stuke," Stubby laughed. "Because, believe me, if you could see her you'd know she's nothing you'd sit down in a game to win!"

"How is Daisy taking it all?" Ada looked with sightless eyes toward the place where Daisy was curled on her pillow, watching with only mild interest.

"She doesn't seem to give a scratch one way or the other." Stubby moved to hunker beside the old dog. Daisy wagged her tail, licked Stubby's hand and opened her mouth in a grin. "Good old girl," Stubby crooned, ''you're a fine old dog. Look at all those teeth, still strong and white, and look at those eyes. Just the finest old thing in all the world, that's what you are.''

''So what else is new out there in the world besides the fact we've got ourselves a new pup?'' Ada probed.

Stubby moved to the couch and sprawled loosely, stretching her legs and grinning. ''Well,'' she said in a deliberately indifferent voice, ''I got to practise with the Women's Senior A team and got a double play and a homer.'' Then, while Ada bent forward eagerly, face alight, Stubby's glee and excitement burst loose. She described in detail every play, and how this one positioned her feet, how that one leaned into the pitch, how this one slid into third feet first and another refused to play without a safety helmet. Sharon came in with the silver tray and the pot of tea, the cold beef sandwiches and thick peanut butter cookies, and when she had poured Ada a cup of tea and placed it in her hand, she sat on the arm of the sofa, listening and smiling. Wright entered, his chauffeur's boots and pants no more out of place in the living room than in the limo, and sat, collar unbuttoned, tie removed, smoking a cigarette and nodding.

Stubby found nothing at all strange in the informal behaviour of the two some considered to be Ada's servants. Ada considered them her friends, part of her family, and so did Stubby. Closer family than Grandmother and Grandfather Fleming and arsletart dipshit Uncle Gordon the Goof.

The next afternoon, as soon as school was out, Stubby raced home on her firengine red five-speed and as soon as she had changed out of her school clothes and into her faded jeans and T-shirt, she started building her Improver. She took a golf ball and placed it in the vise in the tool shed, then carefully drilled a fine hole through the middle and out the other side. Through this hole she threaded a thin piece of strong surgical tubing which she knotted on the short end, flush as she could against the side of the golf ball. She measured off roughly four and a half feet of tubing and took it outside, then climbed one of the pear trees and fastened the tubing to a strong branch. She clambered back down the tree, eyeballed the dangling golf ball, decided it was too low, went back up the pear tree, adjusted the surgical tubing, and went back down again. Three times more she was up and down the tree, tying and retying knots. Then she went back to the tool shed for her Black Diamond hickory softball bat. She took her position, settled herself, changed her mind, relaxed, reached out with the bat, and tapped the golf ball lightly. It sped from the tap of the bat, the surgical tubing tightened, pulled the golf ball back again, jerkily. Stubby tapped it again, harder, and as the golf ball zipped away from her she took her stance, eyes narrowed. The golf ball reached the end of the surgical tubing, stretched it slightly, then whizzed back as the tubing contracted. Stubby swung as hard as she could, the bat hit the golf ball with a thin crack. The golf ball fired away, the tubing stretched as far as it could, and when it contracted, the ball returned faster than it had departed. Stubby swung again, and the process was repeated. Each time the golf ball came back, it came back at a different angle, from a different place, the rubber stretched to a different degree, the snap-back a different tension. Stubby barely had time to return the bat to its original position before it was time to swing again, and by the time Sharon called her for supper, her body was wet with sweat, her shoulders ached and she had blisters on the palms of both hands.

"That's why they have those cute little gloves," Wright teased, "the ones with no fingers in them."

Stubby nodded and threaded a darning needle with a strand of wool. She pierced the blisters with the needle and pushed the point through to the other side, then pulled it through, the wool soaking up the pale yellow fluid in the blister. When she had drained all the blisters, she soaked her hands in a mixture of vinegar and salt water and tried to tell herself the stinging was a sure sign the stuff was doing what it was supposed to do, healing her mistreated hands.

"Fingerless gloves," Ada laughed, "are much like toeless socks."

"My dad wore those lots of times." Stubby tried to smile, but the vinegar and brine was stinging like hell. Which was probably why there were bright diamonds glittering on her lashes.

"My grandmother," Wright mused, "told me once she'd knit a pair of socks that lasted for twenty-two years. Of course," he grinned, "she'd had to replace the tops eight times and the bottoms twelve."

"My dad," Stubby countered, "had an axe my great-grandfather Amberchuk brought over with him from the Old Country. It had a dozen new handles and five new heads, but it was almost as good as new."

"Somebody take the puppy outside," Ada said urgently, "she's starting to squirm!"

On Tuesday nights Stubby had her Teen Town softball practice, and on Sunday afternoons, rain or shine, the Teen Town game. Her hours with the golf ball sharpened her eye, the muscles in her back, shoulders and forearms hardened and when she clenched her fist she could see a little round knob of muscle she hadn't known she had, in her wrists, just below her thumbs. The more she swung the bat, the harder the little knob became, the more it fascinated her. Nobody else in her class, neither male nor female, had it. Her school teachers didn't have it. Wright didn't have it. Sharon didn't have it. Ada didn't have it. But every woman on the Bright's Crossing Women's Senior A team had it. Encouraged, Stubby replaced the Improver's tired length of surgical tubing and switched to a heavier bat.

"Here." Wright handed her two thingamajigs. Each had two red-painted wooden handles on either end of what looked like no more nor less than a thin metal shaft twisted in the middle to form a coil spring.

"What're those?"

"Squeeze one," he suggested. Stubby gripped two of the handles with her right hand, and tried to squeeze. "Harder," Wright urged, "you can't break it."

"Hey. . ." she breathed, grinning happily. "Hey, Wright, thanks a lot!"

"If you're gonna be a batter," he shrugged, "you have to have good wrists." By summertime even Grandmother and Grandfather Fleming had grown used to the sight of Stubby pedalling down the road with Daisy and Stuke in the basket, steering with one hand, squeezing her Wrist Tensor with the other hand. When her right hand was too tired to squeeze any more, Stubby transferred the Tensor to the other hand.

"Hey, Amberchuk," they teased her at school, "what're ya tryin' to do, turn yourself into Popeye?"

"Lookit the wrists on 'er!" they laughed.

"Hey, maybe we could take 'er down to the States and enter her as a dark horse in the wrist twistin' champeenships!"

"Hey, Amberchuk, let's see ya squeeze open yer can'a spinach!"

Stubby just grinned and shrugged and let it slide off her like rain off a mallard's tailfeathers. Who was the fool who decided girls had no choice but to pray to God to give them big boobs, a small waist and an ass like a tame honeybee? Who was the nerd who laid down some kind of law that girls couldn't lift, stack and carry wood? Who was the nosepicker with the need to keep the ball gloves off the female hands, to keep the bats under lock and key? Given a choice Stubby would far sooner any day of the month oil her glove than pluck her eyebrows. Given the choice she would far sooner sweat through a close nine innings than wrassle in the back of a beat-up Chev.

So what if the rest of them were piling as many as possible into station wagons and heading off to the drive-in for dollar-a-carload night? So what if it was popcorn 'n' passion and licorice and french kissing? It might be fun in its own way but it didn't interest Stubby. All that emotion and jealousy and insecurity and powerplay and hanging around with the phone glued to one ear, and what did you get out of it? Pregnant by grade ten like Pat MacKeller. Shipped off to private school in Victoria like Carol Wotzername with the rusty-coloured hair. Two black eyes, a broken nose and gap in your smile like Teddy Carlson when Carol's big brother got hold of him behind Ace Pool and Billiards.

''Phone for you, Stubs,'' Sharon called. Stubby got up from the rug in front of the TV in the living room and crossed wearily to the hallway. She had a hitch in the small of her back and a stitch in her left thigh, and the place on the cheek of her bum where she'd slid into second was downright sore.

''H'lo?'' she mumbled, stifling a yawn.

''Is there a girl at your house plays softball?'' the voice asked.

''Yeah. Yeah, I guess,'' Stubby fumbled verbally, caught off guard. ''Me.''

''Yeah? Great. Listen, my name is Marge Russell, and I play first for the Senior A women. I know this isn't fair, you haven't had any chance at all to get ready or anything, but we've got five injuries and a tournament in Duncan over the weekend, and we're in a real bind, because the rules say you have to have played a league game before you can go into a regional tournament, and Duncan is a regional, so could you play with us in the league game tonight?''

''Uh, yeah. Sure. Where? When?'' Stubby knew her voice was shaking. She could feel every muscle in her body tightening, and sweat was slickering the black plastic receiver in her hand.

''Like. . . ten minutes ago? At the top field by the school?''

''Sure. Right away,'' Stubby blurted, and then the line was humming in her ear, and she was trembling.

''What's wrong?'' Sharon demanded. ''You're white as a sheet!''

''I get to play with the Senior A's!'' Stubby blurted. ''I gotta go! Like right now!'' She raced for the hall closet and her well worn fielder's glove.

''Wright,'' Sharon bellowed, ''get the car!''

If anybody thought there was something unusual in the underage, white-faced and totally terrified replacement third basewoman arriving in a block-long black limo with a uniformed driver to carry her equipment bag to the bench for her, nobody said a word.

''Thanks, kid,'' the coach smiled.

''Amberchuk,'' Stubby managed to choke past the tight lump in her throat. ''It's Stubby Amberchuk.''

She didn't have time to get any more upset, excited, or nervous than she had been when she hung up the phone. She was surrounded by the Bright's Crossing Women's Senior A team, and behind a modest screen of team jackets and equipment bags, she was helped out of her jeans and faded shirt, and helped into her own real live honest-to-god ball uniform. When she was sufficiently covered, the team members grinned, dropped the privacy screen and went back to lacing on their spikes, adjusting their socks, loosening or tightening belts and carefully unwrapping and folding sticks of Doublemint gum which they placed in their mouths and chewed with all the solemnity of a sinner receiving the communion wafer.

Stubby sat on the bench and adjusted her white socks with the beautiful blue stripes around the top. She hadn't seen the limo leave and she didn't know Wright had hurried home to get Ada and Sharon, who had been left behind in the mad rush to get out of the house and to the ball field, and she didn't see the limo return. Nor did she see Wright open the trunk, pull out and unfold the wheelchair Dave Amberchuk had once used, then lift Ada from the back of the limo and place her gently in the chair. Sharon covered Ada's knees with a cotton bedspread and on the bedspread placed Daisy. Wright pushed the chair across the grass followed by Sharon, with Stuke on a thin red nylon cord, and the first Stubby knew about any of it was when Ada's thin, clear, unmistakable voice rang through the pre-game buzz of comment and advice.

"Hey, Amberchuk," she called, "let's get out there and just *do 'er*, eh?"

"Yeah, Amberchuk," Wright echoed. "Let's show them how the little kids are doin 'er right these days, eh?"

Stubby's eyes stung and her fingers shook. She waved, suddenly shy and awkward, then, reassured in places she hadn't known needed reassurance, turned back to the very serious business of lacing and tying her shoes. Good, well oiled, top-of-the-line black leather athletic shoes with molded soles and solid cleats. Ada had presented them to her at the beginning of the season with the smiling comment that nobody moved as well or worked as hard in bad shoes as they did in good ones. She picked up her glove, top quality cowhide, securely stitched and laced. Again, Ada's contribution. Stubby realized, not for the first time, that Ada never buried Stubby in a bunch of shit and stuff that wasn't wanted, needed, or used, but any chance there was to provide Stubby with the things that would make life easier, more enjoyable or more convenient was seized; Ada never made a fool of you by giving you junk for a present.

"Okay!" the coach yelled. "Let's just get it all together!"

Stubby stood up and moved hesitantly toward the clustering group of women. An arm reached out, a strong tanned hand gripped her by the beautiful sleeve of the beautiful team shirt and Marge Russell, first basewoman, tugged Stubby and pulled her to a place next to her. "Hey," she laughed, "get your butt in here, you're on this damn team now, aren't you?"

It wasn't a tight game, it wasn't even a close game—the Bright's Crossing Women's Senior A team had Shawnigan Lake outclassed from the first pitch—but it was a good game, not a joke of a game; there were enough good players on Shawnigan Lake to keep Bright's Crossing on its toes and to make any mistake a serious mistake. Stubby played as if it were the World Series and her life were at stake.

Ada sat in the wheelchair with a very happy, very old dog on her lap, while Wright on her left and Sharon on her right did game commentaries which more than described to her the action on the field, and Stubby's contribution. When the left fielder threw a sizzling ball to third, Stubby gloved it competently, and the thwack of the ball hitting glove leather was clear and satisfying, as clear and satisfying as the umpire's "Out."

"Way to go, Amberchuk!" Ada called. "Way to be, Stubby!"

Stubby's grin was brief and nervous as she wiped her ungloved right hand on the leg of her uniform pants, smearing dust on the beautiful cloth. Her uniform was her armour, her protection, her identification, her dream come true, but she wasn't aware she had wiped sweat and dust on it. When she obeyed the base coach's command, "Take it!" and left second digging hard for third, her uniform and what it meant to her was the reason she ignored the obvious consequences of it and, twelve feet from the third base bag, dove, feet first, arms curled to protect her head and face, and, landing on her right hip, landing on the hip already sore from a similar manoeuvre in a Teen Town game, slid safely under the glove of the basewoman, her extended foot connecting solidly with the flat canvas bag. "Safe!" the umpire yelled. Bright's Crossing Women's Senior A stood as one woman and cheered loudly, Wright and Sharon jumped up and down hollering, Ada clapped her hands and cheered and both Daisy and Stuke yapped excitedly. Stubby stood, retrieved her cap, slapped it on her backside to knock off the dust, then used it to slap the dirt, chalk and lime from her aching hip.

"You okay?" the opposition basewoman asked.

"Oh, you know how it is." Stubby shrugged. "Aches, pains, agony, broken bones, torn ligaments . . . nothing worth talking about, really." They grinned at each other, uniform colour forgotten. Temporarily.

Stubby soaked in a hot tub, then went to bed with an ice pack for her sore hip and a cup of hot tea to calm her. The tea was hours cold in the cup when Stubby wakened sufficiently to put the rubber bag full of melted ice water on the bedside table. She rolled onto her sore hip, winced sleepily, closed her eyes and was once again sound asleep.

Ada Richardson yearned to make life as easy for Stubby as possible, yearned to make up in some way for the upset and difficulties of Stubby's early years. But she knew if she put money into the team it would look as if she had bought Stubby a place on it and nobody, not even Stubby, would remember she had been accepted before Ada made the contribution. Ada herself had never been the least bit interested in the game of softball. If Stubby hadn't been a ball player it would never have occurred to Ada to sponsor a player, let alone an entire team. Ada didn't know a shortstop from a centre fielder or a butt from a line drive, and except insofar as it concerned Stubby, Ada didn't really care.

"What to the families of ball players do?" she asked Wright.

"I don't know," he admitted, "but I can probably find out for you."

"I would appreciate that."

"You have to go to bed now, Ada," Wright insisted gently. "You're too old and too tired for so much excitement."

"I think," Ada laughed, "we had better start getting ourselves used to all this excitement. And I think we should get some rule books and some explanation of the history of the game so we don't disappoint Stubby or make her feel we're ignorant."

In the morning Wright went to every bookstore in town and managed, by good luck and stubbornness, to find one thin book of rules. None of which made any sense whatsoever to him, to Sharon or to Ada, although they studied it determinedly before the tournament in Duncan. "The families of ball players," Wright said, "help with transportation, give moral and actual support, make sure there are oranges, drinks, and picnic lunches, liniment and bandages if needed, celebrate when the players win a game and encourage and commiserate should they lose.

"Transportation and food," Ada said firmly. "We can handle that."

And so it was five of the members of the Bright's Crossing Women's Senior A team arrived for the tournament in a shining black limo driven by a uniformed chauffeur.

"Might as well arrive looking like champions, right?" Marge raised her eyebrows and peered comically down her nose.

"Might just as well," the third basewoman agreed. Stubby blushed. She had almost forgotten her own awe when she had first seen the car, and had definitely forgotten Ada did not live the way all of Bright's Crossing lived. She almost made the mistake of apologizing for the size and splendour of the limo and the rest of her own life, but she avoided the pitfall, grinned like the kid she was and settled back against the well-cared-for leather upholstery. "I'm working overtime," she admitted, "just trying to convince myself someone isn't going to realize who and what I am, stop the car, open the door, and pitch me out into the dingleweeds."

"We won't tell," Marge promised, "if you don't tell on us."

The weekend tournament in Duncan was one of those hell-inspired round robin marathons that exhausts players and officials alike and leaves the spectators sunburned, hoarse, and half gibbled from the beer guzzled to replace lost body fluids.

Inning by inning, call by call, play by play, Stubby did her best. She played capably, with increasing confidence, as she learned the strengths, weaknesses and style of play of her teammates.

When, between the second and third games, they took a one-hour break for lunch, there was Wright with a cardboard box in which rested potato salad and two cold roast chickens. By itself, it was nowhere near enough to feed the team. Had that been all there was, only the catcher and pitcher would have enough to eat. But combined with the food the families of other players had contributed, it was an appreciated and appropriate gesture. Ada had been careful not to overdo the food, so determined was she not to build barriers Stubby would have to overcome.

"How'd you wind up living with Ada Richardson?" the right fielder asked.

"Lucky," Stubby said firmly. "Very lucky."

"What's it like? Her bein' rich and all?"

"It's nice," Stubby laughed. "It's how we should all live."

"Amen," the woman said soberly. "A-bloody-men. And one of these days . . ."

"Right," Stubby agreed. "For all of us, eh?"

In the last of the ninth in the final game of the tournament, with Bright's Crossing ahead five to three and the knowledge there was no way they could lose warming her belly, Stubby Amberchuk got a chance. Ada was sitting in Dave's wheelchair with a glass of cold beer in her thin hand, smiling broadly and proudly, with Wright on her left and Sharon on her right providing the play-by-play. Ada had not been at any of the morning games, in fact none of Stubby's family had been in evidence, although, unbeknownst to her, Wright was watching the game from the vantage point of a nearby hill with a pair of first quality German binoculars, reporting back to Ada by telephone at the end of every inning. When Bright's Crossing moved into the semi-finals, Wright drove to get Ada and Sharon and, of course, Daisy and Stuke, both of whom preferred the cool interior of the limo to the dry heat of the ballfield.

Stubby was tired and sweaty, she was thirsty and covered with dust and grime, her cherished uniform was filthy and her feet were sopping with sweat and swollen with the heat, and she had never enjoyed herself more. She watched the pitcher, as hot, tired, sweaty and happy as herself, and when the ball left the pitcher's hand, Stubby knew again, with that same weird clarity, exactly what was going to happen. She swung. She swung from the shoulder and put her entire stocky body into the swing. She didn't hear the crack of the ball against the bat, she didn't even feel the vibration through the cured hickory, she swung, and when the swing was finished she was running as fast as she could, with the last energy she could draw upon, and the noise from Bright's Crossing Women's Senior A pushed at her like a loving hand, down to first, around first to second, on to third, cleats digging, legs pumping, and as she rounded third, her cap began to slip on her head and she pulled it off, holding it in her hand, gripping it grimly, knowing she had no need to run, no need to slide, knowing she could have danced *en pointe* and still have been home in plenty of time, but wanting to get to home, get it over with, do it and do it the way it ought to be done, one foot in front of the other down the pike. It didn't matter that it wasn't the winning run, it didn't matter they didn't need her run, it didn't matter at all, it was her run and she ran it, every step of the way.

"Way to *go*!" Ada shrilled, and Stubby was over the plate, the women of her team pounding her back, shaking her hand, telling her she'd done it, and done it extremely well.

"Yer lookin' good, kid," the coach smiled widely. "Lookin' real good." Stubby Amberchuk beamed.

The officials made the presentations, starting with the fourth place team, working through third and second, and then Bright's Crossing got the cup for first place. They held it aloft, grinning and cheering, and happy family members took colour snapshots. Doris, catcher and captain of the team, ripped open a case of beer, popped the caps off several bottles and started filling the cup with suds; everyone on the Bright's Crossing team got a drink, then the cup was offered to the captain of the second place team; she drank and handed it to the assistant captain. While the rest of the team took turns drinking and toasting Bright's Crossing, Doris and Madge opened more bottles of beer and by the time the trophy had been refilled several times and the shortstop of the fourth place team was getting her gulp, the setting sun was glinting on as fine an array of tilted amber bottles as was ever seen.

Wright moved forward to ask Stubby if she would need a ride home. "Here, fella," someone burped, handing him the trophy. He looked in, saw several inches of inviting golden suds, grinned, nodded his thanks and took a drink. Then he handed the trophy to the umpire, who looked at Wright's uniform, puzzled, opened his mouth to ask a question, thought better of it and drained the trophy.

"Beach party after this," Madge grinned, handing Wright a bottle of beer. "You know how to get to Flicker Point?"

"Sure do," Wright agreed, holding the bottle of beer but not drinking from it.

"If the old lady needs any help with that chair of hers, there's lots of muscles to help carry it." Madge pointed at the grinning cluster of hairy-chinned males busily stuffing equipment into canvas bags, lugging it to pickups and the trunks of highly-tended Chevrolets and Fords.

The beach party kicked off with a general hunt for good firewood, and when the fires were blazing, the real celebration started. They put steam-cleaned square metal cans from the garage in the middle of the fires, added sea water and, when it was boiling, dumped in scrabbling crabs transported from the boats in wet gunnysacks carefully piled in the back of a pickup. They soaked corn, husks and all, in water, then pushed it into the blistering hot sand around the fires, and while the corn roasted, they ate hot buttered crab and drank beer.

Stubby cracked crab for Ada until the old woman grinned and shook her head. "Not another mouthful," she sighed, "or I'll burst open and make a public display of myself." Ada listened happily to all the jokes, joined in the singing, had her picture taken sitting in her chair with Daisy on her lap and Stubby's beloved baseball cap on her head, and when she left the party, yawning, it was in Wright's arms, with Stubby carrying the folded wheelchair and Sharon bringing the lap robe and Daisy. "You could stay longer if you wanted," she told Stubby. "I'm sure you'd have no trouble getting a ride home."

Stubby hesitated, tempted, then reached over, scooped up Stuke, sighed happily and shook her head. "Enough is enough," she said. "Maybe next time." She climbed into the limo after Ada. The team members shouted their goodbyes. Stubby waved out the open window until even she knew there was no chance at all anybody could see her, then she settled back against the leather upholstery, pushed the button to close the window and grinned all the way home.

Bright's Crossing Women's Senior A made it all the way to the quarter finals of the Provincial Championships before losing to the Vancouver East powerhouse and throughout the season Stubby acquitted herself well. She never got the hit that brought in the winning run, she never got a homer with the bases loaded, she didn't win any awards or trophies, she just did her job, played her position and wore her uniform proudly.

"See you next year," they said, slapping her on the shoulder.

"Hey, Stubby, you ever played soccer?" Peanut asked.

"We're formin' up a basketball team if you're interested," proposed somebody else.

"Great," she agreed. "Great. Let me know when and where, okay?"

8

In grade ten Ada suggested Stubby might think about taking a few courses in business and commerce. "I know it's as dull as dishwater," she sympathized, "but you might not be as lucky as I've been in finding people you can trust, and it never hurts to be able to just walk in, ask to see your portfolio and check it over without having to depend on them for an explanation of everything."

So Stubby took courses in things she didn't really find terribly interesting, until Wright thought to give her one hundred dollars worth of stock in a company that had never raised any eyebrows or made any hearts flutter with excitement. "How's your enterprise today?" he would ask, sipping his first cup of coffee. "Bearish or bullish?"

Stubby, at first, laughed and made jokes about her big hole in the ground. In January her stock went up; she was worth one hundred and twenty-three dollars. In March it dropped; she was worth sixty-three dollars.

"Why?" she raged. "How come?"

"Find out," Ada said unsympathetically.

"If I sell it now, I lose money," Stubby reasoned. "If I buy more, I might make a dollar or two. They'll think someone really has faith in it and knows something they don't know and maybe they'll all rush out and buy and send the price up. Or they might not and I might lose more. What do you think?"

"I think you ought to figure it out for yourself."

Stubby asked her commerce teacher, who, in many more sentences, convoluted and virtually undecipherable, said pretty much what Stubby had already reasoned. Which was no help at all.

"That teacher," Stubby mused out loud, "has never done anything with what he thinks he knows. He put his money in a motel, with his mother as manager. He hasn't got anything in the stock market himself. So what can he tell me?"

Ada just nodded, and waited.

"Everyone says," Stubby continued, "that it only makes sense, in a world starving for protein, to find ways to use what is already being wasted. A factory that turns fish guts into edible protein is a real good idea. If you can figure out a way to talk people into eating protein that used to be fish guts. Which you won't do unless you find a way to make it taste at least as good as soybean paste. But everyone says that every year there are less and less fish being caught, so of course there's less and less fish guts. Then there's the dog food people, who can't make money selling dog food if they don't have fish guts to turn into dog food."

"All of which means . . . what?" Ada probed.

"Means nothing at all," Stubby decided. "You could talk yourself into and out of anything at all. Nobody ever fed the poor of the world before, and I don't believe they really want to feed them now. They just want to make money. And they can make it just as fast, or faster, with dog food for poodles than protein for poor people. The money is in stuff *rich* people want, not in what poor people need." She turned to Wright. "I'm thinking of selling those stocks and investing what I can get for them in something else."

"What?" Wright asked.

"Caviar company."

She sold her stocks the next day, for sixty-one dollars and fourteen cents, and halfway home changed her mind and went back downtown. In the half-hour interval the computer which registered the sale conveyed the news to the brokers, consultants and experts, who interpreted the minor transaction as a sure sign confidence in the project was failing. Failed confidence means uneasiness; who knew what, and why didn't the experts know? Was this a portent of a bath yet to come? Stubby bought back her own stock for thirty dollars because of the minor panic and, with the thirty-one dollars and fourteen cents profit, bought some panic-stricken expert's stock in the same supposedly failing company.

"It'll go up now because there's been what they call activity. Besides," she grinned, "I'm lucky."

Ada looked worried, tapped her fingernails against the arm of her chair, then wheeled herself to her study, closed the door and got on the phone.

"Stubby," she announced at breakfast the next day, "I want you to take a couple of weeks off school. I want you to go to Montreal."

"Me? Montreal?" Stubby swallowed her toast, gulped her orange juice and stared.

"Montreal," Ada repeated, and that was just about all she would say about any of it other than to assure Stubby she would be met at the airport by a friend of Ada's and would have a place to stay in the city.

Stubby stepped off the plane in what she considered to be just about the finest outfit she had. Jeans, new enough not to be faded, used enough not to be stiff as boards. White cotton shirt, a V-necked long-sleeved virgin wool sweater in pale yellow, a warm jacket and a fine pair of Frye boots. The elegantly dressed older woman who met Stubby covered her shock with admirable calm, smiled one of the most charming smiles Stubby had ever seen and, expensive fur coat worn with careless and familiar ease, led the way to where her limo waited. Stubby, accustomed as she was to the limo at home and to Wright in his uniform, was still struck by the rig waiting for her. One look and she knew Ada had deliberately toned down her usual style when she moved back to Bright's Crossing.

Emilie Bliss had learned at an early age to keep her thoughts well hidden behind a pleasant expression. If she thought Stubby was a short, square, semi-literate blob, she at no time gave Stubby any reason to suspect this. If Emilie thought Stubby's clothes more suited to the trash bin than the closet of her quietly elegant home, Emilie gave no hint of it. And because Emilie never blinked so much as an eye, nobody else did either; when Emilie was in the vicinity, no eye blinked until hers had blinked, no jaw dropped as long as Emilie's jaw didn't. Emilie's money and Emilie's power opened doors and closed them, cleared sidewalks and made headwaiters fawn. And when Stubby was with Emilie, Stubby was treated just as well as Emilie.

They went to the art galleries and Stubby stared at colours, swirls, lines, even recognizable objects, and waited to feel some kind of reaction. When there was none, Stubby decided the fault was in her. They went to opera and ballet, they went to concerts and theatres and everywhere Emilie went, Stubby followed dutifully, waiting for some kind of big city polish to rub off on her.

"For god's sake, Ada," Emilie snapped into the long distance phone, "if you *had* to find yourself an heir, couldn't you have found one that had some . . . potential?"

"Stubby has potential," Ada laughed.

"Ada, she is undoubtedly charming, in a very strange way. She smiles and everyone around her responds with smiles. She's like a boxer puppy, so funny-looking it's cute. She's convinced the world is a wonderful place full of wonderful people, she believes if she's nice to others they'll be nice to her, she's as innocent as . . . whatever it is innocent people are compared to! But Ada, for god's sake!''

''Emilie, tell me what it is Stubby is doing or not doing that has you so upset.''

''I don't know,'' Emilie admitted. ''But there's something out-and-out weird, Ada, in this day and age when a young woman decides at two in the morning to go for a walk because she likes the lights of the city. . . and she doesn't get mugged, she doesn't get raped, she doesn't even get frightened. And when I asked her about it, she looked totally puzzled and said nobody had *ever* hassled her. Hassled? Hassled, Ada? We're talking assault, we're talking possible bodily harm, we're talking potential murder! And your heiress thinks of it as hassle. . . .''

''Stubby,'' Ada said quietly, ''can bench press two hundred and eighty-six pounds. Stubby can run. Stubby can kick. Stubby can throw a punch. Stubby can swing, and with the edge of her palm, crack and break a two-inch-thick fir plank. Stubby can even break bricks with her heel kick.''

''But *would* she, Ada? I know how to shoot a gun, but that doesn't mean that in an unexpected moment of danger I would do it!''

''Stubby would.''

''You don't *know* that and neither does she! This is Montreal, Ada, not Bucolicsville, BC!''

''If Stubby can walk through Montreal at night and not get bothered, then not only does Stubby believe she can take care of herself, so do the people in Montreal who might be tempted to jump at her.''

''Ada. . . give this kid a few thou and send her back wherever in hell it is you found her and get yourself someone who can look after your fortune properly. This kid will spend it all on the first whim that comes along. She's a peach. And someone is going to pick that peach and eat it.''

''Get her into a game of poker,'' Ada said and hung up the phone.

Emilie stared at the dead receiver and wondered if Ada was showing the first signs of Alzheimer's Syndrome. But Emilie had tripled her fortune by paying attention to Ada and wasn't about to turn her back completely on her old friend. Muttering about the inherent weakness of the Old Girls Network, Emilie replaced the receiver, then lifted it again and made a few more phone calls.

The men who arrived that evening were the kind of men most of us only get to see from a distance. One glance and you know you are looking at old money, at private schools and private tennis lessons, at all the right clubs and organizations, at establishment and elitism. Usually these men are asking us to vote for them so they can, they promise, represent our interests in the carpeted corridors of the nation's capital.

"Well, dear," they smiled, "would you like to join us in a friendly little game?"

"Oh, that sounds great," Stubby smiled, eyes wide, and one of the men, clearing his throat constantly, asked her if she had ever played cards before.

"Oh, sure," Stubby burbled, "I played snap with my dad when I was little, and sometimes I play stuke. I'm really very good," she said seriously.

The men smiled indulgently and each made a mental note to try to find a way to suggest to Stubby that she not tell anyone she was a good card player. Only the worst players in the world ever say that. And while none of them doubted Stubby might well be the worst player in the history of the world, they all enjoyed the chance to give a little bit of fatherly advice to so unpolished a gem as this little girl from the back bush.

Five hours later they left as smiling and urbane as when they entered. Two of them, as soon as they got home, phoned their brokers and arranged for transfers and sales to cover the incredible skinning they'd experienced.

"I'm very lucky," Stubby told Emilie. Then Stubby had a bath and went to bed without even bothering to add up the figures on the little stack of IOUs she took from her shirt pocket and carefully locked in her small metal box. She put the box under her pillow and fell asleep quickly and easily.

"Okay," Emilie admitted happily on the phone that night, "you were wrong. I was right."

"Exactly the other way around, my dear," Ada laughed.

"That's what I said from the start," Emilie agreed, and then both women were chortling. "Ada, you should have *seen* it! First she tells them she's a very good player, so of course they figured her for a jerk. Then she won a few hands and said she was very lucky, and they had to agree, but they all thought that was just beginner's luck. Then she stopped being little miss butter 'n' eggs and took 'em for everything they had on them. After which she smilingly agreed to take paper."

"That's my kid," Ada agreed. "Tell her she can come home any time she wants. Then I'll tell her myself that she doesn't need to try to study business or commerce. She'll do okay."

"Ada," Stubby hazarded tentatively when she got home, "I think stocks and bonds and investment portfolios and stuff like that are only a science up to a point. After which, I think it's all just another way to play poker."

"Is that what you think?"

"Yeah. Except there's part of it is like shooting craps. So," Stubby took a deep breath, ''I'd like to learn to shoot craps. And play pool, too.''

''I'm sure Wright would be able to teach you what you want to learn,'' Ada agreed easily. ''When I first met him he was hustling in a billiard hall in Saskatoon, dreaming of bigger and better things.''

The dice Wright showed to Stubby were like any dice anywhere in the world. Wright had bought them in the smoke shop for three dollars and forty-nine cents. He showed Stubby everything she would ever need to know about shooting craps, and when she was through staring in wonder, Wright began to teach her how to do what he had just finished demonstrating. ''Soft wrist,'' he urged, ''easy with it. Don't clutch them as if you were drowning and they were a lifeline. Hold them. Feel them. Think about them. Think about the spots on them. Think which spots you need, which ones you want to see.''

''Are you telling me I can think these things into doing what I want them to do?''

''I'm telling you that they weren't kidding when they said faith can move mountains. And if people can bend spoons or lift papers with the power of their minds, if people can find water with the help of a willow wand, if people can dream, Stubby, of things that haven't yet happened . . . you can throw a seven any time you want. *If* you concentrate.''

''Wow, eh?'' Stubby licked her lips, swallowed, and decided to trust Wright in this as much as she trusted him with her life every time she sat in the limo and he drove it out into traffic.

The pool table Wright had installed in the basement was not bought in the smoke shop for three dollars and forty-nine cents. Nor for three hundred and forty-nine dollars. Nor yet three thousand four hundred and ninety-nine dollars. The pool table was imported from New York and the freight bill alone was three thousand plus. Stubby's first pool cue cost two hundred dollars. ''Get you a good one,'' Wright promised, ''when you can play a half decent game.''

''Concentrate,'' he said softly. ''Examine all the angles. Remember, for every action there is an equal and opposite reaction.''

''Like batting a ball,'' she guessed. ''Your feet and how they're placed are as important as your hands.''

''There's hope for you, Stubby.'' Then he took off his jacket, rolled back his shirt cuffs and chalked the tip of his own cue. ''You've got two months,'' he warned, ''and then we start playing for money.'' He bent over the table, looked at every ball carefully and then started. When the last ball was sunk Stubby just stared. ''Two months,'' Wright repeated firmly.

''I'll never be that good,'' Stubby declared.

"No," he grinned. "You never will. But with a lot of work, you might come second."

Sometimes Ada sat in a chair in the basement and listened to the sound of the cue tip hitting the ball, the ball hitting other balls, the comments and silences of the players. Sometimes she thought she could see the balls moving across the green felt. Sometimes she almost thought she could move to the table herself and with or without a cue, make the balls obey.

But most of the time she just listened and thought of other things. Of Joan and the way her eyes crinkled at the corners when she laughed. The touch of her, the smell of her, the taste of her. Ada no longer cared whether she was alone in her room in the protective darkness or not, she visited her own inner world more and more frequently.

"Stubby," she said quietly, patting the side of her bed, feeling it dip under Stubby's weight, "I want to tell you some things. Things I think you really have to know."

"Ada," Stubby's voice quavered, "is this going to be heavy?"

"Probably," Ada pulled no punches, "but you'll live through it, as the woman said." She held out her hand and Stubby took it in her own. Ada could feel the calluses on Stubby's palms, the muscles in the back of Stubby's hands. "I never had a child of my own and you have to know, I never wanted one. Never felt I was missing out on anything at all. The only thing in my life I ever really wanted, I was lucky enough to find, and lucky enough to realize was precious, and so was lucky enough to get it, enjoy it and not waste any time bullshitting around about the cosmic cookie and whether or not it was going to crumble. No angst about did I deserve this or not. Of course I did! We all do! But we don't all get it. And when it was gone, I almost betrayed it all by letting myself sink into a depression and then wallow around in it like a sow in thick mud. But I was lucky. I had my memories. I could pick and choose those, Stubby. I kept them all, but concentrated on the best ones, and knew that even though it was gone, it wasn't gone forever and I'd get it back again, all I had to was wait my turn. And my turn is coming soon."

"Aw no, Ada," Stubby protested. "Don't say that."

"Don't hide from the truth, Stubs, please," Ada sighed. "I almost regret having met you. I'd have gone a long time ago if it hadn't been for not wanting to miss out on any of our fun together. I would have had it back again, you see, and had it a long time ago. But I took the wrong turn and instead of walking home, I was walking myself into riding double on an old bike and nothing has been the same since. Lucky again, I guess."

"Ada." Stubby took a deep breath and dared. "Ada, I want you to know I love you. I'm grateful for everything you've done for me, for everything you've given me and for all the stuff you've taught me, but that's not why I love you. I just love you because I love you.''

"I love you, too, Stubby," Ada smiled. "I love your laugh and your giggle and your guts. But I can't hang around much longer, you see. I'm overdue. I really am. And I'm tired, my Stubby. Christ on a crutch, but I am tired."

"We can get a doctor," Stubby blurted.

"Spare me," Ada growled. "I'm older than your Grandma Amberchuk. I'm older than your Grandfather Fleming. Let us not get unnatural about things," she grinned.

"Okay," said Stubby.

Ada nodded again. "It'll all be yours. Not right away, but at the right time. Enjoy it, Stubs. Enjoy it and know that you do not *ever* have to do anything you don't want to do. Most of the world spends its time on earth eating garbage of one kind or another, with dirty spoons, just to be able to keep body and soul together. They work at jobs they don't like to get the money to buy a house in a neighbourhood they don't really want to live in. Then they have to buy a car to get back and forth to the job they hate. But they need the job to pay for the car and the house and the furniture and the food. People stay married to people they do not like or respect just because someone taught them that was what God wanted. People don't live with people they adore because society frowns on it, or the people think society frowns on it. Or they're afraid, probably rightly so, that if they live with the person they love, they'll lose the job, and then what do you do? None of that has to come down on you, Stubby Amberchuk. I don't want thanks or gratitude or any of that stuff. I just want to know I can die and you'll enjoy your life and your money."

"Okay," Stubby nodded, and tears fell to her shirt front. "I'll try to do that, Ada. And I'll make a point of not doing things I don't want to do."

"I don't regret meeting you at all," Ada yawned. "One of the two luckiest things in my entire life."

It was like a replay, only somehow more horrible because this time there were no buffers, this time there was no safe place to go and hide, no warm nest, no protection. Ada Richardson was dead, and both Wright and Sharon looked to Stubby for direction. All the arrangements came down to one final thing: Stubby's decision. She wanted to protest, she wanted to say, "Hey, hang on, this is a bit much, I'm only sixteen and a half years old; yesterday I wasn't considered adult enough to decide what kind of toothpaste to buy, today the world is sitting on my head. Back off, will you?''

Instead, she listened as the lawyer explained what Ada had said she wanted done, and only when Stubby nodded and agreed did the lawyer reach for the phone.

"Private services," Stubby echoed, and the relief she felt was enormous. No need for all those cars, all those people, all the deadlines and schedules and arrangements and plates of sandwiches and glasses and drinks and cups and mugs and saucers and spoons.

The ambulance attendants lifted Ada's body from her bed and loaded her gently onto a stretcher while Sharon stood dry-eyed and Wright wiped his face with a big white hanky. They covered the frail husk with a white sheet, strapped it in place and took it down the curving staircase to the ambulance, then drove away with it, lights not blinking or revolving, siren silent. Drove it to the funeral parlour, where it would be readied for cremation. No flowers by request. Donations may be made to your favourite charity.

They sat in the living room, all three of them, lost in their own worlds. When Stubby got up to go to bed, Wright and Sharon roused themselves and moved at their own pace to their own separate quarters. In the morning when Stubby went downstairs, Sharon was making breakfast as if everything were the same as it had always been. Only of course, nothing was the same. The entire world was forever altered.

"Your grandma phoned," Sharon said softly. "She wants to know if it's okay for her to come over this afternoon. She asked if there was anything you wanted."

"Guess I'd better phone her back," Stubby mumbled, her throat aching.

"Eat your breakfast first," Wright said, pouring coffee.

"Yeah. I'll try." It all tasted like sawdust. It stuck in her throat. It sat nastily in her stomach, threatening to fly back up her throat again. "I don't think I can eat," she finally admitted. Sharon nodded understandingly, and Stubby put the scrambled eggs, bacon and toast down on the floor for Daisy.

Three days of telegrams, flowers arriving at the house from people who hadn't known of the request for none, phone calls and visits from the neighbours, and at the end of the three days Stubby was exhausted. But she pulled on her new clothes, made sure her hair was brushed to a gleaming shine and, with Sharon and Wright, she drove to the funeral parlour for the memorial services. Grandma Amberchuk held her hand and patted it comfortingly, Grandpa Amberchuk blew his nose loudly and looked completely ill at ease and Ada Richardson's friends flicked glances from the corners of their eyes at the young woman, girl really, who had just inherited a fortune estimated to be positively enormous. The music played quietly and Stubby tried hard not to think that at that very minute the crematorium was going full blast and Ada Richardson was finally going back to the sun, the very sun that had stolen her sight. Stubby hoped Ada would be able to see now, to look upon the face of God and not be hit with blackness.

Back at the house again, with the bronze urn in a tasteful little grey cardboard box, Stubby stepped from the limo into the unexpected embrace of nobody else but Earl himself.

"Sheilagh," he said heavily, "you should have phoned us."

"Why?" she blurted, stepping back, trying to evade his embrace without dropping what was left of Ada on the gravel driveway.

"Baby!" Vinnie grabbed her, and Stubby was caught between the two of them. If she pulled away from Vinnie, she'd walk right into Earl's unwelcome clasp. So she stood, hanging on to Ada's ashes, while Vinnie fussed over her and said things like Oh my, you're so tall, I never dreamed you'd be so tall, why you've grown a good six inches since I saw you in August, somehow I always thought you'd be a little woman, but my heavens, just look at you, oh this is all just so awful, isn't it, why didn't you phone, we'd have flown down in a minute if we'd known, there was no need for you to have to go through all of this alone, and Oh, baby, it's been so long, let me have a good look at you.

"Driver," Earl said coolly, "you may put the car away."

Wright looked at Earl and smiled, then nodded, tipped his hat and moved to the limo again. Stubby managed to get herself disentangled from Vinnie's embrace and started up the stairs to the house.

"Perhaps," Earl said to Sharon, "you could arrange to have lunch served immediately. I'm sure Miss Sheilagh is in need of some food."

"I'm fine," Stubby said. "We ate before we went down."

"We didn't," Earl reminded her.

Stubby looked at Sharon and shrugged, and Sharon smiled, much as Wright had done, nodded at Earl, and went off in the direction of the kitchen.

"Our bags," Earl said to Stubby, "are still at Grandmother and Grandfather Fleming's place."

Stubby nodded, although she didn't see what any of that had to do with her, and started up the stairs with Ada in her hands.

"What are you doing with that?" Earl demanded.

"Taking to it my bedroom," Stubby answered. "Why?"

"If that's what I think it is, your bedroom is hardly the place for it." Earl frowned, and Stubby began to remember all the reasons she didn't very much care for his company.

"Listen, Earl," she said clearly, "don't lean on me, okay? I'm really not feeling up to it." She started up the stairs again, hearing Vinnie hissing at Earl to cool off, calm down and not get his shirt in a knot. When

Stubby came down half an hour later, in jeans, hiking boots and with her backpack in her hand, Earl and Vinnie were sitting at the big dining room table that was usually only used for special occasions, enjoying the lunch Sharon had prepared.

"Where are you going?" Earl asked.

"To do what we're supposed to do," Stubby answered. "It's in the will. We won't be back for about two days but I guess you can let yourselves out when you're finished eating. The door locks on its own every time it's shut, so nobody will bust in, and we've all got keys."

"Going?" Vinnie stared. "But we just got here!"

"Well," Stubby shrugged, "you should've phoned, I could've told you we'd be gone." She held the door open for Sharon, who had also changed into outdoor clothes.

Wright had the car ready and was lounging against it in jeans and a clean white shirt, a cigarette in his hand. He opened the door and Sharon, holding Stuke, slid into the front seat first, followed by Stubby, who carefully placed the backpack at her feet, then spread the blanket on her lap for Daisy. They drove off immediately, leaving Vinnie and Earl standing in the open doorway, their napkins dangling from their hands, waving in the breeze. "I hope they do their own dishes," Stubby growled.

The big limo drove to the airport. They parked it against the side of the ticket building, then went inside. Minutes later they followed a young man in a blue uniform out to the runway and climbed into a small airplane, Wright lifting Daisy and climbing the stairs with her tucked under his arm.

They flew north to Ocean Falls and checked into a hotel, then, first thing in the morning, they chartered a boat and took Ada salmon fishing. When they caught a salmon, they took the hook from its mouth, sprinkled it with a pinch of ashes, and let it go again. When Sharon brought in a three-foot dogfish shark, they repeated the process. By the time they headed back to town in the charter boat, Ada's urn was half empty and what wasn't in it was well and truly mixed with the creatures and water of the sea.

Sunburned and laughing, they had supper and went to bed early, and the next morning they were again out on the chuck, catching fish and baptizing them with Ada. "What a way to go!" Stubby yelled over the sound of the motor. "Sure beats hymns and big hunks of dirt!"

"She said, 'Wright, I have always deeply regretted the fact I spent so much time making money and so little time enjoying it until it was too late. I can hardly inflict these frail bones and sightless eyes on others, but before the last of me is gone, I want to have me some fun.' That's what she said. 'What about salmon fishing, Ada?' I asked, and she laughed. . . you remember that laugh of hers, a cross between a donkey braying and gravel rubbed on a porcelain sink? She laughed and said, 'Okay, Wright, you see to it for me.' And here we are.'' Wright blew his nose loudly and rubbed his eyes with the back of his hand. ''Ada,'' he shouted to the urn, ''are you enjoying your old self?''

''Here,'' Sharon hiccupped and put her bottle of brandy back in her purse. ''Want to learn to fly?'' She sprinkled Ada's ashes on a piece of sandwich, threw it in the air and laughed when an ever-vigilant shithawk swooped and gobbled it.

''Way to go!'' Stubby cheered, tears dripping from her eyes and mixing with the spray from the waves. She opened the urn, looked at the ashes, put her finger in her mouth, then poked it in the ashes. They weren't soft ashes like the ones from a bonfire or woodstove, some of them were chunky and hard, probably bits of bone not totally transformed, some of them glinting with strange colours, mineral deposits or something. She put her ashy finger in her mouth. Tasted like ordinary ash, though. Then she realized what she had done. For a moment horror battled with a fierce jubilation. Then horror was gone and the jubilation remained. She saw Wright and Sharon looking at her, their faces carefully without expression. Stubby again wet her finger, put it in the ash, then returned it to her mouth. ''Okay, Ada,'' she said aloud, ''the rest of you is free.''

Flying back from Ocean Falls the pilot opened the plexiglass window beside him, and one by one they held the urn, had a private little moment and said goodbye to what was left of Ada. Then Stubby put the urn outside, the last of the ash disappearing in the slipstream of the small plane. She opened her fingers and even the urn was gone from sight, her hand suddenly very cold and stiff. She pulled her hand inside, the pilot closed the window and all the fun of the fishing trip almost vanished.

When they returned home, Earl and Vinnie were still there.

''Why?'' Stubby asked.

''Someone has to look after you,'' Vinnie smiled.

''Look after me?'' Stubby echoed. ''I don't need looking after, I'm fine.''

''I am your mother,'' Vinnie said, her tone reasonable enough, ''and you are only sixteen years old.''

''Nearly seventeen,'' Stubby corrected.

''Nonetheless,'' Earl said firmly, ''you are not old enough to live without supervision.''

Wright looked at Sharon and winked, Sharon looked at Wright and nodded. Stubby looked at Wright and Sharon and they both looked back at her, blank faced. She sighed.

"What about your job?" she said hopefully. "Your house in Vetchburg?"

"I have resigned, and the house is listed for sale. I have already made application for a position with the local school district."

"We'll live here with you," Vinnie smiled, "and you won't have to worry about anything. We'll take care of you."

"Sweet suffering christ," Stubby muttered, but under her breath so there wouldn't be any uproar about it. "C'mon Daisy," she said, and started up the stairs to her room.

"Don't those dogs belong outside?" Earl asked.

"No, sir," Wright said smoothly, "it was Miss Ada's express wish that some things not change."

"Oh," Earl nodded, "of course."

Stubby missed Ada so much she didn't want to pay attention to very much of anything. Something inside her seemed to be asleep or numb or on hold. She went to bed at her usual time, got up just the same as always, had breakfast by herself in the kitchen, said goodbye to Stuke, Daisy, Sharon and Wright, and went off to school as if nothing had happened. After school there was basketball practice or softball practice or lacrosse practice or grass hockey practice or soccer practice, and then she rode home on her bike, the same five-speed Dave had given her, to shower and change for supper.

She tried to pay no attention to Earl while paying decent, polite and dutiful attention to Vinnie who was, after all, her very own mother. If there was one thing Ada Richardson had been big on, it was being polite for just as long as someone's assholiness would permit you to be polite, and Vinnie wasn't really very assholy at all. In fact, Vinnie was often quite a lot of fun.

"Oh, are you reading that?" Vinnie asked, surprised. "There you are, not even seventeen, and you're halfway through! I was, oh, probably thirty before I opened it."

Stubby put down Simone de Beauvoir and rubbed her eyes. "It's kind of heavy," she admitted. "Sometimes, it's as if I know what each individual word means but the sentences don't make any sense. Other times, I think I know what the sentences are saying but. . . some of the words don't seem to belong. Or maybe I'm just missing the point altogether."

"Earl said I was missing the point," Vinnie agreed. "He told me to put the damn thing down before I got impossible to live with. So I put it down when he was around and picked it up when he left. I figured if he wasn't there he didn't have to worry how impossible I was being!''

''Does it get any easier to understand?''

''If anything, it just gets more confusing. I mean, there you are, doing something very ordinary and everyday, like sewing on a shirt button or something, and bang! there's something from the book rattling around in your head, and so you try to figure it out and an hour later, there's the shirt, and there's the button still not sewn on and you're just as mixed up as ever. I think at some point in your life the whole thing will just kind of—click—into place.''

''Yeah?'' Stubby laughed softly. ''Well, in my case it's apt to be more of a clunk than a click.''

''I tried *The Female Eunuch* too,'' Vinnie confessed.

''You?'' Stubby stared. 'You're the very one told me to steer clear of all that women's liberation stuff. You said it was all crap!''

''Oh, poof,'' Vinnie laughed, ''that's not women's liberation stuff! It's a best-seller! Everyone was talking about it, about how it was a new way of looking at things, and the old way didn't seem to be doing me much good. I'd watched so much TV I couldn't tell where one soap left off and another started and, as you know, Vetchburg isn't exactly the best place in the world for amusement, entertainment, or distraction. So I go the book, but Earl had a bird about it. Said the woman had a filthy mind and the vocabulary of a dock-whalloper, and he threw it in the fireplace. I wasn't in the mood for a go-round so I just let 'er burn, had a bath and went to bed. Next day I bought another copy and hid it in the laundry basket. I knew he'd never look in there! He practically drops his dirty clothes in with his eyes shut, as if he can't bear to see the evidence of... something... Anyway, I hid it and I read it, and that was fun. Not because the book was any great hell, you understand, but because it was something Earl didn't want me to do and I could get away with it and he didn't even suspect. When I was your age,'' she admitted, ''I used to buy a *True Confessions* magazine and go down to the creek with it. Sit under the trestle and read every story. My mother would have had a fit if she'd ever found out! However, for all that it was fun, it didn't make much sense to me. The *Eunuch* I mean. I understood the *True Confessions* with no trouble!''

''Maybe we aren't the academic types,'' Stubby suggested.

''Maybe not,'' Vinnie nodded. ''On the other hand, who says being academic is such a wonderful thing? I mean if nobody can understand what they're saying, what's the use of it all?''

''Right!'' Stubby laughed. ''So, how are you at playing cards?''

''Not so good, but I'm hell on wheels with Monopoly.''

The trouble with playing Monopoly was, Earl wanted to play. And he took it all so seriously that it was no fun.

"You can't *do* that!" he raged.

"Of course I can," Stubby argued. "You just saw me do it. Nothing in the rules says I can't do it.'

"You traded over half what you had for one property! One lousy little low-cost Marvin Gardens! You *know* Marvin Gardens isn't worth that much! You just did it so *she'd* have enough to stay in the game!"

"Well," Stubby stood up. "It would hardly have been any fun playing by myself!"

"*I* was still in the game! I *am* still in the game! Where are you going?"

"You win," Stubby shrugged.

"But you can't just *quit!*"

"Watch me," she invited, and turned away, walking into the living room and turning on the TV.

"How are you ever going to get anywhere in the world with that attitude?" Earl raged. "Are you going to let all of Ada Richardson's money go down the drain because you don't want to compete?"

"No," Stubby yawned. "I have people who know more about it than you or I ever will, and they get paid to see to it we don't go broke. If we go broke, they're out of a job, and they don't want to be out of a job so they see to it we don't go broke. It's all very easy, Earl."

"And what if they all cheat you blind?" he sneered. "Then what?"

"That won't happen."

She switched channels, but Earl wasn't about to mind his own business. He started yammering on about wise virgins and foolish virgins, something about hiding money under a basket, something about something else and Stubby wished she had the power to snap her fingers and make him disappear. She tried to tune out her ears and let it all pass over her unheard, but Earl was in full pedantic swing, and she knew he would lecture her until hell froze over given half the chance. She turned off the TV and walked out of the room and up the stairs to her bedroom, where she closed and locked the door and sat on her bed with *The Knights of the Round Table*, which she had to write a book report on for school.

It was too bad the world had changed, tempus had fugited and time marched on inexorably. Where were they when they were needed? And wasn't it just her luck to have been born at the wrong time. She would gladly have given half her inheritance to have a white knight ride up the driveway and spear Earl with his lance. Maybe barbecue him in the fire hissing from the gaping maw of a large glittering dragon. If ever a damsel was in distress it was Stubby every time Earl spoke to her. All she wanted to say to him in return was eff off Earl, but if she did, hell wouldn't hold it, and who needed the aggravation. Still, it was fun to daydream about it. There she'd be holed up in the tower and along would come Galahad on his big horse. Except, somehow, she couldn't quite picture herself in a pointy hat with a veil drifting from the top, clasping her hands and smirking up in adoration at some guy in a tin suit. Maybe she'd hold out and wait for Merlin to come along and do a bit of magic. Hocus pocus alamocus and there's Earl changed into a frog, sitting in the slimy water of the moat, using his endless goddamn tongue to catch flies for supper.

If she could just find a way to wangle that, she could play pool and shoot craps with Wright again, but the way it was now, their games had stopped. You can't study action and reaction with some motor-mouth standing at the doorway giving advice or coughing just before your cue hits the ball. And Earl yapped on about how shooting craps was nothing for any young lady to do, and you can't concentrate on making the right spots turn up with that kind of blether going on around you. Maybe Merlin could change Earl into a silent stone and she could drop the stone in to the deepest part of the ocean. But Merlin was asleep in a crystal cavern, and apt to be there for quite a while.

Stubby looked at the lined notebook in front of her, where her book report had somehow transformed itself into something she couldn't even take to school, let alone hand in to her English teacher.

The night of the king's castration, all the dukes, counts, viscounts, discounts and no-accounts were gathered around the Square Table chewing camel shit—for in those days bullshit had not yet been invented—when up rode David in his diamond-studded jockstrap. "The princess, the princess, where is my princess?" cried David. "Why, she's in bed with diphtheria," they replied. "What, is that wop sonofabitch back again?" David hollered. For this, David was thrown to the lions, but the Lions have never been a team in serious contention and they fumbled the throw, causing the linesmen, referees and both faithful fans to boo heartily and leave the field. David, alone in mid-turf, was declared victor. To the victor belongs the spoils and there was little in the world more spoiled than the princess. "The princess, the princess," David insisted. "Oh fuck the princess," the king replied and a hundred thousand loyal subjects rose to the occasion. "Shit," cried the King, and there was a mighty movement in the crowd for in those days the king's word was law. The shit flew at random, but Random was a crafty old bugger and he ducked. "David, oh David," the princess cheered, and they lived happily ever after.

"Sheilagh!" Earl bellowed, hammering on the door. "I haven't finished talking to you!"

"I'm doing my homework."

"What homework?" he demanded suspiciously.

"The life of King David of Wales," she invented hurriedly. "It's for a book report."

"Oh," Earl muttered, mollified. If it had to do with education he couldn't very well complain, nor could he admit he had never heard of King David of Wales.

Stubby tried as much as possible to pay attention to as little as possible because, as she told herself at least three times a day, nothing is forever and sooner or later she would grow old enough to be able to be on her own and Earl would be out of her life. Forever. She went to school, took the minimum number of courses which would allow her to graduate, did as many of the things she liked to do as the law would allow and Earl tolerate; day followed day, week followed week and the universe continued to unfold.

"Tell Wright to bring the car around," Earl snapped from behind his morning newspaper, "and tell him to be on time this afternoon. I want to leave as soon after class as possible."

"Yes, sir," Sharon replied coolly.

"How come you don't drive yourself to work?" Stubby asked abruptly, feeling as if she had been asleep for a very long time and was just now beginning to come awake.

"Why should I?" Earl shrugged. "It's what he gets paid to do, isn't it?"

"What if you get held up after school and have to stay longer?"

"He'll wait." Earl sipped his coffee. "It's his job."

"You've got your own car," she pressed.

"It's his job," he repeated.

"Oh." Stubby stared into her glass of freshly squeezed orange juice, watching a little piece of pulp settle to the bottom.

"And Sharon," Earl held his cup out for Sharon to refill, "don't forget we'll be fifteen for dinner tonight."

"What dinner?" Stubby asked. "Did I miss something?"

"No," Earl said, disappearing again behind the newspapers.

Earl headed off in the back of the limo about the same time Stubby scratched two sets of doggy ears and swung up on her old bike. She made it to the gate first, got off her bike, opened the gate and held it open for Wright to drive through. He winked at her on his way out and she waved back, but her interest was focused mainly on Earl, who was sitting where Ada had always sat. He was sitting tall, looking at the back of Wright's head, saying nothing in words and everything with the very satisfied look on his face.

Instead of going to school, Stubby turned her bike around and went back up to the house. "Sharon," she asked very softly, "could I have a look at the household accounts?"

"Yes, Miss Sheilagh," Sharon replied, her face set in a professional mask.

"Oh for crying out loud," Stubby snorted, "this is me, remember?"

"Yes'm."

"Sharon . . . what's going on with the yes'm?"

"The accounts are here, ma'am."

Sharon handed over the leather bound account book. Stubby nodded, put it on the table, sat down, and began to look over the details of the past months.

"How'd all this happen?" she asked.

"Where have you been?" Sharon said coldly.

"Oh, wow, I'm in shit, right?"

"Am *I*?" Sharon countered.

"You?" Stubby gaped. "Why would *you* be in shit?"

"You've never asked to see the accounts before."

"I'm not checking up on *you*, Sharon, I'm checking up on *me*. I seem to have had my head up my arse. Could you explain to me, please, what in hell we need with a fifteen-hundred-dollar morocco leather desk set? And what *is* it?"

"Mr. Blades required it for his office," Sharon said, her face relaxing. "No shit?"

"No shit, Stubby." Sharon sat down, looked at the account book, and pointed at a particular item. "You might want to look into this, too."

"Well, Lordy Old Baldy. We're buying his clothes, too?"

"He has very expensive tastes."

Stubby turned the pages of the account books, hearing decidedly hard-edged clunking sounds as any number of dimes began to drop inside her head. "I guess," she hazarded, "there's no use saying anything to someone who had done her best to check out of everything for a while."

"Wright and I figured you were sure to come back sooner or later." Sharon poured them each a cup of coffee and patted Stubby's hand. "We figured it was harder on you than anyone had known, first your father, then Ada . . ."

"I feel like a fool." Stubby stirred cream and sugar into her coffee and stared at it for a long time. "There are stories about people who stepped into Fairyland and they thought they were only there five or ten minutes, but when they came back to the real world years and years had passed. I feel that's what I did, sort of.''

''If you wait for magic to make things happen,'' Sharon said sternly, ''you'll be sitting on your backside for a long, long time.''

Stubby nodded and sipped her coffee, tasting something suspiciously like ashes on her tongue. ''Guess I miss school this morning,'' she sighed, turning back to the account books. ''God damn that Earl, anyway.''

She went to school for the afternoon session but her mind wasn't on her studies and after school, at softball practice, she was so preoccupied she fumbled what ought to have been an easy throw from second.

She came home from softball practice, her jeans grass-stained all up one side where she'd slid into second base, and before she was inside the house, Earl's jaw was going full blast. Why didn't you get home sooner, look at yourself, what if someone saw you looking like that, must you go everywhere with that tatty old backpack hanging from your hand, I thought you went off to school in decent shoes, why are you wearing those dreadful old grey sneakers, you'd better go upstairs, have a bath, wash your hair and show up for supper wearing something fit and decent, and be on your best behaviour if you have any, this isn't just any old body coming for dinner, these are some of the best people in town.

Best people in town or not, Stubby didn't know a soul. Not one of them had ever shown up for dinner with Ada. Stubby walked into the room wearing an almost new pair of cords, a white blouse and a soft wool vest, and while she thought she looked just about as fine as she could, Earl frowned at her and did that thing with his mouth that meant he was ticked off about something.

Vinnie looked gorgeous. A bit out of it, a bit spaced, a bit less focused than usual, but gorgeous. She smiled at all the best people, nodded in what seemed to be appropriate places and drifted like dandelion fluff until it was time to sit at the huge antique table and eat the delicious meal Sharon had worked all afternoon to prepare. Stubby figured the meal was costing her at least fifty dollars per person, and of all the people sitting chewing and swallowing, the only one she really wanted to feed was Vinnie, but Vinnie was hardly eating. The rest of them, strangers all, could starve for all Stubby cared.

But Stubby smiled and held her peace, and Stubby used her ears to listen in on the conversations flying around the table. She didn't feel quite so out of whack listening to what people were saying because, obviously, the whole world was out of whack, or at least that segment of it represented here tonight. They all seemed to be suffering under the mistaken impression that it was Earl, not Stubby, who had inherited Ada's house, Ada's land and Ada's money. They talked to Earl about his house and how beautifully restored and decorated it was, they talked to Earl about his well-landscaped yard and they talked to Earl about his lovely rosebushes.

Stubby ate dinner and talked to the people sitting on either side of her, an alderman and a school board trustee, but her ears were stretched for every word directed to or from Earl, who sat at the head of the table and beamed at everyone. From time to time he would raise his eyebrows and look at Sharon or Wright and one or the other of them would move to his side and bend forward attentively. Earl would whisper to them and they would nod, as if accepting instructions. Stubby could not recall Ada every having to make such a big deal out of so little, nor could she remember any of Ada's guests ever dying of thirst or of hunger. She was starting to feel flushed, but she was sure it couldn't be that the room was overheated, because her hands and feet felt chilled. It was her face and the back of her neck that seemed too warm. She wondered if she were coming down with the flu or an allergy reaction, although she had never had an allergy reaction before in her life.

"Your father," said the alderman sitting beside her, "has a promising future in local politics."

"He isn't my father," Stubby said clearly, smiling her most engaging smile.

"Oh." The little balding man swallowed. "Oh, I seem to have misunderstood something."

"Probably not." Stubby smiled, "Earl doesn't always manage to get the truth totally squared away in his own head, let alone convey much of it in his conversations. He keeps on telling people he's my dad, but he's not. His name is Blades. Mine is Amberchuk." She knew by the way Earl pivoted as if he'd just been goosed that he'd heard her.

"Sheilagh." Earl fixed his gaze on her as if he believed his eyes were pins and she were a rare specimen of moth. "Would you like more chicken?"

"No, thank you," Stubby replied. She smiled at Wright, who winked at her, and at Sharon, who refused to smile but nodded, and Stubby ate the rest of her supper like a good little girl, then excused herself and went up to her room pleading a very heavy load of homework.

As the guests left, the sound of Stubby's typewriter drifted from her bedroom window, and several of the finest people in town complimented Earl on having such a studious and industrious daughter. Earl smiled and nodded and shook hands, and waited until they had all driven away before going up to Stubby's room to give her a piece of his mind.

"Open this door!"

"I'm sorry, Earl," Stubby said, "I've got the door locked so I won't be disturbed."

"Sheilagh, I want to talk to you!"

"No, thank you, Earl. It's late."

"You behaved very badly," he shouted. "I am not pleased at all." When there was no answer, he repeated his message, in that cold flat tone that had worked so well when Stubby was only eight or nine.

"Tell someone who gives a shit, Earl," she laughed. "I'm not the one telling lies. If you don't want your cover blown, don't make out things are any other than what they really are." She went into her bathroom, closed the door and turned on the shower to drown out the sound of Earl's scolding.

"Wright, I wonder if you could please take this ad in to the newspaper for me," she smiled the next morning, handing him a large brown envelope. "I don't know how much it will cost, but I'm sure they'll be glad to bill the household expenses. Everyone else in town has had a fine year from that account."

"Sure," Wright grinned. "Want it in today's paper?" he asked, leaning against the counter and sipping the strong black coffee he preferred.

"Please," Stubby nodded. "What did Ada do when she wanted to see her lawyer?"

"I'll phone him for you," Sharon offered eagerly.

"And I'll pick you up at school." Wright finished his coffee hurriedly and cocked his head toward the kitchen door, through which they heard the sound of Earl's approaching footsteps. "Gotta go," Wright whispered, waving the brown envelope, and then he was out the back door.

"Crispy bacon," Stubby said appreciatively. "Seems like we haven't had it in years."

"Well," Sharon lectured, "if you don't tell me you want it, and Earl says he doesn't want it because it's unhealthy. He wants poached eggs for breakfast. Every morning. That's all he likes. Poached eggs and toast."

Stubby sat at the table and started in on the crisp bacon, scrambled eggs, toast and hash browns. Earl came into the kitchen, sat at the table and gaped.

"Scrambled?"

"Special request from Stubby," Sharon said easily, turning back to the stove.

"Her name," Earl said coldly, "is Miss Sheilagh."

"My name," Stubby said hotly, "is Stubby."

"You make the best crispy bacon in the world, Sharon," she said, her tone altered completely. "Sit down and have some before it gets cold."

"Sheilagh," Earl scolded, "the staff never sits down with the employers. It just is not done."

"It was done around here when Ada was giving the orders," Stubby said easily. "Every breakfast we'd sit together and talk about what needed doing, and if it was good enough for Ada, it's good enough for everyone else, including the Queen of England, and most certainly you."

"I think you and I should have a long talk." Earl's mouth was set tight, a little white line around it, and Stubby knew that meant he had decided to go on the attack. "Your behaviour last night was not what I expect from my daughter, and your behaviour this morning is no better."

"Blow it out your ear," Stubby invited. "I am not your daughter."

"You come straight home from school today," Earl commanded, "and once you get here, you go directly to your bedroom and wait until I get home from work. Then this entire episode will be settled!" He turned to Sharon, his face white with fury. "Have Wright bring the car around," he snapped.

"Wright isn't here," Sharon said politely.

"Where is he?" Earl roared.

"In town. On business," Sharon responded.

"What business?" Earl fumed, "Whose business?"

"Not your business," Stubby assured him. She rose, picked the last two pieces of bacon from the plate, and, carrying them with her, went to get her jacket.

"Goddammit, you get back here," Earl hollered.

"What's going on?" Vinnie asked blearily, coming down the stairs just as Stubby reached for the handle of the front door.

"Oh," Stubby shrugged, "Earl's pitching a fit."

"I think . . . ." Vinnie breathed, turning around and heading back up the stairs, "I think I'll have another shower or something until after he's left for work."

When the school bell signalled lunch hour, Wright was waiting with the limo and drove Stubby to the hotel in town where the lawyer had rented a room for the day. "Hi, Stubby," he grinned, "how did you know I was dying for a chance to get out of the office and catch a flight over to the Island?"

"Little voice told me," she laughed. "You know me, I hear voices."

'Well, one thing about that," the lawyer grinned as he poured her a tall glass of ginger ale, "if you ever go broke, just walk into the welfare, tell them you hear voices, and they'll have to give you a handicapped pension . . . because they'll never be able to prove you don't hear voices!''

''Thank you for the ginger ale, and for coming over on such short notice.''

''So, how much of my highpriced advice do you need?''

''Just enough to get an asshole out of my house,'' she blurted. ''How in hell's own name did Earl wind up in my life again? What's he doing acting as if it all belongs to him?''

''You let him in,'' the lawyer said sternly. ''You let him think he was in charge.''

''Yeah,'' Wright echoed, ''where in hell you been the past eight months, anyway?''

''That long?''

''You think that's long,'' Wright shrugged, ''you should've been on my end of the stick.''

''Does he really have the right to live in that house?'' Stubby demanded.

''Not if you don't want him in it,'' the lawyer assured her. ''Ada might have been old, and she might have been sick, but she wasn't stupid. There isn't a loose end for Earl to pull.''

''I think he's my legal stepdad.''

''And I know you're old enough to appear in front of a judge and say you can't take any more of the man's interference,'' the lawyer said evenly. ''The way Ada set it up, you have me to look after the legal ins and outs, you have a chartered accountant and a bank manager, a whole pile of trustees and financial advisors to take care of the money, there are always Wright and Sharon to make sure you're properly and adequately babysat and supervised, and, yes, Earl can try, but he hasn't got a snowball's chance in hell unless you were to appear in front of the judge to say your heart is broken and won't heal without Earl's presence in your life.''

''Can you draw up whatever papers a person needs to kick another person out of her house?'' Stubby asked.

The lawyer reached into his briefcase, brought out a document and handed it to Stubby, who glanced at it and smiled contentedly.

''Remember what Ada told you,'' Wright lectured. ''Seek and you will find, knock and the door will be opened.'

The evening paper had arrived before they got home and Earl had already seen the advertisement Stubby had given to Wright that morning.

''What is the god damned meaning of *this?*'' Earl raged, shoving the paper in Stubby's face.

''Just exactly what it says,'' Stubby assured him, taking off her jacket and hanging it in the hall closet. ''Come on, you old tart,'' she said, picking Daisy up and giving her a hug.

''An entire page!'' Earl roared.

''Didn't want anybody to miss it. And I don't know why you're having such a fit about it, there's nothing in there but the legally provable truth. My name is not Blades, it is Amberchuk. You are not my father. And this is not now, never has been and never will be *your* house.''

''Look at this!'' he spluttered. ''And at this!''

''That's right, Earl, you are here in exactly the same capacity as a freeloader. You don't contribute one thin dime to this place, it's all taken care of by Ada's setup. The taxes, the repairs, the food, everything comes out of the money Ada left to *me*. Your clothes, too, I understand, and your fancy office furnishings, new leather briefcases, matching watch, pen and pencil sets, imported shoes . . . you're a Scrooge when it comes to your money but a god damned unending maw when it comes to mine!''

''I'm your stepfather,'' he growled threateningly. ''Your legal guardian.''

''Yes to the first,'' she agreed. ''No to the second. You're here because Vinnie is my mother. Which is why she's here. And as far as I'm concerned, Vinnie doesn't really bother me, she can stay here if she wants. You, however, are another matter. I want you out of here. The sooner the better.''

''You can't,'' he stared. ''You wouldn't. You won't.''

''I will,'' she replied, ''just as sure as the pope is Catholic. Come on, Daisy, let's go see what Sharon has for supper.''

Right about then was when Earl hauled off and slammed Stubby across the face. Stubby stumbled, fell heavily against the doorjamb, Daisy's body taking the force of the fall. Daisy yelped, once, and Wright let fly a punch that didn't travel any more than four inches but laid Earl flat on his back in the hallway.

''She bit me,'' Stubby gasped, ignoring the rising bruise on her face and struggling up from the floor.

''C'mon, Stubby,'' Wright said, ''let's get her to the vet, quick.''

When they drove home three hours later, they did not have Daisy with them. She was unconscious in the veterinary clinic, and even the young vet was not sure she was going to live.

''It's my fault,'' Stubby sobbed. ''I was having so much fun telling Earl to get lost I walked right into it, and Daisy paid for me being so stupid.''

''Give yourself a break, will you?''

''It's true, though, isn't it.''

''Yeah, I guess it is. But don't be so hard on yourself, the asshole needed his toilet flushed.''

"Daisy didn't need her toilet flushed. Or her ribs broken or her lung pierced.''

"No,'' Wright agreed. "But that was Earl's doing, not yours.''

"She's as old as the rocks on the beach,'' Stubby mourned. "I mean, no human could live that long and not get on TV for it! I'm nearly eighteen and I bet I wasn't eight when I got her and she wasn't all that young then.''

"She's not that old,'' Wright argued. "Not for a terrier-type dog. I knew a woman one time had a terrier that was more than twenty-one years old. Not a tooth in its head, of course, and so stiff you had to dip it in olive oil every morning to get it moving around, but it was so old it made Daisy look like one of her own pups.''

"Is that true?'' Stubby demanded.

"God's truth,'' Wright insisted.

"What was the name of the woman who had that old dog and where did she live?''

"Her name was Katherine Jane Wright, she was my mother, she lived in Hamilton, the goddam dog's name was, if you believe it, Tinker, and I hated the rotten mutt,'' Wright recited.

"Really?''

"No,'' he said, "I made it all up to make you feel better. I never even *had* a mother, I was just suddenly there one day, full grown and full of lies. I'm not really a human person at all, I am an angel of god come to earth to do good deeds.''

"Hamilton, Ontario?''

"Where else?''

"You poor thing,'' she teased, and was shocked to find herself grinning at Wright, while Daisy lay sedated in a wire cage in the vet's clinic, all broken in pieces from the corner of the doorjamb. Stubby thought ruefully she must have very little sympathy, compassion, loyalty or decency if she could smile at a time like that.

When they got home the whole sideshow was unfolding with boring predictability. Vinnie was huddled on the sofa with her hands over her ears, weeping bitterly, and Earl was raging like a fiend while two policemen stood against a wall looking as if they would give a week's pay to be anywhere else.

Stubby took one look and exploded. "Get that guy *out* of here!'' she demanded. "He doesn't belong here! It isn't his house, it's *my* house!''

The police could hardly believe that. Houses of the size and quality of the Richardson farmhouse do not usually belong to seventeen-year-old hysterics, although they do often belong to fifty-year-old hysterics.

"Arrest that man for assault," said Earl, pointing at Wright.

"Arrest him," Wright suggested, "Look what he did to Stubby's face! Not to mention, yet, the family dog."

"You're fired!" Earl screamed.

"You can't fire me," Wright laughed. "Only Stubby can fire me and she can't do that until she turns nineteen."

"Get me an aspirin," Vinnie moaned.

"Get your own aspirin," Stubby snapped, "it's your goddamn headache!"

"You watch your tongue," Earl threatened.

"You watch it," Stubby suggested, and, to make it easy for Earl to do that, she stuck it out at him. He tried to give her a second helping for the other side of her face, but one of the policemen grabbed his arm.

"What's going on here, anyway?"

"Here." Stubby handed over the eviction notice the lawyer had given her. "This is what's at the bottom of most of it."

Vinnie sobbed and wailed and howled and used up about a half box of tissues. Earl raged and roared but, escorted by the two policemen, finally went upstairs to pack.

"What are you crying about?" Stubby snarled. "It was my dog got hurt, not yours."

"I'm so sorry," Vinnie managed. "All I wanted was some peace and quiet, and now look what's happened."

"You don't have to go," Stubby said. "It's Earl I can't stand. You, I could probably live with. For a while, anyway."

Vinnie blew her nose and wiped her eyes. She stared long and hard at Stubby.

"You're my mom," Stubby said, "and that counts. It counts for a lot. But that husband of yours makes my ass ache."

When Earl left, he left all by himself. Except for the two policemen.

The vet phoned first thing the following morning to tell a dry-eyed Stubby that Daisy had gone to join Dave and Ada in that place where time means nothing and the scent of apple blossoms fills the air.

9

Heading north up what once was a twisty cowpath and is now Commercial Street in Nanaimo, you turn right at the five and dime, go down Bastion Street and turn right again into a small, nameless alley. Six steps into the alley, on your left, there is a small doorway, no name, no number, no identifying mark at all. If you have a key, and only if you have a key, you can unlock the door and step into another kind of world.

The law requires you to be nineteen or over to have a key; the law requires you to be of legal age to unlock the door and step into that different world. Stubby had learned from Ada that what the law said it required had very little to do with what you could have, be, accomplish or get—if you had enough money. Nobody in the club ever asked Stubby how she obtained her key or if she were old enough to have it. Nobody asked for identification, nobody asked that she be vouched for by a member in good standing. Everyone assumed all this had somehow been taken care of, else how could Stubby have the key.

Not much of a club. Nothing fancy at all. Just tables covered with green felt, bright but non-glaring lights, a hotplate with coffee pots, an electric kettle, a refrigerator that looked as if it belonged in somebody's kitchen, and in it, fresh cream for the coffee, fruit juice with member's names or initials marked on it, bottles of ginger ale, Coca-Cola, 7-Up, Schweppe's tonic water, again, marked with names and initials. A couple of sagging sofas the Goodwill and Salvation Army wouldn't have anything to do with, a big stuffed chair with arms stained by so many unidentifiable substances they looked black and felt hard as slate, and a huge motley-coloured cat Stubby was sure got called a different name by every member of the club.

And decks and decks and decks of cards. Still in their packages, seals unbroken. Crates of them.

Every player paid so much per hour to sit at the table and that money went to the house, to pay the taxes or the bookkeeper or something. Ten percent of every pot went to the dealer, which was probably the same thing as having it go to the house. Ten dollars a month membership fee, whether you played or not. And if you wanted a grilled cheese sandwich and fries from the Busy Bee, a package of smokes from the Met or another bottle of whatever was your pleasure from the liquor store, the boy would go get it for you, and it was a matter of pride and honour to tip him. After all, other than a minimal sum every week for sweeping out the place and keeping the crapper clean, that was how the boy made his wages. The boy was at least sixty-six years old, withered and humourless, his eyes so tired of looking at the iniquities of human life they had started to close. He had two favourite jokes: ''You're a fine pair you three if ever there was one, coming in at this hour of the night, three o'clock in the morning, well if you think you're staying here you'd better pack and leave,'' and ''Pare me a pair of pears, dearie, pare me a pair of pears.'' Stubby could not for the life of her figure out what it was about either of those jokes that was funny. One night a prawn fisherman told a joke was about a semiliterate who wound up by mistake at a cocktail party and heard the host referred to as ''the venerable gentleman with the horn-rimmed spectacles.'' Attempting to seem as if he belonged at the party, the semi-literate went out of his way to mention the host and mistakenly described him as ''the venereal old fart with the horny testicles.'' Most of the people in the club howled with laughter, but the boy tsk-tsk'ed and said repeatedly, ''Crude, not funny, crude.'' Stubby was never after sure if the boy had a warped sense of humour or no sense of humour at all.

They sat on the couches and chairs drinking beer or wine or whatever it was they had brought, going to the fridge for their personal mix, rye and Coke, rye and ginger, rye and ice water, gin and tonic, rum and water, vodka and orange juice, tequila and grapefruit juice, mixing their own, many of them more at home here than they were with their families. From time to time one of them would go get the bucket with sand in the bottom and empty the ashtrays full of squashed butts, sodden chewed cigars, gum wrappers and plastic tips from Old Port cigarillos. They talked of fishing and logging, real estate and the clinker-built they had just bought, or planned at some time to buy. They talked of everything except home and family.

Stubby wasn't the only woman in the club. But she was the youngest, and for a brief period of time that was an advantage. They didn't expect her to have the icewater-and-steel nerves of a go-for-the-throat gambler.

The first few times she took the pot they shrugged and said "Beginners luck," or "That'll do for starters, kid.' But all good things come to an end, and soon Stubby was known as a real card player, not just a tourist, a visitor or a sheep to be fleeced.

"Who taught you to play?" they growled.

"I'm still learning," she replied, and they nodded.

Nobody hustled her, nobody stared at the third button down on her shirt, nobody eyed her arse as she walked over for another ginger ale and ice, nobody invited her to go smelt fishing at Departure Bay or bird watching up behind the army camp. They were there to play cards; they weren't there to waste time.

"I don't think it's . . . right," Vinnie said.

"Mom," Stubby spoke gently but clearly, "butt out, will you?"

"But . . . what about school?"

"I've finished high school," Stubby shrugged.

"Well then, what about . . . a job?"

"If I'm real lucky, I'd get a job that paid me maybe four-fifty or five dollars an hour. For a forty-hour week that's at most two hundred dollars. Minus income tax, unemployment insurance, this tax, that tax and carpet tax. I'd be lucky to come home with a hundred and twenty dollars. Times four weeks in a month, that isn't five hundred dollars. For which I would have to grin, shuffle, duck, smile, buck and wing and kiss foot." She would have said ass, but occasionally she remembered to modify her language when talking to her one and only biological mother.

"And I'd have to buy the right kind of clothes, the right kind of shoes, have my hair done a certain way and we must not forget the stuff for my face and fingernails. Which would leave me with how much?" She pulled out the small black leather wallet Ada had given her long years earlier. "Here." She handed her mother five hundred dollars. "The past two nights have been slow," she said easily. "Tonight ought to be better. The herring fleet is in."

Vinnie stared at the money, then handed it back. "Keep it," Stubby laughed. "It's yours. Happy Birthday, or Merry Christmas, or whichever is closest."

"Mine," Vinnie stared. "What for?"

"For being a lot more fun than you used to be."

"Why, what a nice thing to say!" Vinnie blushed, almost bursting with happiness. "I could buy a shovel and some seeds and bedding plants," she planned eagerly, "and maybe fix up that area around the back fence. There aren't many flowers around this place."

"Just a few with lots of perfume," Stubby agreed. "Ada couldn't see them, so she chose by smell."

"You wouldn't mind?" Vinnie hesitated, remembering how Stubby had reacted to Earl's attempts to take control of the grounds.

"Momma," Stubby said clearly, "anything you want to do, you do. If you want a greenhouse, tell Wright and he'll get the nursery guys to come out, find the best place, set it up and get you going."

"Are you sure?"

"Sure I'm sure. Go for it!" She kissed Vinnie's cheek, then went to her bathroom to shower so she could have a good sleep in her room with the blinds closed to keep out the sunlight. She wanted to be wide awake and alert for the herring fleet. Some of them thought they were real live gamblers.

The game lasted three days and when it ended Stubby had a pocket full of money and half interest in a herring boat. The former owner shrugged, no hard feelings, and went home to tell his wife. Stubby didn't waste two seconds wondering what he would say or how his wife would take it. If you can't afford to bleed, don't play with a sharp knife.

She stepped out into the alley and blinked in the early twilight, adjusting her eyes not to the brightness or darkness, but to the freshness of the air. She walked to the lot where her car was parked, unlocked her door, got in and drove from the city down the highway toward Bright's Crossing and home. She parked her car and went into the house yawning, feeling the sand and gravel collecting behind her eyes.

"Want anything to eat?" Sharon offered.

"No, thank you," Stubby grinned. "I've been eating prawn and crab for three days. How is everything?"

"Just fine," Sharon assured her. Stubby headed upstairs, wanting nothing more than a bath and her own bed.

She was in a tub full of hot water, more asleep than awake, when Vinnie came in without knocking. Stubby opened one eye, closed it again and wondered about privacy.

"Three days," Vinnie said dramatically, "sitting in a smoky room with an assortment of males of various ages and natures. Gambling."

"I'm tired, Vinnie," Stubby yawned. "Later. Please."

"What kind of life is that for a young girl?" Vinnie asked, "Is this preparing you for marriage? Is this preparing you for your role as the mother of children?"

"Whoa, hey, hang on." Stubby sat up in the tub, shaking her head. She felt as if she had missed several chapters and installments. "I'm not getting married, and I don't think I'm having kids. Not ever. Period."

"Not. . . but *why*?"

"Why?" Stubby echoed. "You should ask me why? You? Of all people? A better question would be why you want me to make the same mistake you made! What is this, every generation has to reinvent the wheel? Twice you got married, and both times you ended up looking just about as happy as a dog shitting shingle nails. Now you want I should do it too? What are you? My mother or my enemy? All I want to do is go to bed and get enough sleep that when the Yank sailors come down from shooting guns at their little yellow submarine at the test range, I can help separate them from their US dollars.''

''Well, then,'' Vinnie snapped, ''if you don't have any intention of getting married, why are you hanging around that awful place with all those men?''

''Momma.'' Stubby gave up on any idea of having a pleasant bath. She pulled the plug and stepped naked from the water, not even bothering to wrap a towel around herself. Vinnie politely averted her eyes. ''Listen, if you want to write long soap operas in your head, you go for it, but leave me out of them. No more pulp romances about me and all the terrible things that might happen. I am not going to wind up four months pregnant and no excuse for it.''

Vinnie's face reddened. ''That's none of your business,'' she said coldly.

''It must be my business,'' Stubby could feel herself getting very angry, ''if *my* sex life or lack of it is your business. You want me to butt out of your sex life? Then you butt out of mine.''

She walked, naked and still damp, from the bathroom to her bed, and Vinnie followed. ''This,'' Stubby yelled, ''is my room, and I want to go to sleep.''

''Oh god,'' Vinnie mourned, ''where did I go wrong? I'm sorry, okay? Is that what you wanted to hear? All right, Sheilagh, I'm sorry. You hear me? I'm sorry!''

Vinnie sat on Stubby's bed, leaning against the headboard, eyes closed, streaming tears. Stubby lay down beside her and pulled the covers around herself, hoping that was the end, but it was only the beginning. Vinnie set out to explain. Stubby tried to listen. But she kept drifting in and out of the sleep she so badly needed, so what she heard made virtually no sense at all, like snatches of conversations overheard in elevators, or when you walk past a table in a pub or a restaurant.

'' . . . I mean Bunny Pembroke had been doing it for a year and nothing happened to her, and Audrey Shakley and, oh, lots of others, and anyway nobody had ever really said what it was I wasn't supposed to do, as if I was supposed to have been born just knowing. . . .''

'' . . . and even if he wasn't exactly our kind of people, he was nice, and always joking, and had muscles like nobody else I knew . . .''

'' . . . dance at the Speedway Hall, and they had run out of fruit juice and I never did like Coke. . . .''

'' . . . nobody told me it was s-l-o-e, I thought it was o-w, like in slow. Momma had always told me not to be what she called fast and slow is the very opposite of that, so. . . .''

'' . . . it was just that once. . . .''

'' . . . you'd think if a thing was bad, it would *seem* bad instead of. . . unimportant. . . .''

'' . . . couldn't stand the thought of them ranting and raving. . . .''

'' . . . just didn't want to be touched any more, that's all. . . nobody ever seemed to care very much whether or not I *felt* anything. . . .''

'' . . . what seemed unimportant started to seem. . . boring. . . and then. . . unwelcome. . . and then, finally. . . it was ghastly. I guess anything you don't *want* to do can become something you want to *not* do. . . if you take my meaning.'

''Then why did you marry Earl?'' Stubby muttered. ''I mean, if you didn't want Dave to touch you, why would you want that guy. . . ?''

''What was I supposed to do?'' Vinnie said, her voice icy cold again. ''How much would I have made at a job? And who'd have looked after you while I was at work?''

''Then why did you fight Dave for custody?'' Stubby was wide awake now but unable to look at Vinnie in case the sight of her face pushed Stubby into physically expressed anger. Which in Bright's Crossing is called ass-kicking fury.

''You're my daughter!'' Vinnie sounded as if she thought Stubby was paddling backward.

''And so because I'm your daughter you marry Earl, lie to Dave, kidnap me and move to Arsehole Heights?''

''It got us away from Dave,'' Vinnie defended.

''I didn't *want* to be away from him!'' Stubby roared.

Vinnie shrugged helplessly.

''And now look at you!'' Stubby raged. ''Married to Earl, and you don't want to live with *him* either.''

''No,'' Vinnie agreed. ''I don't want to live with him. I don't want to live with him ever again. I thought he was so different from Dave in so many ways he'd be different from him in that way, too, but he wasn't. If anything he was worse. At least Dave understood the meaning of the word no. Earl still hasn't learned that.''

''Jesus love us. . . ,'' Stubby breathed, realizing what it was Vinnie was unable to put into words.

''Well,'' Vinnie forced a smile. ''It isn't all bad, you know. Since the big stink, when you turfed Earl out on his ear, I've been able to wean myself off my pills.''

"Huh?" Stubby's eyes widened. "You didn't say anything."

"Well, a person doesn't like to say she's going to stop something when she's been denying for years that there was any problem," Vinnie blushed. "Besides, I wasn't sure I'd be able to, so why have everybody expecting something that might never happen?" She examined her fingernails as if the answer to all questions was engraved upon them. "I asked Sharon who Ada's doctor was and I went to him," she confessed. "He's an acupuncturist. And I made Sharon and Wright promise not to say anything to you."

"Oh, Momma," Stubby sighed, suddenly very sad and very tired. "All that stuff you didn't want. . .but if I don't want it, you worry. All that stuff you didn't like. . .and if I don't like it, there's something wrong with me."

"But. . ."

"But nothing!" Stubby flared. "Everything I do, you worry. Everything I don't do, you worry. And *nothing* that I do is good enough."

"All I ever wanted was for you to have a normal life."

"Normal?" Stubby sighed. "Where in hell would I learn normal, Momma? My dad ate pain pills and drank himself into a stupor because his leg was on fire twenty-four hours a day. And my mother popped uppers and downers, snapped in and out of absolute nutsiness with boring regularity and was accompanied by a perambulating peckerhead who didn't know no means no. Normal? Me? Momma, things that really happened seem unreal to me, and things that never happened make good sense. For jesus sake, Momma, I spent a lot of my childhood playing poker with a blind woman! Have you thought about that? It was a blind woman taught me how to *see*. And you want normal? I play poker in the club because it's fun, nobody bothers me and it's something I do very well. Very well, Momma. I can hold a deck of cards in my hand and *think* about the hand I want and nine times out of ten, I get it! I can hold dice in my hand and I can *see* them through the skin and bones and meat and muscle and veins. I can *see* the spots, Momma. And if I want a six, I get a six, if I want five, I get five.

"Stop talking insanity," Vinnie hissed.

"Insanity? What *I'm* talking is insanity! Did you hear anything of what *you* said? You want insanity, play back the story of your own life! That is insanity!"

"Sheilagh, you are overwrought," Vinnie said primly.

"Overwrought?" Stubby laughed hysterically. "And you, Momma, are you underwrought or just plain old everyday wrought?"

"All I ever wanted," Vinnie managed a kind of bedraggled pride, "was to just live my life without having everything in a total uproar. Some people bend over backward to avoid boredom; I'd have given my eye teeth for it! Oh, not the day-to-day awfulness of the same stupid jobs over and over again! That isn't boring, it's numbing. It's death come before you stop breathing. But that other kind of boring, where things are so nice and comfortable that you don't want anything to change. Where you can go to bed and relax and drift into sleep because it's welcoming, not because it's a great place to go to get away from everything."

"Momma." Stubby felt almost physically sick. "Momma, you don't have the slightest goddam idea of what you do or don't want. You don't have any idea at all what to believe and what not to believe."

"No," Vinnie admitted readily, "I don't. I mean . . . what is truth, you know?"

"No." Stubby's shoulders slumped. "No, I don't know what the truth is, or even if there is any truth."

"And you have *got* to stop believing those crazy things. Those things about being able to choose the poker hand you get dealt and seeing the spots on the dice right through your fist . . . if people hear you talking like that they'll lock you up and swallow the key."

"That's the trouble with this world," Stubby grumbled. "Every time you find the slightest trace of truth or magic someone comes along and locks you up or numbs you with pills or starts laughing so loud even you can't hear what you're saying."

She pulled on some clothes and left the room, knowing if she didn't Vinnie would stay to talk some more, and Stubby didn't want to talk or think or have to concentrate on not hauling off and giving Vinnie a good bop on the beezer. "There ought to be a law," she grumbled, "that you can't have kids until you know a thing or two!"

She sat on the banks of Haslam Creek watching the sunlight dancing on the water. She could smell the fresh tang of thimbleberry leaves, the heavy scent of wild lupin and the strange cloying perfume from the elderberry bushes. In a few days the elderberry perfume would change, become as unpleasant as tomcat spray, but right now, this afternoon at least, it wasn't the least bit nasty.

She was tired, her eyes swollen, her face stiff, and what she wanted to do was fling herself on the sun-warmed rocks and howl like she had never howled when she was younger. But she had no practice in howling or yowling and so she sat wishing the sky would become a huge school blackboard and the finger of God would write some directions for her.

The shimmering on the water increased as the sun moved higher in the pastel blue sky, Stubby's eyes watered and for a moment everything went wavery and blurred. Then she blinked rapidly several times, and the world looked as it always had.

A woman with curly red hair was walking along the bank of Haslam Creek, smiling softly and watching the silvery grey minnows zipping and darting in the warm shallows.

"I know you!" Stubby blurted.

"No," the woman grinned. "You don't know me, you just think you know me."

"No, I know you," Stubby insisted. "You're a friend of my dad's. Or you were," she amended.

"You've got a good memory," Estelle agreed, "but even so, that doesn't mean you *know* me."

"Oh god, philosophy on the creek bank," Stubby yawned. "Okay, I don't *know* you. But I've seen you before, a few years ago."

"Right," Estelle nodded. "When Dave was dying."

"He said you were his girlfriend." Stubby smiled softly, remembering. "And he said you were an angel of mercy."

"Well, there you have it," Estelle laughed, and sat down on the warm rock next to Stubby. "You look like you could use an angel of mercy yourself."

"No." Stubby managed a small, tight smile. "It's not mercy I'm trying to figure out, it's the truth."

"Oh," Estelle laughed softly, "the truth, eh? In twenty words or less?"

"I don't mind if it's more than twenty words," Stubby squinted, trying to see Estelle's face through the shimmering glare from the stream. "I'd rather have no words at all, mind you, I'm a bit sick and tired of words, words, words and none of them making much sense. But if words are all that you have, I'll take them."

"You don't like words?"

"I don't mind words. Except someties there are so many of them they get in the way. Symbols, now, they're something else."

"So you want symbols? You think symbols will help in your search for truth?"

"Probably not." She rubbed her eyes, but the glare wouldn't go away. She tried to put her back to the sun, but that didn't seem to work very well either. Maybe she was getting heatstroke. Maybe she spent so much time in the artificial light of the card room she was getting unused to fresh air and sunshine. Maybe she would develop an allergy to sunlight and have to live in a basement with fungus and toads.

"Maybe I need sunglasses," she said, rubbing at her eyes.

"Well," Estelle soothed, "not to worry. It's probably just my aura."

"Halo, you mean?" Stubby laughed. "Yeah, I guess an angel of mercy would have to have a halo.''

''Boy, you're thick.'' Estelle shook her head, pulled a package of cigarettes from her pocket, lit one and inhaled the smoke gratefully.

''Angels don't smoke,'' Stubby teased.

''Hey,'' Estelle chortled, ''about one out of every ten got to heaven early because of smoking. And hell is full of smokers.''

''I guess they're too busy shovelling coal into the devil's furnaces to have time to sit down for a cigarette.''

''Don't you believe it,'' Estelle contradicted. ''If beauty is in the eye of the beholder, so is everything else. The pinch-noses and tight-asses might think hell is an awful place, but sinners might think it's an okay place. I have always had a soft spot in my heart for sinners,'' she mused. ''They seem to have a better focus on things.''

''I guess Ada was a sinner,'' Stubby said slowly. ''She gambled for money, had a girlfriend and never went to church.''

''There you have it,'' Estelle agreed. ''She probably went to hell.''

''And Dave was a sinner for sure.''

''Oh, undoubtedly. One of the best.''

''Funny, huh.'' Stubby closed her eyes because the reflected glare from the creek was becoming uncomfortable. ''The best people in my life are the ones everybody's mother warns them are bad influences.''

''Holy Mother,'' Estelle sighed. ''You sure are dumb.''

''I beg your pardon?'' Stubby sat erect, opened her eyes wide, angry. Then closed her eyes quickly.

''Not an hour ago you told your mother you could hold a deck of cards in your hand and think about the cards you wanted and you got them! You told her you could hold a pair of dice in your hand and *see* the spots! You came so close to the truth then that you scared her, and scared yourself I suspect. Now you sit here squinting in the light from my nimbus, denying everything around you. If the best people in your life are sinners, what does that tell you about sin?''

''Are you saying there is no such thing as sin?'' Stubby deliberately avoided asking how Estelle knew about her heated discussion with Vinnie.

''Oh, there's sin all right,'' Estelle sighed, ''but it usually isn't what they'd have you believe it is. Hunger in a land of plenty is a sin. War. That thing over there.'' She pointed, and Stubby opened her eyes again and saw something white snagged to a berry bush overhanging the creek.

''That disposable diaper?''

''That plastic-lined abomination,'' Estelle agreed calmly. ''That plastic will still be cluttering up the surface of the planet when everyone alive today is dust. Disposable! They are about as disposable as nuclear waste. Which is another sin.'' She finished her cigarette, stubbed it out and immediately reached for her cigarette package. She put the crushed butt in the package and took out a fresh cigarette. ''I don't miss these in between trips back,'' she smiled, ''but as soon as I have lungs again you wouldn't believe how I feel!''

''Oh,'' Stubby shrugged, ''you know me, I'll believe anything.''

''No,'' Estelle said sadly, ''unfortunately, you won't believe anything. You're probably telling yourself I'm a bit tetched and you'll humour me in the hope I'll just drift off and you can forget me. You manage to forget a lot of things. And overlook a lot more.''

''Lady,'' Stubby said seriously, ''I am so mixed up right now that I don't know what to believe and what not to believe.''

''Try this,'' Estelle invited, pointing again. Stubby looked and froze. She would have looked away if she had been able, she would have closed her eyes, but they wouldn't close. And so she stared with disbelief at the shimmering light floating just above the surface of Haslam Creek, a shimmering light that almost, not quite, had a form, a shimmering light of silver and gold that drifted against the current, moving upstream in defiance of all the laws of nature.

''What is that?'' she managed.

''You know what it is,'' Estelle said firmly. ''You said you wanted a symbol, and there it is. That is truth. That is fate. That is understanding and compassion, that is . . . truth,'' she repeated.

''You mean it was no accident I found Daisy when I found her? Or that it was Daisy who led me to Ada. Or . . . that . . . ''

''You can't make lists and draw lines,'' Estelle said, her voice fading. ''There aren't any maps, with neat borders. The line between plain old ordinary everyday and magic hasn't been drawn.'' As Estelle's voice faded, so did the shimmering light floating against the current of Haslam Creek. Stubby blinked. She was alone on the sun-warmed rock, sitting a foot or two above the burbling water, watching a kingfisher zip up and down the stream. Just a plain old everyday kingfisher. But for the first time in her life Stubby Amberchuk really looked at the blue, grey, white and black wonder. Nothing magic about a kingfisher. Nothing magic about a rufous hummingbird zizzing around the berry bushes, dipping her beak into the hearts of the flowers, her wings moving so fast it almost looked as if she didn't have any. Nothing very magical about any of that. Stubby rubbed her face, then looked at her hands, flexed her fingers, tightened her fist, watched the movement of muscles in the backs of her hands, in her wrists and forearms. What was it the preacher had quoted at Dave's funeral, we are wonderfully and fearfully made? Wonder. Full.

And what was that thing that had floated upstream, anyway?

Stubby told the lawyer she wanted to travel and see the world for herself, she told her grandparents she felt she needed some experience with life before she shouldered her responsibilities, she told her mother she was taking an extended holiday, but she told Wright and Sharon the truth.

"I'm going in search of the Holy Grail."

Wright nodded understandingly and Sharon grinned.

"Ada would understand exactly." She dabbed at her eyes with a paper tissue. "And she would be glad to hear it."

"I wish I did," Stubby laughed. "I really do wish I understood even a little bit of what goes on in the world, or out of it, but I don't."

She had expected Vinnie to pitch a fit and was almost disappointed when that didn't happen. Vinnie nodded, then nodded again. "Will you be gone long?" she asked.

"I don't know," Stubby answered, "But for as long as you want to, you can live here. If you want to go to school, go to school. If you want to plant flowers, plant flowers. If you want Sharon to teach you gourmet cooking, household accounts and the brokerage business, she will. If you want Wright to teach you law, real estate or pool, he'll be glad to. There will always be money for food, clothes, gas, and the trips you've always wanted to take. The only restriction placed on anything is that, forever'n'ever-amen, that goddamned Earl does *not* set foot on my property or inside my house."

"You must try to learn not to hold grudges," Vinnie advised.

"I will hold grudges as long as I want," Stubby laughed, "and cherish them if that's how I feel. I will nurture them and clasp them to my bosom. I will even feed them vitamins to keep them strong and healthy. Not one foot. Not for a pleasant little lunch, not for supper, not overnight, not for a visit. If you want to talk to him, that's your business. Do it somewhere else. His nose is not to be put anywhere near *my* business."

"Sheilagh, those kinds of feelings can sour your life."

"Vinnie, listen and listen good. Earl can't leave things alone. Earl can't butt out. If you were to invite him here for lunch he'd be ordering Sharon around again after five minutes. He assumes, he presumes, and I've had it to the limit with that guy's buttinsky bullshit. Not one inch of space, not one cent of money. And if you do, that's it. You can go back to . . ." She let her voice trail off, and shrugged.

"I could, perhaps, meet him in town for lunch?"

"Sure. Whatever. But he does *not* come here for lunch! He's wiped, momma, wiped right off the map."

"Oh well, if that's how you feel about it, I guess that's how it'll be."

10

It isn't easy to find something if you don't know where to look. It is even harder to find something if they've told you to look in the wrong place. And almost impossible to find something if they've told you not only one wrong place, but several. The chances of finding something when they've not only given you a dozen red herring wrong places to search for it but managed to give you an absolutely wrong description of the thing, become quite minuscule.

Stubby thought she knew a fair bit about the Holy Grail. It was the silver chalice used by Christ at the Last Supper when he poured wine and presented it to his disciples to drink, saying, "This is my blood." After Christ was hung from the tree, or cross, Joseph of Arimathea took the chalice with him, but was imprisoned by the Jews and left in a dungeon for a year and a day without food or drink or even a toilet, but he remained alive and well and not even constipated, because he had the Grail with him. Stubby wasn't sure exactly what Joseph had used the Grail for, but there was no mention she could find of any festering piles of crap in any of the corners of the dungeon when Joseph was finally released by the Emperor Vespasian, who probably wouldn't have been moved to any kind of charity if it hadn't been for the fact he had started to rot. His fingers and toes had fallen off, his nose had started to disappear, and even though he was the Emperor and nobody dared say too much to him about it, the whispers were getting louder and louder and even Vespasian had heard the word *leprosy* echo in the halls of the palace.

One night, Vespasian was tortured with nightmares in which he saw himself falling apart inch by inch, a morsel, a bit, a piece at a time, and just before he vanished altogether, he dreamed of Joseph of Arimathea down in the dungeon. Vespasian awakened, the vision of Joseph still fresh in his mind, and saw by the light of the small lamp that flickered next to his bed that his fingers, toes, and diverse other extremities had regenerated and the scars and fissures on his body had healed. His excitement when he reached up and found his nose can only be imagined.

Vespasian was immediately converted to Christianity, and just as quickly, was hustling his Empiric self down the steps to the dungeon, key in hand. Clutching the chalice, Joseph was freed, and, as we can well imagine, hustled his butt as far from his prison as he could get.

Somehow, Joseph of Arimathea went to England. He established a shrine at Glastonbury and in the shrine kept the chalice now known as the Holy Grail.

There is no mention in any early records of a description of the shrine, what it was used for or how the Holy Grail figured in anything that went on there, but in any event, none of that matters. The Holy Grail disappeared. As did, it would seem, Joseph of Arimathea.

When next heard from, the Grail was kept in a magnificent temple governed by a queen named Dispenser of Joy. Dispenser of Joy was supposed to be married to a Moor and her son John was supposed to be the founder of the Knights Templar, a pagan group of women-worshipping warriors dedicated to the temple in which the Grail was kept, and equally dedicated to defending women and their religion that honoured women. Eventually they became a very popular group, and everyone forgot the Knights Templar had been started by a John whose father was, as they are apt to say, as black as the ace of spades. Especially since, in all the stories that contain good solid morals, it's the black knight who gets the stuffing beat out of him. Which is, incidentally, what happened to the Knights Templar, especially once the Inquisition caught wind of their ideas about women, who, as we all know, are conceived, born, raised in, prone to and full of sins of all kinds and sorts.

Stubby had some trouble with that part of the history of the Holy Grail. There seemed to be a number of contradictions there, but she wasn't really used to a lot of intellectual puzzling, so she didn't waste much time asking questions, like what was the chalice of a definitely anti-sexual Christian church doing in a temple built on top of a mountain called the Mount of Joy or the Mons Veneris, and how come it was being used as a symbol of sexuality and free love in an attempt to rally support against the Christian priests, who were declaring that even marriage itself was a sin and that the only way to enter the kingdom of God was voluntary, willing, eager, actual castration.

In any event, on Good Friday, 717 years after Christ died on the cross, the story was given by the ghost of Jesus himself to a Cistercian monk, who wrote it all down for posterity. It seems that a group of noble-minded Christian knights, the Knights of the Round Table, got hold of the Grail and in no time flat incredible things began to happen. One of the things Galahad, Parsifal and Lohengrin did was keep an eye on the rim of the sacred cup. Any time a woman needed help, the rim of the Grail would glow, the woman's name would appear in fiery letters along the rim, and one of the knights would ride off to the rescue.

Some said the Grail was a plain silver goblet, some said it had a fish engraved on the lip, some said it was studded with gems and that a giant ruby glowed from the middle. Nobody seemed too sure what it looked like, possibly because only one of the Knights of the Round Table ever got to see it. Only Galahad, who was actually Lancelot reincarnated free of sin in the person of his own son, ever actually saw the Holy Grail, and he left only incomplete and often contradictory descriptions.

Well yes, Parsifal and Lohengrin saw it, but they weren't really Knights of the Round Table, so even if they had been able to describe the chalice, who would have listened?

If she was not exactly of an intellectual bent, Stubby Amberchuk was definitely of an adventuresome bent, and she had everything anybody would need to set out on a quest. Now, it is true, Stubby did not wrap herself in chain mail, crawl into a suit of clanking armour, get herself hoisted up on top of an enormous war horse the approximate size of a full-grown Belgian gelding and ride off clanking and sweating and scaring children, dogs and sober citizens, nor did she yell things like zounds, huzzah and oyez. But she did have several good pairs of jeans, a number of cotton shirts, her team jacket with its collection of crests and awards and a good pickup truck. She also had her softball glove and her inheritance, and a fair bit of experience with people of every possible sort and ilk. What more could you need? It was certainly at least as much as the Knights of the Round Table had, and undoubtedly more than Joseph of Arimathea who, as we all remember, did not have so much as a pot in which to relieve himself.

Stubby drove from city to city in search of the Holy Grail, and in every place where she stopped for gas, for a meal, for a motel or hotel room, or even for a visit to that room usually out behind the gas station, Stubby studied the phone book. In vain she searched for descendants of the ones who had last seen the Holy Grail. She found Smiths and Joneses, she found Thomases and O'Reillys, she found Finkelsteens and Finklesteins, she found Whites, Blacks, Browns, Greys and Greens, but she did not find one single Galahad. Nor did she find even a Parsifal or Lohengrin, although she did find several Percys, Persivals and any number of Parsons but, day by day, mile by mile, week by week, month by month, no sign of any descendants of those who might have managed to pass down any clues to the size, dimensions, appearance or hiding place of the Holy Grail.

Stubby paid cash for an ongoing advertisement to be run in the Information Wanted section of the classified ads in all the major and minor newspapers of the land.

> REWARD
>
> Substantial reward offered for information leading to discovery of Holy Grail. Please contact if you have any information. Discretion assured.

Her advertisement had her up to her ears in discreet and understated business cards from psychiatrists, psychologists and lifestyle counselors and up to her hips in copies of historical texts, novels, compilations of poetry and theses proving and disproving everything under the sun.

A little old lady in Courtenay harangued Stubby for an entire weekend, telling her about the British Israelites, the tribe of Benjamin, the migration of the Celtic people from Persia and the Ukraine through Europe to Ireland and the British Isles. She explained in all seriousness that any Scots tartan which had as part of its pattern a yellow stripe was an identifying mark of the Lost Tribes of Israel and of the clans which once had served as Guardians of the Grail. She showed Stubby a pewter goblet she said was a precise replica of the original Grail, fashioned in the year 62 A.D.

Stubby held the replica reverently. She turned it to the light, her fingers stroking it. Then she turned it over and saw the imprint on the bottom.

"Made in Japan?" she queried suspiciously.

"That," the little old lady said with a sweet smile, "is to fool burglars and those others."

"What others?" Stubby asked.

"You know," the old lady smiled. "You know. Them."

"Oh," Stubby agreed. "Them. Of course."

She paid the old lady two hundred and sixty-six dollars and took the pewter goblet with her. The burly guy at the pawnshop looked at the goblet, tapped it, scratched the rim and shrugged. "Circa 1950," he guessed. "Worth maybe ten dollars."

"Thank you," she smiled.

"No problem. Say, if you're interested in pewter I've got a basement full of it."

"You wouldn't happen to have the Holy Grail in your basement, would you?"

"Sorry," he chortled, "but if you're looking for Aladdin's lamp . . ."

"Maybe later." She headed for the door. "After I've found the Grail."

She got drawings in her post office box, she got paintings, she got embroidered pillowslips and tea towels, she got poems, she got short stories, she even got a gingerbread cookie shaped like a wine glass.

She did not have to combat evil knights, dragons or many-headed monsters, but she did have to get valve jobs, oil changes, new tires, new air and water hoses, and always gas, oil, antifreeze and properly inflated tires. She endured White Spot food, Holiday Inn beds and traffic lights cunningly timed to keep traffic choked and drivers fuming. She drove past mile after mile after mile of waving wheat, waving flax, waving barley and the Pampers tossed with cavalier disregard for civility, politeness and sanitation from the windows of Buicks and Oldsmobiles to land on lawns, flowerbeds, ditches, sidewalks and cemeteries, by people loud in their condemnation of government and industry for non-ecological practices and polluting megaprojects.

As has possibly been said before, through pleasures and palaces though I may roam, over hill and dale as I hit the dusty trail, onward and upward excelsior no matter where you start, how long you go or how far you've come, sooner or later, there you are.

Staring with a degree of dismay at what is left of your once new pickup truck. You'd think you'd be safe parking properly on a quiet street in a quiet town in a quiet province of a quiet country on a quiet spring day while you go in a small, quiet cafe for a grilled cheese sandwich and a quiet cup of coffee. But all it takes is one paunchy Kinsman and several salty margaritas and that, as they say, is that, and nothing left to do but stare in dismay and thank all the saints, gods, and goddesses you weren't sitting inside looking at a road map at the time of impact.

Of course, it's no huge financial upset. But once you've managed to extricate what is left of your stuff from the twisted heap of metal and ruptured upholstery, and checked your justifiably upset self into a modest hotel, there is no way to avoid it. There you are, on a car lot, looking for a replacement.

Do you want help? What help could there be? Six cylinders or eight? Standard or automatic? How about four-wheel drive? CB radio? Tape deck? Ford, GMC, Chev, Toyota, Datsun, long box, short box or standard? Blue, red, burgundy, yellow, pumpkin orange or black and red with white stripes? With or without the little lights on top, the ones they cover up with the plastic or leather happyface hoods? Plain or with options? Diesel, gasoline or propane powered?

"Oh my stars," Stubby sighed, "there has to be an easier way. A better way."

"There is only one Way," he said softly, "although there are many false and seeming ways."

"Huh?" Stubby gaped and turned and gaped all over again. The used car salesman gazed at her as if she wasn't really there or, if she was, he was seeing right through her to something far more wonderful than anything she could ever be or even imagine. "How unfathomable is the Way," he nodded. "It is like unto the emptiness of a vessel, yet, as it were, the honoured Ancestor of us all. Using it, we find it inexhaustible, deep and unfathomable. Pure and still is the Way. I do not know who generated it. It may appear to have preceded God."

"Huh?" she repeated.

"Om," he replied, again nodding, again smiling. "Om mani padme hum."

"Oh," Stubby managed.

"Om," he corrected, still gently.

"Om?" she hazarded.

"Om," he approved, smiling widely, and for the first time during their conversation, if in fact that was what it was, he focused his eyes on her. There wasn't a single thing about him that resembled in any way, shape, or form Dave Amberchuk. Maybe that's why just looking at him reminded Stubby of all the good times she and Dave had shared, before the deranged and deformed cells had begun to spread, before good times became a thing of the fondly remembered past. Dave was blocky and powerful, this guy was slender and probably needed help to twist off his own beer caps. All of the Amberchuks, especially Dave, had been blessed with brown hair and brown eyes, and this guy had very black hair and very blue eyes, a combination Stubby immediately decided was about as gorgeous as you could ever want. Stubby knew that if it wasn't exactly the hand of God sent the Kinsman into her pickup, it was at least the finger of fate. This gave every promise of being something at least as much fun as sliding from second to third, or leaping as high as you could, stretching as far as you could to trap what otherwise might prove to be at least a two-bagger, maybe even a home run.

But while Stubby loved to gamble, Stubby was not a fool. She knew all about drawing to an inside straight, she knew about hitting seventeen when playing against the dealer. Stubby ummed and aahed and killed some time, then went back to her modest hotel and got out the phone book. She didn't look for Parsifal, Lohengrin, Galahad or any of the descendants. She looked for a physician. She made an appointment for ten o'clock the next morning, and by ten thirty, Stubby had been fitted with a diaphragm. By noon she was back at the used car lot. Shortly thereafter she was having lunch with the slender black-haired blue-eyed used car salesman and after lunch they started test-driving pickup trucks.

"Oh, yes," he said, very pleasantly and openly, "it's quite well known although not commonly accepted, women have far more spiritual energy than men do, and a man can achieve realization of divinity only by total union with the female energy source."

"You're kiddin'," Stubby marvelled. "I never heard that!"

"Well," he admitted, "it isn't a Christian concept. It's Tantric."

"It's what?"

"Tantric."

"Tantrum?"

"Tan*tric*."

"Oh."

"Om."

"Yeah, right. Om," she beamed happily. He smiled, and took another good look at her and began immediately to plan achieving some realization of divinity. They had supper together, went for a walk in the quiet park, then Stubby invited him back to her quiet and modest hotel room. Within half an hour, neither of them was either quiet or modest and Stubby discovered that yes, by golly, it certainly was as much fun as sliding from second to third, no doubt about it at all. All thought of hitting the road vanished. All thought of the Holy Grail went right out the window. Stubby applied herself to her new recreation as wholeheartedly as she had ever applied herself to anything, even if she did not chant Om mani padme hum throughout the entire pleasurable endeavour, as did Lotzi, the used car salesman.

"Why do you do that?" she asked, yawning.

"I am trying to achieve realization of divinity," he explained.

"Yeah?"

"It means," he said indulgently, "the Jewel in the Lotus."

"That's going to help you achieve realization of divinity? Humming the Jewel in the Lotus?"

"No," he laughed. "This is the jewel, and that is the lotus."

"So why humm?" Stubby asked.

"A man has to store up his vital fluids. The vital fluids, if they aren't wasted, will rise up the spinal column, up through the chakras, to the head, and that," he smiled smugly, "leads to the realization of divinity. And creative inspiration, divine wisdom and total bliss."

"Wow," Stubby marvelled. "Teach me how."

"Don't be silly," he laughed. "Women can't do it."

"Oh," she said. "Why not?"

"Because," he said.

"Who figured all this out?" she asked.

"The Vratyas."

"The who?"

"Vratyas."

"What are Vratyas?"

"They were the foremothers of the devadasis, or sacred harlots."

"Where?" she demanded.

"India," he yawned, and then he closed his beautiful big blue eyes, and went to sleep. Stubby lay awake wondering how in the name of logic and reason something figured out by a bunch of holy whores could be impossible for a woman to learn. Enough of the women on the ball teams Stubby had played with had been married, or at least involved, that Stubby had grown up knowing all the jokes about Wham, bam, thank you man, and Yeah sure, Don Juan, Juan and he's Don. Stubby had also heard more times than she had wanted to what her mother's opinion of it all was and had, more times than she could count or even estimate, sung at one campfire or another the opinion of a possibly mythical Queen of Spain on the brevity of pleasure, the longevity of pain. So nothing had prepared her for hours and hours and, yes, hours of sensation, pleasure and exhaustion.

"How can it be Tao?" she puzzled. "You said it was Tantric."

"It is." He looked up from his navel, which he had been contemplating for over an hour and a half. "After all, whether it's Catholic, Lutheran, Baptist or Anglican, it's supposed to be Christian, isn't it? Well then," he shrugged, as if that explained it all, and returned to gaze at his bellybutton.

Stubby moved from the quiet, modest hotel room to a little house she rented and filled with furniture. Every day she got up, made breakfast and took it on a tray to the bedroom where Lotzi was waiting, naked and crosslegged in the middle of the empress-sized waterbed. When he had eaten more than you would have thought his slender body could hold, he chanted for a while, lay down and went to sleep. While he was sleeping, Stubby tidied up the house, cooked lunch and took it to him. When he had eaten lunch, he got up, had a shower, shaved, brushed his teeth and went to the living room to watch television while Stubby stripped and changed the sheets, made the bed and then did the laundry. When Lotzi's drawstring pants were dry and his pyjamas ironed to his satisfaction, Stubby started supper. She could, of course, have avoided all this time-consuming twaddle by hiring a maid, but Lotzi said he didn't want any foreign vibrations in the house, he had all he could do to stay in touch with Stubby's yin and his yang and his efforts to attain enlightenment and achieve realization of divinity.

"Yin?" she asked. "Yang?" she queried. And so he explained, but Stubby wasn't at all sure she had understood it all. She wasn't even sure she had heard it all. It took her a long time to figure out something was not happening.

"Oh, no!" Lotzi exclaimed, horrified. "It would dangerously deplete my vital forces!"

"It doesn't seem to be depleting mine," Stubby countered, stroking his back and trying to learn how to direct energy through her fingertips to his various chakras. "I've never felt better in my entire life," she grinned.

"That is because, as I explained to you earlier, women possess far, far more spiritual energy than men do."

"What I'm talking about, Lotzi my love," she purred, "is more on the level of the physical and biological than the spiritual."

"All things are part of the All," he sighed.

"I've heard that," she agreed, spreading warm-scented oil on the soft skin of his buttocks, kneading the flesh with her strong basewoman's hands.

"Everything," he sighed, "is Everything. Even the emptiness of the vessel is Everything."

"If it's empty," Stubby mused, "there's nothing there."

"Om mani padme hum," he droned pleasantly.

"So. . . are you saying Nothing is Everything? Or Everything is Nothing?" But for the next several hours his communication was nonverbal and she never did get that question answered.

Night followed day, day followed night. Lotzi gave up selling vehicles so that he could concentrate totally on trying to achieve realization. He never questioned Stubby about her ability to pick up the tab for the rent, the food, the protein supplement, the vitamins and the books and magazines he needed to research his quest for knowledge. His questions were highly arcane and exotic, and no more involved day-to-day hard-nosed reality than anything you would expect to hear from any five-year-old.

For a time Stubby's every thought, response and feeling was focused on Lotzi, but gradually she began to feel it was almost impossible to focus on a sleeping body. Lotzi slept entire afternoons and evenings, waking only for meals or his favourite TV programs. He said he wasn't really sleeping, he was contemplating, and who knows, perhaps he was, but his contemplations were often punctuated with loud and often adenoidal snores.

There is a limit to how much of your energy can be burned off in the cleaning, washing, waxing and polishing of a house, especially if you are accustomed to entire weekends of softball tourneys and twenty-mile bike rides. Stubby began to look beyond the boundaries of the empress-sized waterbed, beyond the front and back doors of the love nest, and found a library just around the corner.

She had read in school, had read for pleasure, had read for information and read because she was bored and there was nothing else to do. Now she read to fill something in her and her life, something she did not recognize as a great gaping maw. She read poetry and she read novels, she read history and she read the compilations of the mythologies of past, lost and forgotten civilizations.

When not reading, she looked for things to read, and gradually she began again to pore through phone books and city directories looking for any name that even remotely resembled the name of any of the Knights of the Round Table. Mythology, folklore and fiction are full of stories of secrets handed from father to son, clues passed from mother to daughter, and when all is said and done, you just never know.

Once a week she phoned home and talked to Vinnie, Wright and Sharon, and from time to time she sent postcards. She remembered birthdays and her grandparents' wedding anniversaries, but only with the outer edges of her awareness. Basically Lotzi was still everything. Life went on hold while he was asleep and clicked into high gear when he opened his beautiful blue eyes.

Lotzi was kind and gentle, he was warm and loving, he seemed everything she had always hoped other people could be. If some of the illustrations and pictures in his research material bothered Stubby, she had no vocabulary to explain why, and Lotzi just laughed off her tentative efforts to verbalize her hesitation. He told her she was uninformed and unenlightened and anyway, they had both been brought up by people who were so repressed themselves they had been sadly repressive. That certainly seemed true of Vinnie, who made no secret of the fact she considered sex a pain in the ass, and Earl most definitely had been in the front ranks of the repressive and oppressive, and what had Dave ever really known of anything? Stubby knew that she herself was woefully ignorant, so whatever information Lotzi allowed her to have was a bonus. She wasn't going to refuse any of it even if the illustrations did look more than a bit low-rent. But without knowing it had happened, somewhere, somehow the worm of doubt had chewed its way into the apple of contentment.

"Stubby," he crooned, reaching for her. "Stubby, I'm trying for the final flowering of revelation. When it happens, even you will see an invisible light emanating from the top of my head.''

"If it's invisible, I won't see it, even if I have my eyes open,'' she said.

"You'll feel it, Stubby. You'll know.''

"Yeah?''

"Yeah,'' and so she went along with it, but even Stubby knew she was feeling definitely unwilling about it all, not just because of the grotty pictures, not just because of the incipient backache, but because of something else, something she couldn't name, but could taste, like ashes, in her mouth.

"I just don't understand why you go to such lengths to avoid orgasm,'' she said. "It's the best part of it. I mean . . . without it, why bother?''

"You say that because you're a woman, and totally unenlightened.''

"Lotzi,'' she took a deep breath and dared herself to slide right into it. "You told me you could realize divinity only through sexual and emotional union with a woman. With me.''

"Yes,'' he said, with that tone of overly-patient indulgence almost guaranteed to kick off an axe murder.

"How do you expect to achieve any kind of emotional union with someone you consider to be a sap?'' She did not raise her voice, she did not pound her fist, she did not stamp her foot, but the effect on Lotzi was almost electrifying. He actually opened his eyes and sat bolt upright, obviously startled. "I don't feel very emotionally united with you,'' Stubby continued quietly. "You tell me I'm too stupid to understand, you tell me I'm unenlightened and an empty vessel and . . . I'm not. I'm just as smart as you are.'' He shot her a look of what might have been anything from suspicion to envy to hate to distrust to spite. But what she said had hit home. He chewed on it for a while. Then he nodded, took a deep breath, almost thought better of the idea, then risked much in order to have a chance at Everything.

"I probably could achieve realization much more easily if I had a teacher,'' he said, "but it's very hard to find anyone who knows the secrets and can speak English. Especially here, in what can only be called the mid-Bible belt. I told you women possess much more spiritual energy than men do. And a man can achieve realization of . . .''

"Lotzi,'' she sighed, "will you please stop saying the same incomprehensible things over and over and over again as if repetition was explanation?''

"Well, even if all *my* vital fluids climb up my chakras, rise up my spinal column and collect in my head . . . it isn't enough. But if I practice enough, I can learn to absorb with my Jewel the fluids engendered by the orgasm of your Lotus. I can then concentrate and have *your* vital fluids climb my spinal cord, go through my chakras, to mix with my own, and I'll achieve total realization of creation and divinity.''

Stubby stared at him for a long time. A very long time. A dangerously long time. ''Then it wouldn't matter if it was *me* or any other woman on the face of the earth,'' she said quietly.

''Everyone is part of the All,'' he agreed.

''And you aren't really interested in whether or not I enjoy all these goings-on, or whether I attain orgasm, as long as the old Lotus does, right?''

''Om,'' he agreed.

''I not only come second, I come further behind than second, or even third or tenth. I, me, Stubby Amberchuk, don't count at all.''

''Om.''

''I thought we were making love,'' she laughed softly, mocking herself. ''I mean, here I've been all this time working, as they say, under a delusion of my own making. I thought you kind of liked *me*, and wanted *me* to enjoy our lovemaking, but *we* weren't making love at all; I might have been, but you were just lying there sucking up my energy!''

''Yin is known to be much more powerful than Yang. And it regenerates about four times as fast, too. Believe me, Stubby, it would take at least four men to actually *drain* your energy. I'm just . . . tapping into it, that's all.''

''Oh,'' she said, very quietly, ''that's all, huh?'' She wanted to yell, shout, stamp, rage, rant and rave, but she had heard more than once that old truism about catching more flies with honey than with vinegar. ''Well, if Yin is that powerful and everything . . . if I stop having orgasms, and if I withhold and retain my vital juices . . . will I get an invisible white light coming from the top of *my* head?''

''No,'' he said firmly.

''Is that fair?'' she asked quietly.

''We've been advised . . . enjoined . . . ordered, in fact, not to teach women the key to the door leading to the Way.''

''Why?'' She pretended to yawn, as if she didn't have a zip of energy left.

''Because,'' he said softly, ''if women learned how not to have orgasm while bringing men to bliss and climax, they would have all their Yin and our Yang, and would greatly surpass men in wisdom, spiritual enlightenment, and realization. They'd have all that superior Yin magic plus the lesser Yang and . . . '' He shut his mouth quickly. But too late. Stubby was looking at him as if he was so stupid words could not even begin to describe it all.

''Lotzi,'' she chuckled, not deliberately maliciously, ''I have news for you. Every survey I've heard of, from Kinsey to Masters and Johnson to Shere Hite, all say the same thing. Millions and millions of married women in every country of the world are bringing men to orgasm without ever feeling a tingle of it themselves. The amount of Yang being blipped into Lotuses to add force to the Yin is incredible. There is probably," she laughed, getting off the bed and moving to the closet to pull out her packsack, "enough energy being expended in exactly that way to light up the skyline of New York for the next twenty years." When she stopped laughing at that idea, she enlarged upon it, stuffing socks and jeans and shirts into her pack. "It might be the answer to the search for a fuel to power intergalactic spacecraft," she howled.

It doesn't take long to leave a place if you don't care whether or not you take anything with you. After all, you can always buy a toothbrush and a hairbrush. She paid the phone bill and told the company to disconnect, she paid the hydro bill and told that company the same thing. She made sure the rental agency knew that she was on her way, and told them they could keep the damage deposit. "Cheap at twice the price," she said bitterly. Then she went to the other car lot, the one where Lotzi had not worked, and bought the first pickup truck she set her eyes on. She waited until all the forms and transfer papers were signed, then took them to the insurance company and got herself protected from those few things against which there is any protection, after which she was issued her plates. She was driving out of town in less than two and a half hours after leaving the empress-sized waterbed.

"Well," she said to herself, "I hope you learned that lesson." She started laughing, envisioning herself driving home and explaining the Jewel and the Lotus to Vinnie. No wonder Vinnie had always seemed more than a bit nervous, more than a bit hyper; all that Yin stored in her body for all those years, and all that Yang being added, and none of it being directed anywhere except around and around in circles. No wonder Vinnie had spun around dusting, sweeping, vacuuming, joining committees and auxiliaries, no wonder Vinnie had to swallow blue pills and yellow capsules and red tablets and multi-coloured time release spansules. No wonder every time she opened her mouth words tumbled out like jellybeans coming through a sack with a hole in the bottom. All things considered, it was an absolute wonder Vinnie hadn't been short-circuited by the energy overload. "She must have one incredibly efficient and powerful safety fuse," Stubby mused.

Stubby just kept driving. She had absolutely no idea at all where she was going except away, far away, forever. There was a tape player in her new pickup, but she hadn't stopped to buy any tapes, so any singing that got done she did herself. She tried to concentrate on the scenery, but her mind, what was left of it, just kept coming back to the same things, the same few unchangeable and hurtful things. "A year and a day," she growled, "a year and a day. Thirteen menstrual periods plus a day. Thirteen lunar cycles, thirteen full moons and me staring at every one of them like a docile cow, and nobody to blame but my stupid self, either. Presupposing a whole pile of stuff just because. . . just because I thought that, and figured he did; just because I felt that and thought. . . well, the fact and the truth of it all is, I didn't think. Didn't even have anything to think *with* if you get right down to it. I mean, here I am, and I don't know *where* I am, off again on the quest for the Holy Grail and what would I do with it when I found it? Take it to a museum so they could put it in a glass case, I suppose. Put it on the mantle above the fireplace and sit staring at it? Well, wherever it is right now, if anyone is staring at it, I bet you the name they see in burning letters on the rim is Amberchuk, Stubby, because if ever there was a damsel in distress, it's me."

"I ought to have some faith," she laughed, "and just find a nice place to sit and wait and give the Order of the Grail a chance to find me." The idea, born of that kind of black humour we find when our hearts are broken, our minds bent and our spirits flagging, the black humour that helps us keep our upper lips stiff and our backs unbowed, made better sense than anything else Stubby had heard in more than a year. So she pulled in at a gas station, filled her tank, topped her oil and bought a map. She sat behind the wheel of her new pickup truck drinking a lukewarm 7-Up and studying the lines representing freeways, highways, secondary highways, paved roads, unpaved roads and dirt tracks. "Looks like chicken guts," she growled. "Study the entrails, Stubby."

When she had managed to figure out where she was, she figured out how best to start herself off to where it was she had almost decided to go. She finished her 7-Up, took the empty can to the garbage and went back to her pickup. What is there lonelier than a 24-hour gas station on the side of a road in the middle of nowhere, unless it's the person getting into a pickup all by herself, turning the key, starting it up and pulling back onto the road with the unhappy suspicion her energy level had been seriously depleted.

Somewhere between Twin Hills and Manyberries, Stubby stopped long enough to get an aluminum canopy fitted on her pickup, then bought herself a piece of foam exactly big enough to fit the bottom of the shortbox. She didn't want to have to deal with the presence of Vinnie, the reality of Vinnie or the complexity of her own conflicting emotions when with or even near Vinnie, and she had a sneaking suspicion both Wright and Sharon would envelop her in the cotton batting of protective indulgence, would both try so hard not to get in her way while she searched for whatever it was she was searching for that she would feel as if she were tripping over their love and concern with every stumbling step she took. And so Stubby did not go back to Ada Richardson's house.

But Stubby did go home. Not to visit any of her relatives, not to slide nostalgically into third, not to try her luck at the club and not to consult with any of the lawyers or other assorted experts Ada's money had put at her beck and call. Stubby just went home.

The Row was more of a mess than it had ever been, derelict cars and abandoned bits of bicycles, baby buggies, scooters, wagons and half-overhauled motors and engines littered most of the yards. Windows gaped empty of glass and holes showed in the roofs where cedar shakes had rotted through and never been replaced. Fences leaned drunkenly, sagged forlornly, or lay fallen in tangles of thistle and blackberry vine, and savage-eyed cats streaked away when Stubby parked her pickup and moved toward the old house. How could a place wind up so defeated and ruined in so short a time? What was it that made people smash windows, kick in doors and use camping hatchets on door frames just because a dwelling was empty?

The roses Dave had tended so lovingly had spread and rambled willfully, the branches and stems tangled thick in the fence, holding it up long past the time it would otherwise have fallen to the ground and been lost in the mess of uncut grass. Foxgloves and lupin had reclaimed the garden space and evening primrose had taken over what had once been the hen yard. The hydro lines to the house had been cut, the transformer glass twinkled in the dirt on the side of the road. Someone had amused themselves by hacking hunks out of the front steps and some weirdo had entirely stolen the back steps. What in the name of God would a person do with a set of swiped steps?

The back door was gone too, so Stubby hauled herself up on the porch and went through the gaping doorway into the house. Everything was frapped. Spray-painted obscenities and scribbled examples of withering wit were all over the walls, the window sills were chopped and jack-knifed beyond repair, the floor was a threat to life and limb and the stove had been attacked with something hard enough, heavy enough and strong enough to turn it into a heap of wasted metal. Even the brick chimney had been smashed and bashed, one section of it missing, the rest of it sagging toward the floor, pulling the roof and part of the wall between the living room and kitchen with it. Stubby was furious. Some geek-brained half-wit had dared to come in here and make a shambles of her memories.

"Well, we'll just see," Stubby vowed. "We will just bloody well see." She carefully made her way through the destruction to the front door, nodded some sort of reassuring promise to the roses, got in her pickup and headed north to Nanaimo, where she checked into the big old hotel on the waterfront and before, doing anything else, picked up the phone in her room.

When her phone calls were made and the wheels set in motion, Stubby had a bath, went for supper, then drove south again. She visited her Grandma and Grandpa Amberchuk and then went to see Wright, Sharon and Vinnie. She even thought up a good excuse for not staying at the house for the next little while. Whether they believed her excuse or not, they accepted it, which goes to show it's true after all, any excuse will do.

Even with Stubby's money it took a week, but a week isn't long to a woman who has wasted thirteen lunar cycles having her energy absorbed and sent through someone else's chakras without her even knowing it was happening. While the wheels ground, she poked around doing only what she wanted to do, not sure what it was she really wanted to do. She visited Vinnie, Wright and Sharon twice more, briefly each time, and got filled in on the news. There were few changes. Stuke was old and half-blind, and flew in the face of all the legends because she didn't seem to remember Stubby at all, and stayed as close to Vinnie as she could. Nobody had any idea where Earl was, what he was doing or how he was, and nobody seemed to care. Only once, and only to be polite, Stubby went with Vinnie to visit Vinnie's parents. Everyone sat around in the living room balancing cups of tea and speaking politely and then, duty done, everyone was relieved when the visit ended.

"I love them, I guess," Vinnie said, "but I've never been sure I liked them."

"Oh well," Stubby philosophized, "you're stuck with your family, but thank God you can choose your friends." Vinnie grinned as if it was the first time in her life she had heard it. Stubby wasn't sure where she herself had heard it. Was it Dave who had said it, or Ada? Was it Wright or Sharon? Who?

The wheels ground and ground, as they say, exceedingly fine, and then Stubby signed some papers and put some other wheels in motion.

"Leave that fence," she said quietly, "and don't touch any of the rose bushes or flowers. Save the bricks in the chimneys. Anything that can possibly be used again, hang onto it. You might think about heaping it over there." She pointed vaguely and they nodded. "All the rest gets the deep six."

Rumblings and coughings, lurchings and grindings, and the machines moved in, like oddly-shaped prehistoric swamp creatures or space invaders. Rubber tires bigger than Stubby's pickup rolled slowly, treads left evenly spaced cuts in the grass, huge blades were lowered and claw-toothed buckets lifted out and moved detritus, debris and junk.

The catskinner chewed his toothpick, his hands and feet moving in some kind of ballet Stubby didn't understand. As gently as if he were picking up a thin-shelled egg, he reached out and moved a knob. Things moved, gears meshed, the machine moved and one entire side of the house fell to the ground. Another delicate flip, a gentle flick, a shift of position and the other half was down, the chimney left standing naked and awkward. The machine moved on, avoiding rose bushes, lilac bushes and foxgloves, and the labourers moved in, salvaging bricks. Trucks were loaded with scrap metal and rusted trash, then rolled off down the old road, headed for the dump. Stubby sat in her pickup, out of everyone's way, and watched, trying hard not to see what was actually going on, trying hard to cling to her vision of what was going to begin when this massive housekeeping was finished.

It didn't take thirteen lunar cycles, it didn't even take six. In less time than it had taken to crack her illusions and dent her pride, Stubby's vision was ready for her to move into it. So what if the bricks had turned out to be the only things she had been able to salvage? So what if the house was built out of brand new wood and in no way resembled the little place where she and Dave had lived together? So what? The view from the windows was the same. When she sat on her porch and looked out at the sunset, the sky was the same blending of pink, peach, lavender and blue. The roses were the same ones, exactly the same ones, and if a few lupin and foxglove had been bent or tattered, others would spring up in the cleared areas. Already there were janie-jump-ups coming up where the grass had grown wild, and a thousand bulbs were waiting for spring to stir them to life and bloom. The bricks had been carefully sorted and chosen, the old mortar chipped away and the soft greys and faded reds, streaked with black, had been used to build a hearth, chimney and what the mason had called a "feature wall." A wood-burning airtight ruled the entire downstairs, and there wasn't a scrap of linoleum anywhere in the house. To Vinnie's horror, there wasn't a snip of inlaid wall-to-wall, either.

"If I had your money I'd have had carpet on every floor."

Stubby just nodded and shrugged and said, "Yes, Momma, I know you would."

"In fact," Vinnie puzzled, "if I had your money, I'd have built something entirely different from this place. Why would you want to be bothered with chickens when you've got enough money to buy every egg in the world?"

"I like to hear the sounds they make when they're happy," Stubby replied.

"There's nothing in the world stupider than chickens," Vinnie grumbled. "Unless it's turkeys."

"Yes, Momma," Stubby agreed. Finally, Vinnie went home.

When the first orange leaves began to fall off the maples, Stubby announced to all concerned that she simply wouldn't be available until further notice. She said that except in case of dire emergency she wasn't to be telephoned or called on. Vinnie, Wright and Sharon rolled their eyes, took a deep breath, sighed, then forced a smile and nodded. They waited until Stubby had driven off in her pickup before they asked each other what was going on with Stubby anyway, couldn't seem to settle to anything, took off for over a year to God knows where, spent all that time getting that place built, then slammed the door on everyone as soon as it was finished. Kids, they said, they'll turn you grey.

Stubby, meanwhile, was holed up in her new house with a mountain of books. She had no intention at all of seeing anyone until she damn well felt like it. She didn't feel like it all through autumn, and all through winter.

When Spring yawned, stretched, and wakened, and the thousand bulbs began to swell and send green spears toward the light, Stubby roused herself from her near-hibernation and began to take some interest in what was getting ready to go on around her. She set herself a schedule and tried hard not to deviate from it too much. She got up at the same time every morning, she had two cups of coffee, then fed the chickens, gathered the few eggs and cleaned the floor of the hen coop, moving the mess by wheelbarrow to a pile in the far corner of the back yard. Stubby rototilled the garden patch and turned the hens loose to free-range. Even with acres of protectively fenced territory, the hens, of course, made a beady-eyed streak for the garden area and scratched and pecked vigourously. A few worms were lost, but not as many as you would think; they headed downward, chewing their own burrows to safety, leaving a buhzillion rear-guard troops in the weirdness of their own excrement, politely referred to as castings, a much nicer word than shit. As the worms chewed and burrowed, the soil was improved and composted and aerated and the hens were as happy as the mean-natured things can ever be, filling themselves with weed seeds and hair-sized bits of root that otherwise would have grown into six-foot tall thistles and yard-long strands of ground blackberry.

There were flower beds to dig and seeds to plant, there were shrubs to be chosen, bought, brought home and transplanted, there were post-holes to be dug for the new fence around the garden, for the chickens were not going to always have this unrestricted access. And when Stubby had nothing else to occupy herself, there was next year's woodpile.

And always the same few questions to be pondered, to be picked up, examined, thought about and put down again because no answers or even hints of answers had even begun to present themselves. Sometimes Stubby thought of her own mind as a sort of flesh and blood rock polisher, and her thoughts tumbling inside like agates or particularly beautiful, unusual, strange, or downright weird beach pebbles.

Most of the junk and garbage left over from the demolition operation had been taken off and deposited at the municipal garbage dump, but a dozen and a half or so cedar fence posts had been deemed salvageable and stacked against the far wall of the new woodshed. The bottom ends, buried for years in the wet soil, had half-rotted and been cut off by a screaming chainsaw, shortening the posts considerably, but they were still long enough to be used around the garden. Stubby wasn't trying to save money. Most of the time Stubby didn't even think about money. The posts had been there when she was little and the world was good, they had survived whatever disaster had turned the Row into an indescribable mess, and if ever anything deserved a chance, a second or third or even fourth chance, it was the old fence supports.

She was pulling the pile apart, stacking the posts as much according to whim as to length or fitness, and there it was. Looking at her. Looking at her with eyes that reminded Stubby of Myrtle the Turtle's eyes. Stubby didn't waste any time wondering how a creature who had been as important to her at one point in her life as Myrtle had been had managed or been managed to sort of retreat into a background so distant Stubby wasn't even sure what had happened to her. Stubby just reached out with her heavily gloved hand and picked it up. "Well, and what are you, a lizard, a newt, or a salamander? I can never," she admitted, "tell one from the other."

It looked at her. It blinked. It opened its mouth in what, at first, Stubby thought was supposed to be a roar or a snarl or a gesture of defiance or defence, and then it blinked again, closed its mouth and curled up in the palm of her gloved hand, its tail wrapped up over its neck. She almost put it in the grass and leaves against the wall of the new woodshed, but impulse and whim, combined with the growling of her own stomach, directed her booted feet toward her own back door, and so it was Stubby took the little critter into the house with her. She got an old, very soft cotton towel, rumpled it into a sort of a nest on the back side of the table, the side against the kitchen wall, and into the middle of the towel-nest, Stubby laid the dozy little thing. It wiggled a bit and squirmed a bit and opened its mouth a few times, then settled down again, and Stubby began to make herself some lunch. She scrambled a few eggs, made herself some toast, cut a slab of cheese and poured herself a glass of milk. As she put her glass of milk on the table, she slopped some of it but not enough to bother going for the dishcloth and wiping it up; it was just a little spill and could wait until after she'd eaten.

She was almost finished lunch when she noticed the little whatever-it-was flickering its tongue in and out of the milk, lapping eagerly, even making little slurping sounds. Its skin, which had been a sort of old-wood grey-brown, was definitely changing colour, becoming blue or green or greeny-blue or bluey-green, and shimmering.

"Well, look at you," Stubby laughed, "you must be a chameleon!" The little thing paid her no mind, had finished the small slop on the table and was eyeing the glass with what could only be interpreted as a nearly desperate covetousness. "Here," Stubby offered, and she quickly pushed aside the last of her scrambled egg and poured a good dollop of milk on her plate. She shoved the plate toward the little thing and it zipped over, climbed up over the lip of the plate and sat there, tongue extended, lapping and sucking greedily, its belly swelling and swelling and swelling until Stubby began to fear the little beastie would burst. In a manner of speaking it did. The shimmering skin along its back split, a faint hairline at first, widening, widening, widening, and then there was the happy little thing inside, shimmering, quivering and definitely bigger. What had been only three inches from nose-tip to tail-tip and no bigger around than a Ticonderoga pencil was now four-and-a-bit inches long and almost as thick as a Jumbo crayon. It burped, and hiccuped, then sat back, balanced on its tail, and began to shred the tattered old skin from its body. Stubby stared at the little pile of glittering-jewel tissue, then went for a matchbox and carefully collected the discarded hide and placed it in the matchbox. The little beast waddled over to its towel-nest, curled up again, and went to sleep. Stubby shook her head, unable to believe what she was seeing. Even Stubby knew she wasn't imagining any of this, it had nothing to do with did you believe it or didn't you believe it. It was just happening.

The sunlight through the window warmed the little critter and played games with the brightly glittering scales. Stubby watched the rainbow-prism colours shifting with each breath and twitch, and the minutes of her life slipped by. And suddenly it was hours later and time to go outside. She finished sorting the fence posts, muttering about how she had expected to get at least a half-dozen of them set in their holes, where had the time gone, here it was past the time she should have put the hens back in their run and nothing much accomplished, what good did daydreaming do a person. On the other hand, what harm did it do a person?

She indulged herself with a totally irresponsible supper; french fries. No healthy salad, no balanced Canada Food Rules two vegetables, just a nice big heaping platter of homemade french fries. Hardly any salt, a hint of vinegar and no ketchup at all. What was even worse, she ate the fries with her fingers, while reading a book. You can't, of course, read a book, concentrate on turning the pages without getting grease on them, find your mouth and your plate, and still be expected to be aware of absolutely everything else that is going on around you. Busy as she was keeping some things under control and unsmeared, Stubby didn't notice the little critter come from the bed in the towel and approach her plate. It wasn't until the steady tiny noise chipped its way into her awareness and began to annoy her that she even thought about her recently found companion. But the noise was one of those noises that will drive you nuts if it goes on for very long, a tic tic tic much like that enraging sound some people make by picking one fingernail with another. She looked up, all ready to snarl, snap, yell or roar, whichever seemed most appropriate. Instead, she just stared. The little beastie was staring at her, rapping the very tip of its tail against the salt shaker. Tic tic tic the hard little point tapped against the shiny metal lid, tic tic tic. The beastie was sitting back on its haunches, front legs crossed under its chin, tail ticking, eyes staring.

"What?" she said. The beastie stared. At Stubby, then at the last few fries on her plate, then up at Stubby again. "Oh," she said. "Sorry. I guess I. . . didn't think." She moved her hands away from the plate and held them up, indicating she was finished. "Help yourself, I'm sure," she offered, unable to believe that she, Stubby Amberchuk, was talking to a lizard as if it were something every woman did as a matter of course. The little critter moved forward quickly, reached out with its front feet and managed to pull a french fry to the edge of the plate. The little mouth opened, the jaws closed on the very end of the french fry and a small crescent disappeared into the mouth. Stubby stared. The front feet holding the greasy chip had definitely started to grow some claws. She was sure there hadn't been any claws before, certainly not any little ruby red ones. Come to think of it, there hadn't been any hard little tip to the tail, either. And hadn't the little thing been only four-and-a-bit inches long and no bigger than a Jumbo crayon? How had it somehow become more like six- and-a-half inches long and at least as big around as a cheap cigar? Stubby raised herself and looked in the nest the beastie had made in the soft towel. Sure enough, there it was, neatly stripped off and pushed to one side, another layer of glittering skin.

"How often is this going to happen?" she wondered aloud.

. . . quite a few times . . .

Stubby went for the matchbox and added the latest strips of glittering hide. The ones already in the box had dried completely; they rattled when she moved the box, and shimmered and glittered in the light. Mostly greens and blues, like emeralds and sapphires, a few clear diamond-appearing scales, they reminded her of rhinestones. She closed the box and put it on the window sill, then sat down to watch the beastie eat the rest of the french fries. Suddenly she realized what had happened. Her mind sort of froze, then leaped ahead, jerked back, and skipped a few times, like a machine trying to cope with a power surge. She wondered if she'd snapped her twig.

"Do you suppose," she asked carefully, "that the matchbox will be big enough to hold all the discarded skin?"

. . . not a chance . . .

Stubby gulped, turned pale and began to sweat. "How do you do that?" she asked. "Talk without moving your mouth or using your voice?"

. . . I don't know exactly. It might be a little bit like mental telepathy, but if it is, it's only a little bit like it. Relax, you haven't snapped your twig. Whatever that means . . .

"Are you saying I don't have to speak for you to . . . hear me?"

. . . It works much better if you verbalize. I mean, if I have to, I can read your mind, but it's very difficult. I believe the word for what's going on in there is . . . inchoate . . . and it's rather like trying to listen to several radio stations at the same time . . .

"Wow," Stubby breathed, "this is incredible."

. . . It is, rather. I hope you won't think less of me if I tell you that it's very, very new to me, too. And I'm not at all sure how I'm supposed to deal with it all. Nothing is the way I expected it would be. Oh, the sky is blue, and I expected that, and the grass is green, and there are flowers, but . . .

"Scary, huh?" Stubby sympathized.

. . . Yeah . . . the beastie nodded, and reached up with a front paw and wiped its eyes . . . Real scary . . .

"Are you a newt?" Stubby blurted. "Or a salamander?"

. . . No! . . . The creature recoiled, obviously insulted. . . . I am not! . . .

"Then what in hell are you?"

. . . A dragon, of course . . .

"Oh," Stubby nodded stupidly, "oh, of course. I mean, what else, eh? I mean, the world is full of them. Everyone is finding them in their old woodpiles these days."

. . . I know it's hard to get your head around, and I understand your reluctance to accept the idea. I even understand, although I don't appreciate it, why it is you think I'm lying to you. But the truth of it is, I'm a dragon. And you're quite wrong. The world is *not* full of us, and almost *nobody* is finding us in woodpiles or anywhere else . . .

Stubby felt very dizzy and a bit nauseated. "Listen, would you mind very much if I just took myself off to bed? I think I'm delirious, or something."

. . . I think it's a very good idea, you're looking decidedly pale and puny. Don't worry about a thing, I'll be just fine on my own. Although it would help very much if you'd be so kind as to leave that container of white stuff here for me, I'm sure I'll be hungry again before long . . .

Just to be sure there were no unfortunate accidents, Stubby took the milk and poured it into a bowl where the critter could get at it. Then she took herself off to bed and lay there for several minutes shaking, trembling and pouring sweat, straining her ears to hear the sound of the sirens that would herald the arrival of the men in white coats. Then it was as if something astringent and cooling, mint-scented and soothing were wiped across the ravaged mess that had been her mind, and Stubby Amberchuk went to sleep.

When she awakened it was day, and she felt almost fine. She rolled out of bed, dressed herself and went to the kitchen. Stubby actually expected to walk into the kitchen and find out she'd had some kind of mysterious fever that had boiled her brain and visited upon her hallucinations and delusions, and that she would find her kitchen a bit messy but otherwise quite empty of any and all life except her own. Still, she was not at all surprised to find, curled up on the floor in front of the woodstove, her little beastie, now the size of a small dog, glittering in the light, shimmering and shining, looking at her with the most incredibly beautiful amber eyes. The kitchen was spotlessly clean, the dishes were washed, rinsed, dried and even put back where they belonged, all the counters had been wiped clean, the sink had been scoured, the table wiped, the floor swept and the stove was warm. In a box beside the stove was what looked like nothing more nor less than a heap of jewels. Emeralds, sapphires, rubies, diamonds, opals, and others Stubby had never before seen and could not name.

"Again, huh?" she smiled.

. . . and again and again and again . . . , the creature agreed.

"Just how big are you going to get?" Stubby asked hesitantly.

. . . Not very, I'm afraid . . . , the dragon said sadly. . . . There was a time we were huge and strong and ruled the world beneath our feet, but . . . nothing is forever, eh? We used to be as numerous as . . . oh, pick something . . . cows, horses, or oxen, but . . . I guess all the changes had something to do with it . . . there aren't a lot of us left . . . fewer and fewer and smaller and smaller, I guess . . .

"Well, what would you like for breakfast?" Stubby offered, surprising even herself with the ease with which she could now accept the presence of a dragon in her kitchen.

. . . Do you have any chow mein? the dragon asked hopefully.

"Not a shred. But I'll go get some take-out for supper," Stubby promised hurriedly when she saw the look of disappointment pass across the dragon's face.

. . . What do you usually have for breakfast?

"Toast. . . scrambled eggs. . . or poached. . . or. . . ," Stubby shrugged, grinned, "whatever's handy."

. . . Then I'll have that, too. Whatever's handy. . .

While Stubby cooked the eggs and made the toast the little dragon set the table and got everything ready for the coffee; put the little plastic funnel over the pot, asked about and then carefully added exactly the right amount of ground coffee, but when it came to lifting the kettle of boiling water and pouring it slowly over the coffee grounds, the dragon had to ask Stubby for help.

"What a disappointment," Stubby laughed. "I thought dragons were huge, and strong, and had sulfurous breath and could blow fireballs at their enemies, and crush mountains with the sheer weight of their bulk," and the little dragon's laughter tinkled like silvery bells.

. . . Stories. . . , she managed, . . . have a way of growing with each telling. Much has been. . . altered. . . you know how it is, someone tells a story and someone else wants to top it. We *were* much bigger, and there were lots 'n' lots of us, but. . . the same could be said of a lot of things. Trees. . . just as a close-to-hand example. Trees were so *big*, and they started at the very edge of the sea and marched row upon row upon row up the sides of mountains and down the slopes of valleys, and now. . . The beast shrugged. . . . It's very, very sad if you dare to think about it. . .

"And lakes?" Stubby suggested.

. . . Oh, lakes! Oh my, yes. Large, deep, clear, clean and very, very magical. . .

They were eating now, the little dragon perched on her back legs on a chair, using her front feet as delicately and as skillfully as possible, especially when you take into consideration that she might never before have held a knife and fork. Her tail poked between the slats on the back of the chair, then rose up to curl gracefully over the top, the hard, glittering tip almost ruby red and showing what gave every sign of being a split.

. . . This is very good. I don't believe I've ever had it before. Do you think we might have it again?

"Guaranteed," Stubby promised. "What did you mean about lakes being magical?"

. . . Oh well, everything was, you know. You *do* know that, don't you? . . . The dragon tilted her head to one side, and peered at Stubby, who tried to look nonchalant while sitting at a wooden table eating scrambled egg with cheese, chewing toast and drinking drip coffee with a small, glittery dragon.

"I had heard stories," she confessed, "but I guess I discounted most of them."

. . . Well! . . . The dragon leaned forward and gently tapped one clawed digit on the table top, annoyed and annoying. . . . Don't! When one is going to discount something, one should first totally examine it to make sure it is, in fact, the correct thing to discount. Do you know, for example, that this is not the only world in the universe? . . .

"I read a lot of science fiction," Stubby admitted, "so I kind of suspected as much."

. . . That's a start, at least! You'd be amazed how many people think this is the be-all and end-all, the absolute penultimate of creation, with themselves at the top of the heap. Hmph. The actuality of it all is there are universes and multiverses and megaverses and galaxies and other setups for which I have no words you would understand. And while each of these places has its own individual governments and rules and regulations and traffic systems and garbage disposal ideas, there is one overall and inflexible and quite strict either-or rule. Either a world is magical, or it is scientific. Period. No mixing the one with the other. And this world used to be magical. When it was very young, very new and very, very innocent and pleasant . . .

"Then if the rule says either-or, what happened?"

"Accident," the dragon burped.

"You spoke out loud!" Stubby cheered. "You moved your mouth and spoke out loud just like anybody else!"

"Yes," the dragon beamed. Her scales shimmered and the lights from them danced on the walls of the kitchen. "Let's do something to celebrate."

"What?" Stubby asked.

"What do you usually do to celebrate?"

"I go to the beach," Stubby said readily.

"Is it far?"

"Just a hop and a skip."

Stubby had to give the dragon a hoist up to the front seat of the pickup; the dragon's legs were too short and her belly just a little bit too prominent for her to haul herself in place. "I used to go everywhere with my dog Daisy," Stubby confided, "but after she was gone, well, the truth of it is, Stuke was never a replacement. I think maybe you can't replace stuff, you have to give everything and everybody their own importance. I mean,'' she babbled, wondering what she was talking about anyway, ''Stuke herself was a very fine dog. If I hadn't been so busy trying to replace Daisy, Stuke and I probably would have got along just fine. But I wanted Daisy, y'know? And Vinnie, she didn't care one little bit for Daisy, but she thinks Stuke's the best thing since sliced bread. Which is why I left Stuke over at the other house.''

''Thank you,'' the dragon smiled, ''for giving me my own importance in your life. For not trying to fit me into the understandable scheme of things.''

They drove down the long narrow road that led from the Row to the highway, then crossed the highway and drove through the last few patches of trees toward the beach. Arbutus twisted and writhed toward the sky and the ground at the same time, and clacker-crickets snap snap snapped their way through the long grass.

''You seem . . . upset,'' the dragon urged gently.

''I'm mindblown,'' Stubby admitted. ''I have a million questions and no idea of where to start.''

''Where would you like to start? I myself would suggest the most obvious and immediate, that which is, so to speak, right under your nose. Me.''

''What do dragons eat,'' Stubby blurted, ''other than scrambled eggs and milk?''

''Well, I'm very fond of chow mein. And salmon and prawns and cod and halibut if it's properly grilled. I like chicken in all its forms, and duck, and rice pudding. I do not like goose, or bulgur wheat!''

''I promise,'' Stubby laughed, ''no bulgur wheat. Nor kasha, which might even be the same thing, for all I know. What's your history?''

''Me, personally? Why, I was put in my egg and told to wait until it was Time. Now.''

''I was thinking more along the lines of the history of dragons.''

''Oh. Well, for a start, we've always been here. You know, in the beginning was the word and the word was Dragon.''

''Oh,'' Stubby gulped, her hands gripping the steering wheel so tightly her knuckles were white.''

''The orientals have the oldest civilization, and certainly *they* knew about us. We've been called Ananta the Infinite, Kundalini, Mat Chinoi, Kadi of Der, Lamashtu the Daughter of Heaven, Nehushtan, Leviathan . . .''

''Hold on, I thought Leviathan was a whale!''

''Oh, for heaven's sake, it didn't originally mean *big*, you know. It means wiggly.'' The dragon waggled her tail and laughed, sharp tinkly sounds that made Stubby think of wind chimes and tuning forks and the sound of Salish deer-hoof dance anklets. ''Oh,'' the dragon shrilled, ''oh, oh, oh, oh, just look at that! Oh, as gorgeous as ever! And oh look, Sheilagh, the spindrift on the beach!''

''Stubby,'' she growled automatically. ''It's the ocean,'' she explained unnecessarily. She parked the pickup, opened the door, got out and reached back inside for the portly dragon. Immediately her feet touched the sun-bleached grass, the dragon was reaching for the water, her scales sparkling in the sun, and before Stubby realized the dragon was going to do it, she had done it and was in the water, swimming expertly, all four legs paddling, tail whipping sideways, body almost spiralling, wiggling and wriggling, churning the waves to foam and sending the foam to the shore where it lay on the rocks and over the logs. Stubby picked up a handful of the spindrift and daubed it on her cheeks, on her chin, as she had done with Dave's shaving suds when she was little and the world was new and Dave was alive and strong. Then, because nobody had let her do it then and because nobody could stop her from doing it now, she scooped up handfuls and piled it on her head, like a crown. Queen of the shore, Stubby clambered on logs, climbed rocks, tore her jeans on barnacles and, when the sun got too hot, moved to the fringe of brush and began to search for the first miraculous berries of the year.

''What are you eating?'' the dragon asked softly.

''Salmonberries. Want some?'' Stubby offered the dragon a handful of the crunchy-seeded berries.

''Exquisite,'' the dragon grinned, chewing happily and reaching for where more berries clustered on the pale green bush. Stubby was certain there had only been a few early berries, and certain, too, she had picked them all, but now the bush seemed loaded with them.

''What you said,'' she mumbled hesitantly, ''about in the beginning . . . did you mean dragons are . . . God?''

''I can't believe this. I absolutely cannot believe this!'' The dragon rolled her eyes in disbelief. ''In the beginning was the word, and the word was Dragon, and the word was *with* God.'' She eyed Stubby to see if any of it was making sense. It wasn't, so she tried again. ''In the beginning was the dragon and the dragon was with God. Oh boy, when they find out about this there is going to be *hell* to pay! I'll never explain it.''

''But you were fierce and dreadful and horrific and . . .''

''Propaganda,'' the dragon sighed. ''We got some very bad press there toward the end. Oh, we had a few . . . misfits . . . but I mean, really, does Puff the Magic Dragon sound like something you'd want to hide your kids away from?''

''Then what about St. George?''

''*Saint* George?'' The dragon pounded the top of her head with her clenched fist and ground her little teeth in a brief temper tantrum. "There was a *Green* George, or George of the Greenwood. . .one of the spirits of spring. . .supposedly he wore a lot of leaves and lived in a tree. Or trees. Sang songs. Skipped and gamboled on the grass. You know, the springly things. He carried a lance." The dragon looked up at Stubby who looked down in dumb amazement. "Oh, come *on*, Amberchuk! Spring. . .a lance. . .fertility. . .a long pole?" The dragon waited. Finally, Stubby nodded, blushing slightly. "Now, with a bit of imagination and a touch of what I think your culture calls female intuition. . .why do you suppose Green George had to use his pecker-pole to kill the dragon?" She waited, but nothing happened. Stubby just gawked. "Oh god!" the dragon moaned. "A full time job this is going to be. Okay, we're supposed to be open-minded. It's a thing that's built into most of us. Chromosome-linked, most likely. Which can't be said for scientists. They are the most narrow-minded of bastards you can imagine."

"I'm getting dizzy," Stubby complained.

"Well, it's not easy to compress thousands and millions of years of ongoing power play and brinksmanship into a few lucid lines, you know." The dragon gave Stubby a shove, moving her into the shade where she sat down and turned her face to the breeze the dragon was making by waving her tail gently back and forth.

"Sheilagh," the little dragon said soothingly, "you have got more brain cells in your head than there are stars in the sky. Now I know that the scientific arsletarts and linear thinkers have been in charge of your education, but. . .try to put aside everything they told you about rational thought and just infuse your brain with some imagination. The world was magic. But scientists wanted it to be something other than magic. All those magic, pagan people loved Green George and the rites of spring. So the scientists said Green George had converted, and become *Saint* George, and said he used his prick-pole to kill the dragon. The dragon, who was there from the start, with God. . .there you go, they said, our God is stronger than yours. Get it?"

"But why?" Stubby demanded.

"Those who loved the old god and respected dragons were pagan. We could not force people to believe. The scientists had no such qualms. Fire, torture, you name it. I mean, from their tiny-minded perspective, it was damned annoying, puttering around with their noxious compounds, experimenting and failing and experimenting again, tormenting dogs and cats, murdering white mice, always needing huge sums of money for their precious research. And then some magic healer just sort of goes "poof," and no cancer, no gallstones, no arthritis. . .and no ongoing tenured salaries, either."

"And...Arthur?" Stubby gulped.

"Ah, yes, Arthur," the dragon smiled, a particularly nasty little sawtoothed grimace. "Artie the Fink. Artie the Rat-Faced. Art the Louse Brain. Artie Fartie the Turncoat."

"Arthur?" Stubby sat bolt upright. "Round Table Arthur?"

The dragon sat down, curled her tail around her front paws and rested her chin in the cleft. "I always knew I'd have to work for a living, but I didn't think I'd have to work so hard. Okay, Arthur Pendragon. Arthur, Son of the Dragon. Think on that. Think hard! Remember, the dragon was with God from the beginning. And also keep in mind that while many of the terms of reference to this story will seem to be about religion, those terms are false. Religion had diddly squat to do with it. What it had to do with, and still has to do with, is value. Money. Gold, silver, junk like that. Gold and silver are really just rocks, you know, and no matter what you do with them, or with it, as the case may be, it is still there. Whether in the ground or wrapped around your finger, there it is. And jewels, well, they have precious little value when they're so easily come by as they are! So to the pagans, who had their dragons, none of that meant shit. But the scientists, they decided this stuff was good. Tried to make it out of straw and all that necromancy stuff and nonsense. So next time you read about a religious struggle, look for the money. Because money is power and money is freedom and for an asshole to have power *you* have to lose freedom!

"So, with that in mind...way back when, there was Arthur's father Uther Pendragon, the Wonderful Head of the Dragon. Now you might ask yourself how it was a mortal became the "head" of the dragon. He was the firstborn son of the matriarch and, as such, was head only insofar as he was the one who supervised the men of the Dragon clan. Who served the dragons. Us. You know, a sort of symbiotic thing. As the head of a cane is not what helps you walk, and the head of the bed is not where you sleep, so the head of the clan was not really any big deal, but only part of the overall structure, and Uther had no authority except that granted him by his mom.

"Now, at one time, the North Pole star was not in Ursa Minor, it was in Alpha Draconis. But as the heavens spin and the world turns and the universe unfolds, things shift. And eventually, due to the changes of the equinoxes and solstices and such, the star Polaris was replaced by Draconis. The North Pole star became situated in Ursa Minor. And Uther, he had a sick sort of sense of humour. His grandfather did, too, but that's a whole other tale.

"Uther thought it was...funny...that the heavens would shift and Bear would replace Dragon. And when his son was born, he called him Arth Vawr, Heavenly Bear. He was built somewhat like a bear, for a start, kind of short and squat and hairy as hell and anyway, in those days they did that, named their kids after stars, flowers, like that.

"So, what was going on was this. Artie the Fink's mother was, prior to his conception, married to someone else, someone Uther hated abso-bloody-lutely. Uther had reason to know this rival was going to die. Uther had, so to speak, arranged it all. And Uther was thick as can be with. . . a person who for now we will refer to as Merlin. With help from Merlin, Uther sent his spirit. . . his essence. . . to Arthur's mother at the same time her husband was being removed from this vale of tears. By magic. But of course she didn't know that it wasn't her real husband strolling into the bedroom with a big smile on his face! She thought it was all as it was supposed to be. Off with the shift, off with the shimmy and have a glass of wine, my dear. Well, just about the perzactle instant her real husband was breathing his last, Artie the Shithead is conceived.

"So some time later, just as she realizes she is pregnant, here comes a messenger saying her husband is dead. No matter what that woman said, nobody was going to believe her story! Hundreds of unimpeachable witnesses had seen the poor bugger skewered at exactly the time she thought she was entertaining him in bed! Nothing for it but to hide the evidence. Loose-fitting clothes, and a trip to visit dear Auntie in Avalon.

"Now Avalon was, and still is, a very secret place. No old mine shaft or cave in the hill or anything gloomy and unsanitary like that! Everybody who was anybody in those days lived in or near Avalon. And the Queen of Avalon was Herself. The Great Mother. Who had three daughters: Elaine, Morgawse, and Morgana. And a niece called Vivienne who lived a bit further off at the lake.

"Now, if I tell you that Morgawse was Arthur's sister, can you try to figure it out for yourself?"

Stubby blinked. She started wheels turning in her head. It hurt. But finally: "If Margawse is Arthur sister, then they have to share a parent. You told me Arthur's mother was married to someone who got killed so it wasn't a father got shared. So. . . it must have been. . . the mother? But Margawse's mother was Queen of Avalon!"

"Good girl," the dragon smiled. "Now you must remember there are parables at work here. So don't get bent out of shape if things don't quite seem to mesh. Margawse was Arthur's sister, and Morgana was Margawse's sister, and that can only mean Morgana was Arthur's sister, too."

"And Elaine's, I suppose," Stubby dared.

"Way to go, Amberchuk," the dragon laughed. "Everybody is brother and sister to everybody else. And Morgana was known as Morgana of the Shades because she could slip around and change form and be a tree if she wanted or a rock or . . . a withered up, twisted old man with a long beard. . . ''

''Merlin!''

''Right,'' the dragon chortled happily. ''Which is why Merlin had the responsibility of caring for Arthur. It was actually Auntie/Sister Morgana babysitting the little brat, if you must know.''

''But his mother . . . Queen of Avalon . . .''

''The goddess has always been served by a combination spouse/son/ sacred king. Always. And each time this spouse/son/sacred king has been defeated, it has been by a stronger or meaner spouse/son/sacred king. It's how you make sure only the best genes mix with your own. So Uther, who was spouse/son/sacred king, got rid of that husband and fathered Arthur, who was born to usurp Uther! Don't bother with questions, Stubby, you accepted the walking on water bit easily enough and compared to that, this is easy!

''So Artie grows up having a fine old time, and grows to adulthood, and becomes a man. So he put on the deer antlers and danced and sang and drank and inhaled the smoke and chanted like a true pagan and was introduced to what you might call his manly powers by . . . Margawse.''

''His *sister?*''

''Why not?'' the dragon shrugged. ''It's a rotten job, but someone has to do it. And Margawse got pregnant with Mordred. Who was born to usurp Arthur the way Arthur usurped Uther who had in fact usurped . . .''

''Uther's own father!'' Stubby gasped.

''Good girl. So Arthur knew Mordred would have it in for him, see, the way Arthur had done in Uther. So he decides things are going to change right here and now. No more usurping. Sends out this order to have all the baby boys put on this special ship, to make them safe, he said, from an evil that was after them. Then he arranged to have the ship sunk. But Mordred survived, thanks to magic, and was brought up by a lighthouse keeper who never did get proper thanks for it, but isn't that just too predictable?''

''But didn't the people know what Arthur had done?''

''Oh, well, he lied, you see. Not that it did him much good. But, of course, everyone who was anyone, those living in Avalon, knew, and they snubbed Artie for an unnatural bastard. So he snubbed them right back. After all, he'd been going over to the Scientists, anyway, and this just accelerated things. I mean, a man's gotta do what a man's gotta do, right? And the little creep immediately set about making life miserable for his mother, his sisters, even his dear Aunt Vivienne. Rotten little shit!''

''But . . . if the Arthurian legends are a crock and hogwash, what about the Holy Grail? Are you saying that there is no Holy Grail? No . . . chalice, no . . .''

"I'm saying no such thing. I know you searched a long time for it. Your search is why I was sent. After all these years, finally, a believer! Oh, you have no idea how happy you made everyone! We had a party. And teased Vivienne about how her name meant Giver of Life and here she'd given life to a Believer . . . Arthur is hogwash. What they've taught you about him, anyway. Noble, brave and all that. The man was a loser. And what's worse, he was a mean loser. But there *was* a Holy Grail, and he wanted it. God, how he wanted it! Without it, you see, there is no immortality. Without it, life is just a big sack of ashes. And all those stories about the saddling up and riding off and looking for and searching and hoping, and praying and fasting and purifying and cleansing are basically true enough. He turned the world upside down and inside out in his search for it! He even helped spread the rumour the Dragons were the ones had stolen it and that the more Draggies got killed the greater the chance of getting the Holy Grail. And in spite of everything he did, he never so much as saw it. But it's there, Sheilagh. All you need is faith. Faith enough to find out what your name really means, who Sheilagh the First really was.''

"Faith?" Stubby puzzled, "All I need is faith?"

"Faith is what you do when you *know* something and don't have any proof.''

"What you are describing," Stubby laughed, deliberately ignoring the reference to the name she hated so very much, "is how to win at a tight game of five card stud. Those who can't play call it bluffing. Those who can play know there is no bluff at all. Just faith.''

"There is hope for you, Amberchuk," the dragon promised. "But still, you are . . . puzzled. Upset. Threatened," she probed.

Stubby nodded, frowning.

"Can you talk about it?" the dragon invited, but Stubby shook her head and avoided looking at the dragon's jewel-faceted eyes. She began, instead, to pick berries again, popping them in her mouth one at a time, sucking the juice, cracking the seeds between her teeth.

"Are the darkest ones the ripest?" Draconis asked with seeming innocence.

"No," Stubby smiled, "they're all the same, they just look different. Some of them are sort of yellow, some are orange, some are various shades of red, and some are almost black. And I've been told they're called salmonberries because if you pick a lot of them and put them in a container, a basket or bowl, for example, they look like the eggs of the salmon when they're swollen and full and ripe and almost ready to be laid.

Like . . . like ruby-coloured caviar!''

"If you can accept that," Draconis said sternly, "why can't you accept the Great Mother, her daughters and their works. Surely it isn't any harder to believe that one branch of a bush can give berries of at least four separate colours than it is to believe . . .''

"Whoaboy!" Stubby snapped. "You don't let go easy, huh? Give 'er an inch and she'll take a mile. Come sneaking up behind you and—zap!''

"Whose ideas was it?" the dragon said coldly. "Did I go off in search of *you*? As I recall, not all that long ago, someone hi-de-hoed herself off in search of the Holy Grail and huffed and puffed like an absolute jerk, looking in all the wrong places for something she couldn't even describe!''

"Jerk?" Stubby knew she was getting angry, and she didn't care. "Jerk? Me? You want to know what is really stupid? I mean *really* stupid! I'll tell you what is stupid and jerky! It's mothers marrying sons, and sisters getting pregnant by brothers and kids growing up fated to usurp is what is stupid and jerky.''

"Really." the dragon smiled, but not sweetly. "And were both your parents Christian?''

"Yes!" Stubby declared firmly.

"Then they were both the children of God, right? Your father was a son of God and your mother was a daughter of God, right?''

"Right. God the Father.''

"Then they were brother and sister!" Draconis' eyes glittered. "And Vinnie got pregnant with you by her brother. And as for mothers marrying sons, isn't Christ part of God? And aren't nuns children of God? And don't nuns marry Christ? Who is, as I understand it, their father. Or at least a part of their Father!''

"What are you," Stubby screamed, "some kind of Jesuit arguing theology, or . . .'' She stared, her words caught in her throat.

"Amberchuk," the dragon roared, "you watch your step! You are dealing here with a motherlover! And enough is enough. So far this week I've been called a newt, a salamander, a lizard, a critter, a beastie and a slithery little thing,'' The dragon swelled until she was the size of a great dane. A very big great dane. "But don't you go too far. I will *not* be compared to, equated with or called anything that even remotely sounds like, or is associated with, that pack of perverts.'' The dragon swelled to the size of a D-8 caterpillar tractor. Her scales were the size of saucers, and glittered with an icy fire unlike anything Stubby had ever before seen. Was it flame or was it salmonberry juice dribbling from the corner of her very large snaggletoothed maw?

"Amberchuk," she roared, "don't tempt fate. Don't puke into the wind! Remember the words of the sages and wyccas: do not fart against thunder.'' The dragon was bigger than the tire companies' blimp, bigger than the *Graf Spee*, bigger than the USS *Enterprise*.

''I'm sorry,'' Stubby cried. ''Never again, I promise!''

''That's better,'' the dragon smiled, and folded in on herself until she was no bigger than an average-sized cocker spaniel.

''Do you do that very often?'' Stubby quavered. ''Get huge and ugly and godawful and horrific and terrifying?''

''I haven't done it in years,'' the dragon soothed. ''And I won't do it again if you don't step over the bounds of good taste and decency. Now, you just relax. Don't try to make sense of any of it. Just let it sit in your head and sift itself out. I'm going back in for a nice swim, and then, when you're ready, we can go home and get that fence in place so you and I can start planting the garden. And maybe,'' she hinted, ''we could have chow mein for supper?''

Part Two

While God Slept . . .

An abbreviated version of the Real History of the World, as told to Stubby Amberchuk by a representative of that ancient and noble race of sentient servants of the Mother.

Sincere apologies for any errors of omission or commission; it's hard to keep your wits about you when the lamps are turned low and you're listening to the fire crackle in the airtight. Even harder when what you're being told is issuing from a creature the size of a fat spaniel, a creature you have every reason to believe can, when angry, puff herself to such a size your eyes cannot see all of her at once.

This section of this work is pure fiction and is dedicated to those who believe in, possibly even have as friends, daring dragons in one form or another.

AVE DRACONIS! We who are about to believe salute you.

They got so much of it wrong when they took it on themselves to translate the scriptures. The part about a camel going through the eye of a needle, for example. And what about a thousand years being but a day in the sight of God. And on the first day she did this and on the second day she did that, and they'd have you believe that in six thousand years the whole kit and caboodle was together and functional. You don't have to be very smart to see the flaw in that, but the fundamentalists, they're still pounding their fists on the pulpits and declaring that if the Bible says it, that's it, that's *it*, and if you don't believe you'll roast in hell; while the other side still regularly trots out their inaccurate evidence—carbon dating and testing and exponential evolutionary extrapolation—and if they'd both stop jawing on and stop to think for a minute they'd be able to see they're both half right and both half wrong and no need to fight at all. It isn't a thousand *years*, that's all. You'd think between the two of them they could come to some estimation of what the proper figure is. I mean I don't know if it's a hundred thousand or a million or ten million, I'm not even worried about the number. A thousand whatevers are but a day in the sight of God.

So for six whatevers God created the world, from swamps and volcanoes through cavewomen and dinosaurs and all the experiments of one kind or another until there it was, the equivalent of late Saturday night, with the Flood over and done with and Eden maybe out of bounds forever, and people spreading out to do whatever it was they'd been told to do, multiply, be fruitful, fill the earth. Probably about 11:30 Saturday night, and God was tired. She'd been busy for six full whatevers and not a minute's rest, what with Adam being a big goof and getting lofty with Lilith and trying to insist on the missionary position, and Lilith saying she wasn't into that and him getting owly about it. They say Lilith said a magic word, threw Adam to the ground, scorned him and flew off to the Gulf of Aqaba to consort with fallen angels, magical beasts and those men and women she found to be desirable. They don't say what the magic word was, but if you think about it and get subjective and put yourself in Lilith's place, and here's this brand new world full of mystery and wonder, and some bozo wanting to get it on but insisting on getting it on in his way, wham bam thank you ma'am, and getting shirty when she suggested it didn't have to be quite as brief and dry as that, well, draw your own conclusions. I always figured the magic word Lilith said was fuck you, or maybe up yours. In any event, off she went to cavort in the waves with something or someone wonderful, a unicorn or a mermaid or a draggie or something precious like that.

Then there was Eve, who was a bit less what you might call flamboyant than Lilith, a bit more passive maybe. Or indifferent. Oh all right, she said, why not, the way you've got in mind it'll only take about three minutes anyway and it'll give me time to plan supper. Adam figured he was onto a good thing and God, well, she was busy trying to get names for all the animals and rolling in the aisles about the jokes she'd made, like hippopotami and giraffes and rhinoceroses so she didn't interfere or take the time to tell Adam to smarten up a bit. And Eve, maybe she figured God didn't really care one way or the other but she started getting bored, wandering around the garden, listening to that sweet-talking snake. Which is really only to be expected, don't you think? I mean if ever there was someone in need of sex therapy . . . and if that had been on, say, Day Two, God might have intervened, but maybe she was in the middle of designing the narwhal or something and didn't notice.

So there was that kerfuffle to sort out and not a moment's rest until it was done and God was tired. I think I'll take the Sabbath off, she said. Pay no attention to anything at all, maybe sleep in real late for a change. You keep an eye on things, y'hear, she said, and the seraphim and cherubim and angels and archangels all said sure, God, sure. Count on us, they said. Leave it in our hands, they smiled, and so she went to bed.

So if a thousand whatevers are but a day in God's sight, it stands to reason a thousand whatevers are but a night in God's sight, too, right? And it might be just a day (or a night) in God's sight, but it might be something more to cherubim and seraphim and archangels. Maybe, like Eve, they got bored. Oh, I know, the fundamentalists say God is omnipotent and omniscient. Does that mean she can't take a nap once in a while? I mean, we're all made in the image of God, right? So anything we have or do or think or are capable of doing or thinking comes from her, right? And we get sleepy, right? Well, there you have it, God gets sleepy, too.

Took herself off, lay down, pulled a soft cloud over her shoulders, closed her blue eyes and before long, probably, there was the gentlest, most perfect snore ever heard, and God was asleep. Perfectly sound asleep.

The cherubim, seraphim, angels and archangels had good intentions, but, as Sarah Graham often said, "the road to hell is paved with good intentions," a sentiment which may not have originated with Sarah but is none the less true. Maybe it was a game of mumbley-peg kicked off by the cherubim or maybe a pickup softball game the seraphim just couldn't pass up, or it might even have been the angels and archangels playing at something, although one has some trouble imagining they ever have any fun at all, serious and highfalutin as they are. In any event, attention up there wavered.

Down on earth things were progressing logically and evolving slowly but steadily. The women were weaving, potting, gardening, planning nutritious meals, perfecting several different alphabets, studying herbs and midwifery and teaching each other to read and write. The boys were out chasing animals, beating them on the head if they managed to catch them, and on those many times the fellows came home empty-handed, the women fed them vegetables, roots, grains, berries and the occasional fish, then warmed them at the fire and clothed them with the results of their weaving.

It might have gone on like that much longer, progressing through who knows what levels of increasing civilization and culture. We might never have had to live with the results of coal-fired furnaces or the internal combustion engine, we might have avoided the horrors of the Industrial Revolution and any number of slaughters and massacres. We most certainly would not have had to survive the Inquisition and witch hunts, nuclear technology would not have us teetering on the brink of total extermination and pollution would not be a deadly daily factor of life. But God was asleep and the heavenly host became inattentive.

There is, of course, no way to validate any of this. But what validation has ever been done on that other book? There is also no way to know what his name was, the one who inadvertently and in all probability half-mindedly kicked off what might well have been a most unwelcome change in what should have been the course of human development.

He undoubtedly had little patience and big muscles, and probably an inordinate ego. Short of temper and long on audacity, he was hungry. And because of those big muscles, he just reached out and took a bowl of berries away from someone who was smaller than himself. "Gimme," he said. "Hey," said the smaller person. The berry thief clenched his fist and held it under the smaller person's nose and the concept of *might makes right* was born. The first time it happened the glutton ate all the berries himself. Maybe the second and third time, too. But eventually several of the smaller ones decided to stick together to form a sort of protective compact. "No," they said, keeping the berries for themselves. The thug went off to think about it for a few minutes or hours or days, and then made his next move. Not everybody was in the protective compact. He went after someone who wasn't, took their bowl of berries, and with that as a bribe got a couple of other big lunks to help take away all the bowls of berries from all the ones without muscles, including the ones in the protective compact. The berry thief had become a Leader.

It worked so well with berries he began using it for other things as well. Eventually the leader had an army and with that army he went around not needing to hunt, fish, forage or anything else except rape, pillage and plunder and wasn't *that* a lot of fun. Rape usually is for the one on top.

"Hey," he said, "I am the generalissimo around here. You do what I say or I'll have my boys tapdance on your face." When he had a lot of everything he looked around and saw some Others had copied him, set themselves up on the other side of the hill and were doing over there what he'd been doing over here. So he and his boys went over there and did some facial dancing and took everything from the copycats, who immediately joined the army and almost doubled its size. Which meant, obviously, that the army needed almost twice as much food. Which meant, just as obviously, that the generalissimo needed to expand his territory. "Generalissimo," said his eldest son, "six hills over is a guy calls himself King and you should see the stuff *he's* got . . . including, by the way, an army about five times as big as yours.''

The generalissimo wasn't going to tackle anyone with an army *that* big, so he went to the little general to the left of himself and made a deal, then went to the little general to the right of himself and made a deal, and when he had a huge army and a gang of lesser generals ready to follow him, off he went to challenge the king. It doesn't matter which of them won. The winner was then king, with an enormous army and a whole new problem. In wartime, an army is a good thing to have. In peacetime it's an awful expense, so what do you do? Disband it? Someone else will re-form it and pull off a coup and then where are you? The only way to feed an army and keep it quiet is to keep taking stuff away from other people. And the only people who ever seem to have any stuff worth taking are the people who stayed home and minded their own business instead of ripping around the countryside raping, pillaging and plundering.

And of course the people who had been gathering, preserving, gardening, fishing, weaving and potting were the women—who did not have an army.

''Gimme,'' said the king. The women looked up from their work and saw a host of bearded, scruffy, hard-eyed pug-uglies and decided discretion really was the better part of valour, so they handed over a contribution. ''Not bad,'' the king thought. ''This taxes my patience,'' said one woman to another. ''That's what it's called, lady,'' laughed the king, ''taxes.'' So the women, who had developed language, lost their first word.

The king sent his tax collectors around on a regular basis after that, skimming the cream and taking the best potatoes and corn. The women began to drift off, moving their gardens further and further away from the kingdom, hiding the children so the army wouldn't steal them.

''I need some help,'' the king decided. But how do you negotiate alliances when you can barely grunt sentences? It takes a degree of slicks to be able to convince others your intentions are worthy when in fact they are what might be called slimesucking and ignoble.

''Hey,'' said the king, ''hey, you bunch behind that wall.''

''Go away,'' said the abbess.

''You watch your tongue,'' the king warned, ''or I'll send in the boys.''

''Really?'' laughed the abbess. ''Girls . . .'' A host of amazons with bows and arrows, sharp sickles and scythes and decidedly unwelcoming looks on their faces stared over the wall at the dumbfounded king.

''Hey,'' he said, ''I'm supposed to be the one with the army around here!''

The abbess didn't bother answering and neither did the amazons, they simply waited to counter whatever move the king decided to make. He decided to retreat with as much dignity as he could muster, which wasn't much, and off went the ragtag bog-trotting crowd, catcalling and hollering insults about unfeminine radicals, unwomanly and probably inverted as well. Other women heard about the walled town and the amazon army and managed one way or another to walk, run, sneak and generally migrate to it. The most worthy of them immediately set about learning how to defend not only herself but those of the women unable to learn. "Well," the king pondered, "how am I going to get around this one?" For rape is no fun at all when what it gets you is a quick hard kick in the slats. Or worse. To someone who sees his pecker as a weapon, or his weapons as his pecker, disarmament is a four-letter word.

It took a long time to think of a possible solution, for the king and his minions were much more used to thumping than to thinking, and it did not come easy. But after much pondering they came up with a plan. The king disguised himself as an ordinary jerk, which wasn't a bit difficult all things considered, and he disguised his son to look like an absolute lout, which was the easiest part of the plan, and together they went to the area just outside the wall of the town where the abbess and the women were doing their usual things. "Excuse me," the disguised king said, almost choking on his own tone of false reasonableness. "Yes?" asked the abbess. That was her first mistake, but how was she to know?

"I wonder if you could help me," asked the king, who was, you must remember, disguised. "It's about my son here. He's not like other men."

"He looks like a man to me," the abbess said coolly.

"Externally," the apparent ordinary jerk said, "but internally, in his head I mean, he's very different, and life for him out here is very unpleasant. He's gentle, he's sensitive and he's non-threatening, and you can imagine how difficult that makes everything for him. He's a good boy, he's kind, he's fond of dogs and other small animals, but he just doesn't think the way men do. In fact if he wasn't my own son I probably wouldn't have much use for him. He takes after his mother, you understand. He's, well, much as I hesitate to say it, he's more of a woman then a man."

"Hmmm," mused the abbess. "What help do you want from us?"

"Well," the crafty king said, "he doesn't have much future with us and I wondered if . . . well, it would be . . . you'd be saving his life, probably."

The women had been so busy working and studying and finding new and better ways to do things they hadn't taken the time to learn how to recognize a full-blown whopper. Besides, there was some degree of debate and discussion going on behind the walls. The amazons were all for telling the apparent ordinary jerk and his son the absolute lout to get lost, but some of the other women had other ideas. "It isn't *all* men," they said. "You can't hold him responsible for the entire system," they said. "The king and his army oppress men too, you know," they said. Most telling of all they said, "Think of his mother," and "How would you feel if you gave birth to a male child?"

The amazons countered with things like "Who cares?" and "Oh, for crying out loud, don't you ever learn from experience?" and "What do you mean oppresses men, too, even the most oppressed man still benefits from our misery." They were told they were uncharitable, hard-nosed, stiff-necked, heartless, spiritually incorrect and unenlightened. Against their better judgement, they began to waver. "You have got to have respect for and validate our perceptions," they were lectured, "otherwise you will be copying and continuing the negating tactics of the Others." Rather than do anything that might at any time be interpreted as being anything even remotely resembling something like that, the amazons shrugged and, to put none too fine a point on it, they capitulated to their friends. The absolute lout was in.

It took a fair amount of time, and all that time the perfect snores continued in heaven. The heavenly host may or may not have looked down occasionally, but if they did they didn't recognize what was happening. Eventually the absolute lout learned how to read and write, how to plant seeds and recognize weeds and a few other little things like that. And then the absolute lout came out from behind the walls and returned to his father. But before he left he went to the women and spoke his devious words. "There are others out there like me," he said (and that was no lie either), "who could put their energies into assisting you in your work." That one was so obvious even the most gullible of the women felt as if something less than absolute honesty was going on, but they failed to recognize the lie, falling into the trap of thinking this poor gentle sensitive non-threatening absolute lout was going to get an awful shock when he got back to the king's kingdom.

It was a sad shock, but it wasn't the king's son got it. He taught a couple of other supposedly gentle and sensitive men how to read and write and when there got to be a few scribes in the court they started taking the king's most trusted thugs and pug-uglies and teaching them what they could. Knowledge perverted is worse than no knowledge at all; they went back to the walled town with machines of destruction and the carnage was terrible.

"Okay," said the king, "there's more in my army than there is in yours, and mine are a whole lot bigger, stronger, uglier, and meaner."

He proved that very quickly. Down came the wall, in went the army and that was that. They broke the vases, stole the cloth, raided the storehouses and swiped all the books.

''So,'' the king leered triumphantly, ''here is how it's gonna be from now on: the first woman I see reading or writing is gonna have her eyes poked out and be burned at the stake and tortured and made to be real sorry, understand? And any goddam woman I see teaching another woman how to read or write is gonna get even worse treatment!'' And that was it for education for women for centuries.

The king's oldest son and a few scribes could read and write and they had the programs started to teach a few other firstborn sons—they were very particular about the firstborn son part of it—and they began to make treaties and sign agreements and bunch together five or six or even seven or eight principalities and territories to form empires. They ganged up on each other, kicked the shit out of the little guys, stole things, accumulated wealth and were just as happy as pigs in mire.

All that stolen wealth and property had to be kept track of and the oldest son was busy with all the military stuff so the next son was called in and told to learn how to read and write, and while he was at it, find a way to keep those goddam peasants out there from coming in here and taking all the good stuff. Stuff like gold, frankincense, myrrh and bowls of berries. The second son came up with a brilliant plan. ''If you don't want their dirty bodies swarming all over everything and cluttering up the storehouses, get their minds.'' He invented organized religion.

Until then the women had worshipped the Mother Image, had danced and sang, planted crops and dedicated them to the Mother, had enjoyed life and tried to integrate worship into everything they did. That kind of religion wasn't guaranteed to keep the poor poor and the meek meek, so the second son started ranting and raving about sin and punishment, about Jahwah and vengeance, and told everyone if they laid so much as one skinny finger on anything that belonged to the emperor, king, prince, noble, lord or just plain old shithead boss, *Jahwah* would get 'em! Burn forever, they were warned, lake of fire, they were told.

''Jesus Christ!'' the terrified peasants gasped.

''That's a very good name,'' the second son said. ''Let's build us a legend around that, too.'' So they told the people to be meek and honest and fatalistic and, to keep the people from rebelling or sinking into non-productive depression, promised them a better life in heaven *if* they were good. ''Eye hath not seen nor ear heard, neither has it entered into the hearts of man the things Jahwah has in store.'' It worked.

''What about me?'' asked the third son. ''How come I have nothing to do?''

"Give that boy a job," the old man ordered; he didn't want any of *his* sons growing up indigent, artistic, philosophic or any of that kind of crap. So they put the third son in charge of ''commerce.'' He began by trading beads but eventually he got into building banks and stockpiles of stuff they had no right to have in the first place, trading land and even people.

The fourth son was a real challenge: couldn't see well enough to shoot arrows, was too skinny for catch-as-catch-can, too puny to wield a club, and, like many other royal personages throughout history, kept falling off his horse. Too absent-minded for commerce, too mousy and uninspiring for religion, they all despaired of him for a long time until someone noticed this kid never had an idea of his own. ''My father says...'' ''My brother wrote...'' ''My friend thought...'' If cornered by someone who was out-arguing him, the kid would point one scrawny finger at the pages of any old book at all and say, ''It's right there.'' When they were sure he couldn't think original thoughts, they made him the first ''academic.'' He couldn't tell fly shit from pepper, the wrong side of his brain was working overtime while the good side was dormant, he couldn't tell a joke without putting his audience to sleep, but all that only proved they'd found the right job for him. Somewhere he ran across something called *tabula rasa*, the clean slate policy.

''Wherever we go,'' he told his dad, ''we'll deny there is any kind of culture. What there is we'll ignore, and, if necessary, destroy. We'll take their kids away from them and teach 'em to think the way we do, and that way, we won't have to keep the army there all the time; the overseers, drafted from the ranks of the slaves, will do it for us. They'll never find out the truth because we'll wipe out everything of theirs and make sure the ones we put in charge think like us.'' It wasn't exactly an original idea but it worked, and the king, who was by now calling himself Most Chosen Wonderfulness, beamed with satisfaction.

The religious son, the one with the most time to just sit and contemplate, went to his father, old Most Chosen Wonderfulness, and said, ''Listen, Dad, you got the start of a problem here. Sooner or later the generals are going to figure out that if they just have themselves a coup, they can shove you—and us—to one side, and that'll give them just that much more stuff for themselves. ''Great God,'' the king gasped. ''Exactly,'' the religious leader nodded, ''Why don't we get the generals fighting with each other? If we tell them that Jahwah has set certain people in certain positions of power or powerlessness that we aren't supposed to understand, we can keep them afraid of making the wrong move against us; and while they're afraid of us, we can nudge them to be afraid of each other, and get 'em fighting. The most obvious division would be to get the black one over there fighting with the pale one over here, and get the one with slanty eyes in a real snit with the one with red hair. I call it,'' he smirked, ''divide and conquer.''

''It's never going to work,'' the king protested, ''it's too damned obvious.''

''Give me some time.'' So the king gave his son all the time he needed and of course the religious leader was right, what was so damned obvious as to be laughable became deadly serious when it was learned Jahwah had said so.

And so, while God slept, less than four percent of the population of the world gained control of everything. They control the thirty multinational corporations that control all the companies, and through them the jobs, schools, universities, health services, governments, United Nations, World Health Organization and nuclear industry. Less than four percent of the world's population control more than ninety percent of the world's resources.

It's been out of control and unnatural for so long it's hard to believe it's probably just a portion of the whatever that is only a day (or a night) in the eyes of God. She is still sleeping. Still snoring perfectly, and the cherubim, seraphim, angels and archangels are afraid to wake her up because as soon as she rubs the sleep out of her eyes and has a cup of coffee she's going to see a mess and know they were playing Trivial Pursuit instead of doing what they said they'd do, which was watch over stuff. They aren't apt to be in any kind of hurry to waken her.

Not knowing how long a whatever is, it makes no sense for us to just sit here waiting for it to pass and the celestial alarm clock to go off and wake her up to tidy the mess. Obviously, we have to *do* something.

Remember *Peter Pan*? Remember how, when Tinkerbell was dying, they said if we would all just vow, ''I believe,'' she'd pull through and live? Remember sitting in the darkened theatre on Saturday afternoon sobbing, snivelling and snuffling, and then suddenly daring to whisper it, and never mind if the kid next to you snickered at you, whisper it, and, emboldened by the little whispers of others in the anonymity of the popcorn-scented dark, whisper it again, louder. Then, hesitantly but louder still, you said it. And soon, every kid in the Saturday show was on her feet yelling, ''I believe!'' and the music swelled, and the glow flickered, and there she was, Tinkerbell herself, stronger and stronger and stronger all the time, and we *did* it, we all helped save Tinkerbell!

Maybe it'll work again. Maybe we can wake God up if we all just keep on believing and keep on making an increasingly loud noise with our belief, so that the roar of our protest reaches even Heaven itself and God yawns, stirs and begins to come out of her deep, perfect sleep.

A Continuation of the Real History of the World as told to Stubby Amberchuk by Draconis Regina

Long ago and far away in a beautiful land of which we have only heard stories, the People lived in soddies carved into the breast of the hill.

Every spring they turned the soil. They prayed and danced, they dedicated their future harvest to the Great Mother, they planted their barley seed and then celebrated their hope by coupling happily between the furrows, calling on the powers of regeneration and fertility and focusing them on their crops and on their own bodies.

The People gathered nettles, stripped them and twisted them into twine; with the twine they made nets to catch the fish which swarmed in the rivers. Every morning they took their animals up into the hills to graze on the lush grass while the herders lay in the warm sun and entertained themselves by singing, their voices rich and full.

The milk from the animals was made into cheese and the barley was made into barley flour, barley bread and barley beer. The People lived well and happily, their children grew strong and joyous, and from dawn to dusk the People sang.

Then the Newcomers arrived. Tall and light-haired, they in no way resembled the People, who were short and small and had dark skin, dark hair and dark eyes. They left their ships and turned their own animals loose to graze; they cut down the trees and used the wood to build houses in those flat lands where the People had traditionally picked berries and gathered wild roots and herbs. They saw the fields of barley and the fields of corn and happily began to harvest them for their own.

When the People protested, blood was spilled. The Newcomers had weapons of metal and the People had only their own feet and fists and the courage in their brave doomed hearts, so the Newcomers took the land and its bounty and persecuted the People.

The little dark-haired People moved farther from the Newcomers and dug new soddies in the breast of the Mother and cuddled in there close to her, grieving and angry. They watched as their animals were herded out of the hills and penned with the animals of the Newcomers. The earth bled as new land was cut with the plough and utilized for more crops.

The poor brokenhearted People grew gaunt and thin; their children wept themselves to sleep, their bellies aching, their bones stunted.

One evening a woman of the People looked at her child and knew there was less than a week of life left in the skinny little thing. Desperate, she took her child and travelled carefully down to the village of the Newcomers and even managed to avoid the savage dogs. She crept from window to window, peering in until she saw where the firstborn son of the chief of the Newcomers was sleeping in his warm bed. She went in through the half-open window, took this fat blond baby from his bed and put her own starving daughter in his place. Then she left, taking the boy with her. She had intended to slit his throat and leave his body hidden in the forest, but she was a mother and unable to kill so jolly and innocent a child.

The wife of the chief of the Newcomers went into her son's room in the morning and found a changeling in his bed, a dark-haired, dark-skinned, dark-eyed little girl whose flesh barely covered her fragile little bones and whose eyes stared up at her with doomed acceptance.

The wife of the chief lifted this wraith of a child and almost dashed her brains out against the wall, but fear hit her. She knew that if this child were to die her own child would die too. She took the girl with her to the warm kitchen, and while the servants watched in disbelief she gave breast to the little mite and spoke softly, soothing the fears of the child.

The skinny little girl grew healthy on the rich milk and when she was old enough to learn to talk her first word was Momma, directed to the tall, strong, blond woman who was wife of the chief. In the hills, the fat blond son of this woman grew lean and hungry and learned to set snares for small animals, learned to sneak up in the long grass, outwit the fierce dogs and steal lambs and calves from flocks which belonged to what were actually his own people. The language he learned to speak was the language of the dark ones whose midwife he called Mother.

Soon another desperate mother, and another, crept down and exchanged her starving child for a blond child who had at least had several months of good rich milk to give it strength to survive. The women of the Newcomers began to leave food out at night, hoping it would find its way to their own dear stolen babes.

The dark changeling children grew strong and brought joy to their foster parents. Then one day, out of the wilds came the young blond son who had been the first one stolen. He was tall, but so thin his ribs showed, and all he had with him was a harp and the blanket in which he had been wrapped when he was stolen. He was terrified, for all his life he had tried his hardest to stay away from these Newcomers, but he had been raised to honour his mother and it was she who had told him to go down to the village and show the Newcomers his blanket, and so he did as he was told.

The fierce dogs rushed at him but did not attack. They had learned over the years that the wild dark ones could easily grab a dog and snap its spine over their knee. Still they roiled and boiled around his feet, making so much noise all the People came running.

One was the changeling daughter of the chief. She looked on this tall skinny young blond man and knew immediately that this was the child who had been taken so that she could grow healthy. And she knew, looking at him, that his own life had not been easy, for he had the marks of hard work and even of wounds he had got hunting the fierce beasts of the forest. She knew the young man was terrified, knew the stories he must have been told of the savage ferocity of the Newcomers. She smiled at him.

He looked at her and was not frightened. This young woman looked like the People he considered to be his family. She was dark-haired and dark-eyed just like his own beloved mother. He reached out, took the young woman's hand and smiled tentatively. He spoke to her in the language which ought to have been her own. But she did not understand a word of it. Then she said some words in the language of the Newcomers and he understood nothing at all. But he knew, for his dark mother had told him the whole story, that somewhere in this village was the woman who had given him birth. Because he had the sense of humour of the People, it struck him as funny that he did not know his own birth language, and he laughed.

The two young people moved toward the assembled villagers. Then the wife of the chief saw the blanket the young man carried. She thought her heart would break. He should have been taller, he should have been much much heavier and he should never have had to fight wild animals for his food so that he was scarred. Sobbing, she ran toward him and he knew, though he did not understand the words she was trying to say. He did as he had been told by his darling dark Mother. He held the wife of the chief in a gentle embrace and spoke to her kindly.

The Newcomers all embraced the young man and welcomed him—especially those Newcomers whose children had been taken as changelings, for this young man was proof that there was a chance their own children were alive. The chief was overjoyed that he again had a son and he ordered a feast.

During the feast some of the Newcomers began to bellow songs and to dance awkwardly around the fire. The young man smiled and stood up and began to play on his harp. The Newcomers stared, struck by the beauty the young man coaxed from his little instrument. He sang for them, songs of the herders and hunters, songs of those whose poor bloody hearts were cracking under the strain of hunger and homelessness. The Newcomers realized what they had caused by their arrival.

The young changeling woman felt as if something was stirring inside her. She did not know that for months this music had been part of her infancy. She did not understand the words but she was moved to try to dance; the young man, seeing her awkward attempts, demonstrated the steps to her while playing his harp. And some time between the first step they took together and the ending of the song, these two understood there was a bond between them—small wonder, each having drunk the same milk of two women.

The two changelings, the blond and the dark, courted each other briefly. Then they were married, and such a wedding it was! The young man went out into the hills and looked for the People and invited them, promising there would be no danger. When he returned he told the villagers that he, the son of the chief, had given his word, and his father agreed.

The day of the wedding dawned. Out of the forest came the People, moving hesitantly, for they had promised not to bring any of their primitive weapons with them. The young man saw the thin, dark woman who had been his mother. He embraced her and wept with joy, and she called him her own dear baby. The blond woman who was really his mother knew her son had been loved, and in the knowing of that she forgave everything and stepped forward to welcome the woman who was the mother of her own beloved daughter. The dark changeling stared in wonder at her real mother, for it was like looking at her own face, older. She embraced the woman and felt many things, but did not feel a burst of love, for her mother was the woman who had wiped her nose, changed her clothes and tucked her in bed at night.

The combined tribes celebrated this marriage in grand fashion. All the changeling children, blond and dark, got to meet their natural parents. The dark People sang and danced and entertained the blond people for days. Old hatreds were discussed openly and new alliances were agreed upon.

Though it all took time, life changed. The People were no longer persecuted, they were given back some of their land and once again they began to raise their corn and barley. They learned much from the blond people about intensified farming and the blond people learned much about respect for the land, and everyone learned to dance together and sing together. There were other marriages between blond and dark until it was impossible to tell which were the Newcomers and which were the People; all were the People.

Until the Outlanders arrived. The Outlanders moved from their strange ships and set up outposts along the shore from which they raided the villages of the People. The Outlanders were only marginally interested in the crops and livestock. Their interest was focused mainly on the coal under the hills. They enslaved the People and sent them into the burrows to dig the coal. The poor People had to obey or be killed.

The beautiful land became scarred and huge piles of black rock began to grow where the debris from the mines was piled. Bit by bit the beautiful green hills were replaced with ugly black heaps. The People sang songs to the Mother of All apologizing to her for what was being done to her. Every morning they would sing their way into the pits and at night sing their way home again. Everyone was sent—the men, the women, the children, all had to dig, pick, heave and suffer in the coal. Many died when the roof came crashing down, when the picks broke through the rock into water, when the gases in the earth exploded, and through it all they sang the sound of their misery, and their music was as beautiful as their lives were sad.

It might have gone on like that forever, but the Foreigners heard of the wealth of the coal and they came to take it from the Outlanders.

The Outlanders quickly formed up their army and impressed many of the People into it. They taught them the ways of killing, then went out to slaughter the Foreigners. While the two armies were away fighting the People sighed with relief and even took a few days off. Finally the Victors returned and things went back to what they had been, with the brokenhearted buggers doing the work and the Victors reaping the wealth.

But those who had been impressed into the army were not about to just calmly walk back down into the pits. They agitated and argued, and to keep them quiet the Victors headed out to do some more pillaging and plundering, for the problem with having an army is you have keep it busy or it will turn on you and devour you. Soldiers need food and clothes, their beer and their pleasures. The best place to get all this for them is someplace where someone else has to pay for it, so off they went.

And so the People worked in the pits and the army went off all over everywhere conquering other poor buggers and breaking their hearts. The Crazed Ones arrived to try to defeat the Victors. The Victors called back some of their army and prepared to meet the Crazed Ones in battle.

The poor People took the day off work and went up on the cliffs to watch the Crazed try to kill the Victors. They celebrated by drinking a bit of barley beer and eating a few cheese sandwiches and exposing their skins to the warmth of the sun and laughing as the cannon roared and the boats of both sides were blown up and soldiers died. Each soldier that died was one less they would have to feed, so they began to sing, pretending, of course, that they were singing to encourage their side, when in truth they did not feel there was any side down there had anything to do with them.

But then they noticed that there were poor suffering bastards down there chained to oars. There were poor suffering bastards who were being blown to bits by the cannon of both sides, who were being dumped into the water, pulled under by their shackles and drowned in water stained with blood for no reason that had anything to do with them. And as they faced certain death their poor suffering bastard hearts broke and the sound of their hearts breaking rose above the crash of cannon and reached the ears of the People on the cliffs. They realized, name of our Blessed Mother, those are our own dear ones down there suffering as we have suffered and are suffering, dying as we have died and are dying. They raced down the cliffs and got their little fishing boats and set out in the bloodstained sea to save their own. The generals and admirals on both sides misunderstood and thought it was for them all this bravery was being demonstrated, and they fell to fighting with renewed vigour, killing more and more of each other with each salvo.

The poor brokenhearted buggers hauled the poor suffering bastards out of the water and took them to the shore and helped hammer the shackles and chains from their tormented and starved bodies. They embraced them and fed them cheese sandwiches and gave them barley beer to drink and put salve on the places where the chains had rubbed their flesh raw. Nobody seemed to notice there was a distinct difference in complexion; they knew only that the colour of blood is the colour of blood and the sound of a heart breaking is the sound of a heart breaking. They left the rich and powerful to deal with the rich and powerful. The poor brokenhearted buggers took the poor suffering bastards down into the mines and hid them in the darkness where they would be safe.

The Rulers rose from the remnants and decided that the coal mines were just about finished anyway and sheep were the thing of the future. They bought sheep, stole sheep, shipped sheep and put them on the green grass that grew between the huge piles of black rock, and any place they found any of the poor suffering fools they beat on them and burned their houses and raped the women and chased off the children and put sheep on the land to eat the grass and crops. The People were starving, in competition with the sheep for the increasingly poor crop of grass, and life was dreadful for them.

By now there was no need for the People to quarrel about much of anything, for the world had become divided into only two groups, the rich and the suffering.

The brokenhearted decided to kiss off the land in which they had been so foully treated. They took to boats and headed away, leaving the Rulers with their sheep. It was cruel; the sea swallowed as many as it allowed to pass. The hearts continued to break and to express their pain in song but eventually a few of the People made it to a land where the sun was warm, the grass green, the flowers many and the bounty of the One True Mother was there for the taking. They wept together, they danced together and the sound of their joy burst from their throats as the brokenhearted and rejected, the sad bastards and poor buggers set about saving their own lives. They dug soddies into the side of the gentle hills and lived there, and they cleared garden space and planted the few poor seeds they had brought with them. They hunted the animals and clung to life through a long and miserable winter, and in the springtime they started all over again, planting crops and toiling from dawn to dusk, making nets to fish the river and setting traps to get animals for meat and for skins to keep them warm in the bitter winter. And they made their lives better and harvested happily and sang together.

From the forests came some people who said welcome, and the poor suffering bastards stared with shock and amazement. They had been happily taking whatever they needed and using it any way they wanted and thinking the land was theirs, and now they were faced with the realization they were not much different than the Rulers, for the land had never been theirs to harvest but was home to others, others who did not dress as they did, nor talk as they did, nor sing as they did, nor dance as they did, but who honoured the Mother and respected the land and were willing to share and be friends.

A young man from the forest stepped forward, smiling tentatively, and a young woman of the People, who realized they were in fact now Newcomers, stepped out to meet him, took his hand and smiled. He smiled in return, forgetting that his people had suffered because of her people, realizing that the differences were not as important as the similarities, forgiving these brokenhearted souls what they had begun to learn to forgive others for having done to them.

And all might have gone well, but the Rulers heard tales of a land where the poor lived together comfortably, sharing the resources and doing quite well without supervision. By now the Rulers had little to rule, for the sheep had gnawed everything down to the roots, then eaten the very roots. So the Rulers called together their army and their navy and headed off to where the People had found a homeland.

Once again hearts began to break, and in the breaking new music was sent from throats tight with sobs, and the rivers were claimed and and the crops were claimed and the army marched and the mines were dug and the trees were dropped and cities built.

The People heard the sound of their own hearts breaking. They remembered the litany of horrors told by their grandparents and they decided to put miles between themselves and the Rulers. They headed off toward the west, for one thing was agreed upon by all the many people who formed the People and that was that freedom lay westward, in the direction of Avalon, the misty isle where apples grow year round and where Rulers have never been admitted.

Part Three

Royal Divine

Royal Divine was born some two hours northwest of Ottawa, and the circumstances of his birth may be the only thing west coast dwellers do not hold against the citizens and province of Ontario. Well, they say, a person isn't always responsible for what happens in the nesting box, why, I had a bitch once was as good as you'd want a dog to be, but her pups weren't worth the powder it took to blow 'em to hell. Not much you can do when nature goes berserk, they mourn, and save their spleen and ire for arseltarts like politicians and other low life.

He wasn't called Royal by his parents, nor was his family name Divine, all that came later. He was named Clarence for his father, Alfred for his grandfather, and the family name was Gannon. It had originally been Gagnon, but nobody in his right mind would live in the Ottawa valley and hang onto a frog name like that. Of course, as soon as you know the family name used to be French, you know that there are a lot of Huron, Algonquin, Iroquois and maybe even Ojibway influences in the family tree, but nobody smart enough to erase the gallic flavour is going to be stupid enough to admit to being tainted genetically, so the hint was eased out in a couple of quiet jokes and within a few generations everyone knew the Gannons were Black Irish. Most Gagnons are either staunch Roman Catholic or fallen Roman Catholic, but the Gannons had more sense than that. Maybe the Orange Lodge was big in the region, and maybe because of or in spite of that a lot of the Irish were rabid Catholics, but not the rich ones, and, as we all know, with wealth goes respectability, and when you're trying to live down the spectre of French-halfbreed, you strive for respectability. They'd have been Anglican if that hadn't seemed too lonely and tight-assed a life. Protestant would do, and the Baptists have always enjoyed lusty singing.

Clarence Alfred Gannon was duly dedicated to the service of Christ, just as his several brothers and sisters had been, and life went back to normal. Farming takes a lot of time and a lot of energy, and everyone worked from sunup to well after sundown. As little Clarence grew, everyone worked overtime at trying hard not to mention a few unpleasant truths. For a start, the kid was puny. Most of what his mother managed to poke down his gullet was rejected by his gut and spewed out a half hour later in a discoloured and festering projectile that stained whatever it touched. At first this septic stew was thought to be the reason little Clarence usually stank like something that really ought to be returned to the pig pen, but slowly the light dawned and everyone tried not to mention the fact that it was Clarence himself who stank. His mother took him to the town physician, who first checked Clarence's diaper, then handed him over to the nurse, who scrubbed the little horror in strong soap and returned him, wrapped in a sterilized towel. The doctor detected no odor and began to lecture Clarence's mother on the proper kinds of cleanliness. Clarence lay on the examining table in the soft pale sunlight and waved his arms and legs jerkily. Within seconds the faint musky smell began to make itself known again, and the doctor stopped talking Public Health. He checked Clarence's ears, throat and nose for infection. Finally he could only suggest to Clarence's poor mother that she get chlorophyll drops and add them to the smelly little creep's milk. Clarence drank green milk and, eventually, ate green-tinged mashed potatoes and still exuded the same kind of odour sometimes found in the dark corners of musty closets.

His hair came in thick, wiry and black, and it stuck out like a bramble thatch. No amount of washing and brushing flat had any effect and his mother took to anointing his head with goose grease and smacking a stocking cap over it all to try to train the hair to lie down and look like hair instead of a windblown mouldy strawstack. All the goosegrease did was make Clarence's body odour seem somehow healthier.

The kid was covered with large dark freckles which slowly grew into large dark moles, some of which had hairs growing out of them before he was old enough to talk. His narrow little eyes burned with resentment from the time he could sit up, and his brothers and sisters knew Clarence was jealous. At first nobody believed any five-month-old baby would deliberately aim at someone's face before projectile vomiting, but by the time Clarence was seven months old his mother knew for a fact what it was he was doing. "Don't get him mad," she said tiredly, "you know how he gets."

And he got more and more like that. About the same time he learned to crawl, the house cat learned to prefer the barn. The farm dog took to leaving the job of guarding the house to the geese, who would have gladly left too, but geese are very loyal, very stubborn, or just too stupid for words. Luckily for the geese, Clarence wasn't very big and the first time he tried to poke out the gander's eyes with the knitting needle he had snitched from his mother's basket, the gander was able to tip the little christer on his back, stand on his chest and flap his wings viciously in the little snarl-twisted face. Now if a gander did that to your kid, or to mine, it would be roast goose for dinner, but Clarence's mother didn't interfere in the least little bit, and when the gander walked off, head high, and Clarence crawled, snivelling and snotting, back to the house, Mrs. Gannon went outside with a half a loaf of fresh-baked bread and fed it to the gander and his spouses. Then she went back inside, wiped Clarence's snoffily nose and gave him a gingerbread cookie to shut him up for a few blessed minutes.

Dogs came from miles away just to bark and howl at the sight of the grisly little fart, and though the neighbours tried hard to be very Christian about it all, it wasn't easy to keep on inviting Clarence to birthday parties and such. He invariably managed to do something ridiculous, unpleasant or disgusting.

Mrs. Gannon didn't know any more about contraception than any other woman of her time and place, but she did know she wasn't taking any chances. Vinegar, her next door neighbour whispered to her, so Mrs. Gannon took cotton wadding, dipped it in vinegar and shoved it up as far as she could. It burned and it made her feel as if both sitting down and walking were things she didn't want to do, and the smell of it upset her. "Hey, come on," said Mr. Gannon, who wanted his meals on time and his release on command. "What if it doesn't work," she whispered, weeping. "What if it's another one like Clarence?" Mr. Gannon's stiffer wilted at the mere thought.

It wasn't that Clarence took fits. Taking fits is common in the inbred families of the valleys around the nation's capital. Some of the most fantastic fit-takers have had great careers as bureaucrats and civil servants. There's no shame in it when most of the people you know have one or two kids who flop and foam on a regular basis. You just try to see to it that the male fit-takers don't take up with the female fit-takers.

Clarence took fits, sure. Fits were the least of the problems the family had to deal with. Mostly, it was Clarence's out-and-out cussedness.

Nobody knows exactly what it was Clarence thought he was up to, and asking Clarence never got you anywhere close to the truth, but the evidence revolved around a very sore teat on the crooked-horn milk cow, a half-empty package of matches and one of Mrs. Gannon's metal knitting needles, suddenly stained with soot and discoloured by heat. Clearly imprinted on the side of Clarence's ugly little head was the outline of the cow's hind foot. Also clearly marked was Clarence's own arm, which was lying on the knitting needle when he was found. The knitting needle had obviously been very hot when Clarence was dumped, because the blister on the filthy little scrawny arm was large, and the scar, after it all healed, was striking. You could even tell it was a number five needle, although from some angles it looked like a smudged two. After that, Mrs. Gannon kept her knitting basket in her bedroom, locked away in the heavy cedar chest. "He's just too fond of knitting needles," she said, remembering the incident with the gander. Mr. Gannon agreed, and even went so far as to visit Cornell Griffin, who cut the piglets and tom kittens, and asked about the possibility of having Clarence fixed so that whatever it was that had showed up in him, it wouldn't be passed on to the next generation. Cornell was going to refuse, but he had three daughters and while the thought of any of them going crazy enough to get close to Clarence seemed remote, on the other hand, it didn't take much talent for imagining to realize what could happen if Clarence took to leaping out of bushes with his pants at half mast.

"Don't know what good it'll do," he said slowly. "They tell me it don't take the lead out of the pencil so much as makes sure there's no messages get writ, so to speak."

"Better than nothing," Clarence's father sighed. "Any message that little shit is apt to write could only be bad news."

They decided to wait until Clarence was a bit older. He had a very high squeaky voice and a pinched, rat-faced look, and maybe, left uncut, he might grow out of both. They were not hoping to salvage anything, but rather try to make Clarence less disgusting and off-putting.

Clarence went off to school with a grin on his razorlipped little mouth, and a new lunch bucket. He knew before he headed off that nobody was going to want to play with him. And he also knew he was going to find a way to make them do what they didn't want to do. He had a natural knack for it, and it was getting easier with practice.

By Christmas time Clarence could read and write as well as any of them, including the teacher. He couldn't add, subtract, multiply or divide, he couldn't colour inside the lines, he didn't know the Queen of England from the King of France, refused to recite the Lord's Prayer or sing the national anthem, but hot spit, could that boy read. You could ask him any word and he could spell it, but come time to put the words into sentences and Clarence began to really shine. His penmanship was beautiful, full of curlicues and squiggles. He often embroidered his margins with colour drawings of vines and flowers, and more than once, reading over and trying to make sense of the torrent of words poured upon the page, the teacher thought she saw round-eyed and appealing bunnies peeking at her from the large rounded loops of his B's and D's, simpering snakes flirting from his S's, and smiling faces peering from behind the shafts of his H's and L's. Clarence could write sentences until the cows came home and, read aloud, the sentences seemed to flow and spiral, to take on a hypnotic rhythm of their own, until those listening began to wonder were they hearing reading or singing. Mind you, once the reader stopped reading there was no use asking them to explain the sense of what they had read, because there was no sense in it, but by god, while it lasted it was powerful and beautiful.

Clarence himself could take almost anything and read it aloud beautifully. There were some who insisted Clarence could even have taken the local newspaper, read aloud from it and wrench tears from a stone. More than once the boy picked up the big black Bible sitting on the corner of the teacher's desk as if pinning the furniture in place by the weight of all ten commandments, and Clarence would start at Genesis and read until you wanted to beg him to continue. Dabbing his mouth regularly with a grubby handkerchief, swabbing the spit from his lips, Clarence could launch himself and his listeners into transports and raptures, turning even the begats into something other than what anybody else could make of them.

Even more incredibly, everyone would sit and listen, jaws agape, eyes glassy, and though they had little memory of it afterward and might not have been able to tell you what it was Clarence had read to them, they enjoyed it while it lasted, the sound of his raspy little voice taking them up and down the cadences of the sentences, in and out between the rhythms of the phrases.

Clarence had his own secret weapon. As soon as he was old enough to be able to print, he sent off to one of those addresses in the back of certain kinds of what might be called, for lack of a better word, magazines. Not for him the two-way walkie talkie or the vial of holy water from Lourdes. Not for him the lifetime ordination or the Jinx-Off lucky charm. "Learn Hypnotism," the ad said. "Bend Others to your Will," Clarence, you must remember, was determined the kids would play with him whether they wanted to or not. They did. He'd fix them with his beady little snake eyes and start to talk in that nerve-wracking voice of his, and they were sunk. He was the first one picked for teams. He even gained weight on all the snacks and desserts the other kids gave him. It was sickening, really, but on the other hand it kept the little puke happy and quiet, and when Clarence was quiet and happy, life was better for everybody.

Clarence grew slowly, and his appearance did not improve in the least little bit, nor did his disposition sweeten, in spite of the pieces of chocolate cake, slices of pie and array of muffins with which the other kids bribed him. His voice deepened, his moles grew and his body odour became increasingly rank. He started staring at girls, as if trying to figure something out, and everyone in the community shuddered at the thought of what might happen if Clarence came to any conclusions. His father knew the time had come to take his terrible son to see Cornell and his sharp-bladed buck knife. Of course, you can't just invite a kid to gladly journey to his own castration, so Mr. Gannon, in what he considered to be a stroke of sheer genius, set about getting Clarence drunk. "You're almost a man, now, son," he said, with as much phony companionability as he could manage. "Here, have your first real drink." He handed Clarence a pint jar full of an oily yellowish distillation. Clarence took the jar, tipped it, drained it and handed it back. His father waited for the kid to pass out, or at least flip into a fit, but Clarence just blinked. "Have another," his father offered. Clarence drained that, too. A few minutes later he sat down, his eyes glazing, a sickly grin spreading on his awful face. His father picked him up, put him in the back of the wagon and drove to Cornell's place.

Nobody ever talked about what happened at Cornell's place that day. All that was known was that Mr. Gannon and Cornell both wound up with facial bruises and contusions, Cornell had a broken arm, both men were pale and bitter-eyed and they both walked for weeks as if they had hot pokers rammed up their arseholes. Within a couple of months both Mrs. Gannon and Mrs. Griffin began to fill out, to lose the exhausted looks they had worn since the first child arrived, to glow again with that kind of expectant wonder teenaged girls have, and the lines on their faces smoothed out and almost disappeared. They took to laughing together and doing outlandish things, like packing huge picnic lunches and taking their kids off swimming in the river. Even more outlandish than that, the mothers would strip to their underwear and dive into the water themselves, splashing and laughing, as vigourous and energetic as you never expect married women to be, as strong bodied and clear-skinned as any single woman in the world. "Oh, bother the ironing," they'd say, laughing easily, patting their husbands on the shoulders as if they actually almost liked them, "let's take the kids down to the slough and show them the swamp lilies." "Oh, housework," they would shrug, "one thing about housework, no matter how long you ignore it, it'll wait faithfully for you and nobody else will show up and take it away or do it for you! The sun is shining, come on, let's pull the kids out of school and *do* something!"

"Oh, Cornell, come *on*, don't be like that! I'll help you finish your work, you'll be free by noon, and we can just *go*. What's life for if it isn't for living? Come on, Cornell!''

And Cornell would hesitate, then nod, and didn't seem even the least bit ashamed of the fact his wife and kids swarmed all over the farm doing his chores for him so he could pile into the wagon and take them off looking for the first spring violets or pole them out on a raft he wasted a day building, so they could watch the fluffy baby mallards following their parents around in the swamp. Clarence Gannon, senior, was just as worse, they said, having actually been caught dancing in the kitchen with his wife. Middle of the day and a world of work waiting and there he was, laughing and smiling, dancing in his sock feet, and not the least bit ashamed of it, either. Maybe he was laughing and smiling because Clarence, junior, aged twelve, was gone. Ottawa, some said. Montreal, others guessed. In a home, they whispered, in jail they hoped, and though they each and every one of them at some time asked Sam Adams, the local constable, if he knew anything about it, nobody learned anything more. Sam just shook his head, smiled, said there was nothing to worry about, everything was just as it ought to be; he himself had interviewed both Mr. Gannon and Mr. Griffin and everything that was needed to be known was known and that was that. Doc Fridzit said even less. Yes, he'd been called out to the Griffin's place the day the boy left town. Yes, he'd been there several hours. No, there was nothing unusual about any of it.

Years later, in London, England, a small, stubby, homely-as-a-mud-fence evangelist with halitosis, body odour and slick-tongued snake-oil-salesman expertise rented a small hall and began to hold lectures. He had magic lantern slides of Africa, of Borneo, of China, he had pictures, postcards and posters of Denmark, Eretria and Finland, he had geographic and socio-political treatises on Germany, Holland and Iceland, and he had a head full of schemes, ideas and dreams. And he could talk. Oh, my, yes, he could talk! Eye hath not seen nor ear heard, neither hath it entered into the hearts of sane people what Royal Divine could yammer on about for hours on end. Any question on any topic was answered, the words flowed, rhythmic, the metre pinning the audience-cum-congregation to its seats, the cadences lulling them into a state almost identical to that of deep sleep, and Royal Divine talked, eyes burning, body swaying, jerking, writhing.

He spoke of truth and he spoke of beauty, he spoke of fulfillment and he spoke of mystery, he spoke of spiritual enlightenment and he spoke of psychic healing, he spoke of glory and he spoke of eternal life. And he spoke of God. Spoke as if he and God had tea together every day at four, when God asked Royal Divine his opinion and sought his approval.

The sons and daughters of the Empire sat like lumps and nodded like dozy donkeys, they focused their pale blue eyes on this reeking little freak from the colonies and all they saw was eternal life. The learned and the righteous, the cultured and the Christian, the imperialists and privileged reached with weak, pale hands for their wallets, reticules and purses, and showered on Royal Divine their allowances and dividends, their inheritances and their trust funds, their share of the booty of half the plundered world.

Paradise he promised, a land where the hand of man has not yet set foot, a place created by God for you and yours, a land you can call home, a home you can call yours, an Eden unsullied and unspoiled, where you will walk in the protection of the Father, commune with the angels and find the path to redemption and eternal salvation. Nobody, he swore, has fouled or sullied this bit of heaven here on earth, you will be as Adam and Eve, the progenitors of chosen people, and he waved the British Admiralty map like a rallying banner, and the sheep responded eagerly.

Royal Divine bought passage for his flock on a Cunard liner and they trooped on board willingly. Servants wrestled with trunks and boxes, crates and barrels, and those who might have at one time or another actually seen an English country garden, talked confidently of carving life from the wilderness, the unsullied, virgin wilderness. They walked the deck in pairs, trios and groups, waving to their families on shore, who waved back, often with absolute relief, and then the whistle blew and the steamer began to pull away from everything they had known. Within ten minutes more than half of them were puking their guts out with seasickness as the vessel cruised gently down the channel toward the open sea.

Royal Divine spent the entire voyage gambling with anyone who would wager him about anything. When asked by a hardy member of his flock if perhaps gambling weren't less than what one might want to expect of a Neo-Moses, Royal smiled his creepy little dreadful smile and spoke of the seven wise and seven foolish virgins, of the light hid under a bushel, of the talents buried in the field, and of the need for cold hard cash to buy seeds and supplies. He talked of the need to meet possible converts on their own terms, and of how the end was far more important than any examination of the means.

"Why," he asked, "should the Devil have all the money? Is it not God who gave us the abundance of this earth? Is not money also power? Do we not, by leaving money in the hands of the Devil-worshippers also put power into the hands of those who work against God? Will we sit on deck chairs in the sunshine and turn our backs on the chance to take from the Devil that which is God's, that we might use it to buy land and seed and with our love and commitment, our dedication and courage, harvest a crop of Angels? Have they not all been taught a lesson, and might not that lesson lead to other lessons? Having spoken to them of flushes and straights and been proven a winner, might I not at some time also speak to them of God and Sanctity and again be proven a winner, their souls saved from the clutches of the Demon Overlord, their lives recommitted to the one true Father? Perhaps by beating them at cards and temporarily rendering them impecunious, I have shown them the folly of giving allegiance to Satan. A soul may well have been saved at that table, and is not anything at all worth the saving of that soul?''

Flummoxed, the questioner almost swallowed his tongue in remorse, and Royal Divine continued to slide aces from his sleeves, palm honest and toss loaded dice, and hypnotize the other players into believing whatever he wanted them to believe.

Eventually, of course, they arrived where the hand of man had never set foot and Royal moved his flock into what had been barns and chicken coops, and nobody asked how it was all these buildings happened to be on land nobody but them had ever before seen. Nobody asked how it was the E&N railway passed within a mile and a half of this hidden Eden. Nobody asked how it was that a two-lane road went along the fence, and nobody wondered who had built that sturdy dock out there, just past the beautiful three-storey house in which Royal Divine lived with his personal staff, all of whom were female, all of whom were yet to see their twentieth birthdays and several of whom were already pregnant.

Royal Divine and his colony of gentrified loons caused little or no stir of interest in the people who lived near Eden. They'd seen it all before; the whole island from top to bottom and side to side was peppered with religious communes, colonies and cults. From every corner of the globe messiahs came, bringing their flocks of sheeplike followers. In every language known to man and several unknown, they had preached and provoked, harangued and hollered, and, bit by bit, piece by piece, the pattern had unfolded so often the neighbours could almost predict the minute of the hour of the day the next foolishness would commence. Of course there were separate dwellings for men and women, of course sex was forbidden unless to increase the population, and, of course, Royal had the say about who would do what, with which, and to whom, how often, when and in which position. Of course the most attractive women wound up in the big house and of course they were all visited at any hour of the day or night by the active force of the Holy Spirit in the shape of Royal himself.

Yes, he fleeced them, yes he fooled them, and of course he fornicated with the dedication of a mink. Yes, there were whips and yes, there were public floggings and yes, there was a big white yacht with a naked woman captain who ferried Royal to the mainland to recruit new converts, the richer the more welcome. Yes, irate husbands showed up with blood in their righteously indignant eyes and dragged home wives who had fallen under the spell of the warty little freak. Yes, wives fell upon the place with the fury of invading hosts, turning loose groups of hired detectives and stevedores to drag home husbands who had gone bonkers and signed away the family savings. Yes, distraught parents showed up and kidnapped back their children and yes, one family hired a gang of confessed criminals to invade Eden, beat the shit out of anyone who interfered, find and subdue the heir to their fortune and drag him back to his mansion. The thug's task was made easier by the fact that as soon as he saw them and realized why they were there, the heir raced forward eagerly yelling, ''Get me the hell out of this loony bin!'' and a dozen others scrambled in his wake screeching, ''Pick me, pick me!''

Yes, there were unmarked graves in the rain forest and yes, there were sacks weighted with stones and dropped over the side of the yacht to sink into the cold green sea. The disillusioned sneaked away and took what jobs they could find in town, and the island became assured of an educated elite who moved into law offices, judicial chambers and the positions of school principals. The police raided several times and found nothing they could use as evidence to prosecute, and nobody ever got any of their money back again.

When Royal Divine disappeared, nobody was surprised except those few stubbornly faithful fools who had toiled for twenty years to make Eden something other than a tired festering hole ankle deep in goose, duck and chicken shit. One morning it was over, just like that, just as the neighbours had expected. One morning the young women came from the big house looking stunned and unsure of everything, including their own names. The big white yacht was gone, and Royal Divine was gone. So was everybody's money. At least the taxes were paid, at least there was a four-month supply of chicken feed in the storage shed. And at least they had some idea of what needed to be done to make the chicken farm work.

Part Four
Megan

1

Just outside the boundaries of what had been supposed to be the New Eden several roads converged, and at the convergence Paddy King built a store and called it, for reasons he never bothered to explain, the Bright Spot. At first, the only people who used Paddy's store were people travelling from Victoria to Nanaimo, people tired of bouncing and jouncing, people who had stupidly gone right past the artesian spring on the side of the road where the very best water in the entire world bubbles day and night, free for the taking, people who were parched and fed to the teeth with the boring sameness of mile after mile of towering trees, people who welcomed any excuse to stop, stretch their legs, drain their poor bladders in the privy out back and buy something cold to drink. Paddy would smile and talk and go out to his well to pull up a bucket in which rested a dozen or so chilled homemade root beer, which he would kindly and grandly sell to the travellers, all of whom paid gladly, all of whom thanked him, and even in some cases blessed him.

When traffic became considerable enough, Paddy had gas pumps installed and hired a homeless teenaged refugee from the now defunct religious colony to pump gas in return for a place to stay and the chance to push his skinny shanks under Mrs. Paddy's generous table. The poor kid, underfed all his life, thought he had died and gone to heaven and worked so hard and so willingly that Paddy thought he'd had an angel fall on him; he bought the kid new overalls, new shirts, new boots and even socks, which the boy had never before worn in his life.

Eventually this homeless brat grew up strong and happy and married one of Paddy's daughters. Since the groom had no name of his own that he could remember, he called himself by his wife's family name, and the Kings increased at such a rate it might have been called extrapolation if anyone had known the word. One or two neighbours wondered to Paddy if there was any awful chance the boy might be a blow-by of that crazy shit Royal Divine, but Paddy said no, he was damned sure he wasn't, the kid was tall, well built, sandy-haired, green-eyed, straight-toothed, didn't have a mole anywhere on his body—and didn't stink. The neighbours nodded, reassured, and went home to tell themselves the kid was probably the son of one of them landed gentry who had thrown a fortune to the wind following the great and holy prophet of sweet bugger all. But whatever his past might or might not have been, the new King went to bed every night content with the present and hopeful for the future and so in love with his wife his eyes filled with tears each time he looked at her pleasantly plain little face.

Another house was built and Junior King, as the homeless waif was called, was homeless no more. He was accepted, he was respected, he had a wife who loved him and an increasing number of kids who adored him, there was work for his hands and peace in his soul. He, who had known misery and hardship, worked like a fool to keep both away from his family, he who had never had reason to smile was determined his kids would spend their days laughing, and he took them on hay rides, piled them into the car and drove them down to the river to teach them to swim, went off with them all to dig clams and stuff them in gunny sacks and considered the passing on of fishing lore to be a joyful duty ordained by nature. And then, on the mudflats, he found another refugee from the ramshackle Eden, and brought him home, telling Paddy, "I couldn't just walk away, Dad, it would have been like turning my back on myself."

Within three days, Paddy understood completely. It was exactly like having Junior show up all over again. The scrawny little mutt almost drooled for the chance to work in return for room and board, trembled for the chance to scoop a place for himself in the setup. "Can't call him Junior," Paddy laughed, "we got us a Junior," and so they called him Aiden, which was their own little joke poked at Eden. Aiden filled out, calmed down, settled in and married another of Paddy's daughters. And another house had to be built.

The cluster might have been called King's Crossing if it weren't for the fact most of the people moving into and renting or buying houses were miners who refused to live in the company town where union organizing was forbidden. None of them had any use for any goddamn King, thank you, excepting, of course, good old Paddy and his rapidly increasing family. So they started calling it the Bright Spot Crossing, but within no time at all it got shortened down to Bright's Crossing . Gradually, Bright's Crossing grew, not exactly by leaps and bounds, but then few things do. Bit by bit, year by year, baby by baby, harvest by harvest, the place grew. A school was built to keep the kids out from underfoot. Prosperity, as such, never quite managed to find Bright's Crossing, not even after the Post Office made the store a rural delivery spot, but life could have been worse and, for most, it had been.

The coal mines were eventually unionized but, of course, blood had to flow by the bucketful for that to happen. Logging companies set to ripping trees from the hillsides. Some of the trees became boards in a sawmill operation and were sold to people who built fishboats. Every once in a while there would be someone from the former religious colony who crept out of the tangle of salal and elderberry and began to try, timidly and inexpertly, to live like a normal human creature again.

Not all of them managed to rejoin the human race. Some who failed became politicians, some became lawyers who became, in turn, judges sitting with the lives of others in the palms of their hands. Those who failed most utterly became real estate and car salesmen, and one despicable bastard became a member of the RCMP.

This stalwart was sent at public expense to Wainwright, Alberta where he learned his left foot from his right, the front of the horse from the back, and how to sit on top of it and hold a long stick atop which fluttered a pennant. The horse was trained to go through the steps of the Musical Ride no matter what the damfool horse's ass in the saddle did with the reins. The horse did so well the rider was promoted to a senior staff position, where he planned great and devious schemes to steam open other people's mail and read it in search of subversion. Unfortunately, the senior staff officer read so poorly and slowly it was necessary to rent extra warehouses to hold all the unsteamed, unread and thus undelivered mail. This cost so much the price of postage in the entire country has been skyrocketing steadily ever since. The senior staff executive married a woman who didn't know any better and had several children, none of whom would be the least bit worthy of mention except for the fact they were all descended from that warty little fart Royal Divine. And had inherited many of his heinous characteristic personality traits.

The one most cursed with Royal's touch learned to read well enough to be able to get from the front cover of *Argosy* magazine to the back without taking any more time than it took the magazine itself to get out another edition, and so spent most of his growing life poring over wondrously inventive stories about catching fish and shooting deer. No more would Jack get to the end of one Argosy magazine than another would drop through the mail slot and there would be a whole new collection of catch'em'n'kill'em sagas.

Just as soon as he was old enough, Jack headed west again, back to the very place his own father left. Just as he was about to starve to death on an island swarming with deer, an island whose rivers flash and glitter with trout, whose beaches are knee deep in clams and oysters and whose ocean heaves and teems with fish, crab and edible wonders of strange shapes and forms, Jack got a job as a logger, and was sent off into the green hills in caulk boots, tin hat and short-legged work jeans held up by the widest possible galluses. He lived in camp, slept in the bunkhouse and ate gourmet meals prepared by expatriates from every corner of the world. Jack, of course, bitched and complained constantly about everything. He read his *Argosy* magazines and bought expensive fishing rods, expensive hunting rifles and expensive knives made of the finest Solingen steel, but not once did he manage to kill anything. Deer walked past his bunkhouse while he was bent over tying his shoe laces. Bear caught fish in the stream and Jack, fancy rod in hand, stared with resentment. When he raced back to the bunkhouse to put aside the rod and return with a gun to shoot the bear, there was nothing on the bank of the stream but a pile of bear shit and a few scraps of fish. Other people limited out, and Jack cursed. Every year he bought his hunting permit and his tags but never once did he get the chance to slide his tag through a slit cut in the ear of a deer he had actually murdered himself.

Twice a month the eagle shat and Jack headed into town in the back of the company crummy to blow his money as fast as he possibly could. This usually involved a double order of fish and chips and as many beer as could be poured over his tobacco-stained teeth. When he was well and truly shitfaced, Jack headed out to the Speedway Dance Hall, halfway between Nanaimo and Bright's Crossing and, hip flask thrust into his jeans pocket, stood around watching other people having fun. When the sight of their joy could no longer be tolerated, he fixed his reddened eyes on some likely candidate, managed to find an excuse, and picked a fight. Behind the Speedway he would punch and be punched, kick and be kicked, bite and be bitten, and have one helluva good time.

In spite of all his best efforts he usually went back to camp with money still in his pockets. Disgusted at this turn of events, Jack would hand it over to the company accountant, who would credit it to him. So, against his own better nature, Jack saved up money. When snow forced the bush to close, Jack got Unemployment Insurance, which he could spend with no trouble. But when the snow melted he'd be back in camp, ravaging the hillsides until it was so hot and so dry and forest fires so inescapable the Forestry Department would declare fire season, and then it was back into town again, Unemployment Enjoyment until the rains came to soak the bush and the loggers could go back into camp and live the only life they understood.

They were up before daylight, trudging through the mud to the cookhouse to fill up on enormous breakfasts washed down by cups of coffee so strong no ordinary person could have swallowed it. When they had eaten their fill, they filed out of the cookhouse, picking up a metal lunchkit packed to the hilt with sandwiches, slabs of cake, hunks of pie, fresh fruit and even chocolate bars. All day they strained and sweated, risking life and limb, chewing through enormous stands of virgin fir and cedar like so many rabid beaver. And when weather conditions closed the bush there was nothing else they understood except the beer parlours, dance halls, whorehouses and police station drunk tanks. There were, of course, exceptions to the rule, but Jack was in no way at all exceptional.

He woke up one morning in the Queen's Hotel with a hangover of unbelievable proportions and the uneasy feeling he'd done something off-the-wall shit-stupid. He rolled on his side and groaned. His groan was answered by another groan, which shocked his sad eyes open; on the bed next to him, naked as the proverbial jaybird, and obviously at least as miserably hung over as himself, was Loretta Dupuis, the loggers' whore.

"Getcher elbow outta my throat," he snarled weakly.

"Is that," she snapped, "any way to say good morning to your wife?"

"You'd better be kidding," Jack managed hopefully.

"Christ." Loretta managed to sit up without puking. "You sure do make a girl feel welcome." She lurched to the bathroom to gaze with doubt at the mess that was her face.

"You are kidding, aren't you?" He sat up, legs swinging over the side of the bed, and prayed the room would stop spinning.

"No," she said.

He didn't believe her, so he pulled on his clothes, laced up his townie shoes and went down to the beer parlour. The stench of stale beer hit him like a wet sock in the face, and gave him hope he'd survive long enough to get to a table and drink a cold draught.

"Well, hell," his buddies yelled, "if it ain't the bridegroom. Here, ya damn fool, have one on me." They all burst into laughter.

He couldn't get drunk enough. He tried. For the rest of his life, he tried. And so did Loretta, who had a lot more reason to regret the stupidity than Jack did. But they were married, and that was that, so he moved out of the bunkhouse and into a small floathouse. Every morning Loretta kicked him out of bed, then got up, made his breakfast, packed his lunchkit, filled his thermos and saw him off to work. At about the time Jack was climbing into the crummy to be driven to hell and gone up some rocky slope or another, Loretta was climbing back into bed. Sometimes by herself, but not more often than she could help. When Jack came home from work in the late afternoon, Loretta would be up again, dressed, hair neatly done, the house spotless, supper ready. She was a good cook but

Jack never noticed that, he just ate what was on his plate, complained about it and then sat at the table with one greasy pack of cards after another, drinking beer and playing solitaire, which he referred to as Beat the Chink. He usually lost. When the slap slap slap of the cards threatened to drive Loretta as crazy as the Chinese water torture ever could, she screamed at him, ''For chrissakes, stop!'' Then they fought until bedtime.

The floathouses were built on a series of giant rafts secured by massive rust-encrusted boom chains to the towering cedars and firs which lined the curve of the shore. The landscape was so rocky, so rugged, so unwelcoming it was virtually impossible to clear the land and build real houses, and anyway, once the men and machines had stripped the steep slopes, there was no reason for anyone to stay there; the camp would move on to some beautiful bay or cove untouched by industry where, as soon as possible after arriving, the sawing, falling and hauling off would begin again. No sense wasting energy flattening land, putting up foundations, building houses and digging holes for privies. This way, as soon as it became obvious it was time to move on, a tug could hook onto the booms or rafts and float the camp off to wherever the next active destruction was to happen. No worries about mowing lawns, no worries about the goddamn deer ravaging the gardens, no worries about blocked plumbing or where to put the crapper; the chuck was a great septic tank and the tide flushed it all away at least twice a day. The floathouses shifted and bobbed day and night, and when the gale force winds fought their way past the last few trees standing as a windbreak, the houses tried their damndest to dissociate themselves from the logging industry, the camp and the sullen-eyed people living in them.

Their daughter was born in the middle of fire season in the Nanaimo General Hospital and was registered but never christened or baptized. They called her Megan. Loretta had seen the name once in a movie magazine and joked she had liked the name so much she had deliberately got pregnant. ''Then, to be sure it would be a girl,'' she would guffaw, ''I got Jack to drive me up and down the logging roads so's to bounce the balls off if there were any.'' Every time Loretta launched her wit Megan cringed, but the loggers in the audience guffawed heartily, being a breed who will find humour in a snake twisting helplessly in the dust, crushed in the middle by a truck wheel.

Of course there were rumours that Jack wasn't Megan's father, and every faller, rigging slinger, chokerman and second loader in the camp came under suspicion at one time or another. Even the catskinner wasn't exempt from scrutiny. But it wouldn't have mattered one way or the other because Jack was the one lived in the house and had the most effect on Megan's life.

By the time Megan was five she was a sharp-faced, bitter-eyed camp brat with a vocabulary envied by the townies she encountered any time they left camp and had to go in for snow or fire season. She knew about the birds and the bees, she knew about the clap and the dose, she knew you couldn't live in a house after the Hindus had lived in it because you never got the smell of curry out of the wallpaper. She even knew they never used toilet paper, but carried a spare canteen of water and washed their assholes after they shat, which was why they never ate with their left hand, only with their right, their left being reserved for their hind end. What Megan didn't understand was why this was considered a filthy practice; it seemed very clean to her, imagine, one entire hand dedicated and reserved to nothing more than making sure you didn't leave shit skids on your shorts. Too bad Jack didn't take it up, sorting the laundry might not be such a disgusting job. Camel drivers, she knew, let their hair grow long, smeared it with butter, then wrapped a rag around it and were too stupid to take off the rag and wear a safety hat like human people do. Had to get special permission from their priest to join the union, for chrissakes. Live crowded together like rats eating nothing but buckwheat pancakes and brown rice. Never get civilized enough to wear socks. Stupid bastards, they'll pay two hundred dollars for a brand new suit, get a new shirt, a tie, new shoes, then go strutting out as if they were under the mistaken belief they were people, their bare ankles poking out of their shiny new shoes. Make rotten neighbours too, you can live next to them for a year and they still won't have said hello. Stick together like shit to a new blanket.

Their camp closed and everything was tugged and barged north to a new show. The floathouse didn't wind up on floats that time, it was skidded up past the high tide mark and left there, at a bit of a tilt, not enough to really bother anyone, but if you dropped a marble it would be sure to roll to the far wall, the one that looked out over the mountains. Everybody said this meant that the show would stay put for four or five years, steady work, must mean the company's doing real good, boss got himself a timber permit on a great big hunk'a crown land, no more gyppo show moving around the goddamn country like a homeless diddycoy without even a pair of matched mules to pull the wagon.

At first the mountains were all greens and blues, covered with trees, and the light played on the slopes, but every day all the men went out with chainsaws and skidders, with cables and big metal hooks, and the bare brown stain began to spread. Trees taller than the tales told about them were dropped to the ground, the limbs and branches slashed off, the trunks dragged off, the bare rocky earth tortured and gouged, discoloured with spilled oil and diesel, littered with junk and crap of every description, the discarded branches wilting, then drying into stiff, red, brittle tinder. By the time Megan was thirteen, the slope looked as if nothing had ever grown on it, nothing ever would grow on it. The roots rotted, and when they were gone, the soil slid and shifted. When it rained, as it did every autumn, winter, and spring, as it had done since the dawn of time, the mud belched and burped, cascaded and slid down, to bury the sand on the beach, wipe out the spawning streams, stain the ocean, and leave huge boulders exposed to the pitiless glare of the sun when it finally emerged. Somehow Megan accepted this as being the natural order of things. It was all she had ever known; she asked no questions.

Every time Jack and Loretta got to arguing, Megan would hightail out of the house until the noise stopped. Sometimes the noise stopped with the sound of slaps and Loretta crying, sometimes with a dull thud and Jack groaning, his head thwapped flat by a frying pan or similar defensive weapon. Sometimes it ended with the frenetic creak of bedsprings and both of them making odd noises. Until the older kids explained things to her Megan thought the bed bouncing was the same as punching and hitting, slapping and pushing, a way to scare, to hurt, to punish, to make someone else do what you wanted them to do. But the older kids, who had seen it all and learned to scorn most of it, clued her in with jokes and ditties, with biologically inaccurate descriptions and fantastic functions of fevered fantasy.

If Megan didn't scoot out of the house fast enough all the ire would be turned on her, and she hated having to walk around with big welts on her arms and legs where everyone could see and know her dad and mom had whaled the shit out of her. Being hit didn't hurt, not at the time, especially if you didn't see it coming so you weren't tensed and stiff. Something happened when you got hit, the first one scared you so much you felt as if, given half a second to prepare, you could fly, or at least run skedaddle scoot for hours, faster than any car or truck, a surge of bright red energy that seemed to block the pain centres in your brain. And after that first one, which usually burned a bit, nothing seemed to really hurt or sting or anything. You felt it. It was like being pressed in the places being hit, your meat pushed against your bones, your body numbing, and even if your breath whooshed out of you and you doubled over, maybe even falling to the floor, you didn't really feel it at the time. Later, of course, everything ached, even the parts of you that hadn't been hit or punched or slapped or banged or even kicked. Your muscles were stiff, your bruises throbbed and your head, even if it hadn't caught one, your head felt thick, your throat sore and stiff. The awful part was the noise. Lying in bed afterward, trying to figure out what you'd done wrong or forgotten to do right or how you'd managed to piss them off, you didn't remember being hit. Even when it played over and over and over in your head, like a movie looping the same few scenes time and time again, you didn't remember the hurting part of it. Just the noise of the palm of a calloused hand against the side of your face or the thwack of a fist against your back or the crack of a wooden spoon or piece of kindling stick against your ribs, your bum, your legs, your arms, your shoulders. Hitting the floor made a thump, hitting the wall made a thwop. Sometimes Megan would wake up in the middle of the night and hear the wind in the blackness, gusting and whuffing with the same kind of sound her breath made as it was pushed from her lungs.

She would lie on her bed and pray a widowmaker would fall from the greenery, slam Jack on the head and push his goddamn hardhat so far down it would slice off his fuckin' ears and flatten the top of his fuckin' head and kill him dead forever. Maybe he'd get his boot caught between a rock and a stump and be standing there cursing and tugging when a great fuckin' log came zinging, thick end first, and just crunched him against a stump, ker-fuckin'-pow! With any luck at all a chain would break and wrap around his goddamn neck and rip off his ugly head. Maybe a cable would snap and cut him right in two or a chain come flying off the saw and rip his throat open, or he'd trip on his own shoelace, fall into the chuck and get eaten by crabs. Anything. She dreamed Jack and Loretta would kill each other, that she'd be smart enough to get the hell out of the house and run off at the first hint of trouble, then they'd drink and yap, argue and nag, natter and pick and he'd hit her and she'd grab the roast carving knife and slit his gullet, but before he died he'd break her neck. Then Megan would come home and there they'd be, gone, and she could live a normal life.

Camp kids who are the daughters of loggers' sluts usually become loggers' sluts themselves, and usually do it before their fourteenth birthday, but Megan knew enough about the birds and the bees to know about loggers and tugboat operators, about beer, moonlight and bastard babies, and she wasn't having any of that, thank you.

"Hey come on, kid, what you saving it for?" they grinned.

"Not for you, asshole," she answered.

"Don't be like that," they coaxed.

"That's what I'm like," she replied, leaving quickly.

"Hey, I'll show you a good time," they promised.

"You? You'll show me fuckall," she promised right back.

"Oh yeah, and what'll you do if I just grab you and give it to you anyway?'' Their smiles were only surface smiles, with an edge she knew enough to fear.

''I'll wait until you're asleep and cut your fuckin' balls off,'' she answered, and they looked at her with bitter eyes and knew she meant every word of it.

''Crazy twat,'' they snarled. ''Ya been livin' in camp so long ya got no idea how to live like normal people.''

''And I suppose you're normal,'' she hooted. ''Christ, you're so fuckin' pathetic ya can't even get yerself laid!''

''Fuckin' bitch,'' they growled.

''Yeah, but I'm not fuckin' you,'' she vowed, and she didn't. Not any of them. It had nothing to do with morals, it had nothing to do with a good family foundation, it had nothing to do with anything but a deep and heartfelt determination to leave all of this crap as far behind her as she could.

Show her a good time. A good time. She knew what they thought a good time was. She wasn't blind. MaryJean Castle had fallen for that line of malarkey, and what did she get in the way of a good time? She went out of her cabin after supper and walked by herself along the path, around the curve of the cove and then up to the bluff that stuck out into a point, where you could lie on your belly and peek over the edge and watch the waves pounding against the black rocks, maybe even get a faceful of spray. And there was that smartass of a chokerman with a case of beer and one of those little transistor radios, and he had a bright plaid blanket spread out and even a couple of packages of potato chips. So MaryJean sat down and tucked her feet politely under the skirt of her dress and accepted a beer and a cigarette and talked about nothing at all, and then had another beer and another cigarette and they talked about the songs on the radio, and then a third beer, and he said have you tried a boilermaker and she said what's that and he said oh, it's good, really good, you'll like it, it's more a lady's drink than just plain beer is, and he poured whiskey into the beer in the bottle and MaryJean, stupid as anybody's garbage can, had believed him when he said it made the beer weaker. And then he opened a package of potato chips and halfway through he started rubbing her leg. And the next thing she knew he rolled her on her back and she said stop, but he laughed, and with one big hand on her wishbone, he held her flat, and he just pushed up her skirt and then pulled her pants down, all of it one-handed, as if even her fear and her resistance were so puny they didn't count, and he stole her underpants and stuffed them in his pocket and undid his belt buckle and zipped down his fly and then slid his jeans down off his arse and he just pushed it into her and she started to cry but he didn't care. And after all that you'd wonder how it could be worth it, he pushed three or four times and then hammered against her and that was it, not even a minute and he was pulling out of her and standing up and pulling up his jeans. MaryJean was sitting up, crying, and he picked up her half-finished boilermaker and drained it, then laughed and waved his arm and another guy came out of the bush. MaryJean tried to get up but the chokerman just put his hand on her head and shoved down and pinned her, sitting, until the second guy got there and pushed her onto her back and she started kicking but they didn't care, and the second guy humped and humped and humped and humped and then a third guy came with a case of beer under his arm.

The reason Megan knew all the details of MaryJean's evening on the bluff was that she'd seen it all, from a tree. In fact, for a while Megan thought she was going to be stuck up that fucking tree for the rest of her life. All she'd been hoping to see was a pod of killer whales; they'd been moving after the herring all week, and she'd gone up to the point and climbed a big shaggy cedar, with her binoculars. The only reason she hadn't said anything to MaryJean the idiot was she didn't want to have to talk to her stupid chokerman boyfriend, and then, before she got a chance to get down the tree and leave them with their stupid beer and chips, it was too late to dare let anyone see her. And a good job she hadn't interrupted them, what with those other guys waiting in the bush, boy, there could have been two raw-end receivers in the hardball game.

MaryJean went home crying and told her mom and dad, and what did they do about it? Gave her shit for drinking beer, and gave her shit for being so stupid as to put herself in a position like that, and gave her shit on general principles. Then her old man went over to the bunkhouse to see the chokerman and there was a shouting match, but one insulted father doesn't stand a chinaman's chance against five single guys; all it was was a gesture and everyone knew it.

MaryJean stayed home for a few days, catching up on her correspondence school courses they said, and then it was back to normal. Except even the teenaged boys figured they could tap on her. And she seemed to think they could, too, that she had given up her right to say no, that going up there and getting gang-banged had put her in a different category. They even made jokes about having a MaryJean party, and jokes about how if she had as many sticking out as had been stuck in, she'd look like a goddamn porcypine. Don't fall in, they'd guffaw. Not likely, they'd say, I'll just nail me a two-by-four sideways across my ass and prop myself where I can crawl back out again, har har.

"Just take your three inches to the cookhouse and see if you can steal a hunk'a raw liver," Megan snarled.

"Grab your can of Dubbin and fuck your lacer holes," she scorned.

"Push your head up your ass and roll down the slope," she invited.

"Set a trap, catch a coon and fuck that," she spat.

"Just shove your pecker out the crummy window and fuck the whole world!" she suggested.

"Rotten little smartmouthed bitch, you'll get yours one day," they prayed.

Megan's fourteenth birthday, and they were living in a rented house in town, out for fire season, living on Unemployment and camp savings. Megan prayed every night for something to happen that would make it possible for her to stay in town forever. Maybe the sun would never stop shining. Maybe it would never rain again. Maybe she'd be walking down Commercial Street and a huge car would stop and someone would point at Megan and say there she is, my own dear daughter, there was a mistake at the hospital, they gave her to the wrong parents, she doesn't belong with those people at all. Maybe she was really the illegitimate daughter of the Duke of Windsor or someone at least half decent. After all, anything is possible.

Loretta and Jack sat around the rented house all day watching television, drinking beer, arguing and nagging, then they had supper and headed off to the pub to swill more beer and find their way home after closing time, sometimes together, sometimes separately. While they were sodden, Megan took the loose change from their pockets and used it to entertain herself. She could go to the Capitol Theatre or to the Strand.

The Capitol Theatre brought in Famous Players movies. They played a new one from Monday to Wednesday, then changed and played a second movie from Thursday to Saturday, and closed Sunday. The Strand brought in Odeon movies and followed the same schedule. Which meant that Wednesday and Saturday nights there was nothing much for Megan to do, she'd seen both movies. She couldn't go to the pool hall, girls weren't allowed inside. She couldn't go bowling, the lanes were all reserved for league teams. She might watch a softball game but couldn't play because she wasn't around regularly enough or long enough at any one time to join a team—just about the time things got interesting they'd be back in camp again. And so she wandered around on those nights, watching faces, watching how other people lived, watching something she didn't feel part of at all.

Then one night there she was, with two dollars from returning the cases of empty beer bottles, standing outside the Civic Arena, staring at the big sign. Not hockey, not lacrosse, not family skating.

TONIGHT!! TAG TEAM SPECIAL!!

What in hell was a tag team special? Oh, well, it was better than sitting on the steps watching the uproar down the street as every dog in town fought and slavered for the chance to father puppies on a motley-coloured bitch in heat. Skewbald, Loretta called it. Skewbald, like piebald, only a piebald had black patches and a skewbald was white with any other colours except black splashed on it. Like a pinto or a paint horse, but Loretta didn't know the difference between pinto and paint. "Lemme alone," was her answer to any question she couldn't explain. And so rather than watch the skewbald bitch yelp and scurry, Megan paid her seventy-five cents and walked inside the arena.

A few townies were walking up and down the steps with little trays full of orange crush and pre-popped popcorn, a few others moving up and down the aisles sold hot dogs and mustard so old it was brown instead of yellow. The floor where the ice ought to be was covered with plywood on which were set metal folding chairs. And at least one-third of the voting public of the entire Island was perched on those chairs or in the bleachers, stamping feet, whistling, clapping, yelling and waiting impatiently for whatever was supposed to happen.

Megan found a seat where she could see the square ring set up in the middle of the arena, so close she could see the weave of the canvas, the big braided ropes, the strong metal cornerposts. She could smell something like old socks or the camp shack when it had been empty for weeks, and the excitement from the others in the crowd was contagious.

Some townie-looking guy in black pants and a white short-sleeved T-shirt climbed into the ring. He started ringing a bell and the people in the seats and the bleachers began to yell and scream even louder. A microphone descended from somewhere up above the square ring and the townie-looking guy talked a while, but you couldn't hear what he was saying for all the whistling and yelling and catcalling and stamping.

And then, great jesus, a woman walked down the aisle and climbed up into the square ring, and as casual as you like she shucked off a satin bathrobe and stood glorious and splendiferous in a bathing suit made of some kind of incredible shiny material with a bust front on it that looked as if it had been made out of the fender of a brand new car. Megan gasped. Hightop sneakers almost halfway up her leg to her knee, and every lace just so, laced to perfection, and brand new, too. Brand new laces as white as chalk in the black leather sneakers. The woman, her bleached blond hair gleaming in the lights, walked around the ring firing the bird at all the people who booed and hissed and jeered and threw paper cups and popcorn bags.

Then another woman climbed in. Brown hair and a bright red satin bathrobe she dropped to reveal a blue bathing suit with a gold-coloured bust front. White sneakers just as hightopped as the other woman's black ones, and brand new laces again, only blue, the same blue as the bathing suit. Everyone stood and laughed and clapped and yelled and cheered and whistled and the brown-haired woman smiled and threw kisses.

The blond sneaked around behind the back of the townie guy, who was talking again, and she kicked the brown-haired woman in the gut, then darted back to her own corner. The townie guy was so busy talking he didn't see any of it. The crowd screamed protest and insult. The brown-haired woman, who had been smiling and waving until the black boot hit her belly, doubled over and groaned and the voting public went nuts. Finally the townie-looking guy turned, saw the brown-haired woman suffering, and he didn't know what to make of any of it. Stupid jerk! When he looked at the bleached blond woman she was busy studying the lights on the vaulted ceiling, maybe looking to see how the microphone had descended so magically.

The townie guy kept talking, the crowd kept yelling, the brown-haired woman got her breath back and the blond woman smirked. Megan hated her. Rotten bitch!

The microphone ascended and disappeared somewhere up in the rafters, a bell went ding ding ding and the two women sprang at each other like enraged tartars. For the next few minutes there was only the ranting and raving of the crowd, the thump and thud of flying bodies, the grunts and oofs and ouches, and the townie guy trying to stay out of the way. The elegant hair styles vanished. Handfuls of hair were pulled and yanked, spit flew from sagging mouths and fists thudded into bellies and guts. The crowd went insane.

The blond woman pulled something out of the bust front of her bathing suit and raked it across the brown-haired woman's eyes. The brown-haired woman screamed, grabbed her face and was thrown to the canvas, her shoulders pinned. One, two, three, the townie slapped the floor and the crowd threatened to rip the arena off its foundations.

Megan bought a red-and-white-striped bag of stale popcorn and gaped. The two women retired to their corners and screeched insults at each other. The bell went again, ding ding ding, and the fight was on with renewed vigour and rage. The blond woman tried to pull the thing-across-the-eyes trick again, but the brown-haired woman pried whatever it was from her enemy's hand and used it herself, blinding the blond and winning the second fall while the crowd cheered as if Jesus was walking on water all over again before their very eyes.

They returned to their corners and glared. The townie rang the bell. Ding ding ding they started for each other and then a woman in a green bathing suit darted out of nowhere, jumped over the ropes, into the ring, grabbed the brown-haired woman from behind and put a choke hold on her while the blond kicked repeatedly at the brown-haired woman's stomach. The townie yelled and threatened disqualification and pointed dramatically for the trespasser to get out of the ring. The crowd was out of its seats, crowding close to the ring, screeching and yelling. And then a fourth woman was in the ring, swinging a metal chair from the audience section, and all shit bust loose everywhere, six, seven, nine women in the ring, no telling who was on who's side, and three more fighting in the aisles, and some gomer in a gas jockey outfit got into it and got himself cold-cocked for his trouble and Megan decided it was all the most magnificent display of asinine stupidity she had ever seen in her life and she wanted more more more.

Men in bathing suits appeared and pulled the women apart, the match was declared a draw and everyone screamed and yelled, hollered and shouted, so a grudge match was set up and scheduled for the next week. Megan knew she'd be there for sure. For sure!

All the women went back to their dressing rooms and the vendors circulated. Then the woman in the green bathing suit was walking toward the ring alongside a black woman in a gold bathing suit. The crowd jeered and hissed. The two women grinned and held their arms up, hands clasped in the champion's salute, working at least half the crowd into a moiling mob of frustrated rage. No more were the green and the gold in the ring than a woman in a burgundy-wine-coloured suit appeared with her partner in a pink suit, and the crowd cheered and hollered encouragement. The burgundy and pink waved, threw kisses, stopped to shake hands with old men and small kids, and by the time they were in the ring almost every family in the arena was ready to adopt either or both of them.

Megan felt dizzy, her pulse speeding, her face stiff with a silly grin she could not turn off or control. It was all so goddamned silly! Like watching the cartoons in the movie and a barn falls on some joker and after the dust settled the joker gets up and weaves off, little birds flying in circles around his head, tweeting and cheeping. In real life the joker would be a mess of bloody mush. And this was the same. Somewhere along the line an unspoken agreement had been reached, not only between the combatants in the ring, but between the wrestlers and the crowd. It gave everybody a chance to be an actor, on stage, part of the circus, and how often does anybody get a chance to really and truly run off and join the circus!

The townie talked, the crowd told him to shut up, the microphone was taken back up into the rafters and the bell went ding ding ding. Only this time there were two teams of women and everything happened much faster. Human flesh was thudding against the canvas, being thrown against the crossbuckles, even heaved over the top rope to land on the floor at Megan's very feet. The woman in the burgundy bathing suit tried to get to her feet, holding her head, weaving off in the wrong direction, while up in the ring the other team held the woman in pink captive in a corner, punching her over and over and over and over again, and then the brown-haired woman from the first match was helping the woman in the burgundy suit get back into the ring. As if a miracle had been enacted before the eyes of the hysterical audience, as soon as the woman in the burgundy suit was back in the ring she recovered, her staggers gone, her dizziness evaporated and she cartwheeled across the canvas, flipped herself in a standing backwards somersault, her booted feet catching both the baddies under their chins, dropping them to the canvas. The woman in pink, not even bleeding, cut loose then, and suddenly the entire arena seemed to be part of it, hot dog buns flying, orange crush cascading, kids wrestling and fighting and two men in the aisle punching determinedly at each other. Megan leaned back in her chair and began to laugh happily. She had seen enough real fights to know just how much damage a crack to the mouth can cause, and while there was for sure lots of blood in the ring, it didn't seem to be coming from any one or two particular place or places. More like something smeared or spilled, like in the movies, everyone knows the actor bites on a little pill and coloured dye spurts from his mouth. All that kicking ought to have at least separated a few teeth from the gums of the wrestlers, but no, not even a loose one. She'd fetched enough bruises on the leg to know how quickly they show up, how plainly visible they are, and, yes, there were bruises, but not the kind you'd get if someone had spent five minutes kicking on your leg. She laughed and laughed and laughed, then cheered and yelled until her throat was sore, and when it was all over and she was walking home in the soft dark of island night, she was still smiling, still reliving in her head the colour and splash, the fun and unabashed phoniness of it all. Something inside her had relaxed. She had found a place, finally, where violence could be controlled, could be tamed and turned into something other than what it really was.

She dreamed that night of satin bathing suits with armoured bust fronts, and of high sneakers like Wonder Woman's boots. The next day she went in and out of every drugstore in Nanaimo, looking at magazines. When she found one with articles in it about women wrestlers she bought it, took it home, settled herself on a blanket on the lawn and read every word, even the ads. Most of the articles were about the men wrestlers, and after she had read all about Betty Gable and Scarlett O'Hare and Lovely Liz and Sally the Storm Trooper and Jungle Janie and Mooba the Queen of the Wild, she read about the men and how they had all decided at some point in their lives that the reason they had never felt comfortable in their ordinary jobs was they had a gift, a talent, and weren't using it, but since taking up wrestling, they had found peace and contentment, tranquility and purpose.

The following week, when the grudge match was held, Megan was right there in the front row, grinning and watching every move. Bugger who won! How did they do it without getting crippled or killed?

According to the magazines, it all had to do with conditioning. Megan got a library card and signed out books on diet, on exercise, on gymnastics, on track and field. She bought a book on martial arts and magazines about kickboxing. She found a paperback that showed, in four hundred and six black-and-white photos, all the moves and turns in karate, with a special chapter on stretching and strengthening exercises.

She no longer sat around bored to tears, she was swimming back and forth, back and forth from shore to the diving float, a steady crawl, back and forth until she ached. She walked right past the bus stop on the corner and began to run, one block, two blocks, three blocks, four. She got a TV guide and tuned in to every wrestling match scheduled, replaying in her head all the best moves.

But it had to end. It rained for a week and they were back in camp again.

Of course, neither Jack nor Loretta knew anything was different. The price of beer and smokes had gone up, groceries were outrageous high, but the kid still got up in the morning, had breakfast, did the dishes, helped tidy the house, then went out to play with her little friends. Came back in time for supper, ate, did the dishes, tidied up and went back out again for a last game of catch or keep-away or whatever they were playing in the evening. There were enough kids in camp now that they qualified for a teacher, and the company let them all take their correspondence courses to one of the empty bunkhouses, where they could study under the supervision of someone who knew what he was doing, and better still, knew what they were supposed to be doing.

"Well, thank god for that," said Loretta. "I mean, I'm tellin' ya, it was gettin' beyond me. I'm the one they make the jokes about, you know, they kicked me outta school in grade four for growing a moustache. I mean, honest to god, if I could'a taught anybody how to do anything, wouldn't I have been a teacher? Besides," she said honestly, "it's more than anyone ought to have to put up with, having a kid around all the time. Know what I mean?"

Megan took her lunch to school. She could easily have gone home for lunch, everyone else did. After all, you could have thrown a rock from the bunkhouse which had suddenly become a school and bounced the rock off the roof of the shack where Loretta was, but Megan preferred to take her sandwiches and thermos down along the curve of the beach where, if you ignored the oil slicks and the clutter of floating debris, you could imagine yourself somewhere else. Besides, she didn't like going home for lunch and finding some cookhouse flunky sitting with his romeos under the table, drinking coffee and grinning as if he knew something Megan didn't. Megan knew. The whole effin' world knew. As if it cared.

Neither Jack nor Loretta found anything different about life in camp, not even the change in Megan. She wasn't playing kick the can or knockie-knockie-nine-doors, she was running in her heaviest boots with a backpack full of beach sand on her shoulders. She went down to the corner box to pick up the mail so nobody but her saw the subscription magazine with women smiling from ear to ear, wearing huge belts with ornate championship buckles, flexing muscles even Jack would have envied, or stepping into or out of pink Lincoln Continentals or Chrysler Imperials. Smiling. Waving. Rolling in money.

Any time there was a fight in camp Megan was right there, watching to see who did what and how and to what effect. She began to practise, at first in her head, then with an imaginary partner, and if Loretta thought Megan was trying adagio dancing, that was Loretta's interpretation, based on nothing at all that Megan had ever said. And when they shut down for snow and headed into town again, Megan didn't even complain about having to change schools.

Two months in townie school, and the kids weren't too bad once you got used to them. Once you'd answered all their questions about life in a logging camp, once you'd proved the stories they thought they'd heard didn't necessarily apply to Megan Crawford, once it became obvious that she knew her schoolwork at least as well as they did. Some of the boys tried to get fresh and found out about Megan's vocabulary and how ill-prepared they were to deal with it. Once all that was finished and done with, it was no sweat at all.

She joined a karate club and went there every night after supper, and Jack and Loretta didn't even know that much about her life. How could they? They were in the pub so much now that often supper was something made by Megan for Megan, and if they ate, it was fast food or takeout ordered through the bartender.

Two months in town, eight weeks of Saturday night at the wrestling matches, but not in the arena any more, that was reserved for the hockey games. The old auction barn, and a smaller crowd because so many of the people who liked to see wrestlers attack and maul each other also liked to see hockey players attack and maul each other and beat their opponents' brains out with a hockey stick. But Megan was glad, a smaller crowd meant fewer bodies between her and the action, fewer obstacles to her studying what she was studying so carefully.

The ones in the white boots are always the good guys, the ones in the black boots are always the bad guys, and always, always, always, the one with bleached hair is a baddy no matter what colour boots he or she is wearing. A step-over toe hold is seldom broken, you crawl until your shoulders are under the bottom strand and then the townie, who is really the referee, breaks the hold. A sleeper usually works, but not always. Elbow to the throat is almost sure fire but if you miss, your funnybone hits something solid and your arm is useless. Bit by bit she began to interpret the hidden rules of the gymnastic display. The rocking chair needs split second timing and if you're off even a little bit, you're in trouble, but if you can pull it off, you've won the match, no doubt about it. And she did not believe for one minute the matches were exactly fixed. Maybe the rules were bendable, sometimes the good guy lost, like if he couldn't get his rocking chair done properly, then the one it was tried on could wiggle free and pull something out of the bag of tricks. Let's pretend, okay, let's have a playfight, but make it look good. And it looked good.

But the snow began to melt and they were back in camp again, and Megan was getting sick and tired of the constant fighting, drinking, squabbling and occasional screwing. She could hardly wait for the sun to start shining sixteen hours a day, day in and day out, turning the bush to tinder and sending them all back into town for fire season.

"What in hell d'ya mean stay in town to do school next year? I never heard of nothin' like it in my life! What in hell d'ya think, we're made of money? You got any idea what it would cost to pay your room and board somewhere? And who'd keep an eye on ya? Think I want you runnin' around town unsupervised? God, kid, just havin' that stupid idea proves you're too goofy to need to worry about goin' to school at all. Get real, willya? Christa'mighty!''

"Leave her alone!" Loretta flared unexpectedly. "Just get off her back, ya hear?"

"What'n'hell's put a bug in your ear?" Jack spluttered.

"Not you nor nobody else is callin' my kid stupid!" Loretta raged. "If ever I heard of shit saying garbage stinks, it's you saying anybody else in the world is stupid! Stop talkin' at her that way! Just because you don't agree don't mean she's wrong.''

"Now listen here . . .'' he started.

"Get the hell outta here," Loretta said quietly, "before I forget I'm a lady and call someone in to lay you out on the floor.''

"Jesus!" Jack exploded. "I tell ya, sometimes my life is made such hell by the monthlies I expect my own fuckin' nose to bleed!'' He stormed out of the house and headed off toward the bunkhouse where half the single guys owed him a lake of liquor.

"Listen," Loretta said to Megan after Jack had left, "you gotta look at it from his point'a view, kid. He hates town. He *hates* it! And so do I. And so does just about everybody else in camp. And the reason you don't hate it is you been lucky, you never had to live there. I mean, Megan, baby, those people worry about the grass that grows outside their doors! You been lucky, you never had to worry about none of that bullshit stuff, and instead of telling him thank you, you're saying you don't like what he's managed to give ya.''

"What?" Megan gaped. "Momma, look around you. Would you just please take a good sober look? Junk and crap and garbage and old bits and pieces of machinery, and dead engines and rusting bits of christ knows what it used to be and shreds of bark all over the place.''

"Oh, Megan, you got near sightedness," Loretta laughed. "Of course there's a mess where the camp is. Christ, you spell camp m-e-s-s, everyone knows that! Look past it. Look, out there, where they ain't logged yet. I mean god, those town pissers would pay a fortune for the chance to just *visit* the place where you live! Any time you want, you can walk down to the beach. You got any idea how much you'd have to pay to live near the beach in town? You can just grab a rowboat and head out to fish for cod, you can do damn near anything you want . . . and they're working fifty weeks a year for the chance to take two weeks holiday in a place just like this. That's why your daddy blew up like that. So don't talk about it no more when he's around, okay?''

"Momma," Megan said quietly, "momma, nobody would pay six cents to visit this dump. But some of us would pay a hundred dollars if we had it for the chance to get out and never see it again!''

"I know, honey," Loretta said, sounding almost sober. "Get me a beer, will ya? I don't agree with ya, but I know what's wrong. The grass is always greener somewheres else. Well, you're growin' up. God damn it to hell anyway. The one thing I didn't want you to do and you've gone and done it when I wasn't lookin'. You want out of here?'' She lifted her beer bottle, drank deeply. "Then you find your own way out, it's the only way you'll ever really leave. If anyone else says they'll take you out . . . you ain't leavin, you're just on your way to the same damn thing set down in a different place.''

"Yes, momma," Megan said, wondering if it would take another sixteen years for her and Loretta to actually have a conversation.

The teeming rain became drizzle, the drizzle slacked off and the sun began to shine, and soon it was burning down on them, making the mud flats boil and stink, drying up the runoffs and creeks, caking the surface of the swamp land. Going for an afternoon swim wasn't a pleasurable big deal any more, it was an absolute necessity. The men went on early shift, the whole camp went on it. They were up and fed and off in the crummy at one-thirty or two in the morning and on the job, ready to work by the time the first thin light began to shine. By noon they were in the crummy and heading out of the woods, the barren slopes shimmering in the hot sun, the place strangely silent, the birds and squirrels stunned by the heat.

They were back in camp by two and out of their sweat-stinking salt-stained clothes quicker than you'd believe possible. A case of beer and a cap opener and they were sitting on the banks of the river, the only place for miles where there was any cool breeze. The younger guys dove in, jeans and all, and surfaced, blowing and laughing, yelling, ''Come on in, the water's great,'' but the older guys just sat drinking beer and shaking their heads, too tired, too numb, too poleaxed by heat and hard work to be able to even remember what it was like to have enough energy to swim. One or two of them dipped their white-spotted red handkerchiefs in the slow moving green water and draped the wet cloth over their heads, some dunked their feet, but most of the older ones just sat, drinking beer, patient, undemanding, worn to some kind of dozy acceptance by too many years of brutal work.

And then they were packing some stuff, heading back into town, might as well, chrissakes, this place'll be the first to burn if the slopes start blazing. They caught a ride in with the crummy driver, jammed in with the single guys, and Megan could taste the excitement and anticipation.

One night in a motel, and the next day they had a furnished suite on the third floor of a main street hotel. The smell of old beer in the stairwell, the sound of a jukebox playing the same few songs over and over again from ten in the morning until one-thirty the next morning. Loud voices and arguments in the hallway, the teenaged whores too young to get into the beer parlour so they waited on the sidewalk until some young guy invited one of them up to his room.

''Sure, why not?'' the girls would laugh. ''I'm easy but I ain't cheap.''

''How much?'' the young guy would ask.

''Ten bucks a go, thirty bucks all night and all the beer I can drink.''

''Come on, darlin', I got a twenty-four in my room right now and there's more where that came from,'' and up they'd go, past the desk clerk who didn't give a damn as long as the underage tarts didn't go into the licensed premises.

''I catch you messing with any of them guys I'll skin your arse,'' Jack warned.

"Don't you talk to me like that," Megan exploded. "I don't do that kind of crap and you know it!"

"Watch your mouth, brat!"

"Nobody insults me like that, poppa, not even you! If I was playing the game you could call me the name but I'm not so you won't because if you ever do, I'll make you sorry!"

"And I'll help 'er!" Loretta screeched, tears pouring down her puffy cheeks, smearing her mascara. "You got no right, Jack. You got no god damned right at all!"

"Hey, listen, I didn't mean it like it sounded, okay? All I meant was . . . ah, hell, look I was out of line, you're right. I'm a fool, okay? All mouth. Okay?" He looked at her with such pathetic hopefulness she could almost have started to cry herself. Christ, he didn't understand her any better than she had ever understood him!

"Don't cry, momma," Megan said automatically. "It's okay."

"Don't talk to her like that," Loretta insisted beerily. "She ain't that kind of girl. Nobody's got no right to talk to my kid like that."

"I said I was out of line, okay?"

'Say you're sorry," Loretta demanded.

"You'll eat shit before I'll say I'm sorry," Jack vowed.

Saturday afternoon and she was sitting behind the arena watching the excursion ferry heading over to Protection Island. Not really doing anything, just determined not to be at home where they were partying with a dozen camp cronies, sitting in the combination kitchen-living room of the cramped suite drinking beer and eating Chinese from take out cartons. She'd bought a hasp and padlock for her bedroom, and Jack and Loretta had watched, wordless, while she struggled to get it screwed onto the door. "You're doin' 'er cross-threaded," Jack growled. Then he got up off the sagging sofa and walked toward her, his eyes like those of a homeless dog who expects to get kicked for licking your hand. "Gimme 'er here," he said. "I'll get 'er in place."

"Good job one of us is thinking," Loretta smiled, a false brittle smile. "Christ, time just kind of scoots away from under you, don't it?" Megan supposed they thought she had one reason for locking up her door, and probably her own real reason was totally different from theirs. She just didn't want to come home to pecker tracks on her counterpane. If they were going to fuck, they could just find some other place to do it than on her bed, by god!

"Haven't seen you around for weeks," a voice said. "You get bored with us?" Megan looked up into the dark brown eyes of the Norse Wonder.

"My god," she said.

"Where you been?" Norse Wonder asked, lighting a cigarette and almost setting fire to all Megan's ideas about conditioning and healthy living.

"We were back in camp," she said, then had to explain what she meant by back in camp.

"Sounds deadly," Norse Wonder mused. "Almost as much fun as being back on the farm."

"So much fun," Megan agreed, "taking a shit seems exciting," and they both howled with laughter.

"It was a big day in our house," Norse teased, "when we made Jello and got to watch it set."

"We'd go down to the beach to watch the seagull shit dry in the sun."

"So I guess you don't plan to stick around once you finish school."

"Not me," Megan said firmly, "I might not even bother finishing school, I might just take off and never mind finishing."

"What you gonna do?"

"Wrestle," Megan grinned, admitting it for the first time.

"Yeah? You any good?"

"I don't know," Megan admitted, "So far all I've done is wrestle this invisible opponent who always gives up because she's scared of me," and they were laughing again.

"Come on," Norse invited, "we'll find out."

It took about two and a half seconds for Megan to find out she wasn't anywhere near as good as she had dreamed she would be, not even anywhere near as good as she'd hoped she might be. Nothing worked. Norse simply was not there when Megan tried to apply a hold.

"It's timing," Norse told her. "And co-operation," she confessed. "Listen, you start off slow, see, and you count. Watch. One . . . two . . . t-urn . . . three . . . reach . . . close your hand on my wrist, okay, six . . . se-ven . . . turn, pull, harder, that's it, twelve, down on your knee, thirteen, lift your shoulder—other one, kid, other one! That's it, now jerk down!" Norse flipped over Megan's back, landed on the canvas and was on her feet again, grinning. "You're gonna catch on real fast," she promised.

"Yeah?" Megan could hardly believe her ears.

"Yeah. You've been working on it at home, huh?"

"Yeah. I got some magazines and books." As she said it she felt like a stupid little kid.

"Want to try again?" Norse offered.

At the end of an hour, Megan ached. Her elbows and knees were red and sore from the canvas. She was dizzy and confused and didn't know what all she had learned, if anything. But she had never been as happy in her life. "I gotta go for a while," Norse said, looking at the big clock above the ring. "You want to come tonight?"

"Oh, you bet!" Megan blurted.

"Here, then," Norse handed her a ticket, not one of the little purple tickets that came off the roll in the wicket and had Admit One stamped on it. A wallet-sized card with a fancy logo in the middle of it and Staff stamped in red. "Don't lose it," Norse teased, "they don't grow on trees."

Megan raced back to the suite, where everyone was starting to think about moving down to the pub for the evening. She locked herself in the tiny bathroom and showered, washed her hair and changed into clean clothes. Everything. Underpants, cotton socks, jeans, shirt, everything fresh and clean. She transferred her wallet from her old jeans to her clean ones, patted her pocket happily, knowing her Staff card was safe in its little plastic window. It was more than luck. More than a real break. It was like a new life.

She cleaned up the bathroom and went back into the suite to fry herself an egg for supper. Only Loretta paid any attention to her, and that wasn't much attention, Loretta had been beering for a week and a half and could hardly focus her eyes any more.

"You okay?" she asked.

"Fine," Megan answered. "Yourself?"

"Fine as silk," Loretta slurred. "Never better."

Megan ate two fried-egg sandwiches, cleaned up her mess, left the cooking nook as tidy as it ever could be, got her denim jacket, locked her room and put the key in her pocket, and headed back out, unnoticed by the boozy bunch still trying to organize themselves to walk down a flight of stairs to the beer parlour.

She sat on a bench in the park overlooking the harbour and wished for the millionth time they lived in a house where roses grew thick and scented the evening air. An old woman was walking along the path between the rose bushes, aided by a well-oiled walking stick. She seemed oblivious to the traffic, oblivious to the motorboats, fishboats, tugs and barges in the bay. She was totally engrossed in the roses, stopping before each bush, examining the flowers, bending forward, smelling the perfume, her wisp of curly white hair turned silver by the light of the sun.

Megan watched the old woman. Then, suddenly, she was overtaken with an impatience and eagerness she hardly knew how to contain. God, what if she got there late and had to sit to hell and gone up in the peanut gallery, so far from the action Norse wouldn't even know she was there!

She wasn't late. She got a seat right up front, and got herself ready, with a big double orange safely tucked under her folding chair and a large-sized bag of popcorn to chew on while waiting for the action to begin. Just a couple of hours of practice and explanation and she could see the glory-holds being put into play, see the choreography, the way it all built to a climax the way the teacher said a play was supposed to build, or a story, or a movie. She nodded approval, she grinned appreciation, she told herself she was a goddamn genius for knowing two minutes ahead of time what was going to happen. And she yelled bloody murder when it was time for Norse to go into the ring and do her stuff.

After the matches, when all the goobers and rubes had left, Megan was invited to go back to the motel with the women. They shared, four to a unit, and relaxed by watching old movies on the flickering TV, eating huge pizzas delivered by a bored high school kid who could barely make change.

"Have a beer?" Norse offered.

"No thanks," Megan blushed.

"Got soft drinks, too, if you'd rather. Or juice. Even got some milk in here." Norse hauled an insulated picnic cooler out from under the bed, opened it and fished around inside. She hauled out a can of pop, held it out for Megan to take, then, grumbling and nagging, lifted the entire cooler, took it into the small bathroom and drained the melted ice water into the tub.

"Chrissake," she growled, "can't anybody else remember to drain this christly thing?"

"I'll go for more ice," Connie the Crusher offered.

"Cheapskate bastards are supposed to supply ice," Norse grumbled, "but they seem to think two inch-square cubes a day are enough for anybody."

"Jesus," said one, "my feet are killin' me. Listen, don't buy your shoes from that beady-eyed Syrian bastard . Him and his professional discount! Christly leather is so thick and so stiff, by the time you got 'em broken in, they're wore out!"

"Do me a favour?" another asked. "Try to find a kind of hair spray that don't smell like cat piss? I mean, bad enough you grab me in a full Nelson, and you taller'n me by a good five inches, but jesus, the hair spray makes my eyes burn!"

"You still want to be a wrestler?" Norse teased.

"More than ever," Megan vowed.

She went home shortly after one-thirty, went directly to her room, closed the door and pushed her dresser against it. The padlock kept the room safe when she was away from the place, but she didn't want to lock herself in the room when she was asleep, with all those yahoos drinking and smoking and passing out on the couch, the last thing she needed to do was come awake in a smoke-filled room and have to fumble around finding a key to unlock the door.

Megan had never been in a fire but she was terrified of the thought. Every year her life was turned inside out because of fire season, hundreds of people migrated like lemmings away from the threat of fire. Everyone she knew, even Jack, was careful with matches and cigarettes in or near the bush, breaking the match in half, digging a little hole with the toe of a well-oiled boot, putting the broken match or the thumb-snuffed cigarette butt in the hole, replacing the dirt, tamping it all flat again, and all the while talking or listening, nodding or frowning, the need to bury the possible fire so deeply ingrained nobody really seemed to notice the precaution, but everybody would have noticed if it hadn't been done. And no more were they in town than they became something or someone else, smoking tailor-mades instead of home-rollies, flopping bonelessly on foam-stuffed couches, boozed to the ears, cigarettes forgotten. Megan had no intention of frying. If anything happened, all she had to do was grab the dresser, heave it to one side and head from her room, across the kitchen-living room to the door to the hallway. And once in the hallway she had no intention of trying to make it down the staircase. It was nothing but an unbricked chimney. There was a small window on the landing, and just beyond it, a metal fire escape ladder, Megan had even counted off the number of steps it would take her to get to it. And she knew, Governor General's Medal for Bravery or not, that when the time came, she was going alone. Jack and Loretta could look out for Jack and Loretta; Megan was going to look out for Megan .

Norse and the others left early Sunday morning to go down to Ladysmith and get ready for the Sunday night matches, and afterward, they drove to Duncan and checked into a motel to catch a good sleep before Monday night in Duncan. Tuesday and Wednesday nights in Victoria, Thursday in Cloverdale, Friday in Vancouver, and Saturday night, back in Nanaimo again.

Megan met Norse at the arena, and for two and a half hours they practised.

"Hey," Norse approved, "you've been practising on your own."

"Yeah," Megan grinned. "I make believe my head is a TV, and I just go over and over everything you showed me."

"Pretty determined, aren't you."

"Norse, if you had any idea what it's like in camp . . . or what it would be like if I just left and didn't have any plans . . . I mean, I can't see leaving and moving into town so that I can wind up slinging hash in a greasy spoon! Even if I finish high school, then what? And if I did get some kind of minimum wage dipshit job, how long would I keep it? And if I kept it . . . how much of the world would I get to see on minimum wage?"

"You don't have to convince me, kid. You're just saying exactly what I thought and felt the day I heaved my last bale of hay and headed off down the highway. Cursing everyone because I was a girl and not a boy. If I'd been a boy, raised on a farm, working like a horse from the time I could stand up, with more muscles than a dog has fleas, I could have stepped into a boxing ring and knocked someone's brains out for the chance to get out of the hole I'd been born in. But I was a girl, so they gave me the choice of becoming a nun or becoming a whore and I wasn't religious and I hate fucking. I mean if there's any fucking to be done I want to *do* it, not be the one it gets done to, right?"

"Oh jesus," Megan started to giggle, lying on her back on the canvas flooring of the ring, "you *were* born in camp!'

Just before they were due to head back into camp at the end of fire season, Megan made her move. No use talking to anyone about it, they'd either tell her to shut up or find some way to stop her. And she'd swallowed as much of it as she could stand. Not one more day of it. Not a minute of it. She packed all her wrestling magazines, her few clothes, her sneakers, and her giant economy box of Tampax, left a brief note on her pillow where they'd find it sooner or later and left. She had fifty-six dollars saved up and in her pocket, and she had a dream she was determined to live.

"We'd best change circuits," Norse told her. "I don't want the cops taking my tag-team partner out of the ring and dragging her back up to Hell Hole to put her in school." Norse phoned her booking agent long distance and explained, very briefly. Megan waited a day and a half, almost chewing her fingers with nervousness, expecting any minute the door would swing wide and the Queen's Cowboys would come in, probably singing "Rose Marie," and haul her back to the bush. Then the phone rang, Norse talked for two minutes, grinning and taking notes, and by eight o'clock that night she and Megan were on a train headed south, into the US of A, and life had begun to take on some kind of meaning.

Megan got her hair bleached almost white and borrowed enough money from Norse to buy a pair of black leathers with white laces and a purple satin bathing suit with a gold bustfront. When she modelled the outfit, Norse grinned and said, "Christ, you look good enough to eat." It was three months before Megan found out what Norse had meant and why the other women had laughed softly.

They were the baddies: the Norse Wonder and her partner Vicious Vera the Valkyrie. They were booed and hissed, they were jeered and insulted, they lost more often than they won and they were paid on time every time. They travelled by train, plane and bus, they slept in motels, auto courts and hotels, they ate as well as they could as cheaply as they could and practised at least three hours every day. Up and down the west coast of the US, four, five and six nights a week they kicked, punched, slapped and were thumped, banged and pummeled. And after eighteen months of it, they knew they were good enough to let their hair go back to its normal colour and become goodies. They even changed their names when they cleaned up their act. Norse Wonder became Jenny Erickson and Vicious Vera the Valkyrie became Flash Crawford. No more make-believe secret weapons hidden down the front of their suits, no more leaping over the top rope to drag some planted goof who was really a male wrestler in civvies out of his seat to deck him in the aisle. And above all, no more shouting insults at little old white-haired ladies who were probably some civilian's dear old gran.

"Hey," Jenny Erickson said, looking up from the letter, "think you'd like to head back home? We can headline! Top billing! All we have to do is sign the contract." She waved it happily.

"You'd better get your signing over and done with fast," Megan laughed, "or I'll crush you in my leap for the pencil."

It wasn't hard finding Jack and Loretta again. Not that she really wanted to, but it seemed a particularly rotten trick to appear in front of the rest of the town and not let them know she was back. What if someone she knew saw her, recognized her, told them and their feelings were hurt?

The inch and a half of dirty snow was slippery and cold, stained in big yellow and brown patches where the dogs had stopped. The sullen grey sky promised more of the same and the damp air from the bay tugged at her jacket. Loud music blasted from the apartment and the sound of loggers har-haring at some stupid joke or another exploded down the long hallway. She almost turned away, but instead rapped politely.

"Don't knock 'er down," Jack's voice commanded. "Just turn the round thing and swing 'er open."

So she did. She stepped inside, closed the door and waited.

"If you're lookin' for money," Jack snarled, "you're shit outta luck 'cause I ain't givin' you any. You made yer bed, now lie in it."

"Why, thank you," Megan answered pleasantly. "It's very nice to see you too, daddy dear."

"So what is it?" Loretta demanded. "You're pregnant, right? And the asshole you ran off with told you to take a walk, right? And you want to walk back in here, right?"

"Jesus christ," Megan grinned. "It's so nice to feel welcome."

"Welcome my ass!" Jack blustered. Then, to show the others just how effin' tough he was, he got up from his chair, put down his beer and moved toward Megan with his hand drawn back to slap her face. "So, after the goddamn stunt you pulled, you want a welcome? Runnin' off like some kind of streetwalkin' slut? Ungrateful bitch." He swung.

Maybe most of what went on in the ring was choreographed and a setup, but Megan really could handle herself in almost every situation imaginable. She grabbed Jack's wrist before the slap came anywhere near close to connecting, and flipped him onto his back in the middle of the floor. It all happened so fast nobody was sure they had seen it.

"Try to pretend," she invited softly, "just for a minute or two, that you're a human person with at least as much brains as God gave the average goat."

He lay on his back in the middle of the little room, gaping at her, while everyone else, including Loretta, howled with joyful laughter. He decided, in view of what had happened and how little control he'd had over his unexpected flight through his own kitchen, to laugh with the others. The alternative might land him in the hospital.

"That's my kid," he bragged. "She don't take no shit from nobody!"

Megan had a beer with them and struggled to answer their questions, but there was no more common ground than there had ever been and, for reasons she could not understand, that made her sad.

"So tell me," Loretta invited, "who was he? The guy you took off with, I mean."

"No guy," Megan answered. "I took off by myself."

"Well, if you don't want to tell me, don't tell me," Loretta sulked.

"Momma, I *told* you," Megan said quietly, "I headed off by myself. I just didn't want any more camp life, that's all."

"Well," Loretta shrugged, "I sure as hell can understand that!"

"You can?" Megan gaped. "But you said . . ."

"So where'd you go and what did you do? Hustle?"

"No, I did not hustle!" Megan snapped. "I wrestled."

"You—what the hell?" Jack blurted.

"Wrestled," Megan answered. She offered Jack a copy of the wrestling magazine that included a feature article on the rising young stars of professional wrestling. "You are looking at one half of the Canadian Women's Professional Wrestling Tag Team Championship Pair." She winked, making fun of her title before anybody else could do it.

"I have never," Loretta said primly, "heard anything so god damned disgusting in all my life." When Megan burst out laughing, Loretta sniffed and opened another beer, gulping it expertly.

"Momma," Megan managed, "if I had told you I was a hooker you'd have shook your head, shrugged, and accepted it as a fact of life. But I tell you I'm not a hooker and you're just about ready to disown me!"

"Who ya shacked up with?" Jack asked insistently.

"Nobody," Megan lied, knowing they wouldn't believe the lie, but knowing they wouldn't understand or accept the truth.

"Aw, come on, a good lookin' woman like you?"

"Who's got the energy?" she shrugged.

To show them how much energy it took to be a champion, she treated the whole bunch of them to front row seats. When the Blond Bombshell smashed Megan on the back of the neck and at the same time kneed her in the stomach, Loretta screamed for Jack to get the hell up offa his fat ass and give a hand to his own flesh and blood. Before Jack could get up off his metal chair, Megan jumped in the air, scissored her legs around the Blond Bombshell's neck and flipped her to the canvas. Somehow, and Loretta was never sure how, Megan landed on both feet, then jumped again, flying through the air to land arse-end first on the writhing blond baddie, apparently knocking her cold as the proverbial clam. She rolled her opponent on her back, pinned her shoulders and—one-two-three—she had the fall. But before she could get up, the Blond Bombshell's partner, Filthy Freda, kicked her in the head.

"Jesus christ," Loretta raged, "is that pissin' referee blind? Or just stupid?"

"Have an eye!" Jack screamed, "Have an eye you sadassed moron!"

That was when Jenny Erickson went over the top rope into the ring, grabbed Filthy Freda before she could kick Megan, who seemed to be bleeding from the scalp, and whip-cracked her across the ring and into the turnbuckles. Filthy Freda stiffened in pain. Jenny rushed her and shoulder-blocked her in the gut. As Freda slumped forward Jenny grabbed her, shifted her across her shoulders and went into her famous helicopter heave.

"Give 'er shit!" Loretta raged. "Let 'er have it!"

Megan got to her feet, shook her head and saw the Blond Bombshell racing toward Jenny, arm drawn back to rabbit-chop her on the neck. Three flips and a kick and Flash Crawford had the Blond Bombshell backing toward her corner, hands up, pleading for mercy. Jenny finished her whirling spin with Filthy Freda on her shoulders, and there was Freda flying through the air, over the top rope, to land in Jack's lap.

"I hope my kid rips yer stinkin' face off," Jack snarled.

"Ah, get stuffed," Freda growled and waded back into the ring.

Jenny and Flash touched hands and patted each other on the back. Flash went out of the ring to stand behind her own cornerpost, hanging onto the short rope, obeying all the rules, so scrupulously clean the crowd adored her. Jenny stood in the centre of the ring, crouched, watching as both Filthy Freda and the Blond Bombshell strode around threateningly and the referee tried to sort out which of the two ought to be in the ring. Both of them refused to leave. The referee threatened them with disqualification. They ignored him, and rushed at Jenny. The referee signalled, the bell rang, Filthy Freda and the Blond Bombshell were disqualified but refused to honour the decision, slamming Jenny against the ropes, working her over, kicking and scratching at her eyes. Flash was over the top rope and into the melee, and the next thing the overjoyed audience knew, Flash and Jenny were going into their Round-the-World routine, bouncing off the ropes, flinging the baddies around like so many wet towels, dizzying them with spins and whirls. Finally Jenny cupped her hands, Flash ran across the ring, stepped into Jenny's hands and was thrown up over Jenny's head to do a mid-air turn, then kick, catching both villains on the side of the head with her carefully controlled feet. The baddies fell to the canvas, not even twitching. Flash landed easily, bounced twice, turned and grabbed Jenny's hand, lifting it high in the victory salute.

"Way to *be*," Loretta screeched. "Way to *be*, baby!"

"Jesus christ," Jack sighed, awed almost to tears. "Who'd'a guessed that skinny little kid would'a done that kind'a thing?"

Loretta just sat watching as the jam-packed civic arena trembled with the approving roars of an audience of fanatic fans. She lifted her glass of 7-Up, sipped daintily and beamed.

"Listen," Jack asked Jenny confidentially, after the last match was done and they were all having a beer together. "Give me the truth. Who's my kid shacked up with, anyway."

"Me," Jenny answered with a wide and gorgeous smile. "We're a team. We work together, we live together, we eat together, we travel together, we train together, we practise together, we even," she whispered privately, "sleep together."

"Well, hell," Jack grumbled, "if you don't want to tell me the truth, why'n't you just say so?"

"Goddamn shame," he mourned to Loretta and the others when they were back at the apartment drinking rye. "Two goodlookin' broads like that and they're so busy makin' money they got no time for what's really important in the world!

"I mean," he continued sadly, "it's such a goddamn waste of womanhood! It ain't right. There's a world fulla guys would be glad to show 'em both a good time and . . . jesus, what if they *all* make that same rotten mistake!" He turned to Loretta, almost accusingly. "You should'a made more of an effort! Maybe you should'a explained it all better to her."

"Oh, for chrissake," Loretta shook her head. "Look at what's talkin! You're the most convincing argument she could'a had," and they were off on another familiar wrangle. But when Jack drew back his hand threateningly, Loretta held her own up, warning him to think again.

''You ever black my eye again,'' she said calmly, ''and I'm callin' my kid and sickin' her on ya!''

Jack gaped, then grinned from ear to ear and started to laugh loudly. ''Jesus, jesus,'' he chortled, ''if any of ya wondered where the kid got her spit and fire, you just got the answer. Can't live with 'er, can't live without 'er.'' Everyone, including Loretta, guffawed and snickered and reached for a fresh drink.

2

It lasted five years and then it was over, all of it, the tag team partnership, the friendship, the trust. It ended the way such things always end, with one heart broken and the other one filled with excitement and passion for a new interest. "We don't have to do it that way," they told each other, but they did it that way. "There's no need to fight," they said, but they fought. "We can remain friends," they promised, but they couldn't. They both behaved as badly as everybody always behaves, until everything they had shared was torn to pieces and the only thing they shared was a mutual dislike. Each of them faced the awful pit that opens when the person who has known you best finds you unacceptable. The one you tried hardest to please tells you your best efforts aren't good enough, and anger sets its claws into that soft place where love used to be.

Megan took an extended holiday. She travelled for months, enjoying very little of it, and returned to learn her booking agent had cleverly circulated the story she was off with a group of expatriate Shaolin priestesses, learning the ancient art of kung fu. She got rid of her purple bathing suit and put on a plain black one. With white sneakers and her hair cut three inches short all over her head she was back on the eastern circuit, working alone, using the name Megan Crawford, playing the squeaky-clean part, and moving steadily up the ranks until she was headlining. If there was little joy in her life there was little sorrow, and no grief at all. At first she told herself that if that was love, they could shove it. Push it up their noses. She, by god, was going to make money! And she did. One hundred and fifty dollars a night isn't much if you're only working one night a week, but if you're working four, five or six nights a week, it adds up to a nice bit. Even subtracting expenses, it's better than pounding a typewriter or getting a new kind of cancer hunched over a display terminal. And when you're a contender, they start to pay more, two hundred, even three hundred a night.

Telling the world to push love up its nose made less and less sense as the hurt faded and the enormous loss began to seem less and less enormous until it hardly even seemed like loss at all. She realized she could remember so much that was good. The laughing and teasing, the joking and cuddling. Oh, there were bad memories, the arguing and fighting, the jealousy and feeling of betrayal, but who wanted to remember that kind of crap. So it had gone bad, well, it should have been expected, after all, when it was good it was very very good, so of course when it stopped being very very good it would seem bad. Better to remember the good things, like the time she wrenched her knee and it swelled up until it looked as if she had a beachball stuck in the middle of her leg. She propped it on pillows, packed it with ice and swallowed some 222s, but god, the leg ached. And ached, and ached until Jenny came back from the matches, and loosened the tensor bandage, put another pillow under Megan's foot, then fussed and babied until Megan relaxed and fell asleep. They milked that leg for all it was worth, Megan limping to the ring for what was billed as the grudge match of all time, a tensor bandage dramatically wrapped from ankle to mid-thigh. Carefully planned and choreographed, she had attempted a mid-air scissor, and missed, crashing to the canvas with a sound that made the audience moan with empathy. How many grudge matches because of the knee that had actually healed in less than a week? And Jenny teasing her, saying, "God, Megsy, I ought to grab you and twist the other one until it puffs up, we'll make a fortune on your bum knees."

There are so many small towns around Montreal that you can buy yourself a good car, rent a comfortable apartment and have some semblance of a real life while racking up enough matches to keep yourself comfortable. Nobody expects the second-best wrestler in the country to fight every night of the week. And nobody expects the second-best wrestler in the country to try for the belt when it's being worn by her former tag team partner.

Megan found herself involved with a woman just coming out the other side of a particularly messy divorce. "God," Lynn shook her head, "can you believe it? The guy walks out, is gone six months, then sues for custody of the kids and I have to prove I can raise them properly! You'd think if I couldn't it would have shown in the six months he was pole vaulting in and out of every available bed in town. Boy," she muttered, "if it had been me had skipped out without taking them, there'd have been no chance of me getting custody! If I'd spent one night away without them, that would be it.''

Megan privately wondered why Lynn wanted the little christers. They whined, they snoffled, they demanded attention constantly.

"Don't they ever just go out and play?" she asked.

"Of course they do," Lynn laughed, "they're just excited because you're here."

But it wasn't excitement. The kids knew it, and Megan suspected it, but Lynn had no idea at all that all the nursery tales about wicked stepmothers were festering in the heads of her kids. Megan collected the debts incurred by Snow White's stepmother and by Cinderella's wicked step-family. She might have been able to shrug that off, but Lynn was no help at all. "I have to be careful," she explained. "All it would take would be just a hint and he'd have me back in court so fast my head would swim."

"Lynn, he doesn't *want* them. He just wants to keep some kind of control over your life."

"Easy for you to say, you don't have to worry about what ordinary people think. You don't have to worry about losing your job and your children."

A few months later Lynn was asking for more freedom, more time to herself. "I have to be sure," she said. "I have to be allowed to find out for sure if this is what I want or if I really need the security of a more . . . ordinary . . . sort of . . .''

"What's his name?" Megan snapped.

"No, Megan, that's not it at all, really!" Lynn protested, her face flaming.

"I bet it's not," Megan laughed. "I bet it's got more to do with being safe, with being looked after, with being protected, with being able to send your own tame bull into the field to fight with that renegade bull who's still trying to bend your brain with his crap about those snivelling goddamned kids!"

And it was no consolation to realize she had been absolutely right, wrong or right she'd said it the wrong way and it was ripped.

By that time Jenny had lost the belt to someone else, so it was okay for Megan to challenge for the title. Back and forth she travelled, winning her matches and after each match loudly stating that the new champion was afraid of her. The excitement and expectation of the paying public mounted, and when the final match was finally scheduled all the tickets were sold out in advance.

Jenny came into the ring before they had even strapped the victory belt around Megan's waist. In front of an arena jammed to the rafters with screaming fans she threw her arms around Megan, hugged her, grabbed her arm and held it up in the victor's salute, and the already hysterical crowd went even madder.

So there you are, and you're the champion, and you're making money hand over fist, just like you always wanted to do, and you're bringing it all in with such regularity you have to hire an accountant to look after it for you.

Megan learned that rock stars aren't the only celebrities who get surrounded with groupies. She learned you may be able to be friends with your lover but it's a stupid idea to become lovers with your friends. And she learned that the best way not to get deeply involved with any one person is to get shallowly involved with several people; then learned that was a guaranteed way to wind up involved in nothing at all, not even your own life.

And then there she was, almost thirty, and the world was full of seventeen-year-old amazons, all of them hungry to get the hell away from the farm, get away from camp, get out of the inner city, get out of suburbia, get out of college, get out of what they had and get what Megan had. And she realized there wasn't really any glamour in it, but it was the only way she knew how to make a living and so she trained a little bit harder because it wasn't as easy as it once was. She trained a little more often and for a little longer, but her pulled muscles didn't heal as fast, her bruises seemed to throb a bit more. She told herself thirty wasn't really old, for god's sake, June Byers was champion when she had teenaged kids.

Then one day, there she was and she was thirty-one, and the word *veteran* had a different meaning, the bed in the motel was lumpy and the sweet young thing sharing it was prattling on about how she had always been attracted to older women.

"Yeah, me, too," Megan grinned, "until one morning I woke up and I *was* one!" Not an hour later she realized she wasn't really enjoying what it was she was doing as much as she was enjoying the feeling of power that came with driving someone else half out of her mind with rampant sensation. Even realizing it, she didn't stop. She watched herself deliberately and skillfully put another woman through an extended sexual pleasure that left the young body slicked with sweat and the young woman herself almost exhausted. Just to prove she wasn't as old as *veteran* made her sound. Just to prove whatever in hell it was she had to prove or thought she had to prove.

The realization left her shaken and unable to sleep, and that meant the next night's matches were harder to get through. So there was something else she had to prove, which gave her something else to lie awake wondering about, and you don't get away with that for very long when the world is full of young amazons just as hungry as you used to be.

Megan knew what was happening but she didn't seem to be able to get control of it. She often felt she had somehow managed to disassociate herself from what she was doing, that she had pulled back, or out, and was watching herself through her own eyes, watching herself spiral downward. She lost her timing. The legendary gymnastics didn't quite click, and there she was one night in the emergency ward of a hospital, with a broken wrist and a shoulder no longer dislocated but aching like hell and strapped with enough adhesive tape to repair the obsolete Canadian navy of floating bathtub toys.

"Three months minimum," the doctor said.

"Three months?" she protested.

"Three months. Minimum. Otherwise, Miss Crawford, you are going to be in serious trouble with that arm."

"Doctor," Megan said, trying to control her own fear, "I am already in very serious trouble with this arm."

She took a cab to her hotel, packed her gym bag and caught a late flight back to Montreal, then another cab took her to her apartment. She had trouble getting her own door unlocked and open, and having one arm taped to her body put her off balance. She banged her shoulder twice before she managed to get herself into bed. It took a double dose of pain killer to calm everything down enough that she could go to sleep. And when she wakened, she knew she had dislocated more than her shoulder. Her whole life was out of whack.

She packed the things she wanted to keep and phoned the Salvation Army to come and get the rest. She phoned the rental agency and gave them the news. And when the Salvation Army had driven off, she phoned the limo service and tipped the driver to carry the two large suitcases and two heavily strapped and corded boxes to the long grey limo. She was driven to the airport, where she tipped a redcap to get the boxes and suitcases to the ticket agent, and watched thankfully as the damned things moved off on the conveyor belt. She had to wait two hours for her flight, and took her pain killer just before she boarded the plane. That gave her three and a half hours of uninterrupted sleep before the codeine wore off and her shoulder and wrist sent red hot pain to waken her.

"Yes, ma'am," the stewardess asked, "may I help you?"

"Could I have a glass of cold water, please?" Megan managed a smile. The stewardess disappeared briefly, returned with a plastic glass of stale ice water.

"This bottle has one of those kidproof caps," Megan admitted, "and I don't think I can get it off one-handed."

"Glad to," the stewardess smiled, and took the bottle. She opened the cap, shook out a pill and Megan swallowed it, draining the water. The stewardess returned the bottle, Megan managed to pocket it, then sat back in her chair trying to figure out how long it had been since she had seen a real live woman with long varnished nails. Ugly damn things, she decided, they look like they've been dipped in blood.

She didn't have to worry about her suitcases and boxes when she transferred planes, and the codeine allowed her to almost forget the agony in her arm, shoulder and neck. She didn't sleep any more, just drifted in and out of a light doze, and before she landed again, a different stewardess helped her with the bottle of pills and glass of water routine. A redcap helped her with her suitcases, a cabdriver took her from the airport to the hotel and a bellhop got the suitcases up to a room on the third floor, overlooking the harbour. Megan tipped him, he left, she put the security chain on the door, pulled the venetian blinds shut, stripped off her clothes and lay across her bed feeling as if she would never sleep again as long as she lived.

She didn't waken until lunch time. She managed to wash up at the basin in the bathroom, then contorted herself until she was able to get herself into a clean shirt. She nearly dislocated her thumb getting the brass button done up on the front of her jeans and there was nothing much she could do with the laces of her sneakers, so she had to open the snaps on her suitcase and get out her loafers. Then and only then could she leave her room, go downstairs, have a cup of coffee, and set about finding a doctor who could do something about the ten pounds or more of tape holding her arm in its socket. Then, maybe, she could move. Or even have a bath.

She found the doctor, who removed the tape, but Megan couldn't move her arm and didn't get to take a bath. Instead, the doctor referred her to the x-ray department for a half hour of take a deep breath hold it breathe again, and some heated argument about whether or not Megan could move her arm or anyone else would move the arm. Then back to the doctor's office with a large brown envelope containing x-ray films and the technician's diagnoses. The physician spent a good five minutes studying the films and rereading the technician's report, then she looked at Megan with very serious big blue eyes.

"Trouble, huh?" Megan dared.

"It's not the best news you'll ever get in your life," the doctor replied.

"Bone?" Megan guessed.

"Nerve, I think."

"You think? You *think*? You don't *know*?"

"Do you?"

"I'm not a doctor!"

"I'm not a magician," the doctor answered honestly. "I want to get your medical record from the physician who saw you at the time of the injury. Then, well, I might want to recommend you to a specialist."

"Oh, god," Megan sighed. "The other guy said three months minimum. This sounds..."

The doctor forced a grin that was supposed to be cheering. "Well, look at it this way: at least you have no choice but to take a much needed rest."

"It shows, huh?" she sighed, tried to shrug but couldn't.

Megan's arm was again strapped tight against her side, but this time it bent at the elbow and poked awkwardly out in front of her. For all that it was as awkward as a festering ingrown toenail, the change in position helped ease the pain in her hand. Her wrist, forearm, upper arm, shoulder and neck were just as bad as ever, but the physician gave her a prescription for a different kind of pain killer. "Just don't take one until you're settled," she advised. "No driving once you start them."

"But I'll sleep?" Megan asked, worried and still frightened.

"You'll sleep," the physician promised.

In spite of her obviously impaired mobility and dexterity, Megan had no trouble at all renting a car. With some money and her credit cards in her wallet, and with her suitcases and boxes in the back seat, Megan drove out of town looking for some place where she could rent a room and enjoy some peace and quiet until it was time to go back to the doctor and get the tape changed. From what she could tell by the pain in her shoulder, neck and back, she'd be goddamn lucky if the arm didn't come off with the tape. "Managed to fuck yourself for sure," she snarled at her own reflection in the rearview.

What she wanted was a nice motel or auto court where she could have some pretence of home and still not need any of the responsibilities or trappings of decent domesticity. What she got was an old renovated cabin at the edge of an orchard in what the sign claimed was Colony Farm Campsites and Cabins.

A bed, a small gesture toward a bathroom with nothing more in it than a toilet, a stained basin, a tiny shower stall and some nails on which to hang damp towels. And a room in which was crowded a wooden table, three wooden chairs, a small fridge that hummed and shook and two old stuffed chairs, one facing a window looking out at the unpruned and neglected orchard, the other facing an old portable TV. The linoleum had been lifted off the board floor, the old boards sanded enough to make them safe for sandalled feet and the sink tap under the window dripped with mind-numbing metronomic regularity. But the bed was comfortable, the old trees beautiful and the path leading down to the beach was thick with fallen evergreen needles, scented with bracken fern and thimbleberry, edged with columbine and small yellow flowers that looked like almost microscopically small snapdragons. At the edge of the clearing, where the high tide left huge logs and bits of treasure, the foxgloves grew six feet tall and the lupins crowded the salmonberry bushes. An osprey wheeled in the sky, circling the small bay, hunting constantly, and a crabby little kingfisher screeched and chattered in a voice almost guaranteed to make you want to throw stones at it. Sometimes a tall, stockily built young woman walked the edge of the lapping water, kicking at spindrift and exercising her fat little cockapoo.

Megan could buy food at the Bright Spot, a sort of mini-supermarket that had obviously at one time been a country store and had been added to over the years until it rambled in every direction at the same time. She could cook her own meals on the three-burner propane stove or drive a few miles down the highway to the White Lotus.

For the first time in years, Megan had no need to pack her bag and hit the road. There was nowhere she had to be, ought to be or should be, nobody she should call, or even could call. She slept, she ate, then slept again. And the old cabin comforted her. When her arm ached terribly, she took one of the new pills the doctor had given her and went out to sit under the rambling old pear tree, sometimes reading, sometimes daydreaming, sometimes just sitting, staring out at nothing at all, floating on the pills and on the pain the pills couldn't even begin to touch, the pain not in her arm, but in those other places, some of which don't even seem to have names.

The doctor had new x-rays taken of her wrist, elbow and shoulder, then others taken of her neck and spine. "You have one or two disks which might be slightly compressed, but not enough to cause this problem. Compressed disks," she smiled, admitting her own limitations, "are very common; they're the price we pay for walking upright."

"Then what's wrong?"

"I want you to see a specialist. Get some tests done that we can't do here."

Megan panicked. "Listen, please, you've got to tell me something! My goddamned arm won't move and it won't stop hurting. Even my ass is starting to hurt! Sometimes it feels as if my legs are going numb. And those pills you gave me are not much help."

"Nerve damage is painful, I know," the doctor soothed, and suddenly Megan didn't even like her any more. "But look at it this way; if there was no pain the news would be really bad. It would mean your nerves were so badly injured they might never heal. This way, at least you still know you've got an arm.''

"Oh god," Megan sighed, "if you knew how pissed off it makes me to hear you say things like that.''

The adhesive tape was replaced by a stretchy elastic riggins, triangular-shaped, that pulled on over her head like an undershirt and helped steady the shoulder joint. Another elastic riggins, this time a tube, fit over her elbow, and the cast stayed on her wrist and hand. The entire throbbing left arm was slung in a wide white canvas belt that hung from her good shoulder and closed with stiff velcro tabs. Her fingers were constantly swollen, the bone in her left arm felt like it had been replaced with a hot metal rod and there was a patch on her back, just over her shoulder blade, that tingled constantly, annoying her more than she thought anything could annoy her.

"You may be developing shingles," the doctor decided.

"What in hell is shingles?''

"Did you have chickenpox as a child?''

"Didn't everyone?''

"Well, it's the same virus. Actually, a form of herpes, we think. Not the venereal kind," she added hastily. "Anyway, it's usually your body's way of telling you to slow down, relax, unwind and get rid of whatever is causing you stress.''

"Well, my lord," Megan snarled, "all I have to do is cut off my arm and then kill off most of the world," The doctor just smiled again.

Megan bought groceries and a couple of pair of denim cutoffs, some cotton T-shirts and a pair of canvas-topped deck shoes with velcro closing tabs. She went into a beer parlour and discovered the camp was still working, so Jack and Loretta wouldn't be in town yet.

She went into a secondhand bookstore and left half an hour later with a Carnation canned milk box half full of tattered paperback novels, then drove back to her quiet little cabin. One-handed, she managed to get together a fruit salad, ate it with half a pint of creamed cottage cheese, then took a book and two cans of half frozen juice down to the beach.

You aren't supposed to sit under an arbutus tree, because, as every Islander has been told a zillion times, the damn things are full of wood ticks, and ticks can give you Rocky Mountain spotted fever, from which you can get meningitis, which will fry your brain and you'll wind up in the chronic care ward, in no better shape than a human vegetable. But then wild cherry, maple, alder and birch trees are also infested with wood ticks and if you're going to spend your life worrying about things like that you'll never set foot outside the house. So Megan, who had never known or even heard of anybody actually getting wood ticks, fever or brain damage, sat under an arbutus, opened her book and tried to lose herself in some story set on another planet, where people with almost telepathic powers did incredibly earth-like things with the help of animals the like of which had never been seen but often imagined. When the pain in her arm got beyond a dull ache and began to approach active agony, she pulled the tab on her now thawed but still cold juice and swilled down a painkiller. The pain receded back to what was bearable and Megan dozed in the shade, her face pale and sweaty.

She wakened slowly, mouth dry and sticky, knowing it was late in the afternoon and her pill was wearing off. Someone was standing in front of her, looking down with a worried frown.

"Are you okay?" Stubby asked quietly.

"I feel like shit," Megan answered, struggling to sit upright, fumbling for her now warm juice.

"You break your arm or something?"

"Something," Megan agreed. "That your dog?"

"Oh, she's not a dog," Stubby chortled, "she's a dragon."

"Yeah?" Megan reached out with her good hand, and scratched the cockapoo's ears. "What's her name?"

"Draconis."

"What else, huh?"

"What else indeed. I'm Stubby."

"Megan."

"You need any help?"

"You know where I can get a new body?" Megan said sourly.

"You might try the body shop in town," Stubby said quietly. "They even have European and import models, you might be able to get something really exotic. But it looks to me as if all you really need is the second hand store."

Megan stared. And then, for the first time in weeks, Megan smiled a real smile.

"That stinks," she grinned.

"Yeah," Stubby agreed happily, "it's just about the awfulest thing I know, but I love it. It's my dad's joke, although I bet he got it from someone else."

It isn't easy to walk on rounded beach stones if you're off balance, and Megan had to move slowly and carefully, placing her feet precisely and firmly, avoiding any discolorations which might warn of algae, seaweed or slime from some oil spill or another.

"You play ball?" Stubby asked.

"No, why?"

"You move real well." The hint of a grin flickered briefly. "You're in wonderful shape for the shape you're in."

"One more like that," Megan promised gaily, "and it's a bop in the beak for you."

"Oh, isn't that some kind of music, that old-time beak-bop rhythm?"

"Careful."

Megan stepped gingerly from the rocks to the damp sand, weighed all the pros and cons, all the fors and againsts, and gambled.

"I'm, uh, I'm a professional athlete," she admitted, half expecting to feel a door close between them.

"Yeah?" Stubby looked surprised and pleased. "But not a ball player?"

"No. Wrestler." Megan held her breath.

"No shit?"

"No shit."

"I'm a multimillionaire and professional poker player."

"No shit?" Megan asked.

"Only a little bit."

"The multimillionaire part, right?" Megan guessed.

"Wrong. The professional poker player part. I haven't played serious poker for about five years. Maybe more."

"But the multimillionaire part is true?"

"Yeah. Do you play poker?" she asked hopefully.

"I hate playing cards."

"You hate playing cards? How can anybody hate playing cards?"

Megan told Stubby about Jack's decades of failure with solitaire, and how nerve-wracking it was to listen to the slip of old cards dealt onto an oilcloth-covered table, and Stubby told Megan about Ada Richardson building a fortune on other people's convictions that they had a foolproof system to beat the odds. Megan told Stubby about life in camp and deciding to leave even if she had to fight her way out, and Stubby told Megan about looking for the Holy Grail.

"You actually went looking for . . . ?" Megan stared at Stubby as if she had never seen her before, although by that time they had been talking and walking together for a couple of hours.

"Yeah."

"Didn't anybody ever tell you that was just . . . a fairy tale?"

"You believe everything anybody tells you?"

"Well, no, but . . . use your brain, woman! The Holy Grail is on the same shelf as unicorns and . . ."

"What makes you think there weren't unicorns?" Stubby asked.

"You're teasing, right?"

"Am I? Why is it that if some scientist of some kind or another holds up a fossilized piece of bone maybe half an inch long and then starts talking and drawing pictures on a blackboard, the world accepts his eventual claim that from that one little scrap of bone —which incidentally not one of us ever gets to even see, let alone hold— he has proved that a buhzillion years ago some new kind of dinosaur roamed the swamps? I mean, good christ, if ever anything was hard to swallow some of those purported critters are! But we hear unicorn and we're conditioned to think pooh-pooh push-tush. And some egghead can talk for half an hour, using words he mostly invented himself, and can rattle off mathematical formulae nobody else in the world could even begin to try to prove, and then he says And so, you see, I predict that in four million years this thing or that will come to pass. Genius, we say! Give that guy another government grant! Pay him more money! Cocktail parties around the world become the place for people who can't add six and twenty-six to use these complicated mathematical formulae to debate whether or not this egghead is right. We accept his bullshit without being able to really prove or disprove it, but we won't accept stuff that can be absolutely positively shown to us.''

''Like what?''

''You ever read the Bible?''

''Yeah, I guess as much as most people.''

''Okay, one of the tribes was called the Benjaminites, right?''

''I'll take your word for it.''

''Well, the Benjaminites weren't allowed to marry among their own tribe, they had to marry outside the tribe. They married and intermarried with the Phoenicians. And the Phoenicians were seafaring people who shipped stuff around and traded it. Well, three times at least in the Bible the Benjaminites get 'exiled'—once for worshipping the Golden Calf on the way back from Egypt with Moses, once when the Levite man is sodomized by a Benjaminite and again when Sodom and Gomorrah got ruined. Now the Benjaminites had a language inside their language, and their holy words and sacred terms were Arabic-Aramaic.''

''What has this got to do with anything?''

''Listen,'' Stubby said, her words tumbling almost desperately. ''Please. It makes sense. To me, anyway. There are inscriptions in the rocks in the south of Mexico that are written in Indonesian script.''

''How in hell did the Indonesians get into this, Stubby? You were talking about Benjaminites and Phoenicians.''

''Listen!'' Stubby's face was flushed, her eyes snapping. ''Listen, Megan, please. There is also Phoenician writing scratched onto those rocks. The Phoenicians and Indonesians had trading alliances, and this is all written in historic records.''

''So the Phoenicians and the Indonesians went to Mexico? Is that what you're saying?''

"And the Benjaminites, some of them at least, went with them!''

"What?''

"The Cree have a holy language, a sacred language, and the root words for all the Cree holy terms have Aramaic-Arabic similarities.''

"You're saying the Cree are the lost tribe?''

"Why not the other way around? Why couldn't the Cree have gone there instead of them coming here? Why is it always . . .''

"Stubby! Calm down.''

"See?'' Stubby shrugged, "you don't want to believe it. It can be proven, and you don't want to hear it. Even though the Indonesians have a seagoing boat they call a phinici. Patterned after the Phoenician trading boat, I'm sure.''

"What's this got to do with the Holy Grail?''

"Everything,'' Stubby snapped angrily. "Everything. You refuse point blank to believe there could be a Holy Grail but you'll listen to these eggheads talk about black holes and big bang and the colonization of Uranus. But you don't want to think about what it means that long before those eggheads will admit it could have happened, people were moving all over this earth. Think what that means! All of those people, every culture, every damned one, has stories about unicorns, dragons and magic. So the scientists have to make sure we discount those stories! Because if we believe the stories, we'll believe in magic and if we believe in magic it will come back and if it comes back those assholes are out of their very well-paying jobs!''

Megan just stared. Standing in front of her was a tall, sturdy, good looking, brown-haired, brown-eyed, clear-skinned woman of some thirty years who was more attractive than she knew she was, who appeared fine, great in fact, in every way including sense of humour and who was out of her goddam skull. Normal in every apparent way, the poor sick bitch believed in magic.

On the other hand, nobody is perfect. One of the women in camp one year spent too much time by herself and decided that the book of Revelations was about to unfold, Armageddon would come with the mushroom cloud of nuclear warfare, the world would be absolutely destroyed but all the good and faithful and God-loving people would be raptured away, carried off by a band of angels to roam around heaven all day singing hymns of praise and humility. And the woman hadn't invented the idea all by herself, she got it from a TV evangelist who had a following of some three million God-fearing Christian souls. None of whom were considered to be out of their goddamn skulls.

"Well,'' Megan managed, "to each her own, I guess.''

They stared at each other. Stubby turned away first, shoulders slumping. ''You think I'm crazier'n a shithouse rat, right?''

''Does it matter?'' Megan reached out with her good arm, touched Stubby's shoulder. ''What difference does it make whether or not I believe what you believe as long as I don't try to make you change your mind? Why do you care what I think? For all you know *I'm* the one who's crazy.''

''Are you?''

''Probably,'' Megan admitted. ''Right now, anyway, I seem to have my head up my arse more often than not.''

That night, with two painkillers numbing her sore arm, Megan dreamed she was some other place in some other time, faced with a challenge she couldn't name, trying to make a decision without knowing the least little thing about her choices. She didn't quite wake up, but was dimly aware of the sound of the wind rustling in the leaves of the old fruit trees, and she wondered, briefly, what it had all been like here before the dispossessed and discounted had arrived looking for their next chance at Paradise.

The arm got no better, but the prefab sling got comfortably grey and less obvious. Megan invited Stubby and Draconis for supper, bought prawns from a fisherman, took them home and cooked them in butter with lots of fresh crushed garlic and a generous splash of white wine. Stubby took Megan out to visit with Vinnie, Wright and Sharon, all of whom seemed to think Stubby had just returned from an extended trip somewhere. Stuke bounced around stiffly but joyfully, Vinnie gave them a guided tour of her rose garden and greenhouses, Sharon cooked the biggest and best meal anybody had eaten in more than a year and Wright sat in a big stuffed chair, smiling contentedly and listening to the conversation. His hair was silver now, and there were lines in his face. His eyes clung to Stubby as if drinking in the sight of her, and every time she laughed, Wright smiled and sighed. Vinnie told jokes, gave hilarious rundowns on gossip real and imagined, and nobody mentioned Gordon or Earl.

''God,'' Megan said enviously, ''your mom is a real hoot.''

''My mom?'' Stubby blurted, nearly taking her pickup off the road and into the ditch. ''My mom opens her mouth and no sense at all pours out in a gush and bubble of blether and blurk.''

''Blurk?'' Megan laughed, ''what in hell kind of a word is blurk? Anyway, your mom's got most of the world pegged in place and deflated. I only wish my mom had been half. . .''

''Crazy,'' Stubby interrupted stubbornly. ''My mom has always been as goofy as a garden toad. She sits down and talks to me, and when she finally shuts up I don't have a clue what she's been yammering on about. Any advice she ever gave me turned out to be the absolutely worst thing I could have tried or done, and her own life has been one ridiculous disaster after another.''

"She's sober, isn't she?" Megan said defensively. "She isn't shitfaced twenty hours a day! You can walk past her and not fall on your fazizzus because of the stink of secondhand hooch!''

"Fazizzus?" Stubby slowed the pickup, looked over at Megan. "Fazizzus? And you thought blurk was a dumb word?''

"Everybody knows what a fazizzus is," Megan scoffed. "Everybody who is anybody at all, that is.''

"No wonder you like Vinnie," Stubby decided, "in your own way you're just as crazy as she is.''

"Why, what a nice thing to say!" Megan teased. "Are you always so silvertongued and swayve?''

The arm continued to just hang there like so many pounds of wet clay, and the pink pills continued to keep the pain far enough from the core of conscious reality that Megan could deal with it. But Stubby had trouble dealing with the pink pills. "My mom," she said quietly, sitting in a comfortable chair on her wide verandah, watching the sky darken slowly and gently, "used to have pills to make her happy and pills to make her sleep. She had pills to wake her up and pills to calm her down. She had 'em in green and blue and pink and yellow, she had them in all sizes and shapes, and she sort of stumbled and lurched from one minute of the day to the next. I think entire weeks and months of her life must have been wiped from her brain. And she was intolerable. I mean it. Not just a pain in the jaw like she is now, she was just totally intolerable.''

"Yeah?" Megan slumped lower on the other big chair, turning slightly so her sore arm and shoulder didn't touch anything.

"Yeah. She doesn't take them any more. Wright and Sharon got her to go see an acupuncturist.''

"And so you think I should give that a try instead of taking codeine?'' Megan challenged.

"I didn't say that," Stubby said quietly. "I just told you what those things did to Vinnie. You made a big thing out of how Vin didn't drink; I'm telling you she might not have been drunk, but she wasn't sober. And I guess I don't see any difference between being shitfaced on whiskey or being shitfaced on valium.''

"Really?" Megan smiled coldly. "I tell you what, Stubbzers. Why don't you wear this goddamned arm for a week and then tell me some more about my painkillers. Maybe Vinnie didn't have a bad arm, but that doesn't mean she didn't hurt somewhere.''

''Yeah?'' Stubby just looked at Megan, then smiled and Megan began to feel uncomfortable, as if she'd just bit a hand extended in friendship. ''My mom,'' she said, blinking at her own unexpected tears, ''has spent almost all her life stuck in some kind of unbelievable . . . circus, I guess. That's all I can call it, a goddamned circus!''

The summer set in on them with determination; entire days passed without so much as one solitary cloud in the pale blue sky. Dandelion fluff floated on the torpid breeze, thistle fluff drifted across the fields and fireweed fluff skittered in the grassy strips at the side of the road, wafting and swirling in the hot air from passing traffic. The level of the water in Haslam Creek lowered, tadpoles grew fat on bugs, midges and mosquito larvae, absorbed their tails, grew their legs, and turned into frogs, and the Forestry department closed the bush because of the fire hazard.

Megan went into town to see the doctor, who wrote her another prescription for more painkillers and suggested they might try some physiotherapy. Megan agreed to try it, made an appointment for the following week, then, instead of getting her prescription refilled right away, walked down the street to check out the Queen's Hotel beer parlour.

Loretta was sitting at a table near the juke box, nursing a glass of draft beer. Her head was back, her eyes were closed, and she was smiling to herself. Megan walked over, pulled out a chair and sat down, putting a ten-dollar bill on the table and signalling to the waiter. ''Ginger ale,'' she said, ''and another round for the table.''

''Took your time getting here,'' Loretta said, her smile widening, her eyes open and fixed on Megan's face. ''I thought you'd'a been here the week before last.''

''What are you talking about?'' Megan puzzled.

''I sent a telegram,'' Loretta explained, lifting her glass of beer and frowning slightly. ''Didn't ya get it?''

''I didn't get any telegram. Where did you send it?''

''That address you give me in Montreal. If you didn't get no telegram, why are you here?''

''I've been here for, oh, a couple of months,'' Megan explained, ''waiting for fire season to get you out of camp.''

''Jesus christ,'' Loretta sighed. She drained her beer, put the empty glass down and reached for the full one. Megan took a deep breath, told herself to hang onto her temper and carefully sipped her ginger ale.

''Let's start all over again,'' she said evenly, managing a stiff smile. ''I got here a couple of months ago and rented a little place south of town.

Hurt my arm.'' She nodded her head at the sling as if it wasn't clearly noticeable. ''I checked here, and the tarbender said you weren't out of camp yet. So, I figured fire season would pry you loose, and I just . . . waited.'' She sipped again.

''Couldn't drive out to see us, I suppose,'' Loretta said stiffly.

''Can't drive very well with this arm.''

''Oh.'' Loretta accepted the lie, shrugged sadly. ''Too bad we didn't do a better job of keepin' in touch. I guess if I'd'a done a better job answerin' your postcards, you'd'a sent more of 'em and I'd'a known . . .'' Again the fatalistic shrug.

''Where's the old man?'' Megan laughed. ''In the john takin' a whiz?''

''Nope.'' Loretta drained her second beer and waved at the bartender to bring more. ''That's what I was tryin' to get in touch with you about.'' She looked at Megan, unable to speak, her faded old beer-boozer's eyes leaking onto her lined and sagging face.

''Ah, shit,'' Megan guessed.

''They let me stay in the house until we all came out for fire season,'' Loretta said dully. ''Said it would give me time to straighten out my affairs. Not much to straighten out. Ain't had an affair in over a year and a half,'' she tried to joke.

''So where you staying?''

''Apartment.'' Loretta shrugged yet again. ''Not bad, I guess. Got a window looks out toward the water. Coupl'a rooms, enough for me. You?''

''Oh, it's okay,'' Megan downgraded her little cabin, her big old fruit trees, her path to the beach. ''What do you figure to do now?''

''Don't really know.'' Loretta, thankfully, did not shrug again, she just looked puzzled. ''I was kind'a thinkin' of gettin' a job, but they disabused me of that notion fast enough. So what's wrong with your arm? I told you, told you from the time you was little, if you didn't stop chewin' your fingernails you were gonna be sorry. Now lookit ya.'' She reached for a cigarette.

''My friend says I should go to the secondhand store,'' Megan said, and Loretta choked on her first puff of cigarette smoke, then coughed several times and, finally, started to laugh.

''Christ,'' she said, ''that's a good one. Come on, kid, buy your old lady some lunch.''

Megan took Loretta to the Businessman's Buffet, and watched as Loretta swelled with pleasure and a kind of pride Megan didn't recognize. ''This is real class,'' Loretta whispered, piling more slices of ham on her plate, spooning on potato salad, five-bean salad and little cobs of corn.

"Seems a waste, don't it," she hissed, "itty bitty cobs like that. If they'd'a left 'em they would'a got ten times the amount of food. Twenty times. Seems wrong, in a way, with so many people outta work and all. But," she grinned wickedly, "since they already done it, no use wastin' it, right?"

"Right," Megan agreed.

"You better eat somethin' more'n that, kid," Loretta warned, "or you're gonna skinny down to nothin' more'n eyeballs'n'asshole. You weren't no skinnymalink when ya lived with me. I made sure you ate. I might'a been the world's worst mother in a lotta ways, but you ate. So do it now, I know you know how! Here, have some'a this stuff." She scooped something onto Megan's plate, then looked at it. "What'n' hell is it? Looks like lime jella with grated cabbage in it."

"That's probably what it is," Megan agreed. "Christly jesus what they won't try to pass off as food, eh? Well, it won't likely kill ya."

They moved to a table in front of the plate glass window looking out over the estuary and the little park built around it. "I can remember," Loretta confided, "when all that was was a dirty sewery river sloppin' through some mudflats. They sure fixed 'er up."

"Why not?" Megan said quietly. "It was them made it a mess. I bet before they started logging and mining and building and mucking around the river was clean and the mud flats didn't stink."

"You think so? Well," Loretta shrugged, "it looks okay now." She applied herself to her meal, eating daintily, smiling often, enjoying everything. Then, with no trace of self-consciousness at all, she reached across the table and quickly cut Megan's slices of turkey into bite-sized bits. "You sure managed to frig up that arm," she said flatly.

"Yeah," Megan admitted. "Yeah, I think I did the ultimate job on it."

"So what is it? More than just a bust bone, right?"

"They don't know what it is," Megan sighed.

"Watch 'em," Loretta warned. "Next thing you know they'll tell you it's all in your head. Every time they don't know what to do and can't justify the christly fees they charge, they try to make you feel it's *your* fault. Why'n't you try somethin' else?"

"Like what? Witchcraft?"

"Well, jesus, look at your arm, kid. Pretend that arm was you. How'd you like to be crammed into a riggins like that, strapped and squeezed and held so's you couldn't move if you wanted to? Why'n't you take off all that crap and garbage and give the damn thing a chance?"

"It hurts, momma," Megan said softly, and again her eyes burned, and tears welled.

"Well, of course it does," Loretta agreed. "That's your arm's way of tellin' you it ain't happy. You just eat up your lunch like a good little girl," she winked, "and momma'll fix your arm for you."

"Christ," Megan shook her head, "if you think I'm gonna let an old tart like you start messing with my arm, you're outta your everlovin' tree."

It was almost night when Megan parked her car in Stubby's driveway and walked toward the porch where Stubby was sitting with Draconis on her knee, listening to Rosalie Sorels on the tape player. "Hey," she said, sinking into the other chair wearily.

"Hey yourself," Stubby replied. "Where's your sling?"

"My mother," Megan laughed, "took it and heaved it in her garbage, along with most of my tensor bandage."

"Your mother?" Stubby gaped.

"Yeah." Megan shook her head. "Christ, what a day!"

"So . . . how does your arm feel? Worse?"

"No." Megan looked at it, just hanging from her shoulder like a stick of wood. "No, it doesn't feel worse."

"Better?"

"I don't know. Feels awful . . . heavy."

"Guess the sling took most of the weight," Stubby yawned. "Put it on your other shoulder, I guess."

"Yeah," Megan laughed, "my good shoulder feels better, for sure."

"Maybe your mom knew what she was doing."

"If she did," Megan said sourly, "it'll be the first time in her life!"

"Oh, I don't know about that," Stubby teased, "she had you, didn't she? Even then, she could have flushed you down the closest toilet."

Megan learned to tuck her useless hand in the pocket of her jeans or in her jacket pocket, to keep it out of the way. She learned to pick weeds one-handed and help Stubby with the garden and the few chickens. She stopped feeling insulted whenever someone cut her meat for her and, although she didn't realize it, she was taking less than half the number of painkillers. Stubby noticed but she didn't mention it. The physiotherapy was as much help as a wet toilet seat on a cold night, but it gave Megan a reason to go into town twice a week and, once the time was wasted in the medical clinic, she could have lunch with Loretta. "My friend's mom is having a birthday supper," Megan said carefully, "for my friend. And she asked if you would like to go to it."

"Yeah? What kind of supper?"

"A birthday supper I told you. Don't you listen?"

"Don't be so damned narky! Christ, didn't anybody manage to teach you manners? I tried and it was a lost cause but I hoped someone else'd have better luck. What kind of party is a nice way of askin' what should I wear? Don't you know nothin'?''

"Wear?" Megan stared at Loretta. "Wear? Mom, what would you expect someone to wear? Clean clothes, for christ's sake!''

"You know," Loretta said conversationally, sipping her beer daintily, "I used to think you had a half decent brain in your head. Now I think someone chucked you over the top rope onto your head once too often. Is this thing a slacks'n'shirt kinda thing or do I got to go down to the bank and cash in the family stocks'n'bonds to buy me one of them cree-ay-shuns.''

"Jeans," Megan said. "Jeans and a nice shirt, that's what I'm wearing.''

"That's no help," Loretta shook her head. "You'd'a wore jeans to your father's funeral if you'd'a been around for it!''

"I wish," Megan said, almost angry, "I wish we could have a conversation, Mom, without all this nattering and bickering. We must sound like a bad dog-and-pony act.''

"Listen," Loretta said firmly, "it might not be much, Megan, but it's a whole helluva lot better than we managed for most of our lives! At least we ain't fightin'! We already did too much of that. Who knows," she tried to smile, her ruined face looking almost pathetic with the attempt, "if we keep tryin' to make jokes and nattering and nagging, we might even learn to say something that means something. It's better'n silence.''

"Is that why you and Jack nattered all the time?''

"Oh, that," Loretta shrugged. "Hell, I never did understand any of that! I'm sure glad you don't drink, Megan," she confided. "I headed out on a weekend party one time and it lasted most'a my life. Woke up, for chrissakes, in a cheap hotel bed married to some sad bugger I never did manage to get to know.'' Again the stubbornly determined smile creased the wrinkles in Loretta's face. "But no use cryin' over spilt milk under the burned bridge, right?''

"Mom," Megan blurted, "you're okay, you know? Mixed metaphors and all.''

Loretta blinked rapidly. "Thank you. But I think you should know I never mixed a metaphor in my life. I never even, got to see a bullfight let alone met the metaphor,'' she winked. The blue-suited, white-shirted, dark-tied businessmen discussing torts and retorts, mortgages and foreclosures, looked up like so many grazing sheep as the two women burst into loud logging-camp guffaws, pointing at each other, shaking their heads and generally acting like almost anything in the world other than ladies.

The birthday supper Vinnie threw for Stubby was one of the highlights of Loretta's life. Megan spoke to Stubby, who phoned Sharon, who asked Vinnie, who understood completely, and when the considered response had gone back along the line in reverse, Megan took Loretta shopping and treated her to an outfit that was so totally appropriate to the occasion it passed seemingly unnoticed. Loretta stopped biting her lip nervously. "I sure do like your roses," she said shyly to Vinnie, who glowed happily and started explaining in detail how she pruned and fertilized them all herself. "Yourself?" Loretta was suitably impressed. "I thought maybe you had a yard boy or something come in to do them."

"I'm the yard boy," Wright flirted outrageously. "I just lie around in the yard looking gorgeous."

"If I buy a yard," Loretta smiled, "would you come lie around in it for me?"

"Lady," Wright said, and everyone knew he wasn't joking in the slightest, "I'd lie around in your yard anytime. And you don't have to buy it, I do rentals, too."

"Really?" Loretta stared at him and Megan realized the face might have spent too many hours draped near the fumes from a glass full of booze, but the eyes were still working overtime and the body was, as Stubby had joked about Megan, in great shape, all things considered.

Sharon had turned herself inside out preparing everybody's favourite food. The cake was rich chocolate with pink and white candles, and nobody looked sideways and sniffed when both Stuke and Draconis were given plates of supper, although Sharon did admit she had never before seen a dog eat cranberry sauce. "I keep telling you," Stubby said easily, "Draconis isn't a dog, she's a dragon, and dragons love cranberry sauce."

"How come when I look at her," Loretta challenged, "all I see is a kind of fat poodly-looking thing." Loretta was being so careful not to drop her endings they almost shot across the table like pebbles.

"She is," Stubby smiled, "an absolute champion of disguise." Megan, who had been waiting all afternoon for Loretta to goof and put her foot in her mouth, was astounded when suddenly everybody except herself started nattering dose guys, dem guys, dat guys and alla da guys.

"I think," she grinned, "I've fallen in with a pack of total loons."

"There is absolutely no reason on earth," Wright said gently, "for any living soul to cling to respectability or seriousness for one minute longer than is necessary. It isn't enough to throw away the Christian work ethic. We have to try very hard to get rid of their conscientious grimness, as well."

"Personally," Loretta said primly, sipping her white wine appreciatively, ''I have always thought we ought to find out where in hell they came from and then ship 'em back there again. I mean, now that we've got rocket fuel and NASA and space flight and all that stuff, surely to heaven we can off-load the humourless bastards.''

By the time they had finished supper, then finished dessert, then finished their after dinner drinks, everyone was too tiddly to even think of driving Loretta all the way into town to her little apartment. ''You might as well just sleep over,'' Vinnie invited. ''There's lots and lots of room, and that way we won't have to cut short the party.''

''I haven't slept over like this in years,'' Loretta admitted. Wright started to laugh. She blushed. ''Oh, you! You know what I mean!'' He laughed harder.

The next afternoon Wright volunteered to deliver Loretta back to town in the limo. She stared at it for several moments, then shook her head. ''I never thought the day would come I'd even get close to a thing like that, let alone get inside it.''

Wright leaned over and whispered something in her ear. Loretta's jaw dropped, her face flamed and for the first time in her life Megan saw her mother stumped for words. ''Come on, Stubby,'' she laughed, ''let's get out of here before the party starts to get dirty.''

They drove up the Lakes road where the logging scars were barely covered with a green layer of brush and scrub, then parked the truck and walked along paths made by deer and raccoons. Draconis scrambled and meandered over logs and rocks, through berry patches and long grass, and any time they were anywhere near water, there she was, splashing and paddling happily, whipping the water to froth and chasing dragonflies and darning needles through the weedy shallows. ''Even logged over and wasted, raped and desecrated,'' Stubby sighed, ''it's so beautiful it makes your throat go all tight.''

''Yeah,'' Megan agreed, but her eyes were turned to Stubby, not to the hillsides and slopes. And, of course, because it was the last thing in the world she had any intention of doing, the last thing in the world she wanted or was looking for, when Stubby turned to smile at her, Megan fell in love. Stubby knew so little about love that it took her all of sixteen seconds to realize what the look on Megan's face meant. ''Oh, my god,'' she breathed, and followed her buddy down that incredible stomach-lurching slide.

''I wish I had two arms to hold you with,'' Megan whispered.

''You're doing just fine,'' Stubby managed between kisses, ''at least you've got the right one. Which means, of course, you've still got one left.''

''One day,'' Megan promised, ''I'm going to kill you because of those corny groaners,'' Then neither of them could say anything the least bit intelligible.

That night, together in Megan's cabin, they made sandwiches with canned salmon, chopped onion and mayonnaise, drank cold milk from the wonky little fridge and, for dessert, shared a chocolate bar. But mostly they just stared at each other in wonder, and grinned a lot.

"You could stay over,'' Megan offered hopefully.

"Want to show me your shower?'' Stubby teased. "Hot tap, cold tap, soap dish, all that complicated stuff . . .''

"Yeah,'' Megan nodded, then blushed and blurted, "I don't know why I feel so damned shy!''

"I don't,'' Stubby assured her. "I'm too close to realizing my maximum attainment of perfection. Invisible white light and all!''

Draconis raised herself from the floor, tiptoed outside and considerately climbed up into the pear tree to sleep in the branches where she wouldn't eavesdrop inadvertently. She tried hard not to hear the sound of spraying water, the soft voices, the throaty laughter, tried hard not to pay attention when the water was turned off and the soft voices moved from the bathroom to the comfortable bed. Instead, she tried to concentrate on admiring the way the moonlight glittered on her jewel-scales, the starlight on her ivory fangs.

Megan and Stubby slept together, limbs entangled, and only their dreams were private and unshared.

3

Draconis lay on the large branch of the pear tree, her tail upraised, the cleft tip of it wiggling, tasting the air. She mourned her lonely condition. The ruby, sapphire, emerald and diamond scales glittered and shone, but there was no joy in her heart.

Oh Mother, she prayed, allow me to return to my own time and my own place. My soul is cramped in a potbellied body which cannot grow any bigger, for the entire world is diminished and depleted and there is nothing with the vitality needed to allow me my real shape. Trees are as small as our rose bushes were, and fewer than you would believe possible. Mother, they drop their shit into their drinking water and pour chemicals in afterward to kill the bacteria, then, because the water tastes terrible, they add artificial fruit-flavoured crystals to it that they can drink it and not puke. Mother, their poor bastard hearts are breaking, and they don't even know it! Every night I travel their world, moving freely while they sleep; everywhere it is the same and in some places, worse. They have learned so much, and forgotten so much more. They are so wise and so ignorant, so schooled and so stupid, and cannot or will not believe what they know to be true, cannot do what they know must be done, will not admit the evidence of their own eyes and ears. They look at dragons and see scruffy dogs, they look at rainbows and cannot hear their song, and neither take responsibility for nor learn from their own immediate past .

I want to go home. I want to go back to Avalon and sleep in the shade of the apple trees, I want to look again on your lovely old face with its lines and wrinkles and I want to listen to the laughter of Elaine, Margawse, Morgana and Vivienne. I want to hear the songs and watch the dances, and, oh Mother, I want to grow to the size I am capable of being! I am a dragon, I am not one of these poor buggers, and I want to concern myself with dragon deeds, not with the silliness of mortals. All the chow mein in the world cannot make up for what is missing. They have been numbed and brutalized, they have been regimented and stifled, entire parts of their brains have atrophied, and they don't even know it.

I am not the one made the mistake, Mother, why should I be the one marooned on this dying loony bin?

Mother, the Inquisition was nothing compared to this, the Fires were nothing compared to this. They played with their toys on an island paradise and were so busy watching the dials and gauges on their machines they did not notice the butterflies falling from the sky and lying dead on the surface of the sea, and how many lives perished then? They did not notice, they did not care if they did notice, and now, Mother, for miles around that little island there are children born who breathe an hour or two and then die, looking more like jellyfish than people. Some have their organs inside their boneless bodies but some wear their organs outside, in a pulsing sac, and these ones cannot understand or absorb or realize what any of it means and have named a bathing suit after that island and I want to go home!

Mother, they have measured the number of cells in their own bodies and counted the genes and chromosomes. They can make graphs and analyse, they can predict and extrapolate their predictions and do not know the mind has nothing to do with the brain, or that the soul is the person, not the body it inhabits. They talk of the missing link and cannot see they carry it inside themselves! They make me cry. I mourn day and night but pretend to be happy. And I want to go home, but I cannot abandon them. Mother, please, relent and allow just a few of them, just a few, those least tainted, those least crippled, allow them to leave with me and we will all live in the Misty Isles. Not forever. Just a week. Please mother, one of your weeks, and then, I promise, I will come back with them and we will start all over again, and this time we'll all be good. We'll all be very very good, Mother, we will, I promise.

They bumble and they stumble and walk right into the stupidity, and those who can see, they lock away and rend helpless. They cut off the top of skulls and look in and count the number of receptors and those with twice as many as most, they call schizophrenic and medicate or imprison. Those who can taste and feel and experience the most, they fill with chemicals and amputate with horrors; and those ones would understand, and would know the magic if you would but relent.

Oh, Mother, this is not my world, this is not my place, there has never been any magic in this terrible little world. Not in this corner of it! How can it not be sterile and incomplete, the rocks have never seen the sky full of dragons swimming in the clouds and sliding off the edge of the crescent moon, and these trees, what few are left, have never felt the surge of joy as Morgana flitted from one to the other, being first this kind and then that kind, and what does this water know of the magic of Vivienne? This land is younger than I am, and even more diminished, and I want to go home.

The young dragon waited, but the Mother did not answer. Draconis sniffled a bit and her tail drooped. She lowered her head and popped her thumb in her mouth and wondered what it was she had done to be so punished.

I don't like it here, she mumbled. I don't like it at all. There has never been any magic in this damned place. All there has ever been here is a bunch of exiles, a bunch of rejects, and it's no wonder they're all stupid, they're the children of discards!

The pear tree trembled slightly. A small rock rolled itself from near the base of the tree and bumped into a slightly larger rock which, in turn, moved a few inches sideways and tapped awake a boulder. The dragon continued to sulk and wallow in her homesickness. The gravel, lying on top of the earth absorbing the sunlight and moonlight, wiggled, and the pebbles beneath the gravel squirmed. The small rocks in the surface of the dirt shifted and the larger rocks further down twisted. Layer by layer the family of rocks was wakened, the message going down, down, down past the breeding boulders, down past the guardian aunties and uncles, down, down to the very old rocks, the huge grandmother chunks and hunks of granite and quartz, down to the very hardpan and bedrock where the wisdom of millennia was stored, and they all did what the insulted little rock at the base of the pear tree did, they all turned over in disgust at the mere idea of a dragon, however young and inexperienced, daring to snivel.

It hit eight on the Richter scale and didn't leave a window intact for miles. Some lives were lost, there was billions of dollars worth of property damage, and the entire crop of pears landed hard, green and punitive on the head of the sulky baby dragon, who had only time enough to squeal a fast apology before passing out with fear and, of course, the concussion of guilt.

Stubby came awake somewhere between the mattress and the floor and saw Megan lying, her bad arm pinned under the overturned chair, staring in horror at a huge crack opening in the ceiling. Stubby knew, in that place that knows, that the next move she made might very well be her last, but she knew something was about to come down where Megan was trapped. Stubby launched herself and landed lying over Megan, trying to protect her with her own body.

The support beam fell from the ceiling at the same time Stubby dove through the air. Stubby's leg hit the tottering table, it fell against the big chair at the same moment the floor bucked and heaved. The floor sent the big chair up, the table sent the big chair sideways and the beam, when it landed, hit the chair. It moved only three or four inches from where it had always stood, but those three or four inches made all the difference in the multiverse. The chair was frapped and Megan's good arm was broken, but she was not squished to goo.

They both passed out with the shock of it all. In the deathly silence that followed the ten-second earthquake and preceded the aftershocks, before the alarms went off and the sirens started, the crabby dragon shook her head, staggered to her feet and looked around groggily. She wanted to say something. Anything. But there was nothing to say. She moved to the wreck of the little cabin, tossed debris aside with her hands, her tail, and then sat next to her unconscious friends, her eyes crossed, her mind whirling.

Another bump, and another, smaller, as the stones settled themselves, and then Draconis got taught a lesson about magic and the various forms in which it can be found in this world.

Stubby Amberchuk opened her eyes and recognized nothing at all. Jagged ends, ruptured supports, glittering shards of what had once been windows. Draconis was whining softly, obviously stunned, hurt and frightened half out of her wits. Stubby could smell smoke and hear a faint sound, like the crinkling of newspaper or the first tentative cracklings in kindling. It didn't make sense. She had been asleep, and then she had been flying. People can't fly. So what was she doing if she hadn't been flying? Falling, that's what she had been doing! Falling out of bed toward the floor, and on the floor someone was lying, pinned under the huge overturned stuffed chair. Oh christ!

"Megan," Stubby managed as she tried to move. Something was across her legs, and Stubby kicked desperately, twisting and straining. Whatever it was fell, and Stubby could move. There was Megan, under Stubby, and on Megan's arm, Megan's good arm, the edge of the splintered wooden kitchen table. "Hang on, please," Stubby prayed. "Just hang on, Megs, okay?" She kicked the ruined table aside, then managed to get to her feet and hook her strong basewoman's hands under the big chair. She heaved. The chair moved, the splintered ceiling beam creaked warningly, and Stubby gulped with fear. She bent her knees, hunkered by the chair, got her hands under it again and straightened her knees, lifting the chair and the ceiling beam, and praying.

Draconis opened her eyes, blinked and saw Stubby, muscles swollen, face contorted, trying to hold the weight of the chair and the roof off

Megan's mangled arm. Draconis knew she couldn't do much, but what she could do, she did. She reached out, grabbed the blood-soaked pyjama sleeve and pulled Megan's ruined arm out from under the incredible weight Stubby had managed to lift.

"Put it down, Sheilagh," Draconis said quietly. Stubby grunted, bent her knees, lowered the chair and, at the last minute, pulled her hands away, saving her fingers. She stared, realizing that the only reason she had been able to get her fingers under the chair in the first place was that Megan's arm had been squished underneath, holding the chair an inch or so off the floor.

"I'm hurt, Stubs," Megan said clearly.

"Easy," Stubby blurted. "Gimme a minute here, Megan. I can't think straight."

"You'd better hurry, Stubbzers," Megan whispered, "I think this shitbox is on fire."

And it was. The small propane stove was overturned, the pilot light still burning. The tablecloth had touched it and caught, spreading to the spilled magazines and the newspaper. The dry, aged, bare boards of the floor were burning, the scattered blankets and sheets igniting.

"I'm gonna grab your shirt at the shoulders, Megan," Stubby explained, "and I'm gonna drag you outta here. There isn't time to do anything else, not kick the junk out of the way or anything, so . . . you're gonna get hurt some more, darlin'."

"Draconis," Megan moaned. "I think she's zonked or something. And Stubs, I can't move either of my arms."

So Stubby picked Draconis up from where she was sitting stupidly, staring at the blood on the floor where Megan's arm had been trapped, and plopped the baby dragon in disguise down on Megan's belly. Draconis immediately grabbed at the bottom hem of Megan's pyjama top and clung desperately. Stubby grabbed the shoulders of the bloodstained garment and started to yard the two of them from the fire that was rapidly becoming an inferno. "Yell if it hurts," she suggested. "Yell if you want."

"Try to stop me," Megan dared. Then her good arm, broken in two places, bumped some debris, and she was white-faced and gasping for breath, unable to yell, being dragged to safety by her love.

Colony Farm Campsites and Cabins was a ruin. Not one of the buildings stood either intact or upright. People were wandering around saying and doing stupid things.

"Don't!" Stubby roared, but the man with the cigarette and book of matches ignored her. His nerves were shot. What he wanted was a drink, what he had was a smoke, so he lit the match and the overturned car he was standing next to exploded, cindering him instantly and starting a fire that made the one in Megan's cabin look like a weenie roast.

"Oh, shit!" Megan sobbed. "Stubs, we've got to get out of here!"

"Right!" Stubby agreed. "But I'm not sure how. We're gonna fry if we try to get to the road."

"The path," Megan said. "Help me up, Stubby, there's nothing wrong with my legs. Then let's get to the beach. We might boil, but we won't fry."

Stubby hooked her forearms under Megan's underarms and heaved. Megan stumbled, then had her feet under her, both arms hanging useless. But she managed a tough grin. "Venus de Milo wound up world famous without much less than this," she gasped.

"C'mon." Stubby picked up Draconis, then put her other arm around Megan's waist, taking as much of her weight as she could. "C'mon, champ," she gritted, "get those legs workin', move those feet."

Down the path to the beach, and every step of it agony for Megan Crawford. No pink-coloured codeine pills, no blue capsules, no nothing but to grit the teeth and keep going. "Come on, darlin'," Stubby encouraged her, "just one step at a time, one foot in front of the other, that's it, one foot, other foot, down the pike, come on, that's it, that's how you do 'er."

"Stubs, I can't feel anything at all in my bad arm."

"Believe me, you're lucky. It's a mess, Megan. I think the only thing that keeps you from bleedin' to death is that it's squished so bad it isn't even bleeding! And," her voice broke, she sobbed harshly, "I don't know what to do to help with it!"

"One foot at a time," Megan tried to grin, but it didn't work, not even a little bit. "Oh, Stubby, I am so god damned scared."

"Me too," said Draconis.

"You'll be okay," Stubby assured the dazed creature, "just take a minute or two and collect yourself."

"I think I got a bang on the head, Stubby," Megan babbled, "because for just a moment there, I thought that dog spoke."

"She's not a dog," Stubby corrected, "she's a dragon."

"Yeah. Right. What else."

The windows in Loretta's little apartment blew outwards, the floor buckled, the ceiling sagged, the water pipes burst and flooded the floor and Loretta wound up sprawled on the suddenly soggy carpet, with Wright falling next to her, practically landing on her head.

"Jesus H. Christ! "she yelped.

"You okay?" Wright gasped.

"I'm squallin', ain't I?"

She struggled to her feet, looked around blearily, rubbing her forehead, smearing the blood trickling from a cut on her scalp. "Come on, lover," she urged, reaching down, taking Wright's arm, helping to drag him to his feet. "See if ya can find yer pants. Come *on*."

Wright moved for the door.

"Put on yer pants and take some time to think," she argued.

"Pants? Oh. Pants." Wright groped in the darkness, found something wet, decided whatever it was the chances were good he'd found his trousers and, fumbling, dragged the sodden mess over his lower body. "Now can we go?" he growled.

"Just a minute," Loretta promised. She hauled on a pair of jeans and a heavy warm sweater, found one sneaker, couldn't find the other, so gave it up as a bad job and headed for the door. Wright stumbled behind her, wishing he'd been smart enough to pay more attention on his way in, it might have given him some chance of finding his way out again. "Gimme your hand," she hissed. She was so frightened she thought her bladder was going to empty, so frightened she knew she couldn't have peed if promised ten dollars for the attempt. She'd been drunk before, she'd seen the floor moving like the waves of the sea, she'd seen walls doing ballet moves and most of her life had put her head on the pillow and watched the room spin like a merry-go-round, but nothing like this.

She stepped through the hole at the end of the hallway, the hole that had once been the front wall. "Thank christ I didn't take a third floor apartment," she mumbled. "Thank christ I grabbed the first floor. The bloody steps is bust off."

"Maybe we should try to help . . ."

"Forget it," she interrupted. "They'll get out or they won't, but there's bugger-nothing we can do to help them. Come on."

"But . . ."

"Wright," she tried to smile, "gimme a break, okay? The entire shiterooni is about to come down. You wanna be in it when that happens?" Wright knew he didn't want to be in it. He nodded and they moved away from the teetering wreck. "Migawd," Loretta stared at the mess that had once been a busy town trying hard to pretend it was a city. "The place was a goddamn horror when it was all in one piece, so to speak. Now . . . what's that thing about a hundred maids with a hundred brooms?" She looked sideways at Wright and grinned suddenly. "You're one hell of a man, lover," she teased. "I mean I've heard about men who are so good they make you feel like the earth moved under you, but I gotta tell you, in alla my life, this is a first!"

"Me, too, darlin'," he agreed, trying but still unable to smile.

They headed up the hill, away from the fractured town and the fires starting in a dozen places. "C'mon," Loretta ordered, turning left at the train track, heading southward, Wright following obediently. "I gotta find my kid," Loretta said determinedly. "I spent too much time already bein' some place where she wasn't. We sure do spend a lot of our lives doin' things we don't really want to do!"

Vinnie looked around dazedly, trying to make sense of it all, trying to make sense of any of it. She was naked, she was standing on the side lawn, she was staring at a heap of rubble and she knew that heap of rubble had once been Ada Richardson's house. In that mess were Vinnie's clothes. And in that mess, god forbid, was Sharon. "Well," Vinnie sighed aloud, "let's get on with it old girl!" She started for the back of the house, where Sharon's bedroom was. The roof had slid backward and was held up by the splintered wreck of a Gravenstein apple tree.

The window was shattered, the wicked shards glittering in the starlight, the wall was smashed, the bureau was tipped and half fallen through the ruin of the outside bearing wall. And Sharon was face-down in the broken glass, limbs sprawled.

Without hesitating so much as a half a second, Vinnie stepped back into the ruin of the house. She knelt in the shattered glass, reaching for Sharon's wrist, searching for her pulse. It was weak, fast and thready, but it was there. "Well, St. John of the Ambulance," Vinnie babbled to herself, "best you revise that handbook of first aid. First rule, as I remember it, is Do Not Move the Patient. But if you think we're staying here, you've got another think coming." She hauled the coverlet off the bed and put it on the floor beside Sharon, then, crossing her fingers and praying, she rolled Sharon onto the coverlet and waited to see if, in moving her, she had also killed her. Sharon just lay there, not making a sound, not moving. Vinnie nodded as if something important had just been proved to her. Then she left Sharon where she was and crossed to the closet, reached around the sagging door and hauled out an armload of clothes. She tossed the dresses on the bed, pulled on a pair of jeans and a thick flannel shirt, then went to the dresser and found warm socks. Back to the closet for sturdy boots, and then she did the whole thing all over again, getting clothes for Sharon.

Only then did Vinnie move back to where Sharon lay on the coverlet, still unconscious. Vinnie dragged the coverlet to the broken wall, heaved the clothes out into the yard, then bent to try to lift Sharon over the mess of support beams, bricks and debris.

But Vinnie couldn't do it. She heaved, she strained, she nearly left her guts on the fractured floor, and she couldn't get Sharon off the coverlet, off the floor and over the heap of crap and garbage. "Son of a bitch," she said clearly. "Dirty rotten no-good stinking heap of bloody-bejezus crap!" She sank to the floor, stubbornly and angrily lacing her boots and tying them. "If at first you don't succeed," she growled, "piss on it!"

The path was broken in more pieces than anybody would ever be able to count, even if anybody had wanted to waste time trying. They had to climb over fallen trees, detour around tumbled boulders, they stumbled, they fell, they got up and tried again, just one foot at a time, down the path to the sea.

"My fault," mourned the baby dragon.

"How do you figure?" Stubby asked.

"I lost faith," Draconis admitted. "I never did that before, not in this life or any other, but I lost faith. I said you were all the children of discards."

"Who isn't?" Megan hissed, not with rage, but with pain. "But you're right. If you said that, the rocks and boulders probably got real mad. After all, it's a known fact the discards and the children of discards are the salt of the earth. And you do not insult with impunity the earth or any part of her."

"I'm sorry," the dragon wept.

"Never mind," Stubby soothed, "we've all made a few mistakes in our time." Draconis nodded, but she wasn't really consoled. She put her thumb in her mouth and sucked furiously, trying to control the terrified shaking of her body, the frightened trembling of her top and bottom lips.

Stubby was mostly carrying Megan by the time they got to the beach. She lowered her to the sand, leaned against a bleached log and looked around, recognizing nothing at all. Somewhere sirens were screaming and wailing, somewhere emergency lights were flashing. Somewhere the army was heading out to try to help those injured or trapped in a mess nature made in a few seconds and the armies of all the nations couldn't have made in hours or even days. The breeze blowing from the sea to the land was pushing the fire away from them, but that wasn't much consolation to Stubby. The fire was being pushed in exactly the direction where Vinnie, Wright and Sharon were.

"Oh, God, I am so sorry!" Draconis wailed

"Hush, now," said the voice. "You heard what Sheilagh said, we've all made mistakes in our time. You're forgiven. How could you have known?"

"Are you . . . God herself?" Draconis quavered.

"No." said the voice. "I'm an archangel. Herself is asleep right now."

"Easy there, Draconis," Stubby soothed, patting the trembling creature. "Easy on there, old girl, we'll get out of this somehow," Draconis realized neither Stubby nor Megan could hear the voice of the archangel.

"The world," Draconis protested, "is destroyed."

"Oh, don't be silly," Stubby forced a laugh. "You know how it is. Like the real estate agent said, a bit of paint here, a bit of paper there, a few hours tinkering in your spare time and it'll all look like new again."

"Christ," the archangel laughed, "another of the crazies!"

"Oh, no," Draconis protested, "she's very brave!"

"Most of them are," the archangel agreed. "But crazy all the same."

Vinnie heaved bricks and yanked on pieces of broken wood, she rolled big hunks of stuff she couldn't even identify and she broke off every fingernail she had. A section of support beam fell and landed on her foot, she cursed viciously and lifted it enough to get her foot out from underneath, not even realizing she had suffered three broken toes. She limped, but so what, lots of people did, and the space cleared still wasn't big enough to drag Sharon to safety. "God *damn*!" she howled, "Do I gotta do everything myself?"

"Hhmmnh. . . ." Sharon moaned.

"Get up, "Vinnie snapped. "Get the hell up, Sharon, and gimme a hand here, will ya?"

She stepped back into the ruined bedroom, knelt and lifted Sharon to a sitting position. "Put your arm around my shoulders, okay?" she ordered.

"Gladly," Sharon whispered.

"Okay, kiddo," Vinnie breathed, "okay, here we go. Upsy-daisy and. . . easy there. . . how you feeling?"

"Like shit on a stick. How's yourself?"

"Similar," Vinnie agreed. "I got clothes waiting for you out on the lawn. What's left of the lawn, that is." With a lifetime history of talking about absolutely nothing at all, Vinnie yapped Sharon over the rubble and out to comparative safety.

"You're one hell of a woman," Sharon managed, slumping to the grass and reaching for some clothing to protect her from the chill.

"You're not so bad yourself." Vinnie sat down suddenly, her face paling, her head spinning. "God," she mourned, "the whole thing is buggered. All my greenhouses smashed. The house frapped, the yard all cracked and pushed up into humps and hills. . . oh well," she decided, forcing herself to look for the bright side, "it could be worse. I don't know how, but I'm sure it could."

"We're alive, that's something," Sharon winced. "I know we're alive because I hurt so bad. Oh shit!" She tried to rise. "Wright...Stubby..."

"Not much we can do," Vinnie sobbed suddenly. "I don't even know where she is or if..."

"Wright," Loretta grabbed his arm, pointed, "Wright, the bush is on fire."

"Fuck me," Wright sighed, almost defeated.

"No time. Sorry," she cracked automatically. "We got about ten minutes and then we're in the cereal box, with all the other crispy critters."

"The river," Wright pointed, "Might as well boil as fry."

They left the tracks, stumbled and slid down the bank to the split in the rock that was the river.

"Come on." Wright took Loretta by the hand, squeezed encouragingly. "Grab a log, old girl, and let's us go for a bit of a dip."

"I gotta tell ya," she gasped, "bein' as how there's no way we can undo this bloody uproar, if I have to be part of the end of the world as she's been known, I'm glad it's you I'm in it with."

"Loretta," Wright shook his head, astounded and touched, "I gotta hand it to you, you're a great date! I haven't had this much fun since the pigs ate my baby brother."

"Yours, too, huh?" She looked longingly at what she had thought for most of her life was firm ground, a sob wrenching harshly from her throat. "God damn," she managed, "if it ain't one pissin thing it's another! And didya ever notice, the time you need a drink most is when there ain't a drop to be had for love nor money?" She jumped into the river, her hands reaching desperately for a floating log.

Stubby was busy in the moonlight, doing what she could to help Megan, who was sitting, white-faced with shock, leaning against a boulder. She managed to splint the broken arm using pieces of driftwood and strips ripped from what was left of her pyjama top, but she didn't dare touch the jellied mess that was Megan's bad arm.

"It's nice," the voice of the archangel echoed in Draconis' head, "to see how some of these kids grow up to be just exactly what you thought they were capable of being all along."

"They're gonna slice it off," Megan said, her voice hard. "Gonna take 'er right off at the shoulder," Stubby couldn't think of a single joke. Megan's eyes filled with tears. "Shit, eh, Stubs? Bad enough when you think it's just a temporary thing, but...there's something so goddamn permanent about amputation.''

''Megan, maybe they won't . . .''

''Hey,'' Megan sobbed, ''you shit your friends, right? And I'll shit my friends. But we won't shit each other, okay. They're gonna cut it off.''

''Yeah,'' Stubby gulped. ''Probably.''

''Well, the best laid plans and all that,'' Megan babbled. ''And here I was looking forward to learning how to play ball and . . . ah, hell,'' she winked. ''Maybe we'll be burned to shit before they get the chance to carve, eh?''

''There was a one-armed baseball player,'' Stubby said, her words tumbling over each other frantically. ''Really, there was! He played outfield. He caught the ball one-handed, then either grabbed it under his chin long enough to shuck his glove or tossed the ball in the air, dropped the glove, grabbed the ball and hucked it in.''

''Bullshit.''

''No bullshit, Megan! I wouldn't lie to you. I really wouldn't.''

''What was his name?'' Megan challenged.

''I can't remember,'' Stubby sobbed, ''I can't remember his name. But he really existed, and he played professional major league ball. Megs, listen, it's the truth. Cross my heart and hope to die. It's true, Megan. And when this mess is cleared up, I promise you, on my word I promise you, I'll look it up and prove it to you.''

''I can't believe this,'' the archangel said sarcastically. ''The world is in ruins and these two idiots sit three-quarters naked in the sand talking about baseball players.''

''Aw, shut up, will you?'' Draconis snarled. ''Don't you know everything is parable? I'd have thought an archangel would have more sense. They aren't really talking ballplayers, they're talking faith and hope and believing and . . .'' Then Draconis remembered just who it was she was telling to shut up. She closed her eyes and prepared to die.

''Way to go, Draconis,'' the archangel said softly. ''Now pull yourself together and I'll carry you all to wherever it is you want to go.''

''You can't do that,'' Draconis gasped. ''A world is either scientific or it is magic, you can't have it both ways!''

''Listen, twerp,'' the archangel said, but her voice was gentle and full of love, ''scientists may think they have taken control, but what have they managed to do? I mean *really* do? Make a mess it might take years to clean up, granted, but these losers have always been ready to clean up messes; even messes of their own making. After all, the Thames is cleaner than it's been in centuries! This world, Draconis, is full of magic! Think of the magic . . .''

"Yes," Draconis breathed. "Yes! Salmonberries, which come in all colours from yellow to black! Huckleberries...kind deeds...wild strawberries...spindrift piled on the lip of the waves... an osprey arching in the sky and eagles giggling...silly jokes between good friends..."

"The sound of a bat hitting solid against a ball," Stubby interjected.

"Thinking you're dead and waking up to find you're only crippled for life," Megan managed, her mouth twisted, but not with pain, with the determined beginning of a small sickly smile.

"Atta girl," said the archangel. She touched Megan with the gentlest tip of her wing and Megan relaxed, her pain sent somewhere else.

"Old faithful dogs." Stubby remembered Daisy. "And loving old women." She thought of Ada.

"Rambling roses," Draconis smiled, "and good blues sung by a voice as rich as cream."

Vinnie knew she was cut in a dozen places, scratched in a hundred more. Her foot was throbbing viciously, her stomach trying to heave itself empty and her head pounding. Still, she'd felt worse in her life. She'd spent days and weeks of her life feeling one whole hell of a lot worse than this; at least, in spite of the uproar and furor, she had some idea of what it was she could do, ought to do, was capable of doing. She pushed herself to her feet, stood wobbling unsteadily.

"What do you think you're going to do?" Sharon asked.

"Well, there's stuff we might need," Vinnie babbled. "I could sure use a jacket. You could use a blanket or two. There's gotta be a pack of smokes in there somewhere."

"I'll help..." Sharon tried to rise, paled, and sat back down again.

"Most help you can give," Vinnie lectured, "is to stay out of trouble. I can handle it. Might be some can handle it better, but none of them are here so it's up to yours truly. Who, incidentally, it has always been up to, in a manner of speaking."

"Come on, fella," Loretta grunted, hauling on Wright's arm. "Just get your feet under you, that's it. Come on, we're closer than we were two hours ago."

"Keee-rist it's cold," Wright gasped.

"Yeah, well, tuck 'er in outta the cold, darlin, there's a time'n'a place for everything."

"Loretta," Wright shivered violently, "when this is all over, remind me to buy you a drink!"

"Sweetheart," Loretta coughed, a phlegmy bar-fly body shaker, ''when this is over you're gonna buy me more than one drink, believe me.''

''If we head over the hill there, past the Row, we're as good as home.''

''Darlin,'' Loretta grinned a twisted little grin, ''I ain't been *home* since about the time they taught me what a thundermug was for. All I want is my kid, safe.''

''Steady on old girl.'' Wright reached out, took Loretta's hand, lifted it to his lips and kissed gently. ''There's nothing so good it couldn't be better and nothing so bad it couldn't be worse.''

Sharon leaned against the trunk of the peach tree, gratefully sipping the coffee Vinnie had given her. ''You're a marvel,'' she sighed. ''I mean here's the whole world tipped on its backside and you manage to make coffee!''

''I'm no marvel,'' Vinnie sighed. ''Just an ordinary person, that's all.''

''Ordinary,'' Sharon laughed. ''Sure you are.''

''You think the kids are okay?'' Vinnie finally put her fear into words. ''Because if they aren't, I don't know what I'm going to do.''

''I can't even think about it,'' Sharon admitted. ''But I'm sure if they're together they're better off than they'd be if either of them was on her own.''

''Are we talking about this damned earthquake,'' Vinnie asked, ''or life in general?''

''Up to you.''

''I thought it would take a lot of getting used to, you know,'' Vinnie confessed. ''I mean, you hear about it, but. . .it's always someone else's kid. And when the dime dropped and I realized. . .it was like part of my mind was waiting for me to really flip out about it and most of my mind was. . .like. . .she's my kid! Christ knows we haven't always seen eye to eye but. . .so what?'' she asked defiantly.

''Someone coming,'' Sharon pointed.

''Oh jesus,'' Vinnie struggled to her feet. ''I'll tell you, a sore toe is a sore thing.''

''But not,'' Sharon winked, ''as sore as a sore thing would be!''

''We made 'er.'' Loretta let it all go then. She sagged to the ground next to Sharon, leaned against the peach tree and began to sob. ''I'm sorry,'' she gulped, ''I'm real sorry, but. . .''

''Have a cup of coffee,'' Sharon nodded, handing the cup carefully, ''and just get a grip on yourself.''

''Thank you.'' Loretta took the coffee mug as carefully as if it were made of gold and silver, studded with jewels and filled with the elixir of absolute truth. She sipped, sighed and handed the cup to Wright. ''Here, save your own life,'' she breathed.

The archangel gathered them up in her arms and Stubby tried hard to see what she looked like. Stubby thought she saw wings and the reddest, curliest hair she had ever imagined. She was sure she saw a gold and white uniform with writing on the back of the team shirt, but mostly what she saw was a bright golden glow.

''Stubby,'' Ada Richardson said clearly. ''Stubby darling, close your eyes. You cannot look at the sun without going blind.'' So Stubby closed her eyes and so did Megan, who was almost unconscious anyway. Draconis kept her eyes open and saw everything there was to see, but she kept it to herself until three days after the unfolding of eternity. They were swept instantly over the tops of trees, past the blazing of the fires, out of sight of the wailing and the terrified, unseen by the firefighters, first aid attendants, civil defence, hospital auxiliary, St. John's Ambulance and all the other volunteers.

''Thank God,'' said Wright, stepping forward and taking Megan from the arms of the archangel. ''Thank God you are alive and well.''

''You're welcome,'' said the archangel. ''But I myself am not God. I'm just an infielder, that's all. But we have met before, Wright. My name is Estelle.''

''I remember,'' Wright smiled. Then he turned his back on the archangel and promptly forgot what he had seen and accepted so calmly. Forever after, Wright, Sharon, Loretta and Vinnie were convinced Stubby had carried Megan to safety. ''People who give their word and keep it,'' chanted Draconis, ''and all turtles named Myrtle. Tap dancing and finger snapping, seaweed and starfish, new-hatched chicks and waddling ducks, dogs with whiskers and dogs with thick fur.''

''Stubby,'' Sharon said firmly, ''you have got to sit down before you fall flat on your face.''

''Sheilagh,'' said Vinnie, ''please, put on this clean shirt, the one you've got on is torn to bits. And then we'll get you some jeans. That's it, baby, that's it, it's okay, everything will be fine, just fine. Mommy,'' said Vinnie, ''will look after everything.''

Stubby looked at the wreck that had been Ada's house and began to cry. ''She worked so hard,'' she blubbered. ''She chose everything so carefully and loved it so much.''

''Better it than you,'' Vinnie murmured.

''Momma,'' Stubby quavered, ''the entire world is in shambles, everything is on fire, Megan is in real trouble and that's all you can say? All you can come up with is 'better it than you'? Can't you please, just for once in my life, say something that makes *sense?*"

"There is no need," Vinnie lectured, "to pitch a fit just because there's been a bit of an accident. Calm down. There is nothing we can do about any of the big problems, so all we can do is take care of the little ones."

"Yes, momma." Stubby sat on the grass. "I guess all my photo albums are gone," she grumbled, "all my pictures of Dave will be ruined."

Most of them were, but not all of them. The albums taken after his accident, the pictures of him shrivelling and shrinking into a wraith, were wrecked beyond any and all hope of repair, but the albums full of pictures of him laughing and strong, tanned and tough, were salvaged.

And yes, they cut Megan Crawford's ruined arm off at the shoulder, but she refused to be fitted with an artificial one. She played outfield, and if she never made it to the major league, so what, how many ever do?

"... kids with chubby fists clenched around crayons," Draconis dreamed contentedly, "and pictures in their hearts, fluteplayers and guitar players, violin players and dobro players, autoharpists and pipe organists and combs with tissue paper folded over them. Bookstores with skylights and Dinner Rock beach, the Lookout and Nanaimo River Rapids, fossils in caves, daffodils and hyacinths and burgundy-coloured columbine, prawn dinners and barbecued salmon and cold beer and moths..."

While Megan was in the hospital, Stubby hired hordes of the people who had lost everything they owned. She paid them twice the going rate, provided them with two meals a day, and they worked themselves to a fare-thee-well putting her house on the Row back in shape. Then she hired them to rebuild Ada's house. Sharon, Wright, Vinnie and Loretta lived in Ada's house, Stubby and Megan lived in the house in the Row and, with their wages, the singing fools rebuilt their own homes.

"Evening sunset and morning sunrise and the sound of the owl in the night, coloured beads and prisms in the windows, jade trees and begonias, land claims and carnations and yellow roses and iris and marigolds, old stumps and young trees, magnolia bushes and herons," Draconis cheered. "Cedar trees and old woman's beard, maple leaves and driftwood, dogwood and firewood and ice cubes and pigtails and new shoes."

"And love," said Wright.

"Yes," said Loretta, "most certainly love."

"Love, for sure," Sharon agreed.

"Most definitely," Vinnie nodded.

''Love,'' Stubby smiled.

''Love you,'' Megan sighed.

''And love,'' Draconis chanted, ''love love love love . . .'' And all the singing fools laughed and sang and worked and loved. The angels and archangels, the seraphim and cherubim nodded and finished stretching and went back to their celestial softball game, and God in her Heaven slept on, resting from her labours.